The silvery ............................................ cheek like an invisibl. ......... .. .... . .... awkward or threatening—in fact, just the opposite.

An intangible aura of protective masculinity wrapped around her, and for a mad moment, she almost gave in to the impulse to lean into him, to feel what it would be like to press against his body again. A delicious tension seemed to build around them as the last flakes swirled in the late afternoon sunlight. She saw the amusement slowly leave Hugo's expression, replaced with something warmer and more potent.

His gaze dropped to her lips, and Julie realized with an almost drugged awareness that he was going to kiss her.

# BOOKED

## Kingsbury Town Football Club Romance
### —— Book Two ——

# Marina Reznor

KINGSBURY TOWN PRESS
BIRMINGHAM, ALABAMA

**Booked**

Kingsbury Town Football Club Romance Series, Book 2

ISBN: 979-8-9850984-2-6 (eBook)

ISBN: 978-0-9994297-2-3 (Paperback)

Copy edit by Denise McInerney at Stone Wall Editing

Proofreading by Jessica Snyder at Jessica Snyder Edits

Cover design by UpdateDiva Design

Published by Kingsbury Town Press LLC

Birmingham, Alabama

Kingsburytownpress.com

KINGSBURY TOWN PRESS
BIRMINGHAM ALABAMA

*For Georgina*

# Chapter One

A BRISK DECEMBER wind blew the door shut behind Hugo Auchincloss as he stepped into the rare books shop on Hampstead Heath, ducking to avoid the low stone doorway mantle. Gladia, the shop's owner, waved a cheery hello and rushed to finish a sale before turning her attention to him. Hugo Auchincloss was not her most famous customer, nor in all likelihood the richest, but he was her only Premier League football player. And after forty years in the business, she liked to have something to lord over the other booksellers on the Heath.

Hugo began browsing the narrow stacks while he waited, enjoying the familiar aroma of old leather, parchment, and the long-ago tobacco smoke that clung to the books. The loaded shelves stretched to the shop's ceiling, and he could have happily spent the entire day there. History and geography were his favorite subjects, just as they had been at Eton, yet he appreciated a variety of writing, especially works authored in French, in which he was fluent.

His personal library was filled with many purchases from this shop, as well as half of his grandfather's expansive library from Wrothesley, the Auchincloss family estate in

Bedfordshire. Five years ago, their mother had declared the house too much for one person and closed it, splitting the contents of the library between Hugo and his younger brother, Ian. Which was the reason for his visit to Gladia's this afternoon.

A handsome 1803 first edition of Vivant Denon's *Travels in Upper and Lower Egypt* caught Hugo's eye, and he began to peruse it.

"Hello, love," Gladia bustled over. "Good to see you."

Hugo bent and gave her a kiss on the cheek. "Thanks for calling me Gladia, I appreciate it. Which one is he trying to pawn now?"

"*The Orchard and Fruit Garden* by Charles McIntosh, 1847. One of the first books on horticulture written for the backyard gardener, rare and valuable. But this copy's been marked up and in rough shape, so it went cheaper at the auction Thursday."

Hugo frowned. "Where is it?"

Back at the register, Gladia took the tattered book from a drawer and placed it on the counter. *Bloody Ian.* It was indeed from their grandfather's library and was one of the old man's favorites. It had sat on his desk for decades, and if Hugo was going to run Wrothesley the way his father and grandfather had, he needed to keep everything the same, to the letter. And that meant keeping the library together.

He nodded curtly and reached for his wallet. "How much?"

Gladia sighed and regarded him over the top of her spectacles. "Eighty pounds, but sorry, Hugo, there's a rub. My grandson, Roderick, was minding the store on Saturday when a pretty girl came in and fell in love with the book. He was smitten and ignored the 'Hold' note, and let her put twenty pounds down on it with the rest due this week."

Hugo shrugged, indifferent. "There you are," he counted out the notes. "Plus an extra ten to the girl for her trouble."

Gladia nodded and deposited the money in the register. "How is your brother?"

"Ian's fine."

"I mean since the accident last month. When he totaled your Jag."

"That wasn't Ian behind the wheel. It was me."

"Fess up, Hugo. Everyone knows it was Ian. Drunker than a skunk as usual he was, called you to hush it up. Very noble of you to take the blame."

Hugo regarded her stonily. "I don't know what you're talking about, Gladia. It was me behind the wheel. It was raining, and I lost control."

"You, lose control? That'll be the day," Gladia scoffed.

Hugo scowled. Of course Gladia was correct. He had taken Ian, younger than himself by seven years, to visit their mother at her converted gatehouse on the Wrothesley estate. As Hugo napped on the sofa after dinner, Ian borrowed his meticulously refurbished 1968 Jaguar and drove into the village, got drunk, and crashed it into a tree a mile from home.

By some miracle, Ian had emerged from the wreck relatively unscathed and called his brother immediately. Hugo ran the entire distance from the house to the scene of the accident, his heart pumping as sirens wailed in the distance. Taking the keys, he arranged the scene so it appeared that he was the driver instead of Ian, and when the police arrived, they found Hugo talking on his mobile phone with his best friend and agent, Tom Bellville-Howe.

With excruciating thoroughness, the police examined every inch of the accident scene, deeply suspicious of Hugo's story that he had been driving his inebriated brother home when he lost control of the car on a sharp turn. Ian sat in silence as ordered, nodding in terrified agreement only when absolutely necessary and leaving the talking to Hugo. A medic tended to a small cut across Ian's forehead, and Hugo was able to produce some nasty scrapes and bruises of his own from the match against Bolton the day before. Still, the questioning dragged on for what seemed like hours.

Eventually the police were forced to concede that it had been raining, the road was full of twists and turns, and there were no witnesses to contradict their story. Undaunted, they pressed charges of reckless driving against Hugo, and four weeks later the courtroom was packed with press and curious onlookers for the arraignment.

Standing solemn and erect in the dock, impeccably dressed in a dark grey bespoke suit, starched white linen shirt, and silk necktie, Hugo had pleaded guilty to the charge.

"Luckily there was no alcohol involved or you would be facing serious jail time," the wizened judge remarked. "But I'm sure you know this."

"Yes, sir."

"Your driving was erratic and dangerous, and posed a serious threat to everyone."

"Yes, sir." Hugo stared back implacably, his eyes an icy grey, his firm jaw set. "I deeply regret my actions and am prepared to take full responsibility for them."

"In that case, I am sentencing you to one year of probation and eight weeks' community service, to be performed at the Haddonfield School in Hampstead, commencing no later than

January of the coming year. You will be required to submit to random drug and sobriety checks, and the school will be filing regular reports on your attendance and contributions."

"What am I to do there, sir?"

"Put that excellent Eton education to some bloody use for once," the old man barked, earning a laugh from the crowd. "You're too clever by half, and I'm sure they'll find something for you to do. Now approach the bench."

Hugo stepped around the railing and stood before the judge, who glared down at him. "You know this has broken your mother's heart," the man whispered. "For God's sake, Hugo, put a lid on that bloody brother of yours. How he escaped with his life, I have no clue."

Cameras flashed as Hugo exited the courtroom, swung behind the wheel of the brand-new black Jaguar XJ Coupe, and sped away in a spray of gravel.

All requests for comment had been directed to the public relations department of Bellville-Howe and Associates, where they were completely ignored.

---

The clanging bell over the shop door announced a new customer, and Gladia looked up, a smile on her lips. "Well, Hugo, today is your lucky day. Here's the girl who wanted your book."

Hugo glanced over his shoulder and saw her in the doorway, her lithe form silhouetted from behind by radiant sunshine. In a rush, everything came into sharp focus: the fresh outdoor scent that accompanied her into the musty shop, the bright blue of her parka, and the sound of the traffic from outside. And, damned if it wasn't true—the world stopped spinning for a fraction of a second so the ethereal image could be etched indelibly in his mind.

Shutting the door behind her, the young woman paused to pull a knit hat off her head, releasing a tumble of hair. It cascaded down her back and around her face, the exact color of the wheat at Wrothesley just before harvesting. Glancing around the shop, she spotted Gladia and smiled, then joined them at the counter.

She stood next to him at barely shoulder-height, and when he looked down, he could see her flawless skin, cheeks pink from the cold, and a fine nose liberally sprinkled with freckles. But it was her blue eyes that held him entranced. They twinkled with life and excitement, and he felt a pleasurable tension begin to fill his body.

Good Lord, no wonder Roderick was besotted. She was enchanting.

"Hello, I was in Saturday and put twenty pounds down on the McIntosh book," the girl said, evidently delighted to see the book on the counter. "I've got the rest of the money right here, my parents sent it as my early Christmas present."

Her accent was odd—British, but with a dose of flat American vowels mixed in. Hugo knew he was staring but was unable to take his eyes off her. In her excitement over the book, she didn't seem to notice.

Gladia grimaced. "Yes, miss, Roderick told me. Unfortunately, this gentleman is also interested in the book."

She turned to him in surprise. "Oh, hello. Do you collect horticulture books as well?"

*Merciful heaven, dimples.*

"N-no," Hugo stammered, his usual cool demeanor evaporating. Words leapt to his lips, ignoring proper order and refusing to form coherent thoughts in their rush to impress her with his intelligence and charm. "Perhaps. No. Books, I... I have some. Yes."

She waited to see if he was going to add any more to the muddled conversation. "Yes, you like horticulture books?"

Hugo swallowed, his mouth dry, and tried again. "There are certain... what I mean to say is, on the subject of horticulture..." He faltered and came to a full stop when he saw the girl pressing her lips together to keep from laughing.

Damn, this was no good, he was behaving like a simpleton. Forcing himself to stop staring at her lips, he turned his attention to the book on the counter before them. With a Herculean effort, he pronounced, "I need this one."

"This one?" She glanced at the tattered copy of *The Orchard*.

"Yes. I've just bought it."

The girl flinched as if she'd been slapped. "But you can't have this one. I've put money down on it. And I've got the other sixty pounds." Digging in her coat pocket, she withdrew a worn wallet and laid the banknotes on the counter.

"I just paid for it, the full amount," Hugo tried to explain, inwardly cursing as he saw her rising panic.

"I'll give you more!" she appealed to Gladia, fumbling again through the billfold. "Here, I can give you another five! That's eighty-five pounds."

"I've already purchased it," Hugo repeated.

"But you don't want this one," the girl countered, opening the book to the mottled flyleaf. "Look, it's not even an 1839 first edition. The vignette title is 1847—it's a reissue, almost worthless."

"I need this one. And I'll make it one hundred."

"You can't do that! Here, here's my last twenty-pound note. That makes it one hundred and five pounds."

"Two hundred," Hugo countered, steeling himself to ignore her shaking hands, gripping the now empty wallet. As pretty as the girl was, the book was his.

"That's not fair!" With unveiled contempt, her eyes coursed over him, noting his handmade Italian shoes, tailored suit, and cashmere overcoat before settling on his hands. "You're an armchair gardener, aren't you?"

It was obviously the worst invective she could hurl. In desperation, Hugo glanced around the counter and grabbed the nearest book that had a pretty flower on the cover. "Look, how about I buy you this instead?"

"Orchids? What would I do with a book on orchids?" She looked in appeal to Gladia, who shrugged and took a twenty-pound note from the register, placing it on the counter next to a notice that read: "Patrons are welcome to put money down on a book but it will be sold to the first person paying the full asking price."

*The Orchard* lay before them, homely and ragged. She turned a few pages, gently smoothing her gloved hand over them. "It's not even in very good condition," she said, doing a heroic job of choking back the tears flooding her eyes. "Look, someone's written in the margins."

"I know. Why would you want a book like that?"

"The notes are the best part."

With shaky deliberation, she tucked the bank notes back in her wallet and gave the book one last, loving look. "It's a very special book," she told him with hard-fought dignity. "Congratulations. I hope you enjoy it."

And with that, she was gone.

# Chapter Two

JULIE RANDALL RUMMAGED through the bedroom closet of her small row house in Finchley, searching for the shoes that would go with the dress she was wearing. *Plum sleeveless cocktail + black pumps w/diamond buckles,* Rosie's note instructed. The bike ride home from Gladia's had done little to cool her irritation over losing the book, and now the blasted shoes were nowhere to be found. Would the brown sling-backs with open toes work?

Dating Mark put huge demands on her wardrobe—as an advertising executive, he entertained clients and depended on having her along. Her meager salary from The Haddonfield School of Culinary Sciences covered her simple lifestyle and no more, but luckily her older sister had come to the rescue. Rosie and her husband, Ken, ran a successful environmental consulting business in Philadelphia and often dined out with clients, and Rosie would periodically ship over boxes of her retired evening wear. The sisters were almost the same size, and Rosie pinned helpful notes to each outfit indicating which shoes and accessories should be worn with it, knowing full well her sister lived in work clothes and wouldn't have a clue.

Julie followed the instructions to the letter and also kept careful note of when and where she'd worn each outfit, not wanting to repeat the mistake she'd once made—wearing the same dress to dinner twice with the same clients. Mark had caught it right away, of course, but stopped her from going home to change. "No, darling, it's too late now, let's hope they don't notice."

The driver from Smith-Wessex would be picking her up in an hour, which was how long it took her to get ready. One of the students had taught her a few hairdos, but the makeup always defeated her. Almost nothing would cover the freckles that dotted her cheeks, and eyeliner was completely out of the question. Mascara to darken her fair lashes and a touch of lip gloss were manageable, but her fingernails were another source of concern. Sometimes all the scrubbing in the world wouldn't remove the clay soil of Hampstead Heath, and it was impossible to grow her nails long enough for polish.

Flopping onto her bed, she muttered a strong yet satisfying oath she'd overheard from the students when they thought she was out of earshot.

The day had been full of rotten luck. This morning at Haddonfield, a basement shelf had collapsed, spilling an entire season's harvest of butternut squash on the packed dirt floor. The repair delayed her trip to Gladia's by two hours, just enough time for that jerk to steal *The Orchard*. There was no helping it, though. Haddonfield ran on a shoestring and these things happened. But where was the justice?

It had seemed like a gift from heaven when she'd discovered the book in Gladia's store three days before. She'd been exhausted from shopping for bathing suits to take on holiday, and a mysteriously captivating peignoir in a shop window had drained her wallet to a single twenty-pound note. Before heading home, she ducked into the bookshop and poked through a box on the counter, spotting *The Orchard* immediately. It took only a quick perusal of the cryptic marks and detailed margin notes to know she'd made the find of a lifetime.

The clerk seemed unsure if the book was even for sale but took the last of her money as a down payment and noted her promise to return with the rest. Back at Haddonfield, she emailed her parents asking for the money as her Christmas present, and they wired it immediately. But that arrogant jerk beat her to it.

Arrogant, handsome jerk, Julie corrected herself. She'd noticed him as soon as she entered the store, and even fancied she'd felt a slight spark between them as they stood at the counter. He was over six feet tall by her estimation, taller than Mark by several inches, with either broad shoulders or a very good tailor who made his frame look lean instead of skinny. He had high cheekbones and blond hair that curled where it was brushed off his forehead. It gave him a scholarly air, like one of her mother's or father's graduate students.

His nose was prominent, with a slight bend near the bridge that spoke of a break in the past, and lips that were full and sensual. The entire image was ruined, however, by his eyes, which were pleasant at first but turned to pale ice as his arrogance grew, completely spoiling his appeal.

The students would call him posh, but there was something about him that didn't fit, a toughness and intensity that belied the pampered impression. Maybe he was one of those bankers from the City that frequented the same restaurants Mark liked.

Or a wealthy entrepreneur. The gleaming black Jaguar parked in front of the shop was probably his as well.

Whatever his occupation, the man obviously wouldn't know a spade from a hoe. Any self-respecting gardener would have a bit of the heavy London clay soil on the soles of his shoes, as she did.

With a flash of inspiration, Julie opened the bottom drawer of her bureau and pulled out the shoe box she'd tucked away when there was no room for it in her small closet. Inside were the black pumps with diamond buckles, and bless Rosie, they really did look nice.

After a final check in the bedroom mirror, Julie couldn't resist peeking in the top drawer of her bureau. The beautiful ivory lace peignoir lay folded on top, and she ran her hand over the thin straps and narrow satin ribbons that held the lace bodice together, the same lace that lined the long, diaphanous skirt. It was slit high to reveal plenty of naked leg, the magical fabric teasingly concealing, then revealing, making the lucky man itch to find out what lay beneath. She had never owned anything like it yet had paid the outlandish price without a second thought.

The peignoir was ready—whenever Mark was.

# Chapter Three

LATER THAT EVENING, Hugo sat in the garden of a Mayfair mansion in an enormous tent, suffering a loud band and the jostling of partygoers cavorting on the dance floor next to his table. Portable heaters had turned the tent into a furnace. He despised removing his evening jacket, but now found himself forced to do so or else become drenched in sweat.

The cream of young British society filled the tent—viscounts waiting to inherit crumbling castles, princesses with bad educations and worse teeth—contemporaries who seemed hell-bent on wasting their lives in Gstaad or St. Barths, or drifting across Africa, barely dabbling in real work. This was his brother's crowd. He had no time for such useless idiots.

According to his Rolex, midnight came in exactly seven minutes, at which time his eighteen-year-old twin cousins would cut their birthday cake and he could politely say his goodbyes and get the hell out of there.

The catering staff tried to move his table back a few inches to make way for the cake, igniting a skirmish amongst the girls staked out around him. Hugo ignored them as they fought to maintain their proximity and instead covertly examined his hands.

What had the girl meant by "armchair gardener?" She had spoken with pure disdain, and he was sure it was the worst condemnation she could think of. He would agree that his hands were the only part of his body that didn't contribute to his magnificent salary, but at the same time, they were also spared the bruises, breaks, sprains, cuts, and other misfortunes the rest were regularly dealt.

Vapid chatter swirled around him as he continued to brood over the morning's events. The girl obviously hadn't recognized him, because if she had, his actions wouldn't have surprised her in the least. His reputation for arrogance and callousness had never bothered him in the past, but tonight it vexed him very much that the girl thought he was an ass.

On the other hand, she didn't seem like the type who would care even if she did know. She'd been intent on purchasing that book, and for the life of him, he couldn't figure out why. When he'd arrived home, he'd immediately gone up to his third-floor library and combed the fragile pages for any clues as to what could make it so special to her. There were long-winded discussions of various fruits popular in the Victorian era —"Persian varieties of melon should not be overlooked"— with terse instructions about planting and caring for them, followed by long lists of cultivars. Peaches alone had twenty-six pages, for God's sake, and his eyes almost crossed reading them. And what the hell was artificial fecundation?

The book had been marked up with cryptic handwritten notes in old ink, and Hugo puzzled over random circled words, irregular geometric figures drawn in the margins, and entire sections crossed out. His grandfather hadn't known anything about the book's origins, except that it had been in the Wrothesley library for generations, along with the four other books in the series. His best guess was that they'd belonged to the estate's head gardener sometime in the nineteenth century and had entered the collection at some point after that.

After two hours, Hugo had given up, but it had bothered him all night and bothered him still. Why had she been so affronted when he offered to buy her the book on orchids? It was double the price of the McIntosh book and with a much prettier picture on the cover. Yet she acted as if he'd propositioned her.

Which wasn't the most distasteful thought in the world.

"Are you sure you don't want to dance, Hugo?" a plump brunette asked from her prized seat next to him, leaning forward to give him the best view of her ample cleavage. Her father was the Member of Parliament from his family seat in Bedfordshire, and his grandmother was her uncle's great-aunt by marriage. In their social circle, they were practically family.

"You know I don't dance," Hugo said, removing his evening jacket from her hands before she could drape it around her shoulders. "But don't let me stop you."

"No, it's too boring. They've already played this song twice." Unwilling to surrender her seat to one of the girls circling nearby, she instead switched topics. "Daddy was wondering if you're coming up to our country house over Christmas. The Harrisons will be there, and the Tarklett-Smiths. It should be a blast."

"No, thank you, Sophie." Harry Harrison would bore him to tears with an analysis of Kingsbury Town's season so far, and Kip Tarklett-Smith would want predictions for the FA Cup. Kingsbury Town would play four fixtures over the holidays, which limited the amount of time he could spend with his mother and Ian, and he'd rather be with them at Wrothesley than anywhere else. Plus, Wrothesley's estate manager, Miles

Dersham, would have a hundred issues that would need to be sorted. Where the patience for that would come from, he had no idea. Fate had thrown the men into their jobs of owner and manager much earlier than anyone would have imagined, and the stress of running the estate properly, the way generations of Auchinclosses and Dershams had done, was exhausting for both.

"Just as well." Sophie sniffed with pretend indifference as she grabbed another glass of champagne from a passing waiter and downed it in one gulp. "I'll probably have to go to Barbados for business. Did you know I'm working at Smith-Wessex now? The advertising firm in Soho? I'm a production assistant—have my own desk and everything."

Hugo didn't bother to stifle a yawn. "Good for you. Glad you're doing something productive with your time."

"Why do you keep looking at your hands?" she asked. Spying a photographer across the tent, she leapt to her feet. "Oh look, here's the photographer from *Tatler*!" In a flash, she plopped onto his lap, crossing her legs and pushing her heaving bosom in his face. "I hope we get into Bystander!"

Several camera flashes went off before Hugo could struggle to his feet, dumping Sophie ingloriously to the floor in the process. "I don't do photographs," he snapped.

"You're in a vile mood, Hugo," Pippa Donnell drawled, exhaling cigarette smoke as she helped her boarding school roommate to her feet. "Where's Ian? It's always much more fun when he's here."

"I think my stepsister Natalie has the most terrible crush on him. Do you know I found his picture in her drawer?" Octavia Swindon offered up archly.

"You mean amongst all the KitKat bars?" Pippa asked, getting a huge laugh from everyone except Hugo. He'd always thought Natalie Swindon was a perfectly nice young lady, regardless of her size. "So where is he, Hugo?"

*Drying out.* "He's home."

"Is he going back to Cambridge after break?"

"No." Hugo had withdrawn Ian after the accident, which had been just a few months before he would have flunked out anyway. Ian was now safely installed in a tiny fourth-floor walk-up flat in Covent Garden and enrolled in International Studies at King's College London, where he would stay until he either graduated or expired from boredom. Whichever came first didn't matter, as far as Hugo was concerned.

Big Ben chimed midnight and a large cake was rolled onto the dance floor. Hugo shrugged on his jacket and began heading for the exit, trailed by Sophie.

"Shall we get out of here and go back to my place?" she suggested, leaning unsteadily on his arm.

There was a time when he would have taken her up on her offer, screwed her senseless, and then left without a goodbye. God knew it might not be a bad idea; it had been some time since he'd had any. Sophie had been making herself very available for a long time, but the sheer tediousness of it put him off and he didn't even consider it.

He liked sex as much as the next guy, but the next guy would have laughed in disbelief if he'd known the real state of Hugo's sex life. A man in his position could have his pick, yet how could he explain that nothing suited him? It was like someone sitting next to a lake and complaining of thirst, just because he didn't like the look of the fish.

Granted, his situation was entirely self-inflicted. Unlike most of his teammates, he steadfastly refused to have anything to do with the groupies that hung around footballers, and he didn't know any ordinary girls like the one he'd met today. That left the women in his social sphere, who were plentiful and interchangeable. His callous disregard for anyone's satisfaction other than his own didn't seem to make a bit of difference to them. He was rich, famous, and owned a stately manor they would kill to be mistress of.

With a few curt words, Hugo returned to the main house to say goodbye to his older relatives, who were enjoying each other's company in the main drawing room.

A platter of sandwiches lay on a buffet and he hungrily ate two, their blandness unnoticed by a bachelor who kept a thinly stocked pantry. With his level of physical activity, he needed to consume thousands of calories a day and rarely cared where they came from. He ate most of his meals at local takeaways, and it was almost impossible to keep his weight up. The team nutritionist had abandoned hope long ago, and his tailor just shrugged. It bothered him, however, that even though he was strong and perfectly fit, he knew he looked skinny and almost anemic.

"Tough luck against Watford last week," an earl, a distant uncle, remarked. "Your mother won five pounds off me, tell her I'll pay up at the next Lady Warwick School trustee meeting."

"Mummy's betting against me?" Hugo laughed.

The earl winked. "Shrewd woman, your mother. She knew your twisted ankle was worse than it looked."

———◦○◦———

The cab followed the midnight traffic as it flowed back to his home in central London, a steady rain making the festive Christmas lights shimmer. If you could call London festive, Hugo thought. He hated the damn place.

London seemed to return the sentiment, in spades. For a city that practically deified footballers, he was an outcast—a toff dabbling in a working man's sport. Yet he was afforded some grudging respect because, after all, the game was the only thing that mattered, and there was no question he'd earned his spot in the Premier League. Consistently ranked in the top twenty Premier League midfielders, he was invariably described as cold-blooded and clinically accurate, defensively steady with excellent technique, and yet creative, with the ability to think on his feet. Getting the ball was one thing— knowing what to do with it was quite another.

He didn't cultivate the image of remoteness he'd acquired. In private, he thought of himself as a pleasant and rather self-effacing chap. The fact that he kept a low profile should have, in his opinion, made him more likable to the general public, but apparently they craved the entertainment his flashy teammates like Mick Carr provided. Carr, Kingsbury Town's bad boy, was a media darling, adored by the masses.

Well, if they wanted a Neanderthal, they were welcome to him. The mess with Trika had cured Hugo of any desire for publicity, and he paid Tom a fortune to keep his name out of the papers, preferring instead the company of his books and venturing out only when there was a duty to the club or his family.

Traffic stopped around Wellington Arch, and a young couple crossed the intersection, the man's arm wrapped protectively around the girl. His other hand held an umbrella over them as she huddled against him. They were laughing and enjoying being together, oblivious to the cold and damp. With a chivalric swoosh, he lifted her over a puddle and was rewarded with a warm kiss.

The lights changed, and the cab drove on.

Where did she live? Probably north London, Hugo mused, up near the Heath. After she'd left the bookshop, he had impulsively driven around for over an hour looking for a glimpse of her, but she had vanished. Maybe she'd gone home to her husband and family—she'd worn gloves, so he couldn't tell if she had a ring on her finger. But if she was married, why was she asking her parents for money to buy a book?

As Hugo replayed that afternoon's encounter, the same potent desire flared, leaving him aroused and impatient. The strong effect she was having on him was startling. There were other women in his life and none so far had left a mark. But after spending less than five minutes in her company, he couldn't get her out of his head.

She was pretty in a fresh, guileless way. It wasn't just that, though—there was an energy about her that intrigued him. She was spirited—an old-fashioned word, but fitting. The brief time they were together was the liveliest he'd spent in ages. Even now, just thinking about her, he felt a fierce urge to find her and take her somewhere private, someplace where they could be alone. It wasn't simply lust. It was a nebulous craving for a lot of things he couldn't put his finger on. He just knew he wanted her attention.

Impatience welled up and he fought the urge to redirect the driver to the north. There were seven and a half million inhabitants in London—what was he going to do, start going door-to-door? *Sorry for the interruption, but I'm trying to locate a lovely girl that I met this afternoon and can't forget. Is she at home?*

Total defeat was a dish Hugo rarely tasted. If the team lost a match, they'd be meeting their opponents again and would have another chance. But now, defeat was being served up to him on a silver platter, and he needed to acknowledge it and move on. He would never see her again. And even if he did, chances were she wouldn't want to see him.

# Chapter Four

JULIE SAT AT her office desk, tapping a pencil on the arm of the rickety wooden chair. From the window over her desk, she looked out at the mansion's original kitchen gardens, where the grid of planting beds she and Clive were recreating was easily visible, if not absolutely to the original plan.

Located on the edge of Hampstead Heath, Haddonfield had originally encompassed a great deal of acreage when it was built in 1847. The owner then hired Charles McIntosh, one of the most famous horticulturists of the time, to design the gardens and orchards. McIntosh's series of five gardening books, the first ever for backyard gardeners, was an overnight sensation, and Victorians became mad for gardening. Queen Victoria herself was an ardent admirer of the man.

Haddonfield was one of McIntosh's first commissions. Over the years, however, the original plans were lost, the gardens abandoned, and parcels sold off until only the mansion, barn, and five acres of land remained. Julie spent hours poring over her hand-drawn map noting clues she'd found of the original planting scheme. Some areas were clearly correct, but the map still contained large empty swathes or later additions that carried the dismissive notation "modern."

The pencil continued to tap a rapid staccato as she stared at the original brick north wall that shielded the garden from the raw winter wind. The mansion house and old staff wing, where her office was located, provided protection from the west and south. Only half of the east wall remained, the missing portion replaced by a post-war glasshouse bursting with vegetable seedlings. A rusted iron gate in the southeast corner led from the gardens to the orchards beyond.

Feeling chilled, she rose to add another log to the woodstove that heated her office. Julie took great pride in the room's sparse functionality, furnished only with a plank table for her desk, a wooden bench, and some chairs for visitors. Two tall bookshelves were filled with her antique gardening books and scholarly horticultural journals. The space she'd cleared for *The Orchard* stood conspicuously empty.

Whoever had marked up that copy had worked at Haddonfield and perhaps even helped McIntosh lay out the orchards. Her heart had beaten feverishly when she thumbed through the pages in the bookshop, recognizing the exact garden dimensions, house layout, and orchard orientation. Varieties of trees were noted, cultivars underlined, and yields indicated. No one had yet recreated a McIntosh design exactly, and if she was going to be the first, she needed that book. Which was probably sitting on a drawing room shelf in a posh house in Notting Hill or someplace swank like that, occasionally thumbed through whenever that bastard felt like looking at his trophy.

"So, where is it?" a petite brunette in crisp chef whites asked from the office doorway.

"Oh, Bonnie, Gladia sold it to someone else right before I got there."

"No! Who?"

"Some man, very rich, very handsome, very arrogant." Julie sighed. "Jerk."

Bonnie, the school's culinary instructor, took a seat on the bench and gratefully lifted her feet onto a low footstool. She was married to Clive, the school's maintenance man, and they were expecting their first child in June, six months away.

"Why would Gladia do that?" Bonnie asked. "You put money down."

"Doesn't matter, first one who pays full price gets it. There are other copies around, but that one has all the notes for McIntosh's orchard plan here at Haddonfield. That book would have saved me ages figuring out the planting scheme."

"That is bad luck. But buck up, something good will come of it," Bonnie said and handed her a white envelope. "A courier arrived while you were out, he said these were the tickets for your trip to Barbados with Mark after Christmas."

Julie opened it and frowned. "Seven days? I thought Mark said we were only staying for four."

"What a slog, poor you."

Julie stowed the tickets in her desk. "That did sound spoiled. Barbados is beautiful, and the Dionysus people were very nice when I went with Mark in September. It's just that he works all the time, and I can't lounge by the pool for more than a day, not like the other guests. The last time, I got so bored I started dead-heading the hibiscus in the planters. Plus, I have so much to do here."

"I thought Mark worked for Smith-Wessex, the advertising firm."

"He does. Dionysus is their biggest client, and he's just been put in charge of all the advertising for their new line of gin.

They throw a huge New Year's Eve party at their headquarters on the island. Mark was invited and insisted I come, too. I'm flying down after I visit my family in Philadelphia."

"Will Rochelle be there?"

Julie winced at the mention of Mark's ex-girlfriend, the world-famous model Rochelle Chevelle. She was the flawless "face" of Dionysus's bestselling liquor, Sam Lord's Castle Rum. The advertisements were everywhere, and it felt like the world was wallpapered with her face. "Mark says no, she has to be in Fiji for a photo shoot with *Vogue*."

"Remarkable how they can still work together after such a public breakup," Bonnie commented dryly.

"They have to. Mark says they're still friends, although I know he sometimes gets irritated at things she does. But they were together for three years, and you can't expect feelings to go away overnight."

"How long have you two been dating? Five, six months?"

"It will be seven months next week. And, Bonnie, he still hasn't..." Julie frowned. "You know."

Bonnie studied her friend. "Made any moves yet?"

Julie's shoulders sagged. "He's affectionate, and we have a great time together, but it hasn't gone any further. Is that normal?"

"Sorry, love, no experience in that department. Clive made it very clear from the beginning what was on his mind. Exceedingly so."

"I'm twenty-six and I've never had a serious boyfriend before. It would be nice if we... got a bit closer. I'm trying, but I don't know what I'm doing wrong."

"Julie, it's normal to want a more intimate relationship. And I'm sure you're not doing anything wrong."

"It's hard trying to fit into his world," Julie confided. "You should see the glamorous people Mark works with, they're so perfect and fragile—it's like they live on a glass shelf somewhere. When I'm around them, I feel like a bull in a china shop. It's why I got those bikinis last weekend, so that I can fit in a bit more. On the last trip to Barbados, I took my one-piece suits and looked like a nun."

"Did Mark say that?" Bonnie asked.

"Not in so many words. He's very kind and says I shouldn't try and compete with the models, that looking gorgeous is their livelihood. They're paid to sparkle—I'm paid to toss compost."

Bonnie's lips formed a thin line. "How considerate of him. Julie, there's nothing wrong with you. You are beautiful. Even wearing three layers of woolies, you turn every man's head."

"Maybe I should get another peignoir."

"Look, I'm a bit older than you. I've seen a lot more of the world, and I know two things for certain. The first is that when a man is interested in you, they let you know. The second is that the right man will make you feel like the most beautiful woman in the world, no matter what you're wearing. When you meet a guy like that, everything will sort itself out."

Her words sounded like good advice, and Julie squared her shoulders. "I'll be patient with Mark."

A student called from the doorway, "Don says he'd like to see the staff upstairs in his office if you two have a moment."

"Thank you, Matthew, tell him we're on our way," Julie said and helped her friend to her feet. "How are you feeling?" she asked as they made their way to the school director's office.

"Much better. The doctor said the morning sickness should be finishing up soon. All of a sudden, I can't bear the stench of sauteing mushrooms. Clive had to come and watch the morning class while I ran out. June can't come soon enough for me."

———◦○◦———

Don Garrett welcomed Bonnie and Julie into his office with his usual boundless energy, motioning them to seats around a large table. Clive, a burly man from the north of England, jumped to his feet to get his wife's chair and fetched a pillow for her back, fussing about her as she got comfortable. Julie watched them wistfully.

"Good news, gang," Don began. "Sir Albert Ross from our Board of Governors called this morning with an offer I think we'd do well to accept. It seems one of the bright young studs from the Kingsbury Town Football Club is in some trouble, and the magistrate has ordered him to do public service for a deserving nonprofit. Sir Albert suggested we'd be very deserving, and I agree."

"A footballer?" Clive asked, crossing his arms across his massive chest. "Would that be the Kingsbury Town midfielder that was in the papers last month for wrecking his vintage Jag?"

"The same. Evidently this one is marginally more educated than the rest, and Sir Albert feels he might be able to do some tutoring. Since our last academics instructor quit after five weeks, it might help take some pressure off until we find a permanent replacement. If nothing else, the students will get a kick out of it."

"How long will he be here?" Julie asked.

"He'll start after the New Year and then twice a week till March, when we end the academics term. They're being very strict. We have to document his hours and affirm he was actually here and did some work. I'll make sure that happens."

Clive frowned. "I've heard of him. He's got a reputation, and I don't mean that in a good way. He's a ruddy good footballer, but he's a cold fish—quite nasty and high-handed. There were also some woman problems a while ago, if I'm remembering correctly. Is that something we want to get mixed up with?"

Don nodded. "Sir Albert brought these issues up himself and assured me this guy would be on his best behavior. I guess he knows the family personally and vouches for him. If it doesn't work out, we're under no obligation to keep him. But academics is our weakest area, I think we're all in agreement there, and frankly, it can't get much worse."

"I hope he's tough, or the kids will make short work of him, like they've done the last four academics instructors," Julie said.

"Agreed." Don nodded. "So as long as he doesn't set a bad example, I can't see much downside to it. I'm hoping Providence is smiling on us. Again."

# Chapter Five

THE CHRISTMAS HOLIDAYS were productive, with Kingsbury Town having wins over Southampton and Burnley, and a third-round FA Cup win over Reading after the New Year. Hugo's own play was decidedly lackluster and uninspired, and for the life of him, he couldn't keep his head together. Ordinary things didn't hold his attention and stupid mistakes began piling up. Giles Roberts, the Kingsbury Town manager, was at a loss to understand him. So he just yelled louder.

Over a three-day break, Hugo took Ian back to spend Christmas at Wrothesley with their mother, who was on holiday from her own busy magistrate's docket. It was just the three of them at her renovated gatehouse on the grounds of the estate, and she'd done everything to make the holiday cheerful. But they all remembered a time not so long ago when the big house down the lane was jolly bedlam, with fifteen living under the large roof and double that number arriving to celebrate the holidays.

Hugo tried his best to be good company but found himself sliding back into a dark mood. He took long walks around the fields in the bitter cold, avoiding Miles with his endless questions and problems. Finally, his mother sat him down for a stern talk and even hinted that he should consider selling Wrothesley if it was too much to keep up. He was appalled by the suggestion and stormed out, eventually finding himself before the mansion's imposing front doors.

He let himself in and paced the empty halls and rooms for hours, the echo of his footsteps disturbing the stillness. The house seemed to be waiting patiently in silent expectation that he would bring back the laughter and love that had once filled the air. In maddening frustration, he kicked the marble newel post at the base of the grand staircase, sending shooting pains through his foot. What was he supposed to be, a bloody magician? Somehow he'd taken for granted that he would meet a girl, that they would fall in love and raise a happy family together within these walls. It would all be easy and effortless, the way his parents had made it seem.

Instead, he was making a bloody bollocks of it and there didn't seem to be any way out.

———◦———

For the past nine months, Kingsbury Town had been training at St Augustine, an old school in Wimbledon that his boss, Sir Frank, was renting while the new training facility was being built in Hendon. Hugo loved Sir Frank like a father, but for the love of God, he was one cheap bugger. While the pitch at St Augustine School was excellent, it was obvious why the rest of the school was scheduled for demolition. And not a moment too soon.

It was Tuesday, the day Hugo was expected to present himself at Haddonfield to begin his probation work. He ran some additional laps after practice in a half-hearted attempt to put the visit off, avoiding the cracked curbs and broken concrete in his path.

The traffic between Wimbledon and Hampstead Heath would be a nightmare. *Bloody Ian.* As if there wasn't enough to do already without tutoring slackers and street thugs in history and maths. And there'd better not be any groupies who wanted his autograph or pictures taken.

Back in the dilapidated locker room, Hugo changed into a charcoal-grey flannel suit and white broadcloth shirt with mother-of-pearl buttons, taking care to avoid a slow drip from the leaking roof. Outside in the weed-infested car park, a few paparazzi looked up when he exited the school, probably expecting Mick Carr or Fernando Garcia-Lopez. One took a few shots with his camera, but Hugo wasn't fussed. Tom would know immediately if anything were going to run in the papers and would shut it down.

On the drive north, he impulsively detoured to Hampstead and pulled into a parking spot in front of the bookstore. Inside, Gladia glanced down from her perch atop a tall ladder.

"She hasn't come back, Hugo," she announced, answering his question before he even asked it.

Hugo cursed under his breath. "Do you know who she is?"

Gladia shrugged. "No, not really. She comes in occasionally to buy a few things, nothing expensive, usually horticulture and agronomy. So I think she's a gardener. Rides her bike, so she must live somewhere on the Heath, but I haven't seen her since you chased her off. Bugger you, I think I've lost a customer."

———⦿———

And this is the kitchens," a student named Lalani told Hugo, pushing her thick glasses back up her nose as she led him on a tour of Haddonfield.

The kitchens stretched along the rear of the house and included a scullery, dish room, and butler's pantry. While certainly not modern by any standards, they were well-maintained and tidy, with floors of polished quarry stone and work surfaces in gleaming stainless steel. There were three long preparation tables in the center of the room, with commercial ranges and several ovens along one wall and industrial-sized refrigerators lining another. An enormous oak trestle table sat under a window overlooking the walled garden, with benches pushed underneath. The constant flow of students reminded him of his dormitory house at Eton.

A set of French doors opened into a glassed atrium that Hugo mistook for a greenhouse since there was barely an inch of space that didn't host a potted plant. A glimmer of water amongst the verdant foliage caught his eye. "A lap pool? Does anyone use it?"

Lalani shivered at the thought. "Julie swims in the evenings after school. She's like one of them polar bears that likes the cold water."

Students dressed in neat chef uniforms were gathered at a prep table, watching a dark-haired woman demonstrate cutting techniques with a large knife. Lalani introduced her as Bonnie, and the students as Matthew, Pax, Jira, Phong, Joanna, Nerida, and Tanda. Hugo shook their hands, amused at their obvious quandary over meeting a Premier League footballer while maintaining their probable loyalty to either Tottenham Hotspur or Arsenal football clubs.

"And this is where we have our dinners for the public every Monday night," Lalani continued, leading him through the butler's pantry and into a dining room with a grand marble fireplace and elegant walnut paneling. Nine round tables with eight chairs each filled the room comfortably, and mullioned windows let in the weak January sun.

"Upstairs are the classrooms." Lalani guided him up the staircase to the second floor, where two former bedrooms were filled with tables, chairs, chalkboards, and bookshelves. The larger classroom's walls were hung with posters of plant life cycles and Shakespearean plays. "This is where we do horticulture with Julie."

"And English?"

"She does them both and maths. She's the smartest person I ever met."

An energetic man bounded to the door and reached to shake his hand. "Hugo Auchincloss? Don Garrett. I'm the director here. Pleased to meet you."

Hugo returned the man's exuberant handshake. "A pleasure to meet you, Don. Quite an amazing place you have here. Lalani has been giving me an excellent tour."

Lalani giggled and twirled a stray piece of hair. "My pleasure," she croaked before ducking out the door and disappearing down the stairs.

"Wonderful girl," Don agreed, leading Hugo down the hall to his office. "Another one of our miracles. Mother overdosed when she was two, no idea who her father is, was in foster care for six years before the Magness Foundation was able to get her out, but by that time she was partially blind from malnutrition. Came to us almost illiterate but has blossomed here. She'll be graduating this year and can expect a very good career as a pastry chef. Her plum tarts would make you weep."

Hugo took the offered seat on a battered settee and Don flopped onto a comfortably threadbare wing chair across from him. "We're very proud of what we've accomplished here. It's only been ten years, but we've been able to graduate over one hundred students in our full two-year program and another three hundred in our certificate program."

Hugo shifted his weight to avoid a spring that was trying to dig its way through the seat cushion. "How did you come to be here?"

"Fifteen years ago, the Haddonfield estate was given to the Magness Foundation—you might have heard of them. They have a much larger operation in London that serves at-risk children, and we operate under its auspices. The house and estate were built in the 1850s by an iron industrialist and stayed in the family until the last owners donated it. The Foundation wasn't quite sure what to do with it, but it's been an excellent match for us, and the local council has been very reasonable since we haven't made any structural changes. It was very well built and always kept up, good roof and dry basements. Still a bugger to heat, though."

Hugo nodded. "I grew up in the family pile in Bedfordshire. Central heating is a miracle."

Don glanced at a paper in front of him. "Says here you graduated Eton. If you don't mind my asking, how the hell did you end up a midfielder for Kingsbury Town?"

Hugo was used to this question. "Football is our winter sport at Eton, and early on, the games master punted me a football and discovered I have quick feet and speed. His brother was a scout for Kingsbury Town, and when I was eighteen they invited me for a tryout. Sir Frank was innovative when it came to building his team and we clicked. That was eleven years ago, and I've been doing it ever since."

"Ever go on in school?"

"No," Hugo answered curtly. "Not many footballers do."

Don nodded and handed him a loose-leaf binder. "Here's what we cover. We do academics from November to the end of February, when the students sit for a small set of exams. We want to do more but for some reason can't keep an instructor. They all have starry-eyed ideals, but the reality is, it's a lot of hard work for almost no pay. Last one threw in the towel two months ago, and the staff have been filling in since. So having you help out a bit for the next eight weeks will take us right up to final exams, and then we'll start looking for a new instructor."

Hugo thumbed through the pages and was shocked by the basic level of material being covered.

Don grimaced. "Obviously, I don't think you'll have any trouble with our curriculum. Prep for dinner service takes all day Monday, so we do classwork Tuesdays through Fridays. It's very basic, and we just try to graduate them with enough language and maths basics to function in the real world. These kids have highly tuned survival skills and don't see the point in doing more."

Sounded like a lot of his teammates, Hugo thought.

"I'll warn you now, these kids are tough. They've seen more hell than you or I could imagine."

"Many discipline problems?"

"Not really. We're very selective. They have to work bloody hard to get here in the first place and don't want to screw it up. Plus, we board them down the road during the week, and that gets them out of their home environments, which is most of the battle. My wife, Gretchen, runs the dormitory house and we live next door with our two girls. The certificate students come up from the Magness Foundation School in the city twice a week. They're a bit rougher, but the full-time students keep them in line. They do food prep with Bonnie. Have you met her yet?"

"In the kitchens?"

Don nodded. "She and I started this school. We dreamt the idea up when we worked together as chefs at a private club in London. I left and traveled around the world, working in every kind of kitchen you can imagine. But we always kept talking about creating a school where deserving kids could be taught a valuable trade. We knew we wanted it to be self-supporting but couldn't make it work until we were offered Haddonfield. Even then, we had no idea what a jewel it was until Julie came."

"Don't think I've met her yet," Hugo said, discreetly picking a piece of lint off his jacket.

"You will." Don grinned. "And you won't forget her. Her official title is Garden Manager, but it's more like Garden Goddess. We knew we wanted to establish a small kitchen garden for the restaurant, you know—some strawberries, tomatoes, basil to have on hand. I think we interviewed every nutty granola from here to the Irish Sea, and then Julie turned up and took us outside. In the middle of winter, mind you, she showed us where there'd been a huge kitchen garden and orchard, and told us it had been designed by some yahoo Victorian gardener who wrote bestselling books and knew Queen Victoria.

"Blew us away, let me tell you. Right before our eyes were antique apple, pear, and cherry trees, as well as the remnants of raised beds, and she even found a few rogue potatoes, knew just where to look. One wall is even plumbed for hot water. She went right to it and took off the top stones and showed us. Then she presented us with a five-year plan with a reasonable budget, and now we're becoming known for the heirloom tomatoes she's growing, plus all sorts of produce and fruit that's too perishable for commercial growers. But let me tell you, it's the best stuff you've ever tasted. She has a remarkable collection of old horticulture books and hunts down the seeds they used—some of the stuff is remarkably rare. It's great publicity and is really setting us apart. When the kids go out into the world, they've got some prestige."

"That sort of thing is very popular these days, I understand," Hugo replied politely, stifling a yawn.

"It's a double-edged sword." Don frowned. "We're almost maxed out on space. She's got every inch of the outdoors planted, but we still can't meet the demand; the school has grown beyond our wildest dreams. The weekly dinners are booked weeks in advance. The neighbors have been supportive, but the traffic and notoriety have started to cause some grumbling. We're overwhelmed with student applications and the Magness Foundation is pushing us to expand. I never thought we'd be so successful that we'd be having these issues."

"Remarkable," Hugo murmured, glancing at his watch.

Don jumped to his feet. "We'll have to get Julie to take you on a tour. But make sure you have enough time, as she tends to rattle on a bit. I think she's out in the barns, let's go see."

"I appreciate you letting me work with your students," Hugo replied formally, wondering when the hell he could get out of there.

Don paused at the door, a faint smile on his lips. "We're glad to have you here, Hugo. I just hope you're prepared for how much this place will change you."

# Chapter Six

"HE'S EVER SO cute," Lalani gushed to Joanna as Julie entered the kitchen carrying a basket of freshly dug potatoes.

"Who's cute?" Julie asked.

"Hugo Auchincloss, the midfielder from Kingsbury Town. He's going to tutor us for a few weeks and I can't wait."

"Oh, is he here? I forgot he was coming," Julie said, weighing the potatoes and recording the data in the produce log.

"You won't forget once you see him. He's smashing." Lalani swooned against a doorway.

"And rich," Joanna added. "He makes millions of pounds a year."

"And ever so polite," Lalani continued. "Don let me give him the tour of the house. He held the doors for me and listened to everything I said, and even called me 'miss.' He asked me questions, too. I don't know why everyone says he's so cold and standoffish. I think he's lovely."

"I got to open the front door for him," Joanna added. "He was wearing the most beautiful cashmere overcoat, must have cost a fortune. Wish he played for Arsenal. My brother would never let me bring home a Kingsbury Town footballer."

"You'll like him, Julie," Lalani said. "He's really smart. He read the Latin motto of the school over the door and knew what it meant without being told."

"What did he think *Ex cineribus resurgam* means?" Julie asked, pulling her hair back into a high ponytail.

"From the cinders I'll come up."

"From the ashes I shall rise," Julie corrected her.

"That's what he said."

"That is impressive," Julie agreed.

"How do you know Latin, Julie?" Joanna asked.

"My father used to teach it. You're all learning it for our horticulture classes, but we can do more if you like."

Lalani sighed and joined Julie at the sink to scrub potatoes. "Sometimes it feels like there's the whole world to learn."

As Julie gathered another armful of potatoes, Don entered the kitchens followed by a tall, aristocratic-looking man dressed in a dark suit and starched white shirt. Julie felt her feet freeze to the floor as the potatoes slipped through her fingers, bouncing dully at her feet. It was him, the man from the bookstore.

Both girls squealed and scrambled to collect the potatoes while Julie dove behind the prep island to help, her heart beating in a flustered staccato.

What in heaven's name was he doing here?

A stray potato rolled towards him and he retrieved it, bending down on one knee to present it to her. "Your S*olanium tuberosum*, miss." His grey eyes glittered in seeming delight.

"It's *Solanum*." Julie snatched the potato from his hand and stood, dismayed at her momentary loss of composure.

Don made the introductions. "Julie, this is Hugo Auchincloss. Hugo is going to be joining us for a few weeks to tutor the students in their subjects. Hugo, this is Julie Randall, our garden manager."

"We've met," Julie snapped and would have jammed her hand in her pocket, but Hugo intercepted it with his much larger one, his strong fingers holding hers in a firm clasp.

The touch was electric, and those grey eyes held hers with a speculative gleam. "A pleasure to meet you again. Julie."

She snatched her hand back while Don glanced between them. "Julie, I thought you might like to take Hugo for a tour around the gardens, show him what we do here."

She frowned at Hugo's custom-made shoes. "Maybe we should wait for a dry day."

"Are there wellies I can borrow?" Hugo countered, pointing to a row of green boots lined up by the back door. "These look like they'd work."

Before Julie could stop him, he pulled on a pair, and Joanna retrieved his coat from the cloakroom. Resigned to get it over with as quickly as possible, Julie put on her own parka and jammed her hat on her head, brushing past him as he held the door for her.

———— ◄○► ————

Julie set off into the blustery January afternoon with Hugo following at her blistering pace. "We do twenty-one crops on a four-year rotation on two point three acres," she recited while staying two steps ahead of him. "Last year's yield was forty-seven thousand pounds of produce, excluding the herb house which has fourteen potted varieties. The orchard is on another two point eight acres and last year yielded forty-four thousand pounds of mixed stone, cane, and seed fruits. Our restaurant seats seventy-two and we served four thousand eight hundred ninety-two covers last year. The garden also provides staff and student meals year-round."

"So you're a gardener," Hugo said cheerfully, easily keeping up with her, much to her annoyance. "That explains a lot."

"So you're a footballer," she said, covering the ground with remarkable speed. "That explains a lot."

As they passed the midpoint of the garden, she gestured to a rectangular patch of earth. "Over there we're planning a twenty-by-sixty-meter polyhouse. When final zoning approval comes and it's built, we should be able to increase our produce yield by fifty-one percent and expand our crops to twenty-seven varieties. In two years we hope to be completely self-producing, through all seasons."

The lightning-fast tour continued past rows of low boxes with glass covers, which Julie explained were the hot and cold frames that functioned like mini-greenhouses.

Hugo peeked into one filled with lush green foliage. "Ah, leeks. I love leek soup."

"What a coincidence. So did Nero."

Continuing her swift pace through the gardens, Julie rattled off details as if she were reading from a phone book, not even bothering to see if he was still following her.

"These are Spanish tunnels." She pointed to several long, low rows of hoops covered with plastic. "There are parsnips, swede, and potatoes under there right now. And these are the carrot beds, which utilize a Victorian method of putting them in raised beds to ward off the carrot root fly. The insect only flies a few inches off the ground, so elevating the beds alleviates the need for pesticide controls."

"Ingenious," Hugo complimented.

Julie ignored him and continued to a line of shallow trenches. "The celery will be planted here in April. They need a lot of moisture, and it's a difficult process, preparing the soil mix to get the performance I want out of these beds."

"Maybe I can be of some assistance." He smiled. "I've been told I perform very well in bed."

Her mouth dropped open in shocked surprise. Snapping it shut, she faced into the cold wind and let it cool her flushed face. After five minutes of a tour that usually lasted an hour, they returned to the kitchens.

"That's our gardens," she announced and held the door for him, but he gently removed her hand and closed the door.

"I'd like to see the orchards," he said. "I've been reading up about them."

That was a nasty shot.

Spinning on her heel, she marched towards the rusted gate in the east wall. It was never used but was the most direct path to the orchard, and she didn't want to spend one more minute with the insufferable man than she had to.

Julie pulled the gate open with a hard yank, making the unoiled hinges scream in protest. She held it open for him, but when she tried to tug it closed behind her, the metal groaned and resisted until the hinges finally snapped and the gate flew towards her.

With lightning reflexes, Hugo snatched Julie out of its path, pulling her against him as the heavy metal crashed to the ground. Her nostrils filled with his scent, like wool and lavender and pepper. Warm and spicy, and not at all unpleasant.

They stood like that for several moments as her heart pounded, his arms around her and his breath against her ear.

The intimacy of their embrace should have been repulsive, yet it wasn't. Quite the opposite, actually.

Recovering herself, Julie stepped away from him. "Thank you. I didn't realize those hinges were so bad."

"That gate hasn't been used in ages," Hugo remarked with cool amusement. "I'm guessing this is a shortcut?"

With renewed determination, Julie marched towards the orchard.

Hugo followed. "Do you keep any chickens or goats?"

"No, it's against the zoning. And I don't do animal husbandry."

"Any grapes?"

"I don't do viticulture either." She tramped on but couldn't resist the topic. "I mean, I can do the basics. I went to Cornell University, which is one of the best schools in the world for viticulture, but you need large acreage to do a decent vineyard and very specific conditions. I specialize in small properties, under twenty acres."

"Is this all organic?"

"No, we're running a restaurant and food needs to get to the table. But by careful planning and observation, we only use a minimum of carefully selected and applied products. We don't use any bio-engineered seed, and all of our plantings come from original rootstock."

"I'm twenty-nine. How old are you?" Hugo asked as they continued down the gravel path. Julie ignored his question and kicked a large stone off the path with the toe of her boot. It ricocheted off a metal tub that held compost and bounced right back onto the path.

"Use your instep next time, you'll have more control." He demonstrated with a casual flick of his foot and the stone landed neatly in the bucket with a loud clank. "You've got an unusual accent. Are you from North America?"

Honestly, was this man from the newspapers? "I've lived in a lot of different places."

"Why?"

"My parents are college professors. We moved around a bit."

Hugo soldiered on. "What of?"

"Mother is mathematics, and Dad is Shakespearean literature."

"So Julie is really Juliet?" Hugo asked, a delighted smile lighting his face. "Any brothers or sisters?"

"Yes."

"Which?" he prodded.

"I have an older sister, Rosie."

"Fair Rosalind," he quoted.

Julie brushed past a cherry tree and let a branch snap back smartly towards him. "Sometimes there's no explaining parents."

Hugo seemed intent on irritating her and it was time to put a stop to it. Ahead in the path lay a treacherously deep, wide rut that would sink the utility cart to its axles. At the moment, it was filled with runoff from the previous night's rain and appeared innocently shallow. *Perfect.*

"Watch your step," she called over her shoulder and without breaking stride, stepped on the one spot in the middle she knew to be the shallowest. Two more steps and she was safely through, but from behind her came a huge splash followed by a foul curse, telling her the man hadn't followed in her exact footsteps.

Julie turned and watched him slog through the channel, the muddy water splashing over the tops of his wellies and soaking the hem of his gorgeous coat and trousers. She didn't even bother to hide her amusement.

Once on shore, Hugo glared at her. Grasping her shoulder to steady himself, he balanced on one foot to empty each boot. "I should put you over my knee for that."

"I did say to watch your step," she reminded him. "Seen enough?"

"Certainly not. Where are the apples?"

Ahead was the grove of established trees, the old limbs twisted and gnarled, some with leaves still hanging on and wet from the rain. "This is all that's left. They were abandoned after the last war and were practically wild when I got here. I think the orchards originally spanned down the hill and over to that line of houses. I've had to rip out quite a bit, but there's a good chance I can save what's left. You can see where we've replanted new stock."

As they walked, she began reciting the names and types of fruit trees, her voice softening to a loving tone. "First are the cherries. This is a Morello. I don't think they were here originally, but McIntosh said every good kitchen garden should have a few. Next to it is a sour Wellington and a sweet May Duke, they've been heavy producers. These are two pears that we're rehabilitating. As you can see, this one lost a limb two days ago in the wind. I've got to get Clive to move it."

"Where would you like it?"

"Over there, but don't try and move it yourself," she cautioned. But he easily gripped the thick limb and carried it off the track as if it were a stick. A satisfied grin appeared on his handsome face.

"I might not be busting out in muscles, but I'm a lot stronger than I look."

They continued farther down the grove. "Here are the apples. These are the Cox's Orange Pippin and the Fearn's Pippin, and in that row are the Court Pendu Plats and Blenheim Oranges. They've come through the best in the orchard, and the students have made some lovely desserts with them. I had to completely replant the Ashmead's Kernel trees, but I got lucky and found some excellent rootstock. We had a small harvest last year."

Hugo ventured under a large tree and peered up at a lone apple on a high limb. "And this one?"

"I'm not sure, it might be a Margil. But you've been studying your book, see if you can identify it." As he stepped closer, Julie tugged sharply on the main branch, releasing the rain captured on the leaves and dousing him in a cold shower.

Hugo stood very still as the droplets ran off him and then shook his head, flinging water in every direction.

"Had enough?" Julie grinned as he raked his fingers through his hair. It had been immature, and she knew it, but there was something about him that raised her competitive spirit.

"Not even close," Hugo assured her, his eyes twinkling with undisguised amusement.

Julie admitted she preferred this disheveled version of Hugo Auchincloss. However, since he refused to be annoyed, she announced, "Then you need to see the view."

———◆———

Julie led the way to the large two-story barn, her ponytail bouncing in the wind. Inside, the old building smelled sweetly of the straw delivered the day before and stacked in the loft overhead.

A sturdy ladder, propped against a massive beam, led to the high loft. "One at a time, it's safer," Julie cautioned and climbed up first.

Under the rafters, bales were stacked almost to the roof on either side of a central aisle. Loose straw littered the floor and muffled her footsteps as she cracked open the sliding door on the west end of the barn, waiting for Hugo to climb up behind her.

"The view from here is spectacular. Stand right there." She pointed to a spot and walked to the east doors. "Ready?"

Hugo stood squarely in the wide aisle. "Absolutely."

Julie drew back the eastern door, and the cold January wind poured through the loft with a dull roar, raising every stick of loose straw around Hugo like a mini cyclone. Millions of tumbling reed shafts filled the air in a magnificent vortex, turning the loft into a glittering, golden globe swirling around him before exiting through the west door.

After a few moments, the maelstrom faded to a faint breeze as the last stray pieces floated to the ground. Hugo, who had remained stock-still during the deluge, was now covered with straw, his wet cashmere overcoat a magnet for straw dust and fractured stalks.

He nodded in appreciation. "The view is spectacular," he agreed and approached Julie, not coming to a halt until they were just a handbreadth apart. A sliver of straw settled in her ponytail, and he reached to draw it out, his fingers sliding the length of the soft strand, his touch somehow tender, yet evocative. "I've never seen a prettier sore loser in my entire life."

His grey eyes held hers, amused and intent.

The silvery vapor of his breath lightly fanned her cheek like an invisible caress. It didn't feel awkward or threatening—in fact, just the opposite.

An intangible aura of protective masculinity wrapped around her, and for a mad moment, she almost gave in to the impulse to lean into him, to feel what it would be like to press against his body again. A delicious tension seemed to build around them as the last flakes swirled in the late afternoon sunlight. She saw the amusement slowly leave Hugo's expression, replaced with something warmer and more potent. His gaze dropped to her lips, and Julie realized with an almost drugged awareness that he was going to kiss her.

"Julie!" a shout interrupted from below. "You're to bring Hugo to meet the rest of the students!"

The spell broken, Julie stepped back and mentally shook off the pleasant sensation. "Unless you'd rather see the bees?"

# Chapter Seven

HUGO DROVE AWAY from Haddonfield with a ridiculously happy smile on his face. It was her, the girl from the bookshop —proof positive there was a God in heaven and that He loved Hugo Auchincloss.

Juliet had fallen right into his lap. A metaphor, but only for the moment.

He laughed out loud at the thought. With a shock, he realized Juliet was the first girl who could actually make him laugh. He'd have to go a little easier on Ian. This was indirectly his doing, after all.

The late afternoon London traffic, which usually taxed Hugo's patience to no end, was almost pleasurable. He whistled to the radio as he turned onto the narrow side street he lived on and pressed a button. At mid-block, a garage door opened beneath a nondescript, nineteenth-century terraced house, indistinguishable from its neighbors.

As he'd predicted, she hadn't been happy to see him again. He couldn't resist goading her and she'd responded in kind. She'd seen her opportunities, too, and taken them. She was smart and clever and even more beautiful than he remembered.

Juliet. He liked the way her name sounded on his lips, the way it rolled off his tongue. A quick glance at her hands had revealed no wedding or engagement ring, and a scan of the staff roster listed her as "Miss." This was all looking very good. Tutoring at Haddonfield suddenly took on a new dimension in his life, moving up from something he'd planned to squeeze in twice a week, to becoming his primary focus, after the team and his family, of course.

Juliet had been caught off guard today and had reacted by trying to kick him out-of-bounds. She was smart, though, and it wasn't going to take her long to regroup and come to the realization that if she wanted the book, she'd have to romance it away from him. He relished the thought of how she might try to do that.

---

As far as Hugo knew, he was the only Premier footballer living in the decidedly unglamorous area of central London called Bloomsbury. He liked it not only because of its proximity to the British Museum, one of his favorite places in the world, but also because it teemed with tourists and students. The bustle of the crowds allowed him to pass unnoticed, which suited him very well.

He'd acquired the neglected townhouse five years ago. The renovations had cost a king's ransom, taking the better part of a year to finish, but the results had been worth it. The brick exterior was kept deliberately plain. A few steps led off the pavement to a nondescript front door, while the finer workmanship and expense was saved for the interior.

The original first-floor plan was left largely intact and upgraded with ornate plaster ceilings and fine woodwork that created a dignified setting any gentleman would feel at home in. A comfortable sitting room opened off the entry foyer, the narrow windows hung with dark velvet draperies. Electronics of any kind were banned in the house, with the exception of an elaborate stereo system hidden in an antique cabinet and a smaller version in the basement gym. All the furnishings were from Wrothesley—thick oriental carpets, antique walnut tables, and gilt-framed oil paintings of trout streams and Bedfordshire landscapes.

The decorator had reupholstered some pieces in soft, muted fabrics but was forbidden to touch his favorite piece, a tufted leather Chesterfield sofa that had belonged to his grandfather. As children, he and Ian had delighted in playing on its slippery surface and lumpy springs, so he kept it in the second-floor study for strictly sentimental reasons. Practically speaking, it was a torture device.

Beyond the sitting room followed a dining room he never used, which in turn led to a period kitchen at the back of the house with cleverly disguised modern conveniences. Even the huge refrigerator had been made to look like a cupboard. A gleaming stainless steel range ruled from the center of the room, but Hugo had no clue how to turn the bloody thing on.

The original staircase had been replaced with a much grander mahogany one. Upstairs, the second floor was reconfigured into a master bedroom suite with a dressing room and a large American-style bathroom. A front room served as a study, and a narrower staircase led to the third-floor library, which housed hundreds of books that lined the walls from floor to ceiling. An enormous oak library table in the middle of the long room held the piles of books he was in the process of reading or referencing. Ian had once tacked a sign on the door that read "British Library Annex," and Hugo agreed.

He found his younger brother sprawled in a comfortable club chair in the sitting room, his laptop computer set on a low Regency table.

"Sit down, Hugo, and watch this," Ian called, pointing to the screen where video footage was playing. "It's some of the best stuff I've ever done."

Hugo flopped down next to him and watched grainy footage of children playing in abandoned lots, running down empty streets, and peeking out of dirty windows. "Who are they?"

"Street kids. I filmed them this weekend."

"They look like my teammates. Aren't you supposed to be doing your schoolwork?"

Ian rolled his eyes. "I hate International Studies. Why are you making me do it?"

"You've got to graduate with a degree in something if you're going to get into law school."

"But I don't want to go to law school either! Just because Mummy's a magistrate doesn't mean I have to be one as well."

"Well, you're not going to be a ruddy filmmaker," Hugo announced, and began sorting through a pile of mail.

"Why not?" Ian retorted. "I could make a good living at it! At least let me take a few classes."

"No, and that's final. Get a degree and then do whatever you like. I don't care. But one of us has to graduate from university."

"Why not you? You're the smart one. Even with the team, you've got lots of time on your hands."

"Not anymore I don't," Hugo said, grinning. "I'm doing your community service at a school up on the Heath for the next eight weeks."

"You don't seem too fussed," Ian observed, gauging his older brother's mood.

"I'm not. Rather looking forward to it, actually."

"Nice to see you in a good mood for once. You were an absolute bear over the holidays, even Mummy said so."

"I've had a remarkable stroke of good fortune. Now get cracking on your homework," Hugo ordered.

With a sigh, Ian shut down his computer and pulled books from his satchel. "My calculator's out of batteries. Do you have any?"

"Upstairs in my desk in the study. Help yourself." Hugo said, slitting open a thick packet from Miles. Another bloody crop report, replete with charts and graphs that made about as much sense as the hieroglyphics in the Egyptian section of the museum down the street. Nothing looked remotely understandable, and Hugo felt the start of a headache.

From upstairs came a loud snap, followed by a sharp curse.

"Mind the booby trap in the side drawer," Hugo called up absently.

Ian reappeared, holding his wrist. "Blasted Grandfather, why the hell did he install that damn thing?"

"Granny said they had a footman who used to pinch the household cash."

"You could disarm it, you know."

"I don't have the faintest idea how. I just flip the switch whenever I open the drawer, I don't even think of it anymore." With disgust, he threw the report back on the table and stood, stretching his back. "I'm going out for a run."

"Don't you get enough of that at work? And what's all that straw in your hair?"

———◆◇◆———

"You've got Hugo Auchincloss coming out to Haddonfield? What a catch!" Mark remarked, checking his tanned reflection in the rearview mirror of the chauffeured car.

"If he's a catch, he should be thrown back," Julie snapped.

She knew she was on edge. The London Symphony benefit dinner they were traveling to was a major event that had taken her two hours to prepare for. And Hugo Auchincloss's appearance at Haddonfield had left her absurdly agitated. The worst part was, the girls were right; he was very charming and handsome. The only saving grace was that after he'd left, the staff agreed they would probably not be seeing or hearing much of him. He had put in his appearance, might show up for a few sessions with the kids, and that would be that. Which was fine with her.

Because the man was disturbing.

Hugo was tall and lanky and from a distance looked thin, but certainly wasn't—he was sinewy, with a sureness about him that many men tried to cultivate, with little success. And he was much stronger than he looked—when he'd pulled her out of the way of the falling gate and held her, it was like being embraced by steel bands.

And later, when they were alone in the loft, his smile had turned lazy and sensuous, as if he were considering some wanton things he wanted to do with her.

Julie smoothed the skirt over her knees. "Do you remember when I went to buy the McIntosh book at Gladia's in Hampstead Heath? He's the one who bought it out from under me."

"But you said he did offer to buy you a nice book on orchids," Mark chided, keeping one eye on his mobile phone.

"Why would I want a book on orchids?"

"Orchids are lovely, darling, you should think about cultivating them. My boss's wife loves them."

Julie didn't know how to respond. Was he hinting about a future together, or was she just reading too much into his comment?

Their trip to Barbados over the holidays had done nothing to lessen her confusion. The beautiful peignoir had been carefully laid out six nights in a row, but Mark kissed her chastely each night outside her ocean front room, explaining that Dionysus was an old-fashioned company and he didn't want anyone to think less of her, had they shared a room. It seemed to Julie that no one cared one way or the other, but she had no idea how to even begin to suggest otherwise.

"Hugo was two years behind me at Eton and used to date Tricia Kent-Ames. Everyone called her Trika," Mark continued. "She was at St Maud's, of course, unbeatable at tennis and a damn good shot with the grouse. Anyway, everyone thought they were going to get married. They were together for ages. Then there was a huge dustup. I think she got caught coming out of a hotel room with another footballer. Huge scandal. Everyone denied everything, but the damage was done. Hugo dropped her like she was on fire."

"Recently?" Julie asked, intrigued.

"Heavens no, that was ages ago. Haven't seen him with anyone else steadily since, but he does make the rounds. Girls throw themselves at him constantly, lucky beggar. Our kind, though. Never any of those ghastly football groupies. He's a good chap."

"No, he's not. He's a smug, arrogant jerk and he's just helping out at Haddonfield for the publicity."

"Hugo Auchincloss? Don't think so, love. The man shuns the limelight like the plague. Keeps Tom Bellville-Howe working full-time to keep him out of the press. We've approached him several times to be a spokesman. Never even gotten a return call."

"Spokesman?" Julie asked.

"For my new Bajan Gin line. We're positioning it to be what British aristocrats want to drink to remind them of the tropics. He's landed aristocracy, mother is a Russell, aunts and uncles galore in the peerage. We tried to get his younger brother, Ian, but he's a boozer and was drinking when he smashed Hugo's Jag. So, of course we couldn't touch him. But if I could get Hugo, it would be a major coup."

"I thought Hugo was driving when the car crashed."

Mark snorted. "Ian was blotto and crashed about a mile from their mother's house. He crawled out and called Hugo. Man's as fast as the wind, he got there right before the police arrived and claimed it was himself driving."

Julie thought about this for a moment. "Surely the police didn't believe him."

"They had to, really. It was his car and he told them Ian was drunk, that he'd been driving his brother home when he skidded on a wet turn. Ian already has one drink-driving citation, and if they'd caught him again, he would have done jail time. As it was, I heard once he sobered up, old Hugo skinned him alive and put him under lock and key. But Hugo took the hit for him and is doing his brother's community service with you. Bloody lucky break."

"For Haddonfield?"

"Heavens no, for me. You'll hook me up with him, won't you?" Mark asked.

Julie had no desire to have anything more to do with Hugo Auchincloss. "You could come out to Haddonfield and visit one day when he's there," she offered.

Mark shuddered. "The students hate me. You know they do. Don't you remember when they put stones in my soup? Look, I know you're ticked at him now, but give the man a chance. He's a good chap once you get to know him. And maybe if you're nice, he'll let you see the book."

He grinned at her, the boyish look that made it impossible to stay annoyed at him for long. "All right," she conceded. "I'll see what I can do."

"That's my best girl." He kissed her hand lightly. "I say, weren't you going to try and get a manicure?"

# Chapter Eight

OF COURSE, MARK was right, and Julie could have kicked herself for not realizing it sooner. Hugo was going to be hanging about Haddonfield in one form or another for the next eight weeks, which was ample time to talk him into selling her *The Orchard*. Or, if he didn't want to sell it, he might be convinced to swap it for a first edition in mint condition Julie had found on the internet. The price was staggering, but she still had the money her parents had sent her at Christmas, and she'd also gotten a small pay raise. She could afford it, barely.

Realizing she might need even more incentives to offer, she explained the situation to Don the next morning and at his suggestion, rode into town with him for a meeting at the Magness Foundation. They got back to Haddonfield in time for staff tea.

"Maybe we should invite Hugo," Bonnie said as Julie sat down at the large trestle table in the kitchen.

"He's here? I thought he wasn't supposed to start until next week."

"So did I, but he said he had some free time and nothing else to do. He arrived before lunch, so I invited him. He ate with the students and then took the afternoon classes for me. I was able to finish the orders and write up the notes from the morning class."

"How helpful."

"You two don't seem to have hit it off," Bonnie observed.

"He's the one, Bonnie, the one who bought *The Orchard* out from under me at Gladia's."

"Oh dear." Bonnie's eyes widened. "That would explain why he came back from the garden tour tarred and feathered."

"I know, it was stupid. I lost my temper and now I'm regretting it. Especially since Mark pointed out that I still might have a very good chance of getting the book from him."

"How do you plan to do that?"

"When we lived in Georgia, our next-door neighbor used to say, 'you catch more flies with honey than vinegar,' so I thought I'd give that a try."

Bonnie blanched. "You're going to seduce him?"

"Heavens, no! I wouldn't know how. I don't even know how to flirt. I just meant I was going to be nice to him. And Don has helped me come up with some options that might entice him to give us the book."

"Well then, why don't you take him up a tea tray? That would be a good first step."

Upstairs, Julie balanced the tea tray on one hand and knocked on the doorjamb to the empty classroom. "Ready for tea?" she asked with a cautious smile.

Hugo jumped to his feet and took the heavy tray from her. "Is there hemlock in it?" he asked pleasantly as he set the tray on a desk.

Julie had the good grace to look ashamed. "No, just Earl Grey. And a plate of shortbread and scones the pastry class made this afternoon. The students haven't quite gotten the hang of the ovens yet, so they're a bit burned on the edges."

"Excellent." Hugo popped a cookie in his mouth. "I love shortbread."

Julie took a seat across from him and began to pour the tea. "We didn't expect to see you back so soon."

"Wolverhampton's not going to put up much of a fight on Saturday, so we had a short practice and I thought I'd get a jump on the classwork," Hugo explained, helping himself to another cookie.

So far, so good; he didn't seem to be one to hold a grudge. Julie looked at him through her lashes and noted he was dressed in another crisp white shirt, this time with French cuffs and handsome cuff links.

"Your family grows wheat?" she inquired.

Hugo's teacup wobbled in surprise, sloshing a few drops of tea on his immaculate white shirt. "How in heaven's name did you know that?"

"Your signet ring and your cuff links." Julie handed him a napkin and indicated the gold disks at his wrists. "They have a family crest with a sheaf of wheat. And Don said you're from Bedfordshire, which produces more wheat per square hectare than another county in England. Unless you're wearing someone else's cuff links?"

"No, they're mine. I mean, ours," he stammered. "I mean, yes. Yes, we grow wheat."

They sipped their tea in silence for a few moments. Julie selected a scone and buttered it lavishly, drizzled honey over the top and bit into it with relish. A drop of melting butter threatened to drip off the edge, and her tongue darted nimbly to catch it. When she was done with the morsel, she licked the honey off her fingers with clear enjoyment.

Hugo stared at her, transfixed.

"Are you hard?" she asked politely.

His eyes grew wide. "Pardon?"

"Are you a hard wheat grower?" she rephrased her question. At his still uncomprehending look, she added, "That's what Bedfordshire does mostly, hard red winter. But some do soft summer."

A strange mixture of emotions crossed Hugo's face, and she could have sworn beads of perspiration broke out on his forehead. "We're hard. I believe. Actually I've never thought to ask."

She nodded and stirred her tea. The conversation seemed a bit odd, but at least he didn't appear to be angry about yesterday, so she plowed on. "I... ah... I'm very sorry about yesterday," she began, looking out the window towards the orchards to firm her resolve. "My behavior was uncalled for and I'd like to apologize."

"For what?"

"For dousing you with rainwater from the apple tree."

"Oh, that."

"And for coating you with straw."

"Don't forget about making me wade across the English Channel."

Julie gritted her teeth. "Yes, I'm sorry for that as well. I was angry about losing the McIntosh book and acted childishly. I'd like to pay your dry cleaning bill."

"I should say not," Hugo retorted, clearly affronted by the thought. "You were right to think I'd stolen the book out from under you, and if taking your anger out on me made you feel a bit better, then I'd say we're even."

Hugo was reacting much more reasonably than she'd dared hope. "But it's your book now, fair and square," she continued. "It was wrong of me to think otherwise."

"And now you'd like me to sell it back to you," he finished helpfully.

Julie swallowed her surprise and soldiered on. "Hugo, all of the notes in the book refer to Haddonfield. I only got to see a few pages, but the notes were about what was originally planted here, following a scheme McIntosh drew up himself that's since been lost. If I have those notes, it would help me reestablish the orchard. I'm sure there are copies of his other books are out there as well, marked up for these gardens, and if I can find them, Haddonfield would be the only kitchen garden in England restored to McIntosh's original design."

Hugo was listening closely, and she was heartened.

"Today Don and I went to the Magness Foundation, and they said if I can prove *The Orchard* was for Haddonfield, they'll see about getting a donor to buy the book from you. They think we can even raise three hundred pounds for it," she announced triumphantly.

"It's not for sale."

"Everything's for sale." It was an assertion she'd heard Mark make many times and it seemed to fit the situation.

Hugo raised his eyebrows coolly. "Is that so? What are you willing to do for it?"

Her heart beat faster and she plunged on. "I can offer you something I think you'd like much more."

"Go on," he said, and she was surprised by the roughness in his voice.

Seeing she now had his full attention, she licked her lips and leaned towards him. His eyes held hers, captivated. "I know what you'd really like," she said softly.

"You do?"

"Of course. I'm sorry I didn't think of it earlier."

Hugo chuckled. "It was that obvious?"

Julie smiled. "Yes, sorry, I'm a little slow on the uptake. You know, a real farm girl."

He traced a finger around the rim of his cup. "I'm a farm boy myself."

"Yes, I guess you are. But you probably have a lot more experience with this than I do."

"I've been around the block once or twice," he admitted, his gaze dropping to her lips.

"Then you'll appreciate what I have to offer even more."

He glanced at the door. "I'm sure any man would appreciate what you have to offer."

"I'm sure they would," she agreed, "but this is only for you."

Hugo's grey eyes coursed over her. "Just for me?"

"Yes, it's something only a man like yourself would like. A very rich man," she continued, her voice almost a purr.

"I'm not that rich, but what does that have to do with—"

"You'd like a big tax write-off," she announced, "and if you donate *The Orchard* to us, I can make sure you get it. I asked the treasurer at the Foundation and he thought it was a splendid plan. That's pretty wonderful, isn't it?"

A sour expression settled on Hugo's face. "I'm sorry. The book is special to me, too. You can't have it."

Julie felt like she was losing the book all over again. "Could I at least see it? Study it for a few hours? I swear I won't hurt it. I'm a professional and I know what I'm doing." It almost killed her to beg, but she needed to see that book.

Hugo stacked the tea items on the tray and carried it to the door. "I'll think about it."

———◇———

Friday afternoon Julie stood in the steaming compost pits, turning the piles with ruthless stabs of the pitchfork.

Clive approached with another load of straw. "Thought I'd find you out here."

"Has he left yet?"

"Not yet. He did all the afternoon classes, now he's grading papers."

"That's a bit excessive. Won't he ever go away?"

"Hope not, it's freeing us up. Yesterday afternoon he lent me a hand repairing the orchard gate and spreading stones in that nasty sinkhole in the orchard you've been on me about. Said you'd taken him for a swim in it Tuesday."

Julie plunged the pitchfork into a fresh bale of straw and flipped it onto the pile. "Wish he'd drowned."

Clive chuckled. "Hugo seems like a nice guy, a lot nicer than his reputation would lead you to believe."

"He seems to be living up exactly to his reputation. What reason could he possibly have for not letting me at least look at the book?" she asked in exasperation.

Clive shrugged. "His book, love, he gets to decide. Let it go, is my advice. You've done a brilliant job without it, why get into such a fuss? It's just an old orchard."

———◇———

Julie worked outside until she saw the Jaguar leave well after sunset. When she returned to her office, a large bouquet lay across her desk with an eye-popping collection of hot pink roses, yellow irises, lush greens, and a brilliant sunflower filling the center. In the drab British winter, their vibrant shades seemed sinfully lavish.

A note was attached, written in a strong slanted hand on thick paper with the monogram "A" engraved at the top.

Juliet,Unless you say that we can peaceably coexist despite our differences, I will bring you a bigger and better bouquet every day until you do.

—Hugo

There was an added postscript: *PS—And don't think I won't.*

Gathering up the bouquet, she carried it into the kitchens where Bonnie was finishing the day's notes. Her friend stopped in her tracks. "How gorgeous. Where did they come from?"

Julie pressed her lips together for several moments. "Our new academics instructor. There was a note."

Clive came into the kitchen and had the same reaction. "Did you win the Derby, Julie?"

Bonnie passed the note to Clive and the two exchanged glances.

"What?" Julie asked in protest. "What am I supposed to say? He's so arrogant he'd probably have an entire florist shop delivered here. Bonnie, why don't you take them home with you?"

"No, dear heart, they're for you. But I'd say he's neatly boxed you into a corner."

At home, Julie put the flowers in a vase and set it on her kitchen table where they filled the small room with riotous cheer. Flowers were, agriculturally speaking, an odd commodity—the only thing you consumed of them was their scent and their appearance, making them a questionable crop for most farmers. Yet there was something more satisfying about this bouquet than a lavish dinner or a fine bottle of vintage wine, and she gave in to the indulgence of just admiring it for a while.

It took a determined effort not to feel flattered by Hugo's attention. It took even more not to be charmed. But what took the most effort was silencing the voice in her head, pointing out that Mark had never given her flowers.

The temptation was strong to just sit and look at them all night, but the driver would be picking her up soon for another dinner out with Mark and his clients. In the bathroom, she splashed cold water on her face, then reached into the closet and pulled out the first dress that came to hand, a dark green chiffon wrap. The driver was knocking on the door as she swiftly dabbed on lip gloss, slipped into the first pair of pumps she came across, and dashed to the door, grabbing her coat and purse on the way.

Their table was already full when she arrived at the trendy restaurant in Notting Hill. Mark stood to greet her with a peck on the cheek.

"Didn't you wear that three weeks ago?" he murmured.

# Chapter Nine

"HUGO! HUGO AUCHINCLOSS! Long time no see!" A loud voice boomed down the tiled corridor of the Westminster Squash Club on Monday afternoon as Hugo and Ian walked back to the men's locker room, both dripping with sweat after their game.

"Who is that?" Ian whispered.

Hugo cursed under his breath. "I'm screwed. That's Mark Brooks, the biggest poon hound at Eton—and believe me, that's saying something. We called him Looks. Roomed with Arthur Swann, nicknamed Don Juan. The two of them together were unstoppable, no skirt left unturned."

Mark bounded up to them, grinning from ear to ear. "Looks," Hugo said, pausing a moment before shaking the eagerly outstretched hand. "It's been a long time. This is my brother, Ian."

Mark spun and shook his hand as well. "What a coincidence running into you here!"

"I shouldn't see why, I've been playing here every Monday afternoon for years. Are you playing with Don?"

"No, Don's in Hong Kong, didn't you know? He's paying alimony to two ex-wives so he needed cold, hard cash," Mark replied, unfazed. "Brilliant game against Leicester City Saturday. Saw you got a goal. Good show, chalk one up for us independent school boys."

"It was a two-two draw."

"And in the small world department," Mark prattled on, "I hear you're also helping out at the same place my girlfriend works, Haddonfield."

Juliet was the only girl he knew to be single, but she was too smart to be dating this lout. "Who are you seeing?"

"Julie Randall. She manages the gardens there, but she's not much of a manager," Mark said with a snort of contempt. "You can tell by the look of her hands, she's up to her elbows in the muck every day herself."

Hugo's dislike of the man grew exponentially. "Oh, Juliet. Yes, we've met. Smashing girl. How long have you been seeing her?"

"Gosh, I guess going on seven months now. I'd like to see more of her, but she's practically married to the place. Convinced she can turn those urchins into productive members of society!" he scoffed before turning contrite. "Look, I'm sorry about the way she behaved in the bookstore. She told me all about it and frankly, she can get a little carried away. She's half American, you know."

Hugo regarded him stonily. "She was completely within her rights. I did steal the book out from under her."

Ian saw a tick begin to form in his brother's jaw and knew from experience that meant trouble. "Hugo, remember I need a lift back to school in time for class—"

"Yes, of course." Mark slapped his shoulder. "Say, a few of us old boys are taking Edward Ponchard out for his stag party tonight, only time we could get him away from the old ball and chain. Don't suppose you're going to the wedding Saturday, but care to join us at Fout's for martinis and steaks? Then we're going to hit a strip club over in Richmond. Should be a hell of a night."

"Haddonfield is having a dinner, and I thought I'd go out and see what that was like."

Mark made a face. "Those ghastly dinners? Shouldn't bother is my recommendation, although they do a fair job on the desserts. Come with us instead, it'll be a carnivore's night out. Around seven at Fout's Tavern. You too, Liam!" With another round of hearty slaps, he continued down the hallway.

"What was all that about?" Ian asked in bewilderment. "And who's Julie?"

"She's a girl that works at Haddonfield, the place I was sent to do your community service penance."

"Oh, that cooking school up on the Heath. Are you really going there for dinner? Can I come too?"

"Might as well. Could be a long night."

⎯⎯⎯◆⎯⎯⎯

After Ian left for class, Hugo pulled up the collar of his recently dry-cleaned overcoat and began the walk home in the misting rain. He found himself humming a tune and realized that London was actually a very lovely city. The fog, the damp, the cold—it was all wonderful.

So, Juliet had a boyfriend. Honestly, it was to be expected. He should count himself lucky she wasn't already married, as desirable as she was. What she was doing with an ass like Looks Brooks was beyond him. The man had always been slimy, and time hadn't improved him. On the bright side,

Looks had said "girlfriend" and not "fiancée." Things were very workable.

Juliet had avoided him since Wednesday afternoon, and both Bonnie and Clive had remarked on her absences from the afternoon staff teas. The view from his second-floor classroom afforded an excellent view of the walled kitchen garden, and Hugo knew she was spending a considerable amount of time in the compost piles at the far end. So she wasn't as indifferent to him as she wanted to be. That was another good sign.

Now that he thought about it, the list of happy omens seemed endless. There was no picture of Looks in her office, where he had taken a moment to snoop around when he'd dropped off the flowers Friday afternoon. The room was neat and orderly and held some interesting clues to her personality. From the music CDs on her shelf, he could see she liked bossa nova, and a framed picture on her desk showed her sitting in the middle of an enormous group of people. Studying it closely, he saw Juliet in the center, flanked by two women who must be her mother and sister. A dignified, grey-bearded man sitting behind them was probably her father, and the remaining people of many nationalities were likely friends of the family.

The most intriguing item, however, was a small photograph of a smiling Juliet sitting next to a large duck.

Had she liked the flowers? The shop where he'd bought Friday's bouquet was just across the road, and he considered bringing her another tonight. In the window there was a dazzling display of yellow roses and blue irises he was sure she'd love, and he wanted her to have them. After some consideration, he rejected the idea. She needed time to accept his challenge. But he rather hoped she wouldn't.

She'd had the weekend to think about him. She might have even caught some of his dazzling performance against Leicester City—as Looks had noted, he'd scored a goal and was back in excellent form. Focused, clinical, tenacious. It was all very acceptable.

As he passed Great Ormond Street Hospital, his mind wandered pleasurably back to the tea they had shared in the classroom. The intensity of the desire he'd felt just watching her lick a drop of honey off a scone was undeniable. There'd been something so artless in the way she flirted with him that even now, just thinking about her as he walked down Great Russell Street, was making him randy as hell.

The readiness of his body surprised him. He was hardly starving for sex, at least not quite, but whenever she was near, he responded like a stallion noticing a mare in the next pasture. The sensation was new and wonderfully unusual, like someone had turned up the volume on every nerve in his body.

——◆◇◆——

"What are they like then, the students at Haddonfield?" Ian asked on the trip up.

"Survivors," Hugo answered as he maneuvered the Jaguar through the evening London traffic. "They're almost all wards of the state, parents either in jail, or dead, or whereabouts unknown. They were left to grow up in the streets. The Magness Foundation took them in, and they've done well enough to make it into the culinary skills program at Haddonfield. They're scrappy, have street smarts, and think God plays for Tottenham Hotspur."

Traffic thinned out as they drove farther north. When they arrived, there were already a dozen cars parked in front of the house and another half dozen spilling onto the grassed lawn. Matthew was directing the parking and waved down Hugo's Jaguar.

"You're late, Hugo," Matthew said, his friendly tone belying a menacing posture.

"Should I park on the grass?"

"Oh no, you said you might be coming, so we made a special spot for you, like a regular VIP. We even put out a yellow cone. Down the drive, past the barn, on the left. You can't miss it."

Hugo didn't like the biting cheerfulness in Matthew's tone. He followed the gravel driveway around the mansion and Juliet's wing, past the large barn to where a spot had indeed been cleared, right next to a steaming manure pile. Hugo couldn't help laughing despite himself.

"Those ruddy buggers!" Ian exploded. "What cheek!"

"Play along, Ian," Hugo replied sensibly. "They just want to get a rise out of me. Ignore it."

"You shouldn't ignore it!" his brother protested. "It's an enormous manure pile!"

Honestly, Ian could be a footballer for all the fuss he made sometimes.

A girl who Hugo guessed was one of the certificate students greeted them inside the door. She took their coats and showed them into the busy dining room, where Don waved them over to a table where he, Juliet, Bonnie, and Clive were sitting with an older couple.

Juliet was wearing a blue turtleneck sweater paired with a trim pair of trousers, and he felt the same potent urge rush through him. She saw him approach and a fleeting look of panic crossed her face before she suppressed it.

Don jumped to his feet and shook their hands. "Hugo! Glad you could come out. Why don't you join us at the staff table?"

Introductions were made, and Hugo noted sourly that Ian was instantly captivated by Juliet. The older couple were trustees of the Magness Foundation and acquaintances of his mother's. Hugo was obligated to chat with them, but out of the corner of his eye, he saw his brother move to take the empty seat next to Juliet's. With an imperceptible movement, he hooked Ian's ankle and dropped him to the floor.

"Clumsy!" Hugo chastised his brother and then gave him a hand up and took the intended seat himself, leaving a disgruntled Ian to take the one next to his. Clive chortled under his breath.

"Hugo. Didn't realize you'd be coming out tonight," Julie said, nervously smoothing the napkin on her lap.

"I wouldn't miss it for the world. The students told me all about it." He bent his head towards hers and lowered his voice. "Have you gotten any deliveries to your office lately?"

"Yes," she replied, staring straight ahead.

"Shall I be sending more?" Hugo inquired civilly.

"No. No, that won't be necessary."

"You're sure? No shortage where they came from."

Julie's smile became even more forced when she realized he was enjoying taunting her. "I'm sure," she muttered, and turned her attention to Ian. "So, you're Hugo's brother. I can see who got the charm in the family. Do you play football as well?"

Ian laughed and shook his head. "No, if I got the charm, Hugo got the speed. I make documentaries."

"You're at university?"

"Kings College, in town."

"And you're studying filmmaking?"

"No, International Studies. I wish, though, that I could—"

"Is this jasmine?" Hugo interrupted, shooting his brother a baleful glare and nodding to the center of the table, where a small vase of twining branches gave off a spicy scent.

"It's wintersweet. The neighbors let me take trimmings in winter in exchange for apples in the fall," Julie explained, glancing between the brothers.

"Is Mark coming out tonight?" Bonnie asked.

"No, he called this morning and said he just found out he has to work very late at the office to pull together a presentation for tomorrow. It was a last-minute thing."

Ian choked on the water he was drinking, and Clive thumped him on the back. "All right there, mate?"

Ian recovered, darting a surprised look at his brother, who was studying the menu with interest. "Do you always do vegetarian?" Hugo asked.

"We don't do shellfish because many people, like Julie, are allergic. Once a month we do a meat or a fish to give the students experience with proteins," Bonnie explained. "It can get expensive, but Don's brother is a fishmonger and helps us out."

Hugo frowned and turned the card over. "There's no prices."

"There's a donation box in the foyer, we ask the guests to pay what they think it's worth," Don explained. "People are very generous. When we switch to the Belevedere in March, it goes to a prix fixe for three courses."

"The Belevedere in Hampstead?" Ian asked. "That's an excellent restaurant. How did you arrange to use it?"

"The owners are very supportive of our program and let us use it on Mondays when they're closed."

"Why switch places?" Hugo asked. "Can't you continue doing meals here?"

"There's several reasons," Bonnie said. "Starting in October, each of the students has one dinner here where they are in charge of everything. They have to set the menu, make a budget, do the ordering, and manage the other students in the kitchen. Then in March we do the same thing at the Belevedere, but we're not there and they are critiqued by a panel of three restaurant industry professionals. The students get a feel for what it's like to be in charge of a full professional kitchen with no safety net."

"So it's sink or swim."

"Very much so," Bonnie agreed. "The Belevedere is their final exam. It's worked out very well, plus the restaurant is larger and we can handle more guests."

"Hope you can handle more cars," Ian groused. "We had to park by the manure pile."

# Chapter Ten

THE TABLE FROZE at his words. "You what?" Julie asked.

"It's okay," Hugo glared at his brother. "The kids were just having some fun. It's not a problem."

"It most certainly is," Julie replied. "You are guests here and it's their job to make you feel welcome. How can they expect you to enjoy your dinner when you've been made to park by the manure pile?" With a curt nod, she excused herself and disappeared into the kitchen, reappearing several minutes later wearing a satisfied smile.

There was a brief tug-of-war as both brothers simultaneously stood to hold her chair for her, with Ian emerging the victor, giving Hugo a triumphant smirk. Bonnie pressed her lips together and Clive coughed, which sounded suspiciously like laughter. Julie was oblivious to the entire exchange, and Hugo sullenly noted that Ian was rewarded with a warm smile.

"That's been sorted out, apologies will be forthcoming, and I've got additional help for the next three days with spreading that pile," Julie announced with satisfaction.

Baskets of freshly baked rolls and pale butter were placed on the table, followed by the first course, curried carrot soup.

"This is delicious," Hugo said, helping himself to another homemade roll.

The soup was followed by the entrée of vegetarian shepherd's pie. The dish was a medley of mushrooms, lentils, barley, and carrots in a rich burgundy sauce, topped with a thick layer of the best mashed potatoes Hugo had ever eaten. The spices were aromatic and the dish served piping hot, which he loved.

"Are these the British Queen potatoes in the mash?" Don asked.

Julie sampled her dinner and nodded. "Yes, I've promised five pounds of them to the rector at St Phillip's. I'm dropping them off Sunday before service, in trade for five pounds of his gooseberries when they come into season."

Hugo cleaned his plate, as did Ian, and both waited in anticipation for dessert. A luscious apple tart with warm caramel sauce and ice cream was served, and coffee poured. Soon the guests began to disperse. Don excused himself to say goodbyes at the door, while Bonnie and Clive returned to supervise the kitchens.

Julie said her farewells to the guests and turned to Hugo and Ian. "Thank you both for coming this evening. I hope you enjoyed it."

"How can we make ourselves useful?" Hugo asked.

She stood motionless. "You want to stay." At his nod she added, "And help."

"We do?" Ian asked in surprise.

"Yes," Hugo replied. "We do."

A dubious smile tugged at the corners of Julie's lips. "All right then, this way."

The men followed her back to the bustling kitchens. "Hugo and Ian want to stay and help," Julie told Bonnie.

Bonnie's eyebrows shot up but she recovered quickly. "Well! Let's put you to work then. Ian, the servers could use a hand clearing the tables in the dining room."

Ian followed the students out of the kitchens. A crate crashed in the dish room and Julie sprinted in that direction. Hugo watched her leave and turned back to Bonnie.

"You're making yourself very useful," she observed.

It was like the woman was looking into his soul. "Like to help out where I can," he mumbled, feigning indifference, but it came off badly.

"I see. All right, you can start out doing the washing-up like everyone else," she said, handing Hugo an apron. "Here, have a blue one. It's her favorite color."

Hugo felt himself flush like a schoolboy but did as he was told. Another student was assigned the task of teaching him how to wash the dishes and seemed to enjoy the image of Hugo Auchincloss with his sleeves rolled up, operating the dish sanitizing machine.

"Wish Niall Eddy were here to see this," the boy snickered, referring to Tottenham Hotspur's star midfielder.

"Bet his teammates wish he could pass farther than ten meters with his right boot," Hugo replied, wrestling with the sprayers.

That shut him up. Hugo worked through the mountain of dishes, stacking the cleaned ones at the end of the counter, where Julie picked them up to return to the dish room. Clive sat with Jira at the oak trestle table as she counted the money from the donation box.

"Someone put a hundred-quid note in the box!" Jira erupted with a squeal of excitement.

Julie shot a suspicious look at Hugo, who pointedly ignored her.

———◄O►———

"Can I give you a lift home, then?" Hugo asked Julie as the kitchens wound down for the evening.

"Thanks, but no, Clive and Bonnie are dropping me off—"

"Sorry, Julie," Bonnie interrupted. "We have to stay late. The Hobart mixer is frizzing and Clive has to look at it."

"It was fine earlier," Clive protested.

Bonnie shot a warning look at her husband. "Tonight."

"Okay." Clive sent his wife a furtive glance, which she returned with a thin smile. "It's been acting funny lately," he muttered.

"But, Hugo, your car is only a two-seater," Julie protested, glancing at Ian who was sweeping the foyer. "How will Ian get home?"

"Not a problem," Hugo answered. "You can keep him."

"I can wait for—"

"I'll come back for him. Get your coat and meet me out front."

———◄O►———

Ten minutes later, Hugo handed her into the car and reached over to fasten the seatbelt across her, his hair brushing fleetingly against her cheek. The Jaguar's luxury was evident as he smoothly shifted and drove off, and Julie noted that man and machine seemed made for each other.

He paused at the gates at the end of the drive. "Which way?"

"Left, then up the high street." She pointed from the comfort of the Jaguar's leather seat. "Sorry about the manure pile, they're just testing you."

"I know. I imagine they've done worse. I'm the fifth academics instructor this year?"

"Fourth. The last one got a bucket of water down his back. The one before him was a vegan and they put a sheep's head on her desk after a butchering class."

"Creative." Hugo nodded in approval. "Dinner was excellent. The kids do a good job."

"They do, don't they? But you didn't have to put the hundred-pound note in the box, a twenty would have done very nicely." At his look of wide-eyed innocence, she reproved, "I know it was you. It was a very nice gesture, but it skews their results, and doesn't give them a true sense of what they took in."

"The meal was delicious. And worth it."

"Maybe at the restaurants you go to. But we won't be getting footballers with multimillion-pound salary packages every week, so a twenty is fine."

Traffic was light as they drove down the high street. "Left here, then I'm the middle of the street, sixth house. That one, right there—you don't need to find a parking spot. You can just let me out at the curb."

Ignoring Julie, Hugo drove past the house and continued down the block. "I'll walk you to your door. This section of Finchley is crime ridden."

She laughed in spite of herself. "Crime-ridden?"

"Absolutely," Hugo continued unperturbed. "Just yesterday I read in the *Times* someone ended a sentence in a preposition."

"But there's never any spaces."

Hugo ignored her and eventually found an opening two blocks away. Julie, in turn, ignored the hand he proffered as she stepped out of his car. Once on the sidewalk, he neatly switched places so he was between her and the curb.

The night air was cold and crisp, and a full moon shone with an array of bright stars overhead. Being alone with Hugo was decidedly nerve-wracking, Julie decided as they walked. Unfamiliar emotions jumbled around inside her as she tried to maintain a cool demeanor.

As if sensing her unease, he looked up at the moon and quoted, *"How sweet the moonlight sleeps upon this bank! Here will we sit and let the sounds of music creep in our ears. Soft stillness and the night become the touches of sweet harmony."*

The familiar verses relaxed her. *"Merchant of Venice."*

"Very good. Your turn."

She settled into the rhythm of the walk and considered a response. *"It is not in the stars to hold our destiny but in ourselves."*

Hugo smiled. *"Julius Caesar.* My turn." They walked in companionable silence for a few more minutes while he thought. *"I never saw true beauty 'til this night."*

A pleasurable ripple, like the brush of butterfly wings, ran up Julie's back. *"Romeo and Juliet."*

"Full marks. You must get that one a lot."

Actually, aside from her father, no one had ever quoted Shakespeare to her. Especially the love quotes. She ducked her head and looped a lock of hair behind her ear.

Hugo cupped her elbow as they crossed the street but dropped it on the other side, his touch almost over before it started. "I bumped into your boyfriend today at the squash club."

"You met Mark? That's right, I'd forgotten you went to the same school." Julie bit her lip, remembering Mark's eagerness for her to hook him up with Hugo. "I wish he could have come this evening. But he's very busy with work, he has an important client who demands all his time."

"So he mentioned. How did you two meet?"

"At a country fair last July. I went with Don and Gretchen and their daughters. Dionysus sponsored a tent and we met there." Feeling the need to emphasize they were in a serious relationship, she added, "He swept me off my feet."

Hugo's lips pressed together in a faint smile. "He has a reputation for that. Hope there was something comfortable to fall back on."

Julie had no idea how to reply. He seemed to be intimating something, but what it was eluded her.

In a short time, they were at her doorstep. "This is me. Thank you for the lift."

"Are you going to invite me in?"

"No," she said firmly, and then relented slightly. He really wasn't as bad as she'd thought and even had some redeeming qualities. Maybe she was being unfair, and there was still hope that he would let her see the book. She turned back to him and smiled. "Thank you for coming tonight. And thank you for the flowers."

"You liked them?"

Julie nodded. "They're gorgeous. Irises are my favorite."

They stood together on the tiny stoop, the evening still and his nearness pleasant. Hugo's gaze fixed on her lips as his own worked in silence, apparently having difficulty forming words. "Welcome. You... You're welcome," he managed to get out.

"And you will think about letting me see *The Orchard*?" she added, letting her eyes twinkle a bit.

Flecks of sweat broke out on Hugo's brow as if he were fighting a terrible inner battle. "The book... I can't... it might be..." he began, his head dropping a fraction closer to hers as his hand brushed her arm lightly. Her own breath tightened in her chest as she realized he might kiss her.

Two doors down, a neighbor emerged with his yapping dog straining the leash, shattering the fragile spell that had twined around them.

With an effort, Hugo regained his usual composure. "Good night, Juliet. See you around." He took a step backwards and promptly tumbled into a prickly bush.

Julie watched in surprise as his long legs flailed amongst the twigs while muffled curses spewed from the shrubbery.

"Are you all right?" she gasped. In a flash, he righted himself and was back on his feet. She stepped forward to help him brush dead leaves off his coat jacket, but he nimbly jumped aside.

"Yes, fine, no problems, good night," he panted, and abruptly fled.

———◦◯◦———

"So, this Julie," Ian enthused on the drive back to town. "She's great."

"Yes," Hugo agreed, shifting in his seat and scratching the places where twigs had poked him.

Juliet was more than great, he realized soberly. She was a sorceress—she'd bloody well have to be, judging by the control she had over him. One flash of her smile and he'd turned into a blithering idiot. Again. She had him behaving like a teenager working up the courage to kiss a girl for the first time. He'd landed in her hedge, for God's sake.

The spell she was weaving was even more confounding because it was making him feel like a hot-blooded knight pursuing an untouched maiden. Which was patently ridiculous. Even if Looks Brooks was completely off his game, he would have bedded her by their third date. She was probably more experienced than he was.

"She serious about that chap we met today? What's his name, Mark?" Ian asked.

"Yes. And I don't know."

"Well, if she's not, I've got dibs on her."

Hugo glanced at his brother. "No. You don't."

Ian sank back in his seat in disgust. "Bollocks. Why do you get all the luck?"

# Chapter Eleven

AFTER PRACTICE THE next morning, Hugo drove to Soho and parked in front of a sleek office building, a bold statement in glass and steel considered eclectic even by London standards. A series of wide ramps led to a red lacquered door, where Hugo paused and nodded at an invisible security camera. There was no sign or identification of any kind to indicate what business was inside. Which was exactly the way Bellville-Howe and Associates liked it.

The door slid open, and a receptionist waved him through to an expansive office, where a man in a wheelchair sat behind the desk, talking on the phone. Hugo grabbed the morning's *Telegraph* from a coffee table, sprawled on one of the leather sofas, and began to read the sport section.

"I ran into Looks Brooks yesterday," Hugo said after Tom Bellville-Howe finished the phone call.

"Get your feet off that sofa or Nancy will have your scalp." Tom jerked his head towards the outer office.

Hugo quickly complied. "Remember him? He was your year," he prompted, but knew Tom's encyclopedic memory would need little help.

"Brooks. Roomed with Don Juan, right?" Tom thought for a moment, then rolled across the office to a low bookshelf and pulled out a yearbook, quickly flipping through the pages. "Yes, that's him. Too right, the pair of them were after every girl in town. Heard he hasn't let up. Where've you seen him?"

"Westminster Squash Club, I think he tracked me down. He's dating a girl at the school where I'm doing Ian's community service."

Tom replaced the book and rolled back to the sitting area. "What's he want?"

"I have no clue."

"Wait," Tom snapped his fingers, "he's with Smith-Wessex, just got put in charge of that horrible flavored gin Dionysus dreamed up. They've called several times, wanting you to be a spokesman. We've blown them off completely. Now he's going through the back door, so to speak."

"Evidently."

"And he's dating one of the girls out there?" Tom thought for a moment. "Pretty, blonde, blue eyes? Really great pair of —"

"Yes," Hugo cut him off. "Her name is Juliet Randall. She does the gardens at the Haddonfield School."

This piqued Tom's interest, and he regarded his best friend with curiosity. "I've seen them around. She seems nice enough, rather quiet. He must be wife shopping."

Hugo frowned at that news.

"That's her bad luck, though," Tom continued. "He's still involved with Rochelle Chevelle."

"The model?"

Tom nodded. "They were a torrid item for years, but he dumped her last summer when Smith-Wessex made it clear he wasn't going to get ahead with a wildcard like Rochelle in the picture. They're a conservative lot at the top, so I guess this new girl is supposed to be the ticket to full partner."

"Bingo."

"It won't play out happily for her. Rochelle didn't take the breakup well. She's been raising hell on shoots and he's had to manage her. She's still Dionysus's top face, after all. He's trying to keep it quiet and out of the country. But if I know about it, then to some extent it's common knowledge."

"Any chance he'll get caught?"

Tom raised his eyebrows at Hugo's obvious interest. "Looks is arrogant. He's bound to trip up sooner than later."

———◆———

The weather that week was horrid, even by January standards. Cold rain lashed the windows and the temperature hovered at freezing. During brief breaks in the storm, students sprinted out to harvest Jerusalem artichokes, parsnips, and carrots from the cold frames, while Julie fussed over struggling celery seedlings in the glasshouse. Everyone returned to the kitchens soaked to the skin and shivering from the cold.

Hugo arrived at Haddonfield every day in time for lunch and didn't leave until after six. He didn't seek Julie out, and the only time she saw him was when the staff would meet for a cup of tea once the students had left for the day. At those times he was cordial, and they chatted pleasantly about the students and their work. There were no more flowers left on her desk.

Julie chafed at the restrictions the bad weather enforced. Clotheslines were strung across her office so the wet clothing could dry before the woodstove. Every inch of the barn and sheds were cleaned, the clay pots scrubbed, seeds inventoried, and her farm notebooks updated. Mark was in Toronto for the week, which left her free to swim in the evenings after the students had gone for the day. But by Thursday afternoon, she was climbing the walls from inactivity.

The weather forecast showed a break in the storm, so when the rain receded to a light mist, Julie grabbed freshly sharpened nippers and headed off to the raspberry bed to thin canes. She worked for over an hour and then was startled to see a man approaching her. He was tall and lanky, and at first she thought it was Hugo. But then she recognized his brother Ian, bundled up against the cold and sheltering a digital camera in one hand.

"Hello, Julie." He waved.

"Hello, Ian, what brings you out here?"

"I didn't have classes today so I came out with Hugo. He's doing composition with the students, which I can't stand, so I thought I'd bring my camera out and see if there was anything doing. Don said he didn't mind as long as it wasn't bothering you."

Julie shrugged and shook the rain off her hat. "No, not at all. Sorry to disappoint you though, I'm just top trimming the raspberries."

Ian took a few steps back and trained his camera on her. "And why do we top trim raspberries, Julie?"

As he began to film, she demonstrated the theory behind raspberry management. "These raspberries gave fruit in the autumn, so the old canes now need to be pruned back to the ground. I did the summer bearing ones over there last November."

"Raspberries are Hugo's favorite. What kind do you grow?"

"Glen Moy for early summer bearing, Glen Prosen for midsummer, and these are Glen Magna for late bearing. If I do it right, we'll have raspberries from June to October."

Ian followed her down the length of the bed, asking questions and encouraging her to explain what she was doing. At the end, he put the camera down and wiped the lens with a small cloth. "This would make a brilliant documentary," he mused.

She laughed. "A documentary on pruning brambles? Maybe on the Insomniacs Channel."

"Not just that, but about these gardens in general. Showing all of the old varieties you're growing here, like those apple trees over there. And telling about the man who did the original design. All of it, it's fascinating."

"Maybe you could make a documentary about your brother being here. That would get a lot more interest. There can't be too many professional football players doing what he's doing."

Ian shivered as if someone had walked over his grave. "He'd skin me alive if he thought I was doing that. And then he'd let Tom have a go. There'd be nothing left after those two got done with me."

"He doesn't like publicity very much, does he?"

"He likes the fans, in his way, but he doesn't give a damn about all the glitz and whoopla that come with being a footballer," Ian confided. "He's actually very shy. It's brutal for him, and he gets a lot of bad publicity he doesn't deserve. He's practically the only educated one on the team, and people think he's a snob because he knows which fork to use. They don't understand how he'd rather spend an evening reading a good book than going out drinking and carousing, unlike most of his teammates. The unmarried ones at least."

Ian followed Julie around the gardens for another hour, filming her so unobtrusively she almost forgot he was there.

Eventually, the dull afternoon light faded, and he went back to the kitchens to film Bonnie, while Julie returned to the sheds to sort dried beans at a worktable. The students arrived to help after their lessons were over.

"Bloody hell," Phong muttered, pulling a stool to the sorting bench and dumping a scoop of beans on a large tray.

"What's up?" Julie asked from across the table.

"Hugo! That's what."

"What's he done?"

"He's going to give us homework! For the weekend!" he snorted in disbelief.

"We don't got to do it, do we, Julie?" Jira pleaded. "Only I've got me nephews to babysit while my sister works. And there's a film I want to go see."

"He's making us learn French, too." Matthew huffed, coming into the room with Nerida. "As if we don't have enough problems with English. It's been every bleedin' day, all week, an hour of French."

"Tell her about the algebra," Lalani added, close to tears. "That's the worst part. Ain't nothing worse than that."

"Algebra? He's really doing algebra with you?" Julie asked in astonishment.

"Yeah, Julie," Lalani whispered, fumbling with her glasses and wiping her brimming eyes on her sleeve. "I was having enough trouble wiff all the other stuff, and now he wants us to be doing algebra and French and composition, and I just don't know if I can do it."

Julie patted the girl's back as she sobbed. "It's not that difficult, not really."

Nerida glowered. "He's nice about it, and I'm understanding some of it, but I looked ahead in the book he brought and it's all numbers and letters, and these funny symbols. Don't make no sense at all. How can you add two letters together? That's rubbish, that's what it is."

"There's no way we'll learn all that lot," Lalani wailed, and the rest nodded in agreement.

"Of course you will," Julie said firmly. "You are all smart and talented and wouldn't be here if you weren't." Looking at the grim faces around her, she relented a little. "But maybe I should have a chat with Hugo and see what he's up to, all the same."

# Chapter Twelve

IT WAS ANNOUNCED at Friday morning practice that Aston Villa's irrigation system had failed and their pitch was under two inches of water, so Sunday's match was being moved to Townsend Lane Stadium. Which suited Hugo's purposes very well indeed.

He drove to Haddonfield in a good mood and arrived to find Clive and Julie at the back of the house, arguing next to a ladder propped against a sagging section of gutter.

"Nay, love, you can't help, it's too dangerous." Clive was trying to reason with her. "Those gutter sections are solid copper and are a lot heavier than they look. It will have to wait until I can get one of the lads from over at the yards to help me."

"But, Clive, the weather today is excellent and we have all afternoon. We can go very slowly," Julie insisted. Clive rolled his eyes heavenward.

"What's up?" Hugo asked.

Julie spun around, obviously surprised to see him. "Bonnie left a message on your mobile saying the visit to the dairy got moved to today, didn't you get it? They've all gone and won't be back until late this afternoon."

"I got it," Hugo said, looking down the length of sagging gutter. "I say, is this original?"

"Yes, and this entire section pulled off in the last storm." Julie pointed to where almost thirty feet had become dislodged. "It's been flooding the beds I've prepared for the polytunnel. This afternoon is the perfect time to fix it, and we've got all the materials. So Clive and I are going to do it."

Clive snorted. "Julie, I'm trying to tell you—it's not as easy as it looks. Each section weighs a bloody ton, and you almost need three hands."

"We have gutters almost identical to this at Wrothesley." Hugo studied them closely, then turned to Julie. "Can we go up into the barn loft to get a better look at them? I've got an idea that might make this job go a lot faster."

"Good idea." With a triumphant look at Clive, she led the way to the barn. At the loft ladder, Hugo motioned for her to go up first while he and Clive waited below. "One at a time, it's safer that way," he reminded her.

When she was safely at the top, Hugo removed the ladder and leaned it against the opposite wall of the barn.

"Hey! What are you doing?" Julie called down from above.

"Keeping you safe," he replied as he and Clive left the barn.

Ignoring her heated retorts, they disappeared around the corner and then reemerged with Hugo wearing an assortment of Clive's old work clothes. Julie fumed as the two men set up scaffolding and set to work, pounding new spikes and ferrules into the wooden fascia before refastening the brackets beneath. There was no way down unless she felt like jumping thirty feet, and no one around besides Hugo and Clive to put the ladder back up. So she threw herself onto a straw bale to sulk and watch the work.

It didn't take long for her to realize it was indeed a tough and bruising job. Each section of gutter weighed at least one hundred pounds and securing it was a balancing act. The men worked steadily through the afternoon, and after she got over her initial indignation, Julie tried to be helpful from her perch, where she could see the strapping and call out directions.

By late afternoon, there was only one more section left when suddenly a retaining bracket broke and the heavy length lashed towards Clive. Julie leapt to her feet and cried out in alarm, and with instant reflexes Hugo grabbed the gutter before it crashed into Clive's ladder. Looking over his shoulder, Hugo grinned at her, and she sat back down, her heart pounding, while the men struggled to reattach it.

---

The sun was setting when Clive and Hugo cleaned up and went back into the kitchens. Julie sat huddled on her straw bale, growing cold while she waited for someone to free her. Soon enough, the barn ladder was propped back against the rafter, and Hugo appeared at the top, carrying one of her garden baskets over his arm.

Julie glared at him. "That wasn't necessary, you know."

Hugo withdrew a blanket from the basket and draped it around her shoulders. "Yes, it was."

Pulling another straw bale next to hers, he sat down and began to unpack the basket. Julie watched in fascination as he laid out a blue tea towel, followed by two plates, utensils, napkins, and two huge slices of apple cake.

"You want to have a picnic in the barn loft you've trapped me in all afternoon?"

"It's the perfect place," he replied amiably, pouring two mugs of steaming tea from a thermos.

"Why?"

Julie could have sworn his eyes twinkled with a wicked smile. "I like the view."

Grudgingly she took the cup of tea he offered. "You didn't have to lock me in the loft like a naughty child."

"I didn't?"

"All right, maybe you did."

"We replaced a section of gutter at Wrothesley two years ago and it took a full team of workers three days," Hugo told her as he tucked into the apple cake with clear enjoyment.

"We haven't got that luxury. It's just Clive and me."

"You've got me now," he added.

"For seven weeks," she muttered and then brightened up. "Maybe we should lay on replacing the septic lines."

He laughed. "*Touché, mon chérie. Vous êtes très intelligent.*"

Julie looked at him blankly. "Sorry, five years of Spanish."

She ate her cake hungrily as Hugo sat across from her, still wearing Clive's work jacket. Julie was surprised how well it fit him—Clive was a large man. Under the jacket, the first two buttons of his shirt were open, and Julie could see a few fair, downy hairs on his chest. Mark didn't have any hair on his chest. Julie suspected he shaved it, which faintly repulsed her.

"The students said you're teaching them French," she ventured after a few mouthfuls. "Why?"

"They're supposed to be going to work in professional kitchens, yes? So I'm teaching them some kitchen French. You know, the names of vegetables, fruit, meats, cheeses. Plus some basic commands like 'empty the trash' and 'turn on the oven.' That sort of thing."

"The kitchens these kids are going to work in won't have French chefs. Or if they did, they won't be talking with them."

"Bonnie's teaching them solid cooking skills. If they can speak some French, they might do better for themselves," Hugo countered.

"But they have so much else to do just to learn basic skills."

Hugo set his empty plate back in the basket and stretched his legs until they almost touched hers. "Do you know what your problem is?"

"I'm sure you're going to tell me."

"You pamper them. You have all the good intentions in the world, but you make things too easy for them. These kids need to be challenged, the way regular kids would be."

"But they're not regular kids. They've grown up doing nothing but surviving. It's a miracle some of them are even alive."

"Which will make them enjoy the challenge even more."

"But what if it's too much for them? Like Lalani. She's a mess, Hugo, terrified that she'll fail. She's delicate, and any disappointment will set her back immeasurably. She came from a horrific background, and Haddonfield is the only stability she's ever known."

"Okay, that's reasonable," he agreed. "But what would happen if she succeeded? What would happen if she learned some French and some algebra?"

Julie thought about that for a moment. "That would be tremendous," she conceded. "But what if she doesn't?"

"Do you think I'd let her fail?" he asked quietly, studying her face. He noticed her blanket had slipped down and leaned forward to pull it back up around her shoulders. "I know I'd have to answer to you."

Julie focused her attention on her tea mug. "You're pushing them too hard."

"I'm only here for eight weeks and then I'm gone. I know I'm working them hard, but let's see what they can do in eight weeks."

"You gave them homework for the weekend."

"Oh, you heard about that?" He laughed. "Of course I did. It's very important. And I told them I expect them to do it, so they will."

"They'll never do it," Julie shook her head. "You don't know these kids, they've never done homework in their life, and they're not about to start now."

"Oh yes? You seem very sure of yourself."

Julie nodded. "I know these kids, Hugo. They won't do your homework."

"Care to bet on that?"

The spark of competitiveness that was never too far from the surface whenever he was around flared again. "Yes, I would." She thought for a moment. "You're completely sure all ten students will have their homework finished by Tuesday morning because you told them you expect them to do it."

"Yes. And you're completely sure at least one of them won't."

"Correct. So if I'm right, you'll give me the McIntosh book."

Hugo raised his eyebrows in cool surprise. "That's a pretty big wager."

"Yes, it is," Julie agreed. "But you've got a pretty big ego, so it seems appropriate."

He leaned forward and rested his elbows on his knees, appearing to consider the wager, their faces only inches apart.

"Okay, and if all of them do it, what do I get in return?"

"What do you want?" she asked warily, sensing a trap.

An invisible friction passed between them, like the sensuous flick of a panther's tail. "A kiss would do."

Julie flushed. "I can't do that. I'm seeing Mark."

"Oh. You're engaged?"

"No."

"Seeing each other exclusively?"

The man was impossible. He sat there so coolly, asking questions Julie couldn't answer. They were, in fact, questions she often asked herself but couldn't bring herself to ask Mark. "I'm not sure... I mean to say, I think we..." she fumbled. "You've kissed hundreds of girls. It wouldn't be anything special."

"Let me be the judge of that."

Julie's mind was racing as fast as her heart. "If I were your girlfriend, would you want me trading a kiss with a man I barely knew?"

"If you were my girlfriend, you would have no doubt that our relationship was very exclusive," Hugo answered. "But since you are neither engaged, nor entirely sure about the status of your relationship, a kiss seems like a rather harmless thing to wager. Especially when the stakes are so high."

"Why would you want to risk losing the book just for a kiss?"

It might have been a trick of the fading light, but Julie could have sworn his grey eyes glinted like a lion's. "Because I think it's the last thing you want to give me. And my book is the last thing I want to give up. So we're even."

"How do I know you won't cheat?"

"A gentleman always keeps his word. No? All right, come to class Tuesday and collect it yourself. Any one of the ten doesn't have it, you get the book."

Julie had never been so tempted in her entire life. She was almost positive that at least one of them wouldn't have the work done, and then *The Orchard* would be hers. She didn't doubt Hugo's word at all.

And if by some miracle they all did have their homework, kissing Hugo would not be any hardship whatsoever. But what kind of person would that make her? "I can't do that. I'm with Mark and that's that."

With as much dignity as she could muster, Julie collected the empty plates, repacked the basket, and climbed down the ladder.

---

Bloody hell, Hugo swore silently, watching her as she left. He knew how badly she wanted the book, and yet she still wouldn't bet.

This was going to be a bit more challenging than he thought.

# Chapter Thirteen

SATURDAY MORNING, THE sun shone brightly in the charming Essex village where Mark's school friend was being married. They had traveled out by train with a jovial crowd of wedding guests, the railcar a rolling party with both men and women producing hip flasks to toast the health of the bride and groom. Julie declined with a shudder—it was only eleven o'clock in the morning.

There was a short walk from the train station to the tiny stone church on the edge of the village green, where more guests greeted them. Attractive women threw themselves into Mark's arms while his male friends greeted Julie with crushing embraces that momentarily knocked the wind out of her. Inside the church, they were escorted to their pew while Mark continued to greet everyone around them, loudly admonishing guests to shuffle over as more people squeezed into their pew.

"Say, I managed to bump into Hugo Auchincloss at the squash club Monday," Mark whispered loudly as the organist began.

"He mentioned that. He won't be here today, will he?"

"Gosh, no. Always invited, always declines, unless of course it's one of his family. Sends a proper gift, though."

A wedding planner wearing a wireless headset appeared near the altar and frowned, evidently a signal to the organist that the wedding was to begin. The soloist took her spot and with a sharp nod from the wedding planner, began to sing a lovely aria. Music was Julie's favorite part of church services and she sat back to enjoy it, relaxing for the moment since it was out of the question that Hugo would be there. Seeing him at Haddonfield was distracting enough.

The soloist finished and took her seat, and a blast from the organ heralded the wedding march. Adorable children began the procession down the aisle, and Julie craned past Mark to catch a glimpse of the little girls in pristine organdy dresses, carrying hoops of flowers and escorted by sullen little boys in sailor suits. They were followed by two older bridesmaids dressed in lavishly ruffled pink gowns with matching hair bows. And then the doors to the church were thrown wide as a trumpet voluntary announced the bride.

With one motion the guests rose to their feet, and Julie's program fell to the pew seat. As she stood on tiptoe for a better view, she felt a tap on her shoulder.

"I think you dropped this, Juliet."

She froze at the sound of that voice. No, Mark had said it was impossible. But sure enough, Hugo stood in the row behind them, an engaging smile on his handsome face as he held out her program.

<hr />

Hugo suppressed a grin as Juliet snatched the program from his hand and spun around, obviously unnerved.

Good.

The wedding service, which he usually hated, was a pleasure to sit through. His seat behind and to the left of Juliet gave him an unfettered view of her, and a fortuitously long-winded sermon afforded him an unequaled opportunity to admire her at his leisure.

She wore a charming dress with long sleeves and a modest neckline that offered an enticing glimpse of cleavage, the skirt short enough to show off her spectacular legs without being vulgar. It was the shade of blue she seemed to favor, he noted with satisfaction.

He had guessed correctly.

Her hair hung in pale gold waves down her back, and pearl earrings dangled from her dainty ears, accentuating the sweep of her neck. Hugo would have been happy to sit there all day as the rector droned on, just admiring her, her expression serene and her beauty ethereal.

Looks, he observed, took no notice of Juliet at all. The man's attention flickered over the crowd like a hungry bird looking for grubs, and occasionally he would whisper in her ear and point to someone. Juliet would nod stiffly, not taking her eyes off the altar.

When the ceremony was over and the organ blared again, Edward and Jillian strode back down the aisle wearing relieved smiles. The guests stood, Juliet whispered into Mark's ear, and he spun around in delight.

"Hugo! What a surprise! Good heavens, to what do Edward and Jillian owe this pleasure?" Not waiting for an answer, Looks bellowed, "Everyone, look! Auchie's here!"

If Juliet had wanted to put as many people between them as possible, she couldn't have chosen a better way. Schoolmates and other hangers-on ambushed him while Juliet slipped out of the pew and disappeared into the crowd.

The slow-moving receiving line to congratulate the happy couple felt interminable, and Hugo suffered greatly. Looks stuck to him like glue and seemed convinced they were old pals. "Is that Pippa Donnell?" Looks pointed at a tall brunette farther back in the line. "In the red dress. She was at St Maud's with Jillian."

Hugo quickly scanned the crowd. "I think so, yes."

"Thought it was! God, I haven't seen her since Flight Night senior year. That was some fun." Looks rubbed his hands together greedily. "Georgeson walked in on us, though. There's some unfinished business there."

From across the church, Pippa winked, a sly grin on her face.

"Aren't you here with Juliet?" Hugo asked coldly.

"Yes, of course. But Pippa's an old friend, and Julie wouldn't begrudge me some catch-up time. You can keep her occupied."

"My pleasure."

———————— ◆◆◆ ————————

As the bride and groom received their guests, Julie made her way across the village green to the old inn where the wedding lunch was being held. A table in the reception area held a hand-lettered seating chart, and Julie was disquieted to see that while all the other tables were set with ten places, theirs had eleven. With Hugo's place written neatly next to hers.

A group of women came up behind her and analyzed the chart, pointing to Hugo's name. "He's at table five, move him with us at seven," one of them directed.

"What am I supposed to do, cross it out with an ink pen and rewrite it?" her friend asked.

"Just go in and move the cards," came the withering reply.

Guests began to trickle in to the large reception room where waiters circulated with silver trays of drinks and hors d'oeuvres. Mark arrived with a crowd, and Julie joined him as he moved from group to group, impressing her, as always, with his memory for names and faces.

Julie's stomach grumbled ominously as empty trays passed by. She slipped away in search of a roll, or anything, to hold her over to the meal. Her search turned up nothing but a bowl of mints, and when she returned she found Mark with his arms around the two bridesmaids. He released them quickly and made introductions and then hailed another passing friend, leaving Julie to make small talk with the women. They, however, were more interested in sizing up the single men.

"I'm going to try and get Hugo Auchincloss to dance with me," one confided, nodding towards where Hugo stood, chatting with an usher who'd been introduced as the groom's brother.

"No chance," the other bridesmaid stated unequivocally.

"I bet I can tempt him."

"What, in these hideous frocks? Besides, Sophie says he never dances."

"Sophie also says he's been after her for ages. She lies. Hugo Auchincloss wouldn't raise a finger to chase after any woman. Look at him. Why should he? We all flock to him."

Julie silently agreed with her.

"Besides," the bridesmaid continued, "he's a cold fish—doesn't give a damn about anything but his own pleasure. Over in a heartbeat then out the door. Even Trika said it was a disappointment, for all he's hung like a horse."

Her partner pondered this for a moment. "Why do you think he's here?"

"No clue. He called Edward yesterday and said he'd like to come after all, so Edward made Jillian move heaven and earth to make a spot for him. That beastly wedding organizer made a huge fuss, the calligrapher was called back to redo the seating charts, it was a frenzy. Jillian was furious, but he'd already sent a good present so there was no choice."

---

From the reception room, Julie watched in amusement as different groups of women nefariously darted into the dining area and could be seen stealing Hugo's chair and place card and moving them to other tables. By Julie's count, he had been moved six times by the time the meal was announced.

Once inside the dining room, she was dumbfounded to see that both the chair and place card had been returned to their original place next to her.

"Juliet, good to see you." Hugo leaned to press his lips to her cheek and held her chair for her. Julie couldn't help but admire how handsome he looked in his flawlessly cut navy-blue suit and starched white shirt. She paused, however, when she realized that the blue silk of his necktie perfectly matched her dress.

"I see you chose to wear Eton blue as well," Hugo noted.

"What's Eton blue?"

"Our school colors. Quite clever of you. You're the only lady here who thought of it."

Julie sank into her chair as Mark appeared with another drink.

"No date, old man?" Reggie Hawkes-Downey clapped Hugo on the back as he took his seat. "You could have brought Sophie, she was angling for an invitation."

"She wasn't invited." A dark-haired girl named Pippa took the chair next to Mark. "Jillian caught her lurking around Edward's bedroom in Gstaad last February, so she's been rusticated."

The bridal party entered to applause, and the speeches commenced. After several minutes, an embarrassingly loud rumbling came from Julie's stomach.

Hugo's hand slid down her arm and settled something in her hand. "These things take forever but I always come prepared and I'll share," he whispered.

Glancing down she saw a candy bar. She couldn't help but smile and ate it hungrily.

The speeches continued, with an occasional remark drawing uproarious laughter from the guests. The jokes were lost on Julie, but Hugo would lean over to whisper an explanation or the identity of the person speaking, or just to make an amusing comment. As time wore on, Julie felt herself relaxing almost against her will.

"Having a good time, sweet?" Mark asked over his shoulder at some point during the fifth speaker.

"Yes, I am." Julie surprised herself by answering honestly.

Finally, it was time to stand and toast the bride and groom. Julie grasped Mark's elbow as he wobbled unsteadily on his feet, and he gave her a silly grin in appreciation.

Jameson, a beefy man with a ruddy face, drained his glass in one gulp and set it on the table with a thump. "Bah, champagne is a girl's drink. Give me a good whiskey any day. Say, Looks, aren't you peddling some new vodka?"

"Gin," Mark replied as they sat, spreading his napkin on his lap with a flourish. "Dionysus wants to branch out beyond Sam Lord's Castle Rum, and they're coming out with a line of tropical-flavored gins. Completely cutting edge."

"Tropical-flavored gin? That's sacrilege," Hugo said, scandalized.

"No, it's brilliant. It's called 'Bajan,' which is what the Barbados natives call themselves. Dionysus has its headquarters on the island. The idea is that good Englishmen like ourselves don't want to give up our gin when we visit the islands and want a taste of the tropics at home as well."

"Can't imagine Tanqueray is losing any sleep over that idea," Hugo muttered.

Waiters circled the room delivering salad plates comprised of lettuce, grapes, cheese and thin slices of melon. Juliet examined the cantaloupe carefully—it was ripe and of good color, and she was intrigued.

"Fancy melons, do you, Julie?" Reggie asked.

"Oh, yes," she answered. "This is a variety of Charentais cantaloupe called 'Magenta.' It's very unusual. They're tricky to grow. They're actually *Cucumis melo* from the Cantalupensis family, a true cantaloupe, unlike the muskmelons which are also named *Cucumis melo* but are in fact a member of the reticulatus family. Although—"

"Darling, don't be a bore, everyone here thinks one melon is the same as the next," Mark said.

"Don't know about that, Looks, I thought you were quite a connoisseur!" Jameson quipped with a meaningful leer at Julie's chest.

The table exploded in ribald laughter, and Julie shifted uncomfortably in her seat.

"I guess that makes you quite a cognoscente of whale flesh, Jameson," Hugo shot back.

The man's laughter faded. "I say, Auchincloss, that was out of line."

Pippa turned to Julie and smirked. "So, Julie, everyone's commenting on your accent. Where are you from? It's definitely not from around here."

Julie ignored the barb. "I guess it is a bit of a mishmash. My mother is British, and my father is American. They're college professors, and we moved around quite a bit. I grew up in America mostly, a bit in Canada, and went to school at Cornell University in New York State."

"Cornell? Never heard of it," Pippa waved her hand in dismissal.

"You wouldn't have, Pippa," Hugo explained. "It's a school for smart people."

Julie had to bite her lip to keep from laughing out loud. The rest of the table focused silently on their plates.

Pippa picked at her salad and glared. "You're being your usual charming self, Hugo. To what do Edward and Jillian owe the pleasure of your company?"

"Edward and I were teammates at school—he's one of the best wingers I've ever played with. He could have gone on and played professionally if he'd wanted."

"Hugo still holds the records for most goals in a season for independent schools," one of the women at the table added importantly. Julie noticed Hugo frown at the comment.

"And Villa Park's pitch flooded so we're at home tomorrow," he continued. "So I rang up and asked if it wouldn't be too much trouble to change my plans."

"How lucky for them. Be careful sitting next to him, Julie," Pippa cautioned. "Hugo doesn't like Americans. You wouldn't believe what he had to say when he came back from the States the last time. But seeing that you're only half American, he might be nicer to you."

"I like Americans very much," Hugo snapped. "Jolly nice bunch. What I objected to was being made to play on an artificial turf field in Texas. That's fine when you've got all that padding American football players wear, but it's practically suicide for us."

Dinner was placed before them, a savory tart consisting of bits of shrimp, potatoes, peas, and carrots. Julie took one look at the shellfish and discreetly put her fork back down and waited for the breadbasket to be circulated.

"Where do you work, Julie?" Jameson asked.

"The Haddonfield School for Culinary Arts, above Hampstead Heath. I run the gardens there."

Pippa snapped her fingers. "My granny dragged me there once to some dinner. It was all vegetarian and bloody awful. I sent my plate back, told them it wasn't fit for a pig."

"Did they find you something that was?" Hugo inquired politely.

Ominous silence filled the table, and for once even Mark's lips were sealed. Without waiting for Pippa to frame a suitable retort, Hugo stood and excused himself, taking his empty wineglass as if to get it refilled. Conversation resumed while Pippa fumed, stabbing savagely at her plate and chewing her food sullenly. A few minutes later, a waiter appeared at Julie's shoulder and deftly removed her untouched plate, replacing it with a selection of more melon, strawberries, and sliced cucumber with a refreshing mint dressing.

"From the chef, miss," was all he would say.

"Thank you," Julie said in bewildered appreciation.

"So you've got Aston Villa tomorrow?" a man named Harding asked Hugo when he returned to his seat with a glass of orange juice.

"Oh, don't be a bore, Harding, you know Auchincloss never talks shop," Jameson shot back.

"Talk shop? I want to know how to lay my bet. Hugo, which is the best team in the Premier League?"

"The one that wins the most games," Hugo replied before attacking his dinner.

Again the table fell silent, with the exception of Julie, who burst out laughing.

<hr />

After the initial attention, Mark's friends lost interest in her and instead told stories and jokes that Julie found childish. Hugo remained aloof, giving Julie the distinct impression he would have rather been anywhere else. But why come at all, then?

Eventually, the dinner plates were cleared and the elaborate wedding cake cut. Several tables were rearranged to make a small dance floor, and a DJ began to pump out pop music. Mark sprang to his feet, anxious to begin making the rounds of the other tables, and Julie followed reluctantly. Her chair next to Hugo was swiftly occupied by a gorgeous blonde in a daringly low-cut yellow dress, and she was soon flanked by more women, each trying to engage him in conversation.

Covertly, Julie watched Hugo as he chatted politely, unaffected and blasé—a bored lion king amid his fawning pride.

# Chapter Fourteen

MUSIC BLARED AND cigarette smoke hung in the air as Julie followed Mark on his endless odyssey of socializing. After two hours her eyes were burning, and she slipped away unnoticed through a French door that led to a lovely cobbled patio. Leaning against the edge of a low stone wall, she gulped fresh evening air.

"Smoke too much for you as well?" Hugo asked from a shadowed corner.

Julie swung around, a shiver of excitement coursing through her.

Not waiting for an answer, Hugo doffed his suit jacket and draped it around her shoulders. "It's chilly out here."

The jacket smelled wonderfully of warm wool and lavender and pepper, mixed with an undeniable male scent. Julie murmured her thanks and drew it closer as they stood in comfortable silence, admiring the moon rising bright and silver in the night sky. From somewhere nearby, a barn owl hooted.

"Looks is quite the social butterfly," Hugo observed.

Julie smiled. "He's just getting warmed up. We'll be lucky to catch the last train back to Kings Cross."

"Are you staying in town tonight?"

"Mmmm. Mark lives in Chelsea," Julie answered, hoping the implication was that she was staying there that very night. Which would be a whopping lie. She had been to Mark's flat exactly twice and had never stayed for more than an hour.

"Are you having a good time tonight, Juliet?"

It took her a moment to work up an appropriate amount of cheeriness. "Yes, very. You? Mark says you don't often come to weddings."

Hugo grimaced. "Too right there. These bloody things drag on for hours and there's no ducking out early."

"You should cultivate some patience," Julie admonished with mock gravity.

"How do you propose I do that?"

"*Assume a virtue, if you have it not,*" Julie quoted, a beguiling smile lurking at the corners of her mouth.

Hugo laughed out loud. "*Hamlet.*"

The laughter transformed his features, she noticed, making his eyes twinkle. "Your turn."

Feigning concentration, he walked around her, his arms folded across his chest. "*Love looks not with the eyes but with the mind,*" he finally declared.

Julie pouted with pretend scorn. "Helena in *A Midsummer Night's Dream.* Can't you come up with anything more challenging? Do another and do it properly."

He nodded, his eyes holding hers. "*All days are nights to see till I see thee,*" he recited. "*And nights bright days when dreams do show thee me.*"

That was from "Sonnet Forty-Three," perhaps the best known of Shakespeare's love sonnets. No man had ever recited love sonnets to her, and certainly no man like Hugo.

Only a handbreadth separated their bodies now, and it would take a mere movement for her chest to brush against his if she wanted to. And she wanted to. Delicious feelings swirled inside her, spreading restless warmth to every part of her body. This is how desire feels, Julie realized hazily, every part of your body yearning for someone. It felt like the most wonderful drug in the world.

From the other side of the French doors, the pounding beat of the pop music finished and changed to a melodic bossa nova. The seductive chords floated out to the patio. "I love bossa nova," Julie said in surprise. "'*Siempre Me Quedará*' is one of my favorite songs."

"What a remarkable coincidence. Would you like to dance?"

Not waiting for a reply, Hugo took her hand and led her back into the room and onto the crowded dance floor, taking his jacket and tossing it on a nearby chair. With a swift motion, he slipped his other hand down her back to rest at the base of her spine and effortlessly drew her into the slow steps.

The romantic song spoke of love and desire, the rhythm both melodic and throbbing. Hugo was an excellent dancer, and Julie followed his lead easily, feeling his lean muscles flex against her body, sinewy and strong. His grey eyes held hers, cool yet somehow tender, his focus on her complete as he smoothly twirled her, pressing her lightly to step back, then forward, then back again, their bodies touching for brief seconds and then parting.

Much too soon, the song was over, and Julie realized everyone in the room was staring at them in rapt astonishment. Dropping his embrace, Hugo bowed deeply, and she had enough presence of mind to effect a quick curtsy. Then a blaring rock song began, and everyone resumed their dancing and talking.

Mark made a beeline for them and grasped her arm, surprising Julie with the rare display of possessiveness.

"Darling, stop monopolizing Hugo. He wants to socialize," Mark admonished and ushered her away.

———————◦○◦———————

Disgusted, Hugo watched Looks maneuver Juliet into a throng of people, the feel of her in his arms still fresh and potent. Goddamn it, what a hell of a night this was turning into.

Coming to the wedding had been a calculated play to find out exactly what the situation was between Looks and Juliet. He'd needed to see them together, and Edward had once again proven himself a good friend and not asked any questions, although Hugo had caught his satisfied grin over Juliet's shoulder on the dance floor. His next call had been to the wedding planner, who was a favorite of his mother's side of the family and had been anxious to do whatever Hugo asked to ensure that Miss Randall enjoyed the day.

It hadn't taken long to surmise that Looks was obviously fond of Juliet, but there was nothing beyond friendship. Juliet, on the other hand, was harder to read. She seemed to be putting on a very good show of enjoying herself, but he was getting to know her well enough to see she was faking it. There was some affection between them, but no chemistry. If the sex was good, it obviously didn't translate into outward affection.

Puck Fitzherbert, a distant cousin, sidled up next to Hugo at the bar and signaled for a beer. "Looks has got the luck again," he said, following Hugo's gaze to where Juliet stood. "Bastard."

"Give a dime to bang her," Jameson joined them, belching loudly. "And he's got Pippa Donnell fawning over him as well. It's not fair."

"Isn't he still with that booze model?" Fitzherbert snapped his fingers. "Roxanne? Michelle?"

"Should sack the lot of them for her." Jameson was practically drooling. "I could spend a month between those tits."

Hugo gripped his glass tighter, feeling very much like smashing both their faces, but contented himself instead with keeping an eye on Juliet as she dutifully followed her idiot boyfriend.

Needing a break from the enforced socializing, Hugo found an empty lounge off a side hallway and flopped into an overstuffed wing chair drawn up to a hearth with a crackling fire. He had just pulled out his mobile to check the results of the day's matches when he heard the lounge door close behind him with a soft click.

"Darling, darling, calm down," whispered a panicked male voice.

*Looks Brooks*. Hugo sat motionless, listening.

"It's difficult to talk now, we're at a wedding reception," Looks continued, obviously speaking to someone on his mobile, his voice barely above a whisper. "Yes, she's here too, but she won't hear us."

After a moment, he lowered his voice. "Rochelle, they don't hate you. Don't you remember, this is the team you had in Fiji? I made sure they used the same hair and makeup people as before. They adore you."

Evidently this was not what Rochelle wanted to hear, as Looks continued in soothing tones. "I miss you, too, darling.

What are you wearing?" A throaty laugh followed, and Hugo cringed in disgust. "That's my favorite one. Do you remember when I bought it for you Tuesday?"

Looks sighed. "I don't know when, darling, but soon. Next week at the earliest. Now say you'll wait."

A tentative knock at the door interrupted the steamy exchange. "Mark? Is everything okay?" Juliet asked from the hallway.

"Hold on one second," Looks whispered. "Yes, darling," he called out, "just a call from corporate I have to take. Damn New Yorkers, they haven't a clue there's a time difference. I shan't be long."

"Pippa's organized a game called Bottle Safari in the basement and they want me to play."

"You go play, darling, have fun."

"Okay. I'll see you in a bit."

After a moment, Looks resumed his conversation with Rochelle. "Reception is lousy in this room, I'm going to move to the other side of the inn and see if it's not any better." The door slid open, and the sound of footsteps receded down the hall.

Well, for God's sake, Hugo thought grimly. Tom was right, as usual. What scum. Turning off the lights, he went looking for Juliet.

———◦———

"How do you play this game?" Julie asked the huge sweating man next to her on the stairs as they followed the crowd down into the dark basement, raising her voice to be heard over the excited chatter.

"They've hidden a bottle of champagne and we've got to find it."

"Will it be very dark?"

"I hope so!" Jameson chuckled.

The loud music from the dance floor overhead was barely muted in the cavernous basement. People continued to pour down the steps, and Julie could see several rooms with many turns and alcoves, just like at Haddonfield.

"Okay, everyone, on the count of three, I turn off the lights and the first one to find the bottle of champagne wins! One, two, three!" Pippa shouted, and the basement plunged into pitch-black darkness.

Random bodies bumped into Julie, accompanied by squeals and hoots of laughter. Groping hands seemed to be everywhere and she ducked them blindly while trying to move along the wall. It occurred to her that no one was paying much attention to actually looking for the champagne bottle.

"Where are you, my pretty?" Jameson's voice slurred drunkenly, and she felt a damp hand grasp her waist. She quickly scooted out of reach, but suddenly a different hand, this one large and strong, clamped firmly over her mouth. An arm wrapped around her shoulders like a steel band as she was pulled against an imposing male body.

Julie squirmed furiously but ineffectively as she was lifted her off her feet and carried through the pitch-black, feeling the light scrape of walls and corners as she was swept through the crowd by the stranger. After several rapid twists and turns, they finally stopped in what felt like an alcove.

It was quieter here but not by much, the velvety darkness all-enveloping and absolute. The man relaxed his grip on her slightly, and she felt a finger press against her lips in a clear message to be silent. She nodded her head, feeling warm breath on her cheek as her breathing gradually came back to normal. Who was he?

His hand moved from her lips to brush the hair back from her cheek and she felt the metallic touch of a thick ring against her skin. It was on his left hand. Hugo always wore a gold signet ring on the little finger of his left hand—she had admired it at dinner.

Relief mingled with intense joy. *Hugo.*

They stood motionless as partygoers ran past, shrieking. Hugo's right arm continued to hold her cradled against him, and she could have easily pushed him away, but instead, she put her hand on his chest, seeking his heart, and felt it leap at her touch.

His fingers slid through her hair, seeming to luxuriate in its feel. He rubbed his cheek against the softness and inhaled deeply, before dropping lower to nuzzle the outline of her ear. His lips grazed the tip, detonating tiny explosions, and with a muffled groan, he claimed her lips.

Her knees buckled as his mouth covered hers. At first he was gentle, almost tentative, but then he pulled her tighter against him as the kiss deepened. Hugo kissed her with expert technique, plundering her with rough and luxurious kisses that she returned eagerly, twining her tongue silkily against his as he was doing to hers.

She cradled his head in her hands, his hair like rough silk in her fingers, his breath warm and tasting faintly of oranges. His arms crushed her to him, and she pulled him against herself madly, loving the feeling of his body against hers. This was nothing like the awkward and sloppy advances she'd been subjected to in the past. She wanted more of this, more of him.

His lips dropped to the smooth skin of her neck, and she rolled her head back to give him more freedom, loving the slight rasp of his beard and the play of his hard muscles under her hands. He devoured her skin as if he owned it, scorching her with the fierce heat of his desire.

Wanting him to kiss her more, she pulled his lips back to her own, shocking herself with her ardor. She thrust her tongue past his lips without preamble and felt a shudder run through his body. He kissed her with possessive thoroughness, his breathing ragged. Pressing her roughly against the wall, his hands dropped to her hips, molding her against the length of his desire, intent and unmistakable. She arched against him and groaned with pleasure, her body unabashedly accepting his.

There was a loud crash, and a man's jolly voice called out nearby, "It's okay! Just a heap of boxes tumbling over! No harm!"

The sound jolted her back to reality. Bodies bumped into theirs and a hand groped roughly down her arm. She twisted easily out of Hugo's embrace to avoid it and heard a sharp punch followed by a man's groan. Hugo reached for her, but she eluded his grasp and fumbled along the corridor, slipping past bodies till she reached the rough banister of the stairs. In a moment she felt the steps and escaped up to the foyer above.

Julie sank onto a secluded bench, her mind working feverishly.

Hugo had kissed her, and it had been wonderful. More than wonderful, it had been so... she couldn't even put a name to all the feelings she was experiencing. It never felt that way when Mark kissed her, this feeling as though her bones were melting.

A couple came down the staircase from the guest rooms, and she was surprised to see Mark. He had his hand on Pippa's waist, and they were laughing.

"Mark."

He almost jumped out of his skin. Pippa let out a small squeak and scurried off towards the main reception room.

"Darling!" Mark hurried to Julie's side, running his hands through his hair and checking his belt buckle. "What are you doing here by yourself? You look upset, what's the matter?"

"Someone kissed me. Downstairs, during Bottle Safari."

"And?"

"And, and... I didn't know that was going to happen."

Mark relaxed fractionally and patted her hand. "Darling, what did you expect to happen?"

"What do you mean?"

"If you go into the basement for Bottle Safari, you can hardly object to being kissed. It's the point of the game, go in for a bit of anonymous snogging in the dark," he explained.

"Does—" Julie clasped her hands in her lap and licked her dry lips. "Does everyone know that?"

"Of course. It's an old game, our great-grandparents were probably playing it."

"Why didn't you tell me? I would have never have gone down."

"Blast it, you're right, I was so wrapped up on that call I didn't think." He took her fingers and kissed them. "Of course I would have stopped you. Can't have my best girl being fondled in the basement, can I? All the same, if you went down, you were open season."

Julie slowly digested this information. So, everyone except her had known the point of the game was to kiss whomever you found. It meant nothing to Hugo; he'd simply kissed the first girl he found and probably hadn't even known it was her.

Hot waves of embarrassment washed over her, threatening to drown her. She was lusting after Hugo just like every girl there. Where was her self-respect? Suddenly she felt very awkward and very, very tired.

"Now that you've explained it, you're right. I overreacted. But from now on, would you let me know these things?"

"Of course, darling. This is the first time you've been around my crowd from school, I forget how wild we can be. Now, shall we get back to the reception? I'm ready to dance!"

Going back to the reception was out of the question—there was absolutely no way she could face Hugo. The sight of him with other women, after what he'd made her feel, would be devastating. "I'm sorry, I'm very tired."

"You want us to leave now? But the party is just getting started," Mark protested.

"No, you don't have to go. There's a train in half an hour, I'm going to take that."

"Well, if that's what you want," he groused, though he didn't seem terribly upset. He looped his arm over her shoulder. "Come on, I'll walk you to the station."

# Chapter Fifteen

HUGO STOOD IN the dark basement as the chaos gradually subsided, his breath coming in hard rasps.

*Juliet.*

He'd never felt such unbound passion. Her reaction had been immediate and untaught, completely innocent, and he'd literally felt the desire ignite within her. The way she touched him left him reeling with pleasure, her artless passion the most arousing thing he had ever experienced.

There'd been no plan when he followed her into the basement except to protect her from the lecherous swine that he knew would be going down as well. He dropped Jameson easily and made short work of Voorhees along the way, then caught her and pulled her into a safe and secluded niche.

At first, she struggled in his grasp, but then went motionless when he touched her face. He didn't plan on kissing her, but good Lord, she smelled so rousingly fresh and sweet, like some magician had found a way to bottle sunshine and wild flowers and woman. The feeling of her, finally in his arms, was too much to pass up, and he hadn't been able to stop himself. He could not stop kissing her.

Never had he ever felt so blissfully out of control. As soon as his lips touched hers, something ignited between them. Then Juliet melted in his arms and he'd been lost. It was totally cliché but damned if it wasn't true—passion simply consumed them.

She fit perfectly against him, her lithe body stronger than he would have supposed, yet softer as well. And her skin—her skin tasted like candied satin. He could still feel the way she'd shifted her hips when he nestled his hardness against her, her movement welcoming and accepting.

An alarming thought occurred to him as he stood in the darkness, struggling to get ahold of himself. She seemed to have enjoyed it, but had she really? Truthfully, it had never mattered to him what the girl of the moment felt about the experience. But suddenly it mattered very much.

Juliet had kissed him back, and it was clear to him that her desire was very real.

That settled it. She was his.

Stealing another man's woman was primitive and barbaric. If he had seen any tenderness between her and Looks, any hint of fondness or attachment, he would have backed off and left her alone. But there'd been none, and his own chemistry with Juliet was more potent than anything he'd ever dreamed. There was no way she could deny that.

Reluctantly, Hugo conceded that the decision had to be hers, but for heaven's sake, the girl wasn't stupid. What could Looks possibly offer her that he couldn't? He was richer, vastly more successful, and socially superior. What choice was there?

He shifted uneasily against the wall. Intuitively he knew that money, success, and social standing meant very little to Juliet.

She was honorable and decent and might worry that she would hurt Looks's feelings or some ridiculous nonsense like that.

*Bloody hell. What to do, what to do?*

Tossing her over his shoulder and marching to the Jag, all the while explaining that they were meant to be together and not to worry, that Looks could manage very well without her, was unfortunately out of the question.

Best to go find Looks and have it out with him. He would ask for a word outside and try to explain what was going on. He'd lay it on the line. Juliet was now his and that was just Looks's bad luck. If Looks took it like a gentleman, he would be rewarded with continued acquaintanceship. Hugo shuddered at that thought but suppressed the squeamishness. It was a fair enough trade.

On the other hand, Looks was already drunk and might get blustery, might demand his honor be served. Granted, it would be distasteful to fight in public, and Jillian would probably never let Edward speak to him again, but he was stealing Looks's woman. Or one of them, at any rate, and etiquette demanded he allow Looks the opportunity to save face. It would pain his ego, but he'd let Looks get a punch in—but no more than one.

After that, he'd flatten the man's drunken ass.

And then he'd take Juliet and leave.

---

Hugo waited a few minutes for his breathing to return to normal before climbing the stairs with the rest of the crowd. He roamed from room to room for over an hour, but there was no sign of Juliet. Eventually, he spotted Looks with Pippa Donnell sitting in his lap, giggling over glasses of champagne.

"Where's Juliet?" he asked with as much feigned boredom as he could muster.

Looks focused a bleary eye on him. "Oh, she left an hour ago, caught the train back to London. Somebody snogged her in the basement and she got upset."

"Oh, really?" he asked coolly, his heart pounding. "Who?"

"She doesn't know, but my money's on Jameson, he's been sniffing after her all night. But she decided she'd had enough and left in a huff. I had to promise to take her to Kew next Saturday as a treat. Honestly, you'd think she was sixteen, the way she behaves sometimes."

Hugo left abruptly without a backward glance.

———— ◆ ————

The train pulled out of the station, and Julie sank into her seat with relief. A newspaper left on the seat next to her was open to the sports page, with a picture of Hugo prominently displayed in an article on Kingsbury Town's match the following day against Aston Villa. The photograph showed him mid-kick, intent, focused, his jersey gaping to reveal his powerfully sculpted abdomen, and a faint trail of hair from his navel disappearing below the waistband of his shorts.

She moved to the next car.

Leaning back in the seat, she closed her eyes, the feel of Hugo's lips still on hers. She felt deliciously warm and happy, like her emotions had been stirred with a magic spoon. And that had to stop immediately.

The kiss had lasted less than a minute, but it was ample time for her to learn that Hugo Auchincloss was a skilled and experienced lover. No wonder the girls were lined up three-deep around him. And they were very, very mistaken about the cold fish part; the man was nothing but raw, powerful passion.

She struggled to extinguish the seductive delusions that were forming, unbidden, in her mind. It was so easy to imagine that Hugo had come to the wedding to see her, made sure he sat next to her at dinner, had the chef make a special plate for her, arranged with the DJ to play her favorite music so they could dance, and then followed her into the basement to kiss her.

It was imperative that she laugh out loud at that because it was ridiculous. It came out sounding like a choked cough, and the lady sitting across the aisle from her glanced up in concern.

It took the rest of the train ride back to Kings Cross station to methodically convince herself that she was behaving like a teenager with a crush. Hugo and the groom were close friends, and Hugo himself said he'd had a change of schedule and could make the wedding after all. The return of Hugo's chair to its original position was obviously the work of the eagle-eyed wedding planner. The waiter probably took the initiative to bring her a new plate, and bossa nova music was certainly mainstream. If she'd been paying attention, she might have noticed the DJ played a wide variety of music.

And no one would dispute the fact that Hugo Auchincloss would kiss the first girl he laid hands on.

Hugo's attraction was undeniable. He was funny and made her laugh. His attention made her feel special, maybe even beautiful. Being in his company was effortless, and she found she enjoyed it very much. Too much, actually. She had to get a handle on that.

A plan, Julie knew she needed a plan. Hugo might come to the dinner Monday night, and she had no idea how she was going to face him. What if Mark was wrong and Hugo did know who he'd kissed in the pitch blackness?

The best defense was a good offense. If he did mention it, she'd coolly acknowledge the kiss and laugh it off, as Mark had. Of course she'd kissed him, wasn't that the whole point of Bottle Safari? It meant nothing. She'd had a bit too much to drink, and so had he. Party games were wonderful, weren't they? But they didn't mean anything. Ha, ha.

The train pulled to a smooth stop and she exhaled. This was good. This would work.

# Chapter Sixteen

MONDAY'S DINNER PREPARATIONS began badly and got progressively worse as the day went on, distracting Julie from her own problems. It was Phong's evening to be in charge, and he was crumpling under the pressure of a full house with half of his classmates laid low by the flu. Wracked with indecision, he repeatedly changed the menu, and things grew steadily more chaotic as the day wore on.

In the midst of the bedlam, Julie drew Bonnie aside and asked her for a ride home after service that evening.

"Of course. But what if Hugo offers you a lift?"

Julie shook her head. "Not a good idea."

This piqued Bonnie's curiosity. "Is everything okay?"

"Everything is fine. I just need to keep it that way." Before she could elaborate, a stack of roasting pans crashed to the kitchen floor, and a shouting match erupted.

By two o'clock the kitchens were mayhem, and everyone's patience was stretched to the limit. The staff watched it all with a careful eye and tried to step in when things seemed close to the brink of disaster, but Phong brushed off all suggestions and dashed from emergency to emergency. Sensible advice from

Bonnie and Julie went unheeded, and even Clive's directions were met with stubborn resistance.

"Look, I appreciate all your help," Phong snapped. "But I can do this myself."

"That's the point, dear, you're not doing this by yourself," Bonnie said. "You're supposed to be the leader, not the one doing all the work." But her advice fell on deaf ears.

Later in the afternoon, Juliet retreated to her office to water some tender seedlings and update her logbooks.

"Seems a bit frantic in the kitchens," Hugo announced from her doorway. He slouched there, handsomely aloof, picking an invisible piece of lint from his suit coat.

His unexpected entrance made Julie jump. "Phong's having a bad night," she said, studying him for any trace of a knowing glint in his eye, but his absorption in his jacket was complete. "Half the students are back in the dormitory with the flu. He has to deal with a full house and short staff, and he's not one to think on his feet."

Hugo nodded and sauntered to the woodstove to warm his hands. "How's he handling it?"

"Not well. He's a good cook and will always do as he's told, but the bigger picture eludes him."

"So what do you do?"

His question was completely devoid of mockery and she relaxed further. "We have to let him deal with it. We'll step in if there's a serious problem, but he needs to figure out how to make it work. You're staying for dinner?"

Hugo shrugged. "I didn't have any plans for the evening. Ian's around here somewhere as well, probably with that bloody camera of his. Let me know if he's being a pest."

"Don't put another hundred quid in the box again," Julie said.

Hugo raised his eyebrows in affronted innocence and leaned over her shoulder to look at the framed picture on her desk. "Is this your family, then?"

His shoulder was by her cheek, almost brushing against it. "Yes, we took that at Christmas. That's me, and Rosie and Ken, and Mother and Dad, and the rest are their graduate students and their families. We sat twenty-two for Christmas dinner. The record is forty-seven."

Hugo whistled. "Do they all live there?"

"Some live with my parents, they come and go. I never knew what it was like to have my own room growing up. The house was always full of people."

"So this is the first time you've ever lived by yourself?"

"Yes. I thought I'd like it but it's a bit lonely. I didn't realize how much I liked living in a house full of people."

"So you'd want a big family someday?' Hugo asked, his tone oddly serious for such an innocuous question.

"I'd mind having a small family," Julie admitted. "Seems very boring."

A series of doors slammed, and Julie jumped to look out her window in time to see Nerida race across the gardens to the glasshouse.

Hugo watched over her shoulder. "What's she going for?"

Julie strained to see. "No clue."

After a moment, Nerida returned, clutching a large basket filled with greens. "Oh, they forgot the chard they cut earlier," Julie explained, turning back around. But Hugo didn't move, and she was trapped between her desk and his imposing body.

With nowhere else to go, she leaned back, and the ancient desk creaked in protest. They were so close, they were almost touching, and she noticed that Hugo's eyes weren't grey at all, but green. With gold flecks in them that seemed to glow with warmth.

"You left the reception early," he noted.

His scent, like wool and lavender and pepper, enveloped her. "Tired," she finally managed to reply.

"Pity, it really picked up." He stared at her lips, his warm breath fanning her face. "Rousing good time. Top notch. None better."

The sound of multiple footsteps in the hallway broke the closeness that had enveloped them. Phong ran frantically into her office, followed closely by Bonnie.

"Julie, I cut chervil instead of dill!"

Julie slipped past Hugo. "Oh, dear," she said, taking the boy by the arm. "Come with me."

◆◆◆

As Phong and Juliet hurried away, Hugo saw he had Bonnie's full attention.

"Staying for dinner?" she asked.

Hugo shifted under her inscrutable gaze. "Might as well."

"Well then, you know where the aprons are. I think we need all hands on deck."

Hugo followed her into the kitchens and hung his jacket on a peg. Rolling up his sleeves, he discreetly observed Juliet as she huddled with Phong, examining pots of herbs in the pool room. Looks was right, he decided, she didn't know who had kissed her. Or at any rate, she was mightily unsure. It didn't take a mind reader to see she had been wary when he'd come to her office earlier—she'd practically jumped to the ceiling when he announced himself.

It was obvious that what had happened at the wedding was weighing greatly on her mind, and that was fine.

More than fine, actually.

Because if she *did* know it was him and wasn't interested, she would have sat him down and firmly told him everything had been a game—she'd had a bit too much to drink, it meant nothing, and wasn't it all a funny lark. Ha, ha.

But she hadn't.

All supposing aside, Hugo concluded as he began scrubbing crusted pans, they had to work together and if she wanted to ignore it, or pretend it didn't happen, there was a reason. God knew every other woman would have been all over him. It was a novelty in itself that this one was running in the other direction.

It was all fine with him. Yesterday's game had been brilliant. He'd been completely focused and relaxed. There was plenty of time to let things unfold with Juliet. He could be patient.

———◦○◦———

An hour before the first guests were due to arrive, Haddonfield was a maelstrom of confusion. The tables were partially bare, baked desserts were taking needed oven space, and no one had noticed the dairy hadn't delivered butter. Phong dashed between the cooks, interrupting them and yelling at no one in particular. But when a basket of onions toppled over and crushed a tray of cooling rolls, Hugo decided he'd had enough.

"Phong! Round here, lad, right now!" he barked, and Phong followed him to a quiet area off the scullery.

"Right! Enough of this messing about!" Hugo said, doing his best imitation of Kingsbury Town Manager, Giles Roberts. "How long until the main doors open?"

Phong glanced at his watch. "Forty-five minutes."

"Have all the tables been set?"

"I'm not sure..." His voice trailed off, eyes downcast.

"So get out into that dining room and make sure they've been done!" Hugo directed, deliberately getting in the boy's face. "Look at me! What else do you need to do?"

"Make sure the reservations and greeters are set?"

"Yes, and who is doing that?"

Phong paged frantically through his clipboard. "It's supposed to be Jira and Tanda, but Tanda is sick."

"Then Jira will have to do double duty. Go tell her."

Phong's eyes widened. "What if she doesn't want to?"

"You're in charge. Everyone will do what you tell them to. But you have to tell them."

"But what if—"

"No ifs. You've got people standing around waiting to be told what to do, my brother being an excellent example."

Ian looked up from his camera. "What, me?"

"Can you wait at table?" Phong asked him in a wavering voice.

"Of course he can!" Hugo snapped. "He somehow passed his A levels; he's not completely useless. And don't ask—tell. Now go back in there and get everyone's feet moving."

From a corner of the kitchen, Bonnie, Clive, and Julie watched as Phong, with a straighter spine and new resolve, marched into the dining room to inspect the settings. "Oi! Need more dinner forks over here!" He pointed at a table. "And these glasses are foggy! Let's get some clean ones out here, Clive! Julie, do you have anything blooming for the tables?"

Julie gaped at the transformation Hugo had made. "I can cut some wintersweet and put it in the glass vases."

"Good job, let's see that." Phong nodded and set off for the dish room, barking more orders.

"Guess we better put a light under it." Clive grinned and they stepped into action.

Service began with a flurry of activity that never seemed to stop. Ian quickly warmed to his impromptu role as a waiter while Julie stepped in to run the plating table in the kitchen. An hour later, she looked up and saw Hugo still manning the scullery sinks, his shirtsleeves rolled up and his blue apron already soaked, the taut muscles of his back working smoothly under his starched white shirt.

"Haven't you gotten your dinner yet?" Julie asked in surprise.

"Not yet." Hugo pointed to the mountain of dishes on the counter behind him. "They don't stop coming."

"We need to find someone to take over. You need to have your dinner."

Hugo grabbed her wrist as she brushed past. "Everyone's got their hands full. I'm fine doing this. We'll eat later."

During the night, Phong would dart back to the scullery to huddle with Hugo and regroup, each time emerging with new determination. When the evening was over, they had served seventy-one dinners and the reviews were outstanding.

After the last guests left, it turned out that no one had gotten an opportunity to eat, so they all gathered around the large kitchen table and devoured the leftovers. Julie watched covertly as Hugo tucked into the roasted vegetable baklava with obvious enthusiasm, Ian seated next to him with his camera by his side.

"Good job tonight, Ian." Clive clapped him on the back. "Have you found a hidden talent?"

Ian grinned. "I think I have. Might go see if I can get a job at one of the swank places in town."

"After you've graduated," Hugo added, not looking up from his plate.

Phong counted up the cash box and stood to give the traditional wrap-up. "Tonight was a very successful evening. Thanks to everyone for stepping up when I asked, but most of all, thanks to Hugo who gave me the best coaching ever." Everyone applauded and Phong waved a bank note. "And we got another hundred quid!"

⸺◈⸺

"I told you to cut it out with the hundred-pound notes," Julie told Hugo later as they stacked plates in the dish room.

"Saves me the effort of going to the ghetto and tossing shillings to the beggars," he quipped, taking the stacks of bowls she passed him and placing them on the high shelves over her head.

She couldn't resist smiling at that. "You were amazing with Phong. Whatever you said to him really worked."

"He just needed some coaching. Everyone does at some point." They stacked for a few more minutes, and then he asked casually, "Need a ride home?"

"No!" Julie jumped, the dessert plates in her hands clacking loudly. "No, Bonnie and Clive are dropping me off."

"Oh. Homework is due tomorrow morning, care to reconsider our bet?"

"Only if you're willing to change the stakes."

"Not on your life."

# Chapter Seventeen

HUGO HAD TO hand it to Juliet, for the rest of the week she did an outstanding job of avoiding him. Every afternoon, she put in perfunctory appearances at the staff tea, where she was cordial and polite, but after a quick cup and a nibbled sweet, she would bolt back into the gardens. Nor did she acknowledge the stack of homework he'd left on her desk Tuesday evening, all ten copies of it. They were returned to his upstairs classroom the next day, slightly out of order, and he was positive she had read them all.

"Crystal Palace is looking challenging this weekend," Clive commented Thursday afternoon at tea, referring to the FA Cup fourth round match that Kingsbury Town was playing Saturday afternoon.

Hugo hungrily selected another slightly burned scone from a plate Julie had placed on the table. With her hair pulled back in a ponytail, she looked no older than a teenager, and he felt the familiar readiness stir in his lower regions as she moved around the kitchen. When she bent over to retrieve a jug of milk from the bottom shelf of the refrigerator, a minor earthquake rattled every nerve ending in his body.

Clive coughed dryly, and Hugo flushed when he saw the glint of amusement in the older man's eyes. "Palace. Yes," he said, forcing his attention back to the conversation. "Quite a dilemma, not sure how that's going to go. They've been all over the place. When we played them in September, we had our arses handed to us, then they rolled over for Everton like lambs."

Out of the corner of his eye, he saw Juliet reach for a bowl on a high shelf. The waistline of her trousers dropped lower on the gentle flare of her hips, exposing a brief glimpse of panties. "Their lace flank, I mean their left flank is weak," Hugo stammered, "but their keeper, Costanza, has got eight arms. It's like kicking against a brick wall. Last match against them I had four shots on goal, and all of them just came back out like he was playing with a tennis racket."

"Hi, gang," Don greeted everyone and took a seat. "Wanted to let you know the town council just called. They're putting our plans for the new polyhouse on the agenda tonight. They've already reviewed them and there's no problems, but they want me there."

"Shall I go as well?" Julie asked. "In case they have any questions?"

"If they had any questions after reading your sixty-seven-page information package, they'd have to be daft," Don laughed.

Hugo saw Juliet's face fall. "Maybe they'd want her there as a show of support," he suggested sharply.

Don was instantly contrite. "I'm sorry, Julie. I just meant that they won't need that level of detail. It's going to be the big picture stuff. I've already spoken with the councilors and they're prepared to let it go ahead. It's just that, while the details are very important to us, they might be confused by the technical stuff."

She tried to smile and nodded in agreement, then hastily excused herself and went back to her office.

"Don, that was rude," Bonnie berated him. "You know how sensitive she is."

"I know, I'll apologize. It's just she does tend to go on, and those people couldn't tell the difference between a cucumber and courgette."

"Then you need to make them understand. It's the foodies that are packing our dinner nights, and we're starting to draw from far away as well. People are even beginning to plan visits here. And did you know that we're going to be written up in one of the big magazines? To them, she's a patron saint. The least we can do is let her talk a bit."

Don nodded. "Okay, I'll take her with me tonight. I'll go tell her."

"After her swim."

"Right."

———◇———

Hugo excused himself, returned to his classroom, and began grading papers. His desk was strategically angled next to the window, which was where he sat every night at this time. If Her Majesty were to suddenly command him to the palace, he would have to politely send his regrets.

Because from here, he could watch Juliet swim.

The glassed atrium was built at a right angle to the main house, and from his window, he had an unobstructed view of the lap pool where Juliet usually swam in the evenings after the students left. She possessed an outstanding collection of bathing costumes, and from his perch he could see that today she was wearing the blue bikini.

Ah, the blue bikini. More like azure, to be completely accurate, with a slight sheen to the fabric that glistened when it got wet. It wasn't one of those gauche thongs, but instead tied at each hip, showing off her round bottom to perfection. The skimpy top displayed the tempting valley between her breasts and was his favorite.

But then again, perhaps the green bikini, yesterday's choice. It had merits as well that required serious consideration. It was crocheted, for one, and if he snipped an end and pulled the string with his teeth, it would unravel in under a minute. And then her body would be his to explore in unhurried leisure.

Such a difficult decision—both suits had their distinct advantages. Each showed off her body brilliantly, the green one having the slight advantage of being a little too small and requiring frequent tugs to pull it back into place. The blue suit, however, was made of a thin, gauzy material that must have been woven by the angels because when she dipped into the cool water and surfaced, as she had just done, her taut nipples were perfectly outlined. And it was the color of her eyes.

There was an orange one-piece that made an occasional appearance, but it was plain and rather prudish and in all fairness, shouldn't be in consideration with the other two. A black high-neck racer style was dismissed out of hand for its dull fabric and excessive coverage.

From his high perch, Hugo watched her while lazily debating the topic in his head as she swam with strong strokes, her body cutting through the water like a mermaid. Today she swam for over thirty minutes, longer than usual, and then pulled herself out of the water and sat on the edge, tucking her legs to her chest. Her unhappiness was tangible, and for some reason Hugo couldn't bear it.

Don appeared and spoke with her, probably about going to the council meeting that night. This seemed to perk her up and she stood, toweled off, and went back to her office. Show over.

Hugo contemplated the now empty pool for a long time before pulling his mobile out of his pocket. "Phillip. Line me up a Cup ticket for Saturday, midfield close. Shake down whomever you have to. I need it by tomorrow."

---

Friday afternoon, Julie was in the glasshouse washing the windowpanes, a messy annual chore. A portable radiator stood just outside and blasted in a steady wave of heat, turning the little building into a sauna. She had stripped down to a t-shirt and jeans, which were now soaking wet. Feeling short-tempered and exhausted, she brushed back a stray lock of hair from her ponytail and moved the stepladder to attack the final section of roof.

Last night had been the opening of an American designer's clothing boutique in Knightsbridge. Several movie actresses were scheduled to appear, and Mark was excited to meet them. But as the hours wore on, it became obvious they would be late, and by midnight Julie was dead on her feet.

Mark's apartment was only four blocks from the store. It would have been convenient to have stayed there, but he didn't offer and she still felt too shy to ask. Instead, she left by herself, not crawling beneath the covers of her own bed until one o'clock in the morning and then up again at five.

Mark called at noon to make sure she'd gotten home safely and gushed excitedly about meeting the stars. "They were lovely. You should have stayed. So much prettier in person."

"I'm sorry, I had been double-digging all day and didn't realize how tired I was. But I'm looking forward to going to Kew Gardens tomorrow. What time shall I meet you there?"

"Kew?" Mark asked. "Oh! Yes, of course. How about two p.m.? Look, darling, have to run, call with Los Angeles is starting. Bye for now."

The squeegee left satisfying cleanliness in its path as she drew it across the old panes.

"Where is everyone?" Hugo asked from the doorway, making her jump. Honestly, the man moved like a cat.

"Don't come in. Everything's wet," Julie cautioned. "Bonnie took some of the first years to the market and the rest are upstairs preparing for your algebra test."

"Oh, good."

Hugo took the squeegee out of her hand and easily reached the upper panes, flicking them clean with deft movements and not getting a drop on himself. He returned it to her with a slight bow.

"Juliet, are you—" He stopped as she pulled at the wet t-shirt fabric plastered against her skin. "Are you all finished then?" he finally got out, gesturing vaguely around the glasshouse. "Shall I give you a hand putting the tables back in?"

"Yes, thanks."

As they worked, it struck Julie that Hugo seemed uncharacteristically nervous. Twice more he started to ask her a question but each time caught himself and reverted to mumbles. When they finished returning the greenhouse to order, Juliet put her wool sweater back on while Hugo turned the heater off.

"Say," Hugo began with what sounded like undue casualness, "we're playing Crystal Palace in the FA Cup fourth round tomorrow at Townsend Lane Stadium. Would you like a ticket?"

"Two tickets?"

"Of course," he corrected himself. "Thought Looks might be out of town."

"Thank you, but no, we have other plans. We're going to Kew Gardens, the *Pyrostegia venusta* is in bloom. It's a South American flame vine."

"Sounds delightful."

Something in the tone of his voice told Julie that Hugo was distinctly disappointed to hear the vine was flowering.

---

Later that afternoon, Julie was in the orchard inspecting the apple trees when she heard her name called. Looking up, she saw Lalani running towards her, crying and waving a paper.

Julie sprinted towards the distraught girl. "What is it, Lalani?"

"My test," Lalani gasped, trying to catch her breath. "My maths test from Hugo."

"What happened? Did you fail it?"

A fresh burst of sobs answered her question. Infuriated, Julie took the girl by the arm and began marching back towards the house. "That's it. He's got to stop this ridiculous nonsense—"

"No! Julie!" Lalani pulled away, taking her glasses off and wiping her eyes with the back of her sleeve. "I got a ni-ninety-two p-percent!"

Julie stopped in her tracks. She reached for Lalani's test paper and read it carefully—the math was basic one- and two-step algebra, and Lalani had done all the problems neatly and well. Hugo deducted a point here and there for missing signs and one incorrect answer, but overall it was very good work.

"Me! Algebra! A ninety-two percent! Can you believe it?" Lalani cried in happiness and hugged Julie.

# Chapter Eighteen

IT WASN'T HUGO'S habit to hit the after-match parties with his teammates, but this particular Saturday night he felt in great need of distraction. Immediate distraction. Actually, any distraction would be welcome.

Kingsbury Town's 2–1 win over Crystal Palace in the FA Cup fourth round that afternoon had been full of surprise plays and ingenious moves from their opponents. Crystal Palace's new manager was an unknown quantity who unfolded a brilliant series of plays that pushed Hugo to play a more forward midfield position than he was used to, causing him to perform as striker on two occasions.

It was one of those rare games when the team played with one head and one heart, and when they won on Marco's penalty kick in the last thirty seconds of injury time, the stadium exploded. The match would rank as one of the best games they'd ever played, and he was bitterly sorry when it was over—he could have played for hours. His heart was pumping, and he felt nearly delirious as they circled the stadium, thanking the fans and applauding Crystal Palace's fans as well, all of whom had sat for two hours in the pouring rain.

Back in the locker room, he toyed with his mobile phone, the urge to call Juliet almost impossible to resist. The great victory filled him with supercharged adrenaline, and he wanted to tell her all about it. Instead, he found himself sitting on a velvet lounge in a penthouse nightclub just off St James's Square with a beautiful woman on either side, bored to tears and agitated beyond words.

"You were brilliant today, Hugo," one purred in his ear. "Crystal Palace never stood a chance."

Stupid cow, they had stood every chance, and if their right wing hadn't been recovering from a bout of the flu and tired early, Crystal Palace might have drawn the game.

"Just brilliant," repeated the other, her unnaturally round breasts pressing heavily against his arm.

They were a gorgeous pair of birds, scantily clad in almost identical dresses and spiky high heels. Hugo knew they were his for the night if he were interested. It wouldn't be a bad idea. He'd been so horny lately—maybe some relief would be in order.

It had been some time since he'd had a woman, and perhaps that was the problem. Remembering the last time was difficult, and the times before that, impossible. And the time before that? Faces and names failed to materialize. It was all a blank. There was only Juliet.

The entire week had been tender hell, seeing her every day, being around her but always with others. Watching her afternoon swims filled him with an ungovernable mixture of emotions—impatience, rampant desire, and a mystifying sense of tranquility. Then yesterday he'd gotten more than he'd bargained for when he found her in the glasshouse, soaked to the skin, her wet t-shirt clinging to her body like a second skin.

She looked toothsome, one of his favorite words. Luscious, delicious, innocently provocative. Jesus, just the memory was making him as hard as an iron pike.

A painful throbbing started in his temple, helped along, no doubt, by the battling perfumes the women were wearing. Each was assaultive in its own right, expensive but obvious. And their hair was brittle, he noticed, looking as though it would snap at the touch. Hugo remembered burying his hand in Juliet's golden locks, and the sensuous way the silken strands slid around his fingers as he kissed her. And he knew without a doubt her hair would feel like the most luxurious satin against his naked skin.

Why was he so cursed? It should be Juliet sitting next to him on the divan as they looked out over the lights of London, her fingers caressing him, teasing him, her attention fully on him. She would burn with a desire equal to his, letting him know that she, too, chafed to be alone with him.

He wanted her anxious, excited, and willing. And he wanted her immediately.

Rutting, his grandfather would have called it. Rutting like a stag in heat, his blood surging hotly, making him stupid and impulsive. And he did feel like banging his horns against something, preferably Looks Brooks's ass, and then dragging Juliet off to a very secluded and private place where he could seduce her properly.

*Patience*, a part of him cautioned. Where was Icewater Auchincloss now? He was dangerously close to blowing it and he damn well knew it. Juliet was right, he thought ruefully—assuming the virtue of patience was his only chance in hell of achieving it.

The brunette on his right dropped her hand to his lap, her eyes widening as she felt the length of his rampant arousal. "Wow, it is true what they say about you," she murmured appreciatively, moving to explore further.

"Let's get another bottle of champagne," the one on the left suggested.

"No, let's not." Swiftly removing the hand from his lap, Hugo abruptly stood and motioned for the bill, paid it quickly, and stalked out of the lounge.

"Oh, come on, Hugo," one of the women cajoled as the pair caught up to him outside in the foyer. "Let's go to Bash Club."

Hugo reached in his pocket and gave each a hundred-pound note. "Here you are then, go and have fun, drinks are on me. Goodbye."

A cab dropped him off two blocks from his house, in front of an all-night fish and chip vendor he knew well. Dinner in hand, he walked to the British Museum, his favorite place in the world ever since he'd been a small lad. It was magnificently lit up, the colonnade grand and bright. Sitting on a nearby wall, he ate his supper and considered his miserable plight. Somewhere in the city, Juliet was probably out with Looks, enjoying herself immensely without a thought for him. And here he sat, able to have almost any woman he wanted, except the woman he wanted most.

This was a problem, and feeling sorry for himself was not going to solve it. He rolled up the chips wrapper and tossed it into the rubbish, and put his mind to finding a solution.

———◦◦———

"Mark, that guy just pinched my bottom!" Julie yelped as she trailed Mark through the crowded dance club.

"That's nice, darling," he yelled over the incessant techno music. Neon lights pulsed to the beat, and Julie felt a headache coming on.

"No, it's not!" she protested, flinching as a woman's high heel crushed her toe. "Can we find a seat somewhere?"

"Of course, darling, I'm looking for our friends now."

Finally Mark steered them to where a group of fashionable men and women from Mark's office were perched on padded stools, sipping elegant cocktails. They greeted Mark and Julie cheerfully and then returned to their animated conversations.

Mark offered her an empty spot on a sofa and gave a drink order to a passing waiter. "Sorry about the mix-up today, love, I so wanted to go to Kew with you," he apologized again. "But that damn call dragged on for hours, I barely made it home in time to change for tonight."

"It's all right," Julie said, trying to forget the disappointment she'd felt when Mark called at noon to say an important issue had come up and he couldn't meet her. "I got a lot of things done around the house."

"You are my angel," Mark consoled, taking his drink from the waiter and waving to a group of models that wafted by.

"I'm just glad I didn't take Hugo up on his offer of tickets for the match this afternoon," Julie added. "It would have been miserable sitting in Townsend Lane Stadium in that rain."

"Pardon?" Mark paused, his drink almost to his lips.

"Hugo offered tickets to the FA Cup match this afternoon, but I told him we had other plans."

"Why?" Mark sputtered. "Tickets to those things are jolly difficult to get. They're sold out months in advance."

"But we'd made plans to go to Kew."

"We can go there any time," he replied peevishly. "Not every day you can go to an FA Cup match, especially when you know one of the players. He might have gotten us into the after-party as well."

It occurred to Julie that it wouldn't have mattered either way, as Mark was supposed to have been on a call all afternoon. "Next time he offers, I'll take him up on it," she said.

His taciturn expression lasted a few more moments before being replaced by his charming smile. "You're right, darling, as always. We would have been drenched, and what fun is that? Oh look, there's Zhang Cho, I need to give her my mobile number. Won't be a sec."

Mark vanished into the crowd, and Julie sat alone. The waiter returned with her wine but couldn't get through the throng to deliver it, so she got up and stepped behind a wide pillar to accept it from him. Turning back, she saw that two women from Mark's office had taken her seat and were deep in conversation.

"I just got told I have to go on the Lisbon shoot to babysit Rochelle next month," one complained.

"Sorry to hear it," her friend sympathized. "I was with her in Fiji in January, biggest headache of my life. Bobby gets the duty in Rome next week."

From behind the pillar, Julie stood motionless, unseen yet close enough to hear every word.

"Worst was Miami two weeks ago. It wasn't until Mark showed up and—"

A loud burst of laughter from another group drowned out what the woman was saying for several moments.

"—and that set the entire schedule back a day and a half."

"That's exactly what happened in Fiji. You know," one continued confidentially. "She's been absolutely impossible since they split up. And now that he's got that new girl—the boring one,—I think Rochelle is scared she's not going to get him back like she has all the other times."

"His new girlfriend's not boring, she's just quiet. Refreshing change. I quite like her."

"Dull as dishwater. And an absolute fashion moron—do you know she was wearing Manolo Blahnik shoes at the symphony dinner last week and didn't even know it? And Talia was wearing that amazing sequined caftan..."

The women moved on to other topics, and Julie remained behind the column. Mark had gone to Toronto two weeks ago, not Miami—she remembered it clearly because she had teased him about coming home from Toronto with a sunburn in winter, and he had been very annoyed. He certainly didn't mention he went anywhere else, or that he had seen Rochelle.

Julie looked across the room to where Mark was holding court, making jokes and laughing along with everyone. He was the complete opposite of Hugo, she observed. In public, Hugo was aloof and reserved, yet very charming and friendly in person. Mark, on the other hand, was the life of the party, but when they were alone he seldom had anything to say. Then again, they were rarely alone.

The students had never warmed to Mark, and if truth be told, could barely conceal their contempt for him. He, in turn, had made no secret the feeling was mutual. But they had immediately taken to Hugo and now accepted him wholeheartedly, even after he assigned them homework. It was very odd.

She chastised herself for being unfair to Mark. Hugo had all the time and money in the world, while Mark had a very responsible job that, as he frequently reminded her, required him to be in three places at once. It was natural that he might have forgotten to tell her he'd gone to Miami instead of Toronto. If Rochelle were having problems, he might have felt he owed it to her to help.

And Hugo Auchincloss needed to get out of her head, she admonished herself sternly, because she was hardly the kind of girl who would fall for someone like him. Tonight she was on a date with her boyfriend, and they were having a good time. Which could turn out to be a great time if she applied herself a bit.

Squaring her shoulders, she edged her way to Mark's side and slipped an arm around him. He gave her a quick squeeze while keeping up his discussion with an exotic Asian model.

Soon a couple joined the group, breathless and giddy. "And where have you two been?" Mark teased.

"Upstairs in the VIP club with the Kingsbury Town players," the girl giggled. "That was a lark."

"I'll say," her companion added heartily. "They won today, two-one over Crystal Palace. People are calling it the match of the decade. They're all there, living it up."

"All of them?" Mark asked. "Even Hugo Auchincloss?"

"He was there, but left over an hour ago with two brunette birds on his arm," the man confirmed.

"Hugo took two women home! Lucky bastard," Mark crowed approvingly, but swiftly backtracked when he caught Julie's look of surprise. "But not as lucky as me, darling. Not when I've got you."

"Lucky girls," a French model corrected in halting English. "I hear rumors about him."

A Brazilian model sipped her vodka and winked slyly. "S'no rumor..."

Julie's eyes narrowed dangerously.

For the rest of the night, she resolutely stuck to Mark like glue, trailing him from group to group as he chatted with everyone in the club. By the wee hours of the morning, the place began emptying out and Julie could barely see straight.

Mark patted her on the back. "You've been fantastic tonight. Had a good time?"

She nodded, exhausted. "Best ever."

"Come on, I'll take you down to fetch a cab."

It was now or never. "You know, I could go back to your place with you."

Mark stiffened and began walking her towards the stairs. "Oh, darling, that would be wonderful but the flat is a complete mess. I haven't been home all week and I'd hate for you to see it like that. And I have to be at Heathrow to catch my flight for New York at seven."

"Is Rochelle going to be in New York?"

"Who knows?" Mark quickened his pace, eyes straight ahead. "You know, darling, you should stop fussing about her. She's out of the picture. There's only you. I'll introduce you to her sometime, and you'll see."

He gave her a quick peck on the cheek and handed her into a waiting cab. "I'll be back Thursday. Don't forget we're having dinner with the Mendozas. I'll have the car sent round."

Mark shut the cab door and ran to catch up with a group of friends.

# Chapter Nineteen

THE SUN WOULDN'T be rising for another hour, but Julie abandoned the pretext of trying to sleep and padded down to the kitchen to make some breakfast. Hugo's flowers were on the table, still fresh and remarkably vibrant. A few yellow rose petals littered the table, and she idly rubbed one between her fingers, releasing its delicate scent.

To her dismay, a tear rolled down her cheek.

She brushed it aside and fingered a lock of her hair. It was blonde—a warm, rich shade she had always thought was pretty, but now seemed unremarkable. Rochelle's hair was cut dramatically short. Mark said it was a "signature style" that women around the world imitated, and that she had to get it trimmed every week so it always looked the same. Where Rochelle found the time, Julie had no idea.

Hugo had gone home with two brunettes. Maybe he liked them better than blondes.

More unbidden tears welled in her eyes as she struggled with emotions that were alarmingly out of control. Her boyfriend was flying to New York, perhaps to be with his ex-girlfriend. A guy she barely knew was having sexual adventures most men only dreamed of. And she was sitting alone at her kitchen table with a cup of lukewarm tea and piece of toast, wearing a prim white cotton nightgown trimmed in lace with a single pearl button at the top. Could she be more pathetic?

No matter how hard she fought, tears continued to spill over her cheeks. She finally gave up and cried her heart out, the sadness pouring from some unidentifiable place deep within her. Eventually the storm subsided but left her mystified.

She found the tissue box and blew her nose, telling herself she was acting like a spoiled child. *That* was going to stop immediately. Mark had to go to New York for work, not to romance Rochelle. And Hugo was behaving exactly like the rich, famous, and handsome football star he was. If she was miserable, it was her own fault for letting herself live in a fantasy world for the past week, thinking he fancied her. Of course he did—he fancied every girl.

Dabbing at her eyes, she searched for explanations. Maybe she was jealous of Rochelle. She'd never felt jealousy before, but everyone said it was awful and she certainly felt that way. Rochelle did make her feel insecure, but she had to give herself some latitude—not many women had to deal with ex-girlfriends who were supermodels. It might help if she met Rochelle and got to know her a bit. Who knew, they might even become friends. The thought cheered Julie up, and she blew her nose again.

Which left Hugo. What did a man do in bed with two women? Julie wondered, painfully aware of her own inexperience. Wasn't there enough to do with just one? Her upbringing had been relatively wholesome, and no topics in her parents' house were particularly taboo, but lively discussions usually ran towards ideals of Renaissance love or theoretical mathematics. They'd never had a television, and trips to the movies were infrequent. She was woefully naive about the varieties and nuances of making love—even Lalani was worldlier than she was.

But Julie knew from firsthand experience that Hugo had more than enough passion for one woman, so maybe two made sense. The French model was right, lucky girls indeed.

A wave of anguish crashed over her, and she buried her face in her hands as the flood of tears began anew.

After what felt like ages, she finally pushed the tissue box aside and stood. It was no good crying the morning away over some man who was completely wrong for her. Today's weather was supposed to be very pleasant, and Sunday morning service at the neighborhood church would be a good way to begin the day.

Upstairs, she splashed her face with cold water and brushed her hair till it shone and then selected a smart navy-blue sweater dress that she paired with low heels. Pulling on her dress coat, she locked her front door and resolutely started off on the short walk to church.

The rector was a frequent dinner guest at Haddonfield and greeted her warmly. The church was about half full and she found a seat in a middle pew. Lovely music from the pipe organ filled the stone building.

Did the women Hugo took home last night have short hair or long? Julie firmly resisted thinking about that and instead chose to be grateful she had found out about his activities in time. Really, she cautioned herself sternly, she'd have to be more careful. She couldn't rely on luck to remind her how far she needed to keep away from him. Hugo Auchincloss was off-limits.

The music began to lift her spirits. Late arrivals filled out the pews and the congregation stood to sing the opening hymn. As she sang, she became vaguely aware of the man next to her, his voice deep and rich. She glanced left and felt the hymnal slip from her fingers.

Hugo stood next to her, singing clearly and powerfully. He looked handsome, clean-shaven and apparently well-rested.

"What are you doing here?" she whispered, not even trying to effect coolness.

"It's Sunday, and this is a church. Where else should I be?" He looked down at her with a mischievous glint in his eyes before retrieving her hymnal and politely presenting it to her.

Julie snatched it from him and frantically tried to regain her composure. The congregation sat, and she fumbled with the book but jerked it away before he could assist. She forced her gaze to the rector and the beautiful stained-glass window behind him, noting with surprise that the illuminated colors looked brighter than before.

*Mark has never come to church with me.*

The liturgy proceeded in a series of rote responses that she barely comprehended. During the sermon, she caved in to temptation and cast a sidelong glance at Hugo, who sat beside her, relaxed and attentive, his hands resting on his legs mere inches from her own. He looked dashingly handsome, dressed with his usual impeccable sophistication in a dark navy suit with a starched white shirt and expertly knotted tie.

What did she expect to see, she rebuked herself, him covered in lipstick and claw marks?

In the blink of an eye, the service was over, and they were singing "Land of Hope and Glory." She had no choice but to allow him to help her into her coat, and together they walked stiffly down the aisle, his hand resting on the small of her back. It took a superhuman effort not to shove past the people in front of her and run out the door as fast as she could.

The reverend greeted Hugo enthusiastically and Julie made the introductions. The men shook hands and chatted for a few moments about Hugo's win the day before, then the reverend invited him back anytime.

"That was completely unnecessary," Julie snapped as they walked down the flagstone path. "By tomorrow, it will be all over the neighborhood that you were here."

"I don't see a problem with that," Hugo said. "Should set an example for Arsenal. I didn't see any of them in there. Now, I need to take a drive out to my family's farm today and I thought you might like to ride along. Stop and have lunch. What do you say?"

A pathetic flare of delight leapt within her, achingly sweet, which Julie tempered by summoning a mental image of him lying naked in a bed with two writhing women. At the sidewalk, she turned on her heel and began walking quickly towards home. "Thank you, but I've got a lot of things to do today."

He followed her. "With Looks?"

"No. He left this morning for New York."

"There's an interesting little event going on at a school I know. I thought we might stop in on the way. You might enjoy it," he said, matching her brisk pace.

"I doubt it."

"But you don't even know what it is."

Gritting her teeth, she walked faster. "Sorry you went to the trouble of coming to church, but I've got a lot to do today and couldn't possibly take the time."

"It wasn't any trouble, and I like church. Always have."

She knew she was behaving oddly, but she had to get away from him. They were forced to stop at the corner as several cars passed through the intersection. She tapped her foot impatiently.

"How was Kew yesterday?" he asked as they waited.

"We didn't go," she replied primly. "Mark had to be on a call. A very important call. But we went out to Jester's later."

There was a pause, and Julie felt smug. Maybe now he'd get the picture.

"You were there as well? I didn't see you."

"We got there late. Evidently you and your friends had already left."

"What are you talking about?" With no compunction he grabbed her arm as she attempted to dart between cars. "I didn't leave with any friends. I left by himself."

Her eyes widened at the bald-faced lie. He searched her face, the picture of injured innocence, and then swore a blistering oath. "You think I went home with two women, don't you?" He gave her a shake to emphasize his point. "That's what you think, isn't it?"

"It's absolutely none of my business what you—"

"I didn't."

This was too much. "Everyone saw you leave with the two girls—it was all anyone was talking about it. Mark was very impressed." Julie tried to sound casual and worldly, but it came out all wrong.

"I'm sure he was," Hugo spit out venomously.

"How you spend your time outside of Haddonfield is of no interest to me. Just don't be surprised if I decline your offer to spend a Sunday with you." She flushed and glanced away. "I might catch something."

"Juliet. Look at me," he demanded, cupping her chin gently with his hand. "Yes, I was at the club. When I got up to leave, two women followed me out, and yes, they wanted to go home with me. I made it clear I wasn't interested, but they were... well, insistent. So, in the outside hall I gave them money and told them to go away. Then I got a cab and went home. Alone."

He watched her intently, but she refused to accept his explanation. Reaching into his wallet, he pulled out a taxi receipt and handed it to her. "Here, this is the cab receipt."

"You don't have to show me any proof." She pushed it away, her heart pounding.

"Look at it, damn it!" he practically shouted, his cool demeanor replaced by an anger hotter than anything she'd ever seen in him. "When I got to Bloomsbury, I bought fish and chips for dinner. Here, here's that receipt as well."

Julie reluctantly looked at the papers he was jamming into her hands. One was indeed a taxi receipt for a ride from Jester's to an intersection in Bloomsbury, for one passenger, close to midnight. And the other showed a single large order of fish and chips, five minutes later. Unbidden relief flooded through her.

"There! Who takes two birds home and stops for fish and chips on the way?" he demanded.

"It's none of my business," she said, handing them back to him.

"It is your business. I teach your students."

"Does that happen to you a lot? Women coming on to you like that?"

"All the time. Bloody nuisance," Hugo groused. "The worst part is people getting the wrong idea about you and making rash accusations," he added for good measure.

Julie bit her lip and nodded. "I'm sorry. It was wrong of me."

"It was," he agreed in an injured tone. "Chap's reputation is all he has."

"Yes, it is. Please accept my apology."

"The situation seems to require more than an apology. I think you need to make it up to me."

An involuntary smile tugged at her lips. "I do?"

"Yes. You impugned my good name, and I'll only forgive you if you'll go out to Wrothesley with me today."

She laughed out loud. "That's a bit much. And I am busy."

"Doing what?"

Her shoulders drooped. "Paying bills."

He grinned in satisfaction and steered her back towards the church car park. "I promise I'll have you home in plenty of time."

# Chapter Twenty

HUGO SETTLED JULIE in the Jaguar and got them onto the motorway before she could change her mind. For the love of God, London was a city of seven and a half million people. How did she find out where he had been the night before?

"You won yesterday," Julie said.

"It was the best ever. Crystal Palace has a brilliant new manager. He studied us and came up with some inspired plays that forced us to play completely outside of our normal roles," he said, aggressively cutting and weaving through the Sunday morning traffic.

"Do you drive the way you play football?"

He saw she was clutching the armrests for dear life and immediately slowed to the legal limit. "Yes, actually. Sorry."

Her grip relaxed. "Tell me more about your match."

Hugo readily complied, and if a reporter from the *Telegraph* had been sitting in her seat, they would have gotten the interview of the year. He told Julie everything, every detailed nuance of the match, every mistake they'd made, every Achilles' heel they had. It was obvious she didn't understand a word, but there wasn't anyone he could talk to, really, who didn't already have an opinion on how he'd played and what the team had done. Even Mummy would have remarked that their defense fell apart in the last ten minutes and he'd not properly cleared a corner kick, letting Palace almost back-heel one in.

Instead, Julie listened, occasionally asking a question, and just let him talk.

Within an hour, they were leaving the highway and traveling narrow country roads, passing through picturesque towns and rolling fields before pulling into the crowded car park of a village school.

"Here we are then."

Julie looked around curiously. "Where's here?"

"Let's go find out," he answered mysteriously and held the car door for her.

Inside the school, a faint, violet-like scent hung in the air. Julie sniffed and looked questioningly at Hugo, but he shrugged and gestured down a narrow staircase. At the landing, Julie sniffed again.

"Irises?" she asked in faint wonder and skipped down the remaining steps to where a hand-printed sign announced "East of England Regional Iris Society Show."

"It's not Kew, but I thought you'd enjoy it," he said, holding the door for her.

Hugo paid the admission fee and followed Julie into a large room filled with the most lavishly colored flowers he'd ever seen. Exquisite irises in every shade and hue of blue were present, dotted with bursts of yellow and white. There were easily three hundred in pots arranged on tables around the basement room, the colors dazzling even under the fluorescent lights.

As they walked the aisles, Julie carefully examined rare varieties and exclaimed over new cultivars, patiently explaining to Hugo the difference between one flower and the next. What had first looked like a bunch of pretty flowers now sorted themselves into families and classifications: the smaller reticulata, the taller and fuller bearded varieties, and the slim and elegant Siberians, all forced in greenhouses. It was remarkable.

After an hour, a loud rumbling erupted from Hugo's stomach. "There's a tea table. Shall we get a bun?"

Julie looked up from her intent study of a rare Turkish variety and blinked. "I've got a better idea, give me a moment." She spoke with the woman who'd sold them their tickets before returning to his side. "The lady said there's a restaurant around the corner, the Crofton, which does a nice Sunday lunch. May I treat you?"

She smiled up at him, making the breath catch in his chest. "You want to treat me to lunch."

"Coming here was a lovely idea, and lunch can be part of my apology. And you're in luck, I just got paid, so I'm flush. What do you say?"

He knew he was looking at her oddly but couldn't help it. "Is the Crofton not to your liking?" Her smiled faded, and she began to fumble in her pocketbook for her wallet. "I might be able to do a bit better, let me check—"

With a quick motion, his hand gripped her wrist, staying it. She wanted to buy him lunch. No girl had ever wanted to pay for something, ever. A funny feeling rushed over him, a current of emotion completely beyond his control, not unlike being on a roller coaster.

He loved roller coasters.

"I've already made plans for lunch," he said, his voice rough. "Local place, it's very exclusive and the chef is a bit opinionated, but it's got an excellent reputation. I was lucky to get reservations at such short notice. You're to be my guest."

———————◆———————

After some chiding, Hugo finally allowed Julie to buy some buns to hold him over until lunch. He hungrily ate two before they got back in the car and drove farther north.

"Tell me about Wrothesley," Julie said.

"It's a farm—actually, three farms—the one with the house plus two others that are very close but not contiguous to the main property. The principal crop is wheat, although the farm manager, Miles Dersham, has been nagging me about adding other things. Miles's family has lived on the land as long as we have. His father was the estate manager before him, and his father before that. Actually, no one remembers when it wasn't that way."

Julie nodded. "Any grazing land?"

"It was about half grazing at one time, I remember the herd vaguely. The barns are still there, and Dad and Miles's father were considering restarting an Angus cattle herd."

"Did they?"

"No. They were both killed in a plane crash nine years ago, coming back from Aberdeen after looking at some breeding stock. They had picked up my best friend, Tom, who was at university there, to bring him home for break. He's the only one who survived the crash. But he's in a wheelchair."

Julie glanced at him, and he waited grimly for the gush of sympathy that such news usually produced. Instead, she nodded and seemed to be considering something.

"I'm so sorry for your loss," she finally said. "But how on earth did you learn to run a commercial wheat operation? Did you work on the farms growing up?"

He kept his face emotionless but felt a swell of pride. "Perceptive question. I see you've noticed I wasn't born with a green thumb. No, I didn't have much to do with the farms. Dad always thought there would be plenty of time for me to have my career and take over running the estate when I was older, the way he had. When the accident happened, Miles was in the Royal Marines, and I was up to my neck with the team, so Grandfather ran things for two years. Then he died, and I took over."

"But you had a full-time job as well."

"Dad and Grandfather had a good system going, so it wasn't like starting from scratch. The harvesters were scheduled, and the seed, and the rotations. We've just continued doing everything exactly the same way ever since."

They drove through a town and Hugo pointed out local landmarks and then turned down a narrow road bordered by lush fields and tall hedgerows. Around a corner, they came upon an old tractor partially blocking the road, with two trucks pulled in behind it and several men peering at the engine. A dour old man wearing ancient tweeds stood slightly apart from the group, his hands jammed resolutely in his pockets while he puffed furiously on a pipe.

"It's Old William," Hugo said, pulling the Jaguar in behind the other vehicles. "William Sproul. He used to work on the estate."

He held the car door for Julie, and they walked towards the group of men who shook hands with Hugo. He introduced Julie to each individually, naming the local farms where they lived. Miles Dersham was one of the group, and she was startled to see he was as young as Hugo but with the weathered face of a seasoned farmer.

"Hello, sir," Hugo greeted William. "Good to see you. What seems to be the problem?"

William jerked his head towards the tractor, muttering a few unintelligible words.

"Old William here was on his way to the Hart and Dove," Miles said, "when this old relic packed it in."

"Couldn't you have waited an hour 'til I picked you up?" A neighboring farmer clapped William on the back. William grumbled darkly about the pub opening at noon and not wanting to be late.

"Well, the engine's flooded for the moment," Miles informed them, and the men fell into animated conversation while Julie looked closely at the old tractor.

"That's a Massey-Ferguson 135," she said. "We had one of those at school with a fussy carburetor. They're very sensitive to the float. May I?"

The group paused in mid-sentence and then parted to let her approach the machine. Standing on tiptoe, she stuck her head under the hood, poked around the inner workings for a moment, and then reappeared. "Does anyone have a wrench and a cloth?"

Hugo smothered a grin as the men scrambled to fulfill her request. Miles won, reappearing with a tool kit and a set of rags. The farmers gathered around, eager to see what she was going to do. Even Old William came closer to get a better look.

It took ten minutes of prodding, but she reemerged with a smear of grease across her brow and a satisfied smile on her face. "Your valve's become very worn," she told William, "and is trying to close at an angle, just like ours did. It needs to be replaced. I'm going to clean it out and reseat it, and it should get you home without a problem."

Taking a cloth from Miles, she disappeared again and after two loud clanks, shut the hood. "Try it now."

Miles climbed onto the seat and turned on the engine, which gave a few tentative sputters before bursting to life. The men helped William into the driver's seat and watched as he drove slowly back down the lane the way he had come.

"Is that the safest thing?" Julie asked.

"Safe enough to get him home. We won't be seeing that ancient heap out again, not after Hugo's girl fixed it. He won't live that down any time soon," said one of the farmers with a laugh, and was joined by the rest.

A discussion ensued, and the farmers included Julie, dropping their usual taciturn reserve. In fact, Hugo had never seen them—all of whom he had known his entire life—warm to a stranger so quickly. They were hanging on her every word as they discussed the unseasonably warm temperatures and the lack of rain, which confused Hugo since it seemed like he'd been doing nothing but playing in the sodding wet.

After several minutes, Hugo interrupted. "I'm going to take Miss Randall round to Wrothesley and let her have a look at the place," he announced, resting his hand on the small of her back.

"I'll come too," Miles said. "We can swing by my house, I've got soil analysis and seed profiles you might like to see."

"That would be interesting—" Julie began, but was cut off as Hugo steered her back to the car. "She doesn't have time for all that, just lunch at the Lodge, and a quick visit to Wrothesley. Perhaps another day."

---

Back in the car, Julie caught a glimpse of herself in the mirror. "Oh, dear. I'm covered in grease from the tractor. Is there someplace I can wash up before lunch?"

Hugo revved the Jaguar. "I know just the place."

Farther down the road, Hugo turned onto a wide gravel lane lined with stone walls and massive oaks. A charming, two-story stone house stood on the right, and Hugo pulled into the curved driveway in front of it. The house had obviously been recently renovated with modern transom windows and repointed stonework. From where they parked, Julie could see a small patio and garden tucked around the back.

He helped Julie out of the car and opened the door to an attached garage.

Julie stopped, seeing a gleaming Mercedes parked inside. "This is someone's house. I can't go in there."

"They won't mind. And there's a sink in here you can use."

"You're sure?"

"Completely." He took her hand and led her to a scullery.

"I can use this sink," she said, stopping by a large utility sink in the corner.

"There's a better one in here," Hugo countered, and she reluctantly followed him into a charming modern kitchen.

"This is nice," he commented, wandering around the room before stopping in front of an aromatic roast, cooling on the counter. "Roast beef, my favorite." He plucked off a morsel and popped it into his mouth, holding another one out for her. "Care to try?"

Julie stood at the edge of the room. "Have you gone insane? This is someone's house!"

The click of high heels from the hallway came towards them. "Sherry's in the pantry, darling. Pour yourselves a glass while I find your grandfather's carving knives." A beautifully dressed woman accepted a kiss from Hugo. "My, you've gained some weight! Thank goodness."

Turning to face Julie, the lady smiled warmly and extended her hand. "And you must be Julie."

Julie nodded, her mouth dry. The woman embodied the definition of stately grace and poise. She was wearing a tailored wool dress with a beautiful jeweled brooch, and in an instant Julie saw the strong resemblance between her and Hugo.

"Where are my manners?" Hugo said, moving next to Julie. "Mummy, this is Julie Randall. Juliet, my mother, Cynthia Auchincloss."

"Mrs. Auchincloss." Julie hid her dirty hands behind her back, mortified. "It's a pleasure."

"Please, call me Cynthia." The woman looked her over with keen interest. "Hugo, what have you done to this poor girl? She's covered in grease."

Hugo snorted. "Juliet did Old William Sproul a service and repaired that ancient tractor of his along the Bramford road."

Cynthia sighed. "Oh, dear. Not heading to the Hart and Dove again, I suppose? We took his license away three years ago. Rather you had pushed that bucket of rusted bolts into the Ouse."

"The tractor or Old William?" Hugo grinned.

"Both," Cynthia replied firmly.

"Juliet did better than that. She fixed his tractor in front of all of his draughts chums—he'll never live it down. I bet we never see that tractor again."

Cynthia laughed. "Then that is a service. Well done, Julie. Now I suppose you'd like to get cleaned up? Sensible girl. Tell you what, come this way and we'll get you fixed up. Hugo, carve the roast, and I expect at least half of it to still be here when we get back."

"You'd never know it to look at him, but he can eat you out of house and home," Cynthia continued as she led Julie through the house and up the stairs. "Between him and Ian, I'm marketing every day over the holidays. Here's the guest bedroom with en suite bath, use whatever you like."

"Thank you, Mrs... . Cynthia. Your brooch is beautiful. Is it a morning glory?"

"Yes, thank you, they're my favorite. It was a gift from Hugo's father. You'll find Auchincloss men are very generous." She winked and closed the door behind her.

The guest bedroom had a full-size bed and a small but modern bath with every appointment a guest could want. Julie scrubbed off the grease, brushed her hair, and carefully straightened her skirt before heading back downstairs.

Hugo was at the counter with his sleeves rolled up, carving the thick roast while his mother transferred potatoes to a chafing dish. He finished stacking slices of roast beef on a platter and handed her a glass of sherry. "Okay?" he asked quietly.

"Lovely. Why didn't you tell me this was your mother's house?"

"What would you have done?"

Julie thought for a moment and smothered a grin. "Run away."

"I thought as much."

Lunch was delicious, and Julie ate hungrily. Cynthia was a charming and down-to-earth lady, and the banter between mother and son showed a true affection between them.

Cynthia was very curious about her. "Now about the gardens you run at Haddonfield School. You're doing an amazing job. We're all rather in awe. I'm glad Hugo ended up there."

"He's fit in well," Julie said. "He's a natural teacher. He's gotten more out of the students in three weeks than we have in six months."

"That's because you all have other jobs, in addition to the academics," Hugo countered, helping himself to more potatoes.

"No, it's not that. The students respond to you."

"Because I'm a Premier League footballer."

"That was true at first but lost its glamour after the first round of homework assignments. The kids had never been given homework until Hugo assigned it. It caused quite an uproar," Julie confided to his mother.

"Brilliant!" Cynthia said. "Darling, you could go to university and get your teaching degree."

"No, I couldn't," Hugo snapped in irritation. "University is for the young."

"My father didn't start college until he was almost thirty," Julie said. "He worked while my mother finished her doctorate. Then he got his degree when he was forty."

Hugo shifted uncomfortably in his chair and stretched his left leg out, unconsciously massaging the muscles.

"I think it's a brilliant idea, Hugo," his mother said. "Best to have a plan. Your body isn't going to hold out forever."

A twitch of irritation pulled at Hugo's mouth. "I am not an invalid."

Cynthia glanced at her watch and went to his chair to give him a kiss on his forehead. "Don't be cross, darling, I'm just being your mother. Now I've got to run into the village. The vicar is having a card party at four and I said I'd play. There's an iced cake in the fridge for pudding, and Hugo, you are to let Julie eat at least a slice."

Hugo and Julie walked to the door with her. "It was lovely meeting you, Cynthia," Julie said.

Cynthia hugged her. "It was lovely meeting you as well, Julie. A gardener is always welcome in this house. Please do come back and visit."

# Chapter Twenty-One

HUGO HUGGED HIS mother goodbye and followed Julie back to the kitchen, tucking a dishtowel into his trousers and finding an apron for her. They chatted as they worked, and after the dishes were dried, Hugo suggested a walk.

"Oh, yes. After that meal I'm afraid I'd need a nap if I didn't keep moving," Julie agreed, and Hugo silently cursed himself. A nap could have led to some very pleasurable things.

Hugo helped her on with her coat and found a pair of his mother's boots for her to wear. They set off on a winding path leading through a small copse, the damp earth smelling fresh and alive as they walked close beside each other. Hugo buried his hands in the deep pockets of his coat to keep from taking her hand in his.

"Have you really had a lot of injuries?" Julie asked.

"Eleven years of wear and tear, plus I had groin muscle surgery last summer. Two winters ago, my shoulder dislocated, and I was out for six games. I go to a specialist in Lyon every three months to keep an eye on it. But by Premier League standards, I'm practically untouched."

"You still have a lot of years ahead of you, right? I have no idea how long people can play football professionally."

"My career is almost over," he admitted. "I'm turning thirty and that's ancient. Mummy's right. I am thinking of retiring in the next three years, and I do need a plan."

Birds flickered overhead in the tall trees that bordered the path. Julie would pause occasionally to look at an interesting botanical specimen or point out the names of trees and plants as they passed. Her knowledge was encyclopedic, and he felt like he was seeing the woods he'd played in all his life through new eyes.

"Juliet, how did you learn all this?"

She stopped and considered his question. "I don't know. It's just that everything has a name, almost like a first name and a last name. Like this tree, it's an *Acer rubrum*, or red maple. I bet you can do the same thing with football players on other teams. You know almost all of them, don't you?"

"Yes," he said, enjoying the analogy. "Have you ever been to a football match?"

"No. Cornell has very good men's and women's teams, but I was out at the farms so I never went to a game. I did play a table game in the Student Union building, though. It had rods with little players on them and you moved them back and forth to make the players kick a ball."

"Foosball."

"Yes, that's right. Which one are you?"

It took every ounce of control not to wrap his arms around her and kiss her soundly, there and then, because she desperately needed to be kissed. Instead, he covered his laughter with a cough. "I'm in the second row at the end of the left side."

The path emerged into a wide meadow. Across the grassy expanse, a handsome mansion sat on a rise, its mullioned windows glinting brightly in the late afternoon sun.

"This is Wrothesley," Hugo said.

"How beautiful," Julie breathed. "Is this where you grew up?"

"Yes. There's been a manor here in one form or another since at least 1140. This house was built about 1720 and has been added to and subtracted from ever since."

As they walked across a broad lawn towards the house, Hugo pointed out the various wings and noted how the architecture became less formal towards the back. While it was certainly grand, the different styles and eras hung together handsomely. Several outbuildings, including a large cow barn and garages, were visible farther down a gentle slope.

Juliet frowned as they passed bare patches of lawn and overgrown shrubbery. "No one lives here now?"

"No. Fifteen years ago, eleven people lived under this roof. Our family, Dad's parents, a staff of five, and occasionally Mummy's father—she grew up about twenty miles away, near Woburn. We closed up the house five years ago and renovated the gatehouse for Mummy. She took some things and I have a bit. The rest is in storage."

Wide steps led up to a columned portico. Taking a key from his pocket, Hugo opened the main doors, noting that the thick hinges squeaked slightly and needed to be oiled. Inside was a marbled foyer with reception rooms on either side, each with a handsome fireplace and soaring ceilings. A grand staircase made of dark oak led to the second floor, with a gallery overlooking the foyer.

They walked through empty rooms lined with exquisite wood paneling and ornately plastered ceilings, their footsteps echoing off the well-worn floors. Heavy curtains blocked the late afternoon light, and ghostly spots on walls showed where paintings had once hung. A long room at the back of the house overlooked a terraced stone patio and formal garden, which in turn led to a broad lawn and rolling fields.

"It's spectacular," Julie said, standing before the wide French doors. "Who laid out the gardens?"

"Not sure, it was done sometime in the nineteenth century. My grandfather remembered them being much larger, and the rose bushes were his mother's pride and joy—until one morning, when there was a break in the fence and the cattle herd was found devouring every rose in sight. That was the last of the cattle on the property for a generation."

Julie inhaled deeply and closed her eyes. "My parents would always rent old houses. I love their scent."

"What can you smell here?"

"Beeswax... and varnish... and old wood. But it's missing wool rugs."

"Ha. I've got a few at my house, but the really big ones are rolled up in storage."

In the dining room, Hugo showed her where several prime ministers had carved their initials in the side of the fireplace mantle. "My great-grandparents threw a house party that got a bit out of hand," was all he could offer by way of an explanation.

Julie laughed, the sound echoing around the paneled room. "I don't know how to say this correctly, but your house is a lot more comfortable on the inside than it looks from the outside. You'd think it would be cold and grand, but it's homey and comfortable."

Her observation pleased Hugo immensely. "That's because it was never built to be a grand stately manor, like Cleveden or

Chatsworth. It's always been a home first, and no one titled has ever owned it." He looked around sadly. "Now it's like a museum of what it used to be."

They climbed the main staircase to the second floor, where the bedrooms were spacious with lovely views of the surrounding countryside. Hugo checked for any roof leaks and broken windows and satisfied himself that all was in order.

The shadows were growing long when Juliet paused at the top of the staircase and looked down the curving stretch of polished banister. "It's almost too tempting."

Hugo grinned. "Go ahead, we used to slide down it constantly."

With a smooth movement, she hitched a hip onto the wooden railing and slid gracefully to the bottom, landing lightly on her feet with a whoop of joy.

Hugo applauded and followed her lead. "My turn."

He began to slide swiftly, but with a panicked yelp, his long legs became tangled in the balusters and he pitched backwards over the edge. He heard her gasp as he caught himself at the last second and swung upside down over the foyer, grinning like a Cheshire cat.

"You've done that before," she said disapprovingly.

"Used to give my grandmother heart attacks," he admitted, and she laughed.

Effortlessly hoisting himself upright, he slid smoothly to the end and jumped down next to her with a self-satisfied smile. "It's good to hear laughter in these halls again."

She reached up to brush back a stray lock of hair that had flopped over his forehead, her fingers cool and smooth on his skin. A sensual shiver ran down his spine at her touch. He swore he could smell her skin, and the memory of how warm and sweet it tasted came back to him vividly.

An effortless chemistry drew them together, and he saw her eyes darken and lips part. A bevy of invisible ghosts silently urged him to close the short distance and kiss her. It seemed like the most natural thing in the world to do, and he bent his head to oblige.

A truck's headlights drenched the foyer in rude light, breaking the spell. Julie took a hasty step backward as he mouthed a silent curse at the interruption.

"Thought I'd find you here," Miles called from the doorway, a canvas bag slung over his shoulder and long rolls of paper under his arm.

"Miles, good to see you," Hugo bit out, glaring at the man. "Again."

"Sorry for the interruption," Miles continued, obviously not sorry at all, "but I was wondering if Miss Randall might be willing to take a look at some of the soil reports I mentioned earlier."

Hugo started to shut the door. "Later."

"This can't wait," Miles countered, elbowing his way past Hugo. "I'm don't mean to impose, miss, but you did say you'd be willing to look at my reports."

"Of course. But large-scale crop management isn't my field, really."

"Yes, sorry, Miles, it was good to see you again all the same," Hugo said, but Miles cast a pleading look towards Julie, who interceded.

"I did minor in soil science, so I might be able to give some help."

Hugo sighed in defeat. "Let's go back to the Lodge," he said sourly and locked the doors behind them.

———— ◆ ————

Space was tight in Miles's truck, so Hugo sat in the passenger seat and pulled Julie onto his lap before she could protest. He felt her stiffen, but she remained quiet on the quick trip back to the Lodge and then jumped out quickly. Once inside, Miles unrolled the maps on the kitchen table while Julie put on her glasses and twisted her hair back in a tight bun, a look Hugo found overwhelmingly alluring.

"This here is the main field. We eke out seventy-one bushels per acre of hard red wheat a season, that's down from eighty-nine three years ago," Miles began, pointing to an area of a large map.

Julie frowned. "Are you alternating with soybeans?"

"Yes, miss. Those yields are down as well."

Julie took out some paper from her bag and began taking notes as she and Miles launched into a rapid agricultural shorthand from which Hugo could catch only a few spare words.

"What's the soil profile?"

"Calcareous medium loam over chalk at about an eighty to one hundred-centimeter depth."

"Clay loam?"

"Medium clay to medium silty clay loam."

"At what point do you hit hard chalk?"

"One meter, miss."

Julie studied the map for a few moments and pointed to an area. "Drainage problem?"

"Not really, gets a bit swampy down in that corner, but the rest is fast draining."

Julie nodded and paged through Miles's notebooks. "And your average rainfall?"

"Close to seven hundred millimeters a year."

"Good for your wheat." Tapping her pencil thoughtfully against her cheek, she flipped pages and read something that made her blanch. "You can still get this seed?"

Miles's face grew red and he glanced angrily at Hugo. "It's a special order now, but yes. Most of it goes to developing countries who can't afford better."

Hugo sulked against the kitchen doorway, hating his farm manager.

Juliet noted the exchange and motioned to the seat next to her. Hugo took it grudgingly, glowering at the maps and notebooks scattered across the table.

"Miles is worried that you have a serious fusarium infection," she explained. "It's very common and can wipe out entire wheat crops but is easily treated with targeted fungicide applications and by switching to some of the newer strains of seed. We're going to look at your application schedule and rates now."

Miles handed her three thick notebooks and she referenced all at once, turning pages rapidly. "You were obviously too late here," she indicated on one page while pointing to another page in another notebook.

As she and Miles flipped between records and maps, she occasionally paused to explain to Hugo what they were seeing and discuss the implications. Gradually, Hugo began to get a glimmer of understanding about how his farms worked. He ventured to ask a few questions that Julie answered patiently, and after just one hour he realized she knew more about his estate than he did.

As they studied the data, Miles's sense of relief grew palpable, and he became more animated than Hugo had ever seen him. Julie listened to his ideas and added insights of her own, and it struck him that Miles seemed to be pouring his heart out to her. There was a subtle magic about her, an honesty and patience that drew people to her. That, of course, was in addition to her beauty, and she had a jolly good head on her shoulders along with being sensible and down-to-earth. No wonder Looks was intent on her. She'd be the jewel in any man's crown.

Jealousy consumed him as he considered his rival. What did she see in Looks? And just how bloody serious were they? Was she in love with him? Was she getting sick of him? He ran over the pieces of the puzzle in his mind, but they were odd and didn't fit together at all. There were obviously key pieces missing, big ones. He brooded over the questions, which just seemed to spawn even more questions with no apparent answers.

# Chapter Twenty-Two

JULIE AND MILES worked for hours. Hugo seemed to have gotten past his obvious resentment of Miles's interruption, Julie noted, and caught on quickly to the condition of his farm. The two men were uncomfortable with each other, but as they worked together, she began to see both sides of their situation. Miles was appalled that Wrothesley was still being run on an agricultural blueprint from twenty years ago, a plan that Hugo clung to out of devotion to his father and grandfather, as well as an ignorance of any better way to do it.

They were deep in a discussion about an outbreak of cephalosporium leaf stripe at a nearby farm when the clock chimed the hour. Miles looked at his watch.

"Eight o'clock! I'm sorry for taking so much of your time, miss," he apologized, and began packing his papers in his satchel. "But this has helped an amazing amount."

Julie shook his hand. "My pleasure. I'll email you a list of possible non-cereal rotations you might want to consider."

Hugo shook Miles's hand as well, apparently mollified, and walked him to the door while Julie gathered her notes and put them in her bag.

"It's getting late. Shall we head back?" he said when he returned to the kitchen. "We could also spend the night—Mummy offered."

Julie pushed the image of the large bed in the guest bedroom out of her head. "I have to get back, I have an early morning."

Hugo appeared to be in a pensive mood as he drove. Julie supposed he was thinking about his fields.

"I'm sorry, I didn't intend for you to have to work so hard today," he said after they merged onto the main motorway.

"I had a good time. Miles is a talented manager and has some very good ideas. But I think he's intimidated by you."

"Whatever for? He's two years older than I am, used to beat the living tar out of me when we were little."

She framed her words carefully. "He's very aware of the way things have always been done at Wrothesley, but he's got some excellent ideas for changes. You might want to consider them."

Hugo frowned. "Our fathers and grandfathers had things down to a system, and it worked well."

"I'm sure it did," she agreed, "but agriculture has come a long way, even in the last year. I have to read three journals a month to keep up. What they were doing twenty years ago was cutting edge, but modern practices keep progressing."

He kept his focus on the road and considered her words. "You're sure about all this?"

"You shouldn't take my word for it. I told you, large-scale cereal cropping is not my area of expertise," she said, trying not to sound put out, but it was rather basic stuff. "I can hook you up with several experts and you can talk with them."

"I didn't mean it that way," Hugo apologized. "Whatever you and Miles come up with is fine with me."

As they drove it became obvious to Julie that something was on Hugo's mind. Maybe he understood more than she was giving him credit for—there were serious consequences for the way his farms were being run, and it was going to take several seasons before they were productive again, or double that if the weather didn't cooperate. But if Miles began an aggressive program of rotating cultivars in varying tillage systems, and—

"When does Looks come back from New York?"

This was the last question Julie expected. "Thursday. We're having dinner with his boss and his wife."

Hugo made a noise that sounded suspiciously like a snort. "If you don't mind my asking, how do you afford dating someone like Looks? I mean, on what I'm assuming is a princely salary from Haddonfield."

"You mean all the entertaining he does? My sister Rosie and her husband have their own company and entertain a lot, and she sends me her old things."

"Hand-me-downs."

"They're a bit more than hand-me-downs, Rosie's got expensive taste. Which works well because Mark's rather particular, and he knows all the designers."

"It sounds like he's more your boss than your boyfriend," Hugo observed.

That truth stung a bit more than Julie would have supposed, but she let it pass.

"Has Looks met your parents?"

"No."

"Have you met his?"

"No." Cynthia was the first parent she'd ever met, but that hardly counted. Hugo was just a friend.

It was almost midnight when he turned onto her street and parked, finding a rare open spot in front of her house. "I had a really good time today, thank you," she said as he walked her to her door.

Hugo stood silently as she fished in her bag for her house keys. "Juliet."

"Yes?"

"Today..." he began, and then stopped, and then began again. "Did you like the people you met today?"

"Yes, of course, everyone was lovely."

Her answer didn't seem to be the one he was looking for. "What I mean is, do you think..."

She waited, trying to make sense of what he was asking. "Do I think what?"

"Do you think that I, I mean you..." He searched her eyes, seeming to will her to understand his conundrum. Finally his shoulders slumped and he sighed. "I'm sorry, it's been a long day and I think we're both exhausted. Good night."

The urge to stand on her toes and kiss him was overwhelming, the same way it had been when they'd stood in the foyer at Wrothesley. Instead, she nodded and pulled the door closed behind her and leaned back against it, her legs feeling like jelly. She could see the box of tissues on her kitchen table and with a stab of surprise remembered the despair she'd felt that very morning. Never in a million years would she have dreamt that the day would have turned out as wonderful as it had.

<hr />

Dinner preparations were running smoothly when Hugo arrived at Haddonfield the next afternoon, which was not a surprise since Alex was in charge. The lad had a cool head and sharp judgment that didn't waver easily, and the kitchens hummed efficiently under his eye.

Also not surprising was the news that Juliet was running errands the entire afternoon and wasn't expected back until just before dinner service began. Because as surely as night followed day, Hugo knew she would be regretting enjoying herself with him while Looks was supposedly toiling in the advertising mines of New York. The drawbridge would go up, the wonderful day would be trivialized, and she would redouble her attention on her idiot boyfriend.

But he was getting closer.

He hung his overcoat and suit coat on a kitchen peg and put his apron on and at Bonnie's request began fetching crates of carrots from the barn. He dumped them into the scullery sink where Matthew toiled with a vegetable peeler, concentrating ferociously on the task.

Matthew nicked himself and muttered a curse under his breath. "Bloody vegetables. I hate the lot of them."

"Bad attitude to have for someone who's going to be a chef," Hugo observed as he dumped in the next crate.

"I don't want to be a chef," Matthew confided.

This piqued Hugo's interest. "Sorry to point out the obvious, but aren't you in the wrong place?"

"No, not at all. I need to know how to cook, and this is the best school for someone like me to learn. But I don't want to do just that. I've got plans. I want to run restaurants."

"What kind of restaurants?"

"Proper restaurants, like the Belevedere in Hampstead."

"You want to manage them."

"Yes. Be the manager. And eventually own them. But to do that I need the business part, all of it, the lending and the planning and everything. I need to go to a business school."

"That's not hard. There are lots of business schools around."

"No." Matthew scowled at Hugo's obtuseness. "Not just any. I want to go here." Glancing furtively over his shoulder, he pulled a rumpled brochure from his back pocket. "Hampshire College of Management Science. They've got a degree in Restaurant Management that's the best in the country. I want to go there."

Hugo read the flyer. "Doesn't look cheap."

"Not a problem, they've got scholarships for the poor and downtrodden like me. But they want entrance exams and they won't waver. I need all five GCSE's." Matthew pointed to the list on the brochure, where the requirements for the General Certificate of Secondary Education were outlined. "I can do the maths, but I'll never pass the English parts."

"Why?"

"It's too bleedin' hard! I can barely speak proper, let alone write or read up to snuff. I know I could do really well if I can just get in there. I'm a hard worker, Hugo, but I need help. I need someone to work with me, someone who's already passed all those subjects. Would you tutor me?"

Hugo paused, momentarily taken aback by the request. "When is the test?"

"End of May."

"That's less than three months away."

"Don't I know it. Look, I've been working on me own, I bought some books to help study, but I'm getting bloody nowhere. And I can pay you a bit—not much, but a bit."

Hugo was deeply offended. "I don't want your money, Matthew. But when would you have the time?"

"Nights. Weekends. Whenever you say. I live with me gran in Tottenham Green. It's a special arrangement, seeing as how she's old and ailing. So I've got some flexibility. Only thing is, we can't tell anyone."

"Not even your grandmother?"

"'Specially not her. She'd worry and think I wasn't smart enough, and not want me to be hurt if I didn't get in. So we'd have to keep it a secret. That way if I don't pass, no one will make fun of me."

It was beyond Hugo why anyone would make fun of him for trying, but that was another issue. "All right, I'll help. But you'd have to do all the work I give you, no excuses."

"I will, no problems there," Matthew agreed. "But I can't not pay you."

"I won't take your money."

"Then I have to do something for you."

Juliet came into the kitchens carrying a large basket of lettuce, her cheeks pink with the chill and her ponytail bobbing fetchingly.

"We'll think of something." Hugo said.

---

The evening's menu featured sorrel soup, pumpkin ravioli, and chocolate torte for dessert. It was a full house, and Alex kept the kitchens and staff running smoothly, nimbly substituting a sage browned butter for a cream sauce that curdled.

From his seat at the staff table, Hugo covertly watched Juliet across the room, her back to him. She had greeted him pleasantly enough in the kitchens and then neatly sidestepped having dinner with him by arranging to sit with members of the local garden club who were eager to discuss heirloom tomatoes.

With an effort, Hugo pulled his attention back to the table and realized Clive was asking him a question. "Pardon?"

"I said, care to go down the pub with me for a drink after service?"

Hugo got the distinct impression it was more of a command than a request.

"You can drive me," Clive continued, "and Bonnie can drop Julie off."

It seemed to Hugo that everyone at the staff table was waiting expectantly for his answer. "Certainly," he replied, and forced his attention back to his plate.

———◦———

At the pub, they took a table and Clive signaled for a round of beers.

"That was quite a game," Clive said, nodding to the television behind the bar that was playing highlights from the Kingsbury Town versus Crystal Palace match.

"Amazing," Hugo agreed. "One of the best. It sent Giles back to the drawing board, that's for sure."

They watched in companionable silence until two pints of beer were delivered.

"Don asked me to tell you, on behalf of all of us, how grateful we are for what you've been doing for the kids," Clive began. "You've got a talent for teaching."

Hugo was profoundly touched. "I'm not a teacher. I never went to university."

"You are a teacher and a sight better than most we've had. And I never went to university either. I was assigned to Haddonfield by the courts, just like you."

Hugo raised his eyebrows in surprise. "You? What for?"

"Car theft. They actually got me on a very minor offense. I'd been doing lots worse for a long time. Started as a juvenile offender. My specialty was boosting posh cars. Yours is very nice by the way." Clive grinned. "I went to Haddonfield knowing it was my last chance. Met Bonnie the first day there, and it was love at first sight, just like in the books. Completely turned me around. They ended up hiring me, and I've been there ever since."

"You dated while you were doing your public service?"

Clive snorted. "Hell no. Took me three years to get her to even agree to have coffee out with me."

"Is this your first child?"

"Yes," Clive said, but changed his mind. "No. We've had over two hundred, because Bonnie considers all the kids in the program hers. She's very possessive of those she loves—we both are. And that's why we need to talk."

Hugo leaned back in his chair and regarded the large man across from him warily.

"What are you up to with Julie?" Clive asked bluntly.

"Who wants to know?"

"We all want to know—Don, Bonnie, and me. I've been deputized."

Hugo considered Clive's question for a moment. "Juliet is a lovely girl. Why do you think I'm up to something with her?"

"You took her to meet mother yesterday, showed her the ancestral home, stayed for Sunday lunch. I'd wager you're not doing that with every lass you meet."

"She's helping us with a problem we're having with our wheat crop. We've got a fusarium infection," Hugo quoted from memory.

"Call it consulting, call it whatever you like, but you look at her like a dog in a butcher's shop. And it's very obvious to everyone except her."

"So what if I am? She's not married, not engaged. I'm not breaking any laws."

"No, you're not, but you are dealing with someone who's a bit clueless when it comes to men. Look, I know about you footballers. I grew up on the streets of Birmingham with Bev and Joss Jenkins. They're still my best mates. I play draughts with Bev every Saturday night at the Black Thistle. I saw what it was like when Bev played for Fulham, and Joss is still with Birmingham City. I know the kind of women that hang around, and that you blokes get more than your fair share of—"

"Like to see menus, gentlemen?" the barmaid interrupted. Both men declined.

"I might get more than my fair share," Hugo said, "which is not a quarter of what the rest get. But I'm not after her for that."

"Look, I don't blame you," Clive commiserated. "She's smart, sincere, loving, and all of that in a spectacular package, and you needn't go repeating that to Bonnie. But I'm not blind."

Hugo nodded.

"Julie is not naive—far from it, in fact," Clive continued, leaning forward and dropping his voice to a gruff whisper. "But look, mate, you need to know that she's a—"

"Are you Hugo Auchincloss?" an attractive woman interrupted, holding out a pen and notepad. "Would you mind?

Only it's for my niece."

Hugo complied while the woman practically danced in excitement. He then returned her pen, her notepad, and the scrap of paper on which she'd written her phone number. She flounced away in a huff and he turned his attention back to Clive. "She's a what?"

Clive watched the exchange and frowned. "A little sheltered," he finally said. "And extremely focused. Sometimes it's like she has blinkers on and the most damnably obvious things go right over her head. Like this bloke she's been going out with, Mark Brooks. We think he's bad news."

"How so?"

"You tell me."

"Why do you think I'd know anything?" Hugo parried.

"Julie says you're thick with him, and you toffs stick together. What's he up to?"

This put Hugo in a pinch. He wasn't at liberty to repeat Tom's appraisal, and he had no actual proof that Looks was still dallying with Rochelle, and Pippa, and God knew who else. "He wants her because he thinks she'll make the perfect little wife, and that's what he needs to keep going up the corporate ladder."

Clive thought about that for a moment. "Makes sense. But he seems to still be making time with that piece of baggage." He jerked his head towards a poster of Rochelle smiling seductively, a glass of Sam Lord's Castle Rum in her hand. "Julie says they broke up and simply work together, but we think he's lying through his teeth. And Bonnie thinks it's more than just that bit of muff. She's heard rumors from the kids about his shenanigans at the bars. And we think you know more than you're letting on."

"What if Juliet is in love with him, Clive? What then? What if he truly loves her and gives up his other, er, interests, and they live happily ever after? Do you want to interfere with that possibility?"

"No, I don't," Clive conceded.

"If she can't see through that clown, then maybe they deserve each other. And you're right, I've not made any secret of the fact that I'm interested in her. Either way, it's her decision to make."

"And what would she do with you?" Clive asked reasonably. "Find herself on the cover of every tabloid in the UK?"

"I would never let that happen. I can protect her."

"You're a footballer. You might not have a choice."

"I employ someone full-time to keep me out of the papers."

"Well, they've done a good job, I'll give you that." Clive finished his beer and set it before him with a thud. "Julie deserves a nice guy who will love her for the wonderful person she is. She doesn't deserve to get her heart broken, and if it is, I will personally start breaking the first thing that comes to hand. So, this is a warning. At the first sign that Julie is being hurt or is upset, you are shut down. That comes from me and Don and Bonnie. And I suggest you pay attention to that—the woman is a demon with a knife. And that's after I get done with you."

Hugo heard the warning, loud and clear.

# Chapter Twenty-Three

WEDNESDAY NIGHT'S MATCH against Tottenham was technically an away fixture. The team coach was scheduled to depart from St Augustine School promptly at 5:00 p.m. for the 8:00 p.m. kick-off, so Hugo ended classes at three to give himself time to fight the traffic. He fussed mildly that it would have been easier for him to drive directly to White Hart Lane Stadium from Haddonfield than to do the circuitous route via Wimbledon in tortuous traffic, all to end up exactly one mile from where he started.

As he packed his satchel, Hugo realized another thing that irked him about the midweek fixture—Juliet could reliably be counted on to swim Wednesday evenings, and there was an excellent chance the blue bikini would be putting in an appearance.

The first floor was buzzing with certificate students who came up from the main school twice a week for basic cooking classes with Bonnie and horticulture with Juliet. He had seen them out in the orchards with her an hour ago, stamping in the cold as she tried to teach them pruning techniques. Don was right—they were a rougher group.

Turning the corner, he collided with two burly boys wearing Tottenham Hotspur t-shirts. "Hey, give us a hand, would you, mate?" one student asked. "Julie said she needs the parsnips from the clamp right quick, and there're three crates and only two of us."

"What's a clamp? Sounds like a jail."

The boys didn't miss a beat. "It's a storage room in the basement. Ever been down there before? It's pretty amazing."

Hugo followed them down the steep stone steps into the low-ceilinged cellar, astonished by what he saw. It was like an Aladdin's cave of produce, room after room full of hanging burlap bags of potatoes, braided ropes of onions and garlic, wooden shelves stacked with apples wrapped in paper and gourds lined ten-deep. One room alone contained nothing but shelves of glass jars filled with dried beans, pickles, applesauce, jams, and tomatoes. It staggered the imagination.

"This is the cool and dry part of the cellar," the first boy explained as he led the way through the labyrinth. "Pretty ingenious how it's all laid out, how stuff stays so fresh without a fridge and all. Julie says ventilation is really important."

"The best part is the cool and damp cellar down those steps," the second said, pointing to the most remote part of the basement. "That's where the clamp is, it's a big pile of dirt and sand that the root vegetables can stay fresh in. It's pretty old, and Julie thinks it was part of a house that was here before Haddonfield, a long time ago. She said the brickwork is all different. Take a look. We've got a moment."

Fascinated, Hugo followed as they descended a short set of stone stairs into the lowest part of the cellars, noting that indeed the brickwork did change halfway down. At the bottom, the boy pushed an ancient door open to reveal a small room lit by a faint bulb hanging from the ceiling and let Hugo step past him into the gloom.

A few dusty, cobweb-laced crates lay scattered on the earthen floor, telling Hugo this room had not been used for anything for years. The rest of the basements were immaculately clean, and he knew immediately Juliet wouldn't store a tin of beans in this place. Instantly alert, he spun around —just in time to see the door close shut with a resounding thud, followed by a quiet click. He was two seconds too late. Now he was trapped.

Hugo sprang at the door and pushed it furiously, jiggling the handle with all his might, but the bloody thing wouldn't budge. Rotten little buggers, they'd locked him in the cellars knowing he had to leave by four o'clock, which was in exactly thirty-seven minutes. A string of curses poured out of him, mostly directed at himself for falling so easily into their plot.

"Julie said she needs the parsnips from the clamp right quick," they'd said. He'd needed no other bait and well they knew it.

Being late to a game was an unforgivable sin and the fine would be the least of his problems. Missing a game because he let himself be locked in a basement by a bunch of Tottenham supporters, and kids at that, would end his career. In fact, he would welcome a quick, merciful death instead of the heap of scorn and ridicule he would be subjected to. *And* deserve.

He spent several minutes venting a furious tantrum, bellowing at the top of his lungs and kicking several crates, scratching his new Italian loafers in the process. Shoulder-butting the door didn't make a dent, except to cause shooting pains where he'd dislocated it the year before. The door was solid oak and at least four inches thick, with lateral iron bracing straps and hand-forged nails. It refused to budge.

Breathing hard, Hugo forced himself to calm down and focus. There had to be a way out of here, but he was never going to find it by acting like a madman. With a sudden epiphany, he fished in his pocket for his mobile phone. It swished to life with a blessed trill but took an eternity to initialize and then paused to search for cellular reception. Seconds ticked by until finally one bar appeared, the invisible waves somehow finding their way into the depths of his basement prison.

Damn, who to call. Tom had taken Cassandra to Cap d'Antibes for her birthday, and Ian was in class and would have his phone turned off. His teammates were out of the question—he'd never live it down. The police would create very unwelcome publicity. There was only one person, Juliet. He hoped to God she had her mobile with her.

The call began to go through but was dropped. Pressing closer against the door, he tried again, and this time her mobile rang twice before the connection dropped cut off. The next five attempts never got that far, leaving Hugo roaring with outrage.

Forcing himself to be calm, he stacked two crates and stood on them in the hope of somehow improving his chances. Amazingly, this seemed to work, and the call went through smoothly. He fought growing panic as her phone rang and rang, and just as all hope seemed lost, he heard her angelic voice on the other end.

"Hugo?" she asked, bewildered. As well she should.

"Juliet. Thank God you picked up. I need you to come get me."

"But you're here. I can see your car parked outside. Shouldn't you be leaving for your match soon?"

"I can't. They've locked me in the basement."

There was a long pause. "Hugo, I can barely hear you. It sounded like you said you're locked in the basement."

"I am!" he yelled. "I need you to come let me out! The last one, the furthest one—"

The phone fell silent and he saw that the single bar was lost. He moved the phone frantically around the door, but it failed to produce any more. Sitting down heavily on the crates, he waited and prayed.

Minutes ticked by until he began to hear faint noises. They got steadily louder and he pounded on the door. "Juliet! I'm in here."

Her voice was muffled from the other side. "Hugo, are you all right?"

"Yes, I'm fine. Just let me out. I have to get to St Augustine."

"What happens if you're late?"

"You don't want to know. I don't want to know. Now lift the bar."

There was a slight pause and his heart pounded in his ears. "Have you given any more thought to letting me look at *The Orchard*?" she asked pleasantly.

"What?" He ran his hands through his hair in complete exasperation. "No. I haven't. Would you hurry—"

"It's just that I would really like to at least look at it."

"Woman, have you gone completely mad?" came the heated reply. "Oh. I see. All right, you can have an hour. Now let me out."

"A day."

He swore, if he didn't kiss her he'd strangle her. "Two hours. I can also call the Hampstead Constabulary to come let me out."

"The reporters will follow them," she countered cheerfully. "Four hours."

"This is blackmail."

"I prefer white mail. Get it? The pages of the book are white, and—"

"All right! Four hours, just get me out of here!"

"Your word? As a gentleman? You said a gentleman always keeps his word."

"My word as a gentleman," Hugo agreed through gritted teeth.

"Thank you. Now look at the door. Can you see the interior latch? Underneath the crossbar there's a small catch on the bottom, flip it to the left and push the bar up at the same time."

He knelt to peer closely under the thick wood and saw the old-fashioned locking mechanism she described. "You mean I could have opened it myself?"

"Well yes, obviously. The hinges are on your side—that should have told you something."

It was a good thing she wasn't present to hear the words that escaped his lips as he saw what she had just pointed out. But the small catch was rusted and moved with protest, and when he pushed on the crossbar, nothing happened. "It's not working."

"You have to do both at the same time or it won't work. Give it a good whack, it might be a little stiff."

There was a loud thump, and then another, and suddenly the door was yanked open and Hugo sprang out. Julie jumped back up the stone stairs and he leapt to the top in two bounds, grabbing her by the arms and placing a very warm, very grateful kiss firmly on her lips.

"I love you," he told her fervently, and bounded out through the cellars like the hounds of hell were on his heels.

⸻ ◆ ⸻

The Plaid Elephant, a popular pub on the east side of Finchley, was packed with Tottenham supporters singing bawdy football songs as they waited for the start of the Wednesday evening match. Julie slipped in unnoticed, cleverly disguised in a black and white Hotspur scarf she'd found in the school's Lost and Found bin. A quick read of Clive's daily paper had given her an overview of the game and the names of two Hotspur players, either of whom she was prepared to list as her favorites if pressed into a discussion.

She found an empty barstool and sat down with many misgivings. It was wrong to be here while Mark was in New York, and it was wrong to want to see Hugo play. But the urge was so overwhelming, she knew she had to give in or go mental. She needed to get over this infatuation immediately and tomorrow would be soon enough. For tonight, she would yield to temptation.

Fans continued to stream into the pub, and as the server delivered her a pint of ale, she glanced around the room and saw no other patrons wearing Kingsbury Town yellow and black. The pub had a large screen TV over the bar where two commentators were discussing the night's match, and they seemed to feel that Tottenham held a slight edge due to the questionable status of Marco Cantamessa's groin muscle. She vaguely remembered Hugo saying Marco had seriously injured it during their match against Crystal Palace and that they would be in trouble if he were to be sidelined since they had almost no forward depth. Her ears perked up as the commentary moved to Hugo.

"The wild card will be Auchincloss," an announcer was saying. "He had a rather lackluster first half of the season, but suddenly he's come on fire."

"Aye," his partner, an announcer with a heavy Scottish brogue, weighed in. "Something's reignited the lad."

The other commentator sagely agreed, and the camera panned to the teams as they lined up on the White Hart Lane pitch. Julie couldn't help but smile when she saw Hugo looking calm and composed as he sang "God Save The Queen". Quite a difference from a few hours ago.

Play began, and Julie sat on the bar stool, enthralled. The Tottenham supporters in the pub kept up a lively commentary of their own, seeming discontented with a Hotspur back who was "dogging it," and a forward who would "kick at anything." The intricate footwork was mesmerizing, and she gradually realized that when the pub moaned in unison it was because something good had happened for Kingsbury Town, and cheers meant the opposite.

Late in the nineteenth minute, there was a flurry of activity as Tottenham crowded the Kingsbury Town goal. The keeper blocked a shot, but unfortunately, it ricocheted off the bar above his head and back into the pack, and immediately a player on the far right shot it into the net. The crowd erupted, and the Tottenham players celebrated as Julie saw Hugo pat the Kingsbury Town keeper on his back before jogging to his position midfield.

Play continued, and Julie saw how fast Hugo truly was. His motions were fluid and sinuous, as opposed to some of the much larger men on the pitch, and he seemed to breeze through opposing players like the wind. Much of the time he would stay in one place, appearing to jog sluggishly or not at all, and then would move with a blinding burst of speed and boot the ball three or four strides ahead of the closest opponent. Once, he and an opposing player landed on the ground in a tangle, but he was immediately on his feet and cleared the ball to a teammate.

The score was 1–0 Tottenham at halftime and the server came around to deliver more drinks, frowning pointedly at Julie, who had barely touched hers. She took several swallows and listened attentively as the people at her table evaluated the game so far. Heaps of derision were piled on the Tottenham manager, who they seemed to either love or hate, while ideas for his strategy for the second half were put forth.

Back on the field, Kingsbury Town quickly pressed, and within two minutes, a series of blur-like passes ended in Hugo taking a shot at the Tottenham goal. Score!

"Wow!" Julie slid to her feet, staring at the television in rapt awe until she suddenly realized the pub had gone completely silent. All eyes were trained on her. She slunk back onto her stool, abashed. "He's cute," she added.

A red-faced man next to her was nonplussed. "Hear that? Lass thinks Auchie's cute. More like a bloody menace. Like to know what cold storage they found him in."

Julie almost burst out laughing because she knew exactly which cold storage she'd found him in. While his teammates flashed smiles, he remained resolutely aloof, his expression giving away nothing. The cameras switched suddenly to a pair of pretty girls in the stands waving KTFC flags and cheering lustily, both wearing jerseys with Hugo's number. Jealousy seared through Julie, hotter and sharper than anything she'd ever felt in her life, and she was gripped with an urge to rip the flags out of their hands and pull their hair.

Tottenham went on to miss a goal ten minutes later when a player was ruled offside, and the game ended in a 1–1 tie, much to the disgruntlement of the patrons. It was widely agreed that a more forward attack had been needed, and that it was only by luck that three of the Kingsbury Town shots on goal were deflected.

Back at home, Julie changed into her white cotton nightgown and lay in bed, deliciously tormenting feelings bubbling through her. It meant nothing, absolutely nothing, that Hugo had kissed her when he freed himself from the basement. The flowers also meant nothing. That moment in the grand foyer at Wrothesley, when everything had been still and magic, meant nothing.

Sitting up, she punched the pillows and collapsed back against them, staring at the ceiling, eventually falling into a dreamless sleep.

# Chapter Twenty-Four

LOUD KNOCKING AT the front door jolted Julie awake. The illuminated clock read 11:02 p.m., and she stumbled for her robe as the knocking continued. Flicking on the hall lights, she hurried down the stairs to find out who was raising such a racket at this time of night.

Through the side window, she saw Hugo standing on her stoop, dressed in his club warm-up suit with streaks of dirt from the match still on his face. She yanked the door open, her heart pounding. "Good heavens, what's the matter?"

"What's the matter?" Hugo asked with mock indignation. "You're not dressed is the matter. Come on, we don't have all night."

"All night to do what?"

"You want to see the book, don't you?"

"Yes, but it's almost midnight."

"Then you better get dressed," he said, his eyes coursing over her. "Unless you'd rather go in your nightie, which is very lovely by the way, and I'd have no problem with that."

Julie pulled the thin robe around herself. "Where are we going?"

"To my house. The book doesn't leave there, you have to come to it."

"I can't go to your house! It's the middle of the night."

Hugo slumped against the doorjamb with an elaborate sigh and crossed his arms. "You should have negotiated that as well."

"Mark is in New York, I'll wait till he's back and can go with me."

"It's now or never, Juliet. You've got five minutes to get ready."

She saw he was completely serious. Turning on her heel, Julie flew up the stairs, shedding the nightgown and pulling on a pair of jeans and a dark blue V-neck sweater. In the bathroom, she brushed her teeth and hair, and without stopping to think, dabbed two tiny droplets of cologne behind her ears. Bolting back downstairs, she stuffed a bag with a blank notebook, a pencil, and two reference books.

"Ready," she announced.

Hugo helped her into her coat, held the door for her, and hustled to keep up with her as she ran to his car.

"Great game tonight," she said as he settled her in the passenger seat.

"You saw it?" Hugo asked, helping her with the seatbelt. "I didn't think you had a telly."

Julie backtracked. "It was on in a shop. You scored a goal."

Hugo turned the ignition, and the Jaguar roared to life. "Sometimes I'm the luckiest man in football. Connors missed his pass and it went long. I was half a step ahead of my defender and had a clear shot."

He continued to tell her about the game as they drove into the city, and she laughed at his funny observations and imitations of his teammates. In no time, they turned down a side street in central London lined with identical three-story brick, terraced houses. Midway down the row, a garage door opened, and Hugo pulled in.

"Here we are then." Grabbing their bags from the trunk, Hugo led the way through a well-appointed basement gym and up the stairs to the first floor. At the top, he fiddled with an elaborate control panel, flicking switches at random.

"Gosh," Julie said in awe, "what do all of them do?"

"I actually don't have the first clue," he admitted. "The house is smarter than I am. But I do know that this turns on the downstairs light, this one is the second-floor landing, and this is the basement. The rest I just toggle and hope for the best."

Lights came on randomly, illuminating the magnificent townhouse. A dazzling chandelier lit up the adjacent dining room, while discreet sconces highlighted magnificent oil paintings. The polished dark wood floors, tall ceilings, and intricate moldings reminded her of Wrothesley, but without the worn patina of centuries of family life.

Hugo threw his kit bag in a hidden laundry room off the foyer. "Are you hungry? I don't have much in the house, but I'm starved and was going to order in. What shall we get?"

"Nothing on my account. Where is it?"

"Upstairs. Follow me."

At the top of the mahogany staircase, he paused to give her a tour. "This front bedroom I use as an office—that's my grandfather's desk. This next room used to be two bedrooms, but I had it combined into a bedroom, dressing room and bath."

Hugo's bedroom was high-ceilinged and handsomely appointed, its masculine luxury apparent. An enormous four-poster bed dominated the bedroom, made up with snowy linen sheets and plump pillows with a thick down comforter folded at the bottom.

"I brought that bed from Wrothesley," he said, standing at her elbow. "It's over three hundred years old—we had to raise the ceilings to make it fit. I gave the original crewelwork hangings to the Victoria and Albert Museum."

It was the kind of bed a king would sleep in, Julie thought. Tearing her eyes away, she followed Hugo up a narrower staircase to the third floor and gasped in pleasure as they emerged in a room brimming with books of every size and age.

"Do you like it?" he asked.

"It's beautiful."

The attic stretched the length of the house and was lined with shelves on every available inch of wall. A large, round library table in the center was stacked with more books, surrounded by a pair of comfortable reading chairs. Thick oriental carpets muffled Julie's footsteps as she wandered around the room in awe.

Hugo held a chair for her at the table and went to a nearby bookshelf, carefully removing *The Orchard* and placing it before her.

"Your four hours starts now."

———◦———

Hugo watched as Juliet laid her hand on the book's cover and opened it. She smiled, a tender, loving look he felt a fierce need to be on the receiving end of. Without taking her eyes from the book, she pulled her notebook and pencil from her bag and twisted her hair up, securing it with an elastic. A few delicate tendrils of hair dangled provocatively as she moved her head, daring him to tease them.

"I'm going to get cleaned up. Will you be all right?" he asked, his voice rough.

"Yes, of course," Julie murmured, putting her glasses on her pert nose as she peered at the first few pages. "I don't believe it! There were no peaches! None! And I've been killing myself trying to get them to grow in that horrible clay soil."

Back in his bedroom, Hugo called a local pizza shop and ordered two with an assortment of toppings, unsure of what she liked.

Once in the shower, he quickly scrubbed himself clean, anxious to return upstairs. Juliet was here, in his house, and he intended to take every advantage of the opportunity. The idea had come to him during the second period of play, and he acknowledged its brilliance. He'd wanted to see her after the game, wanted her in his house, wanted her to get used to it and start to feel comfortable here. Seeing the book was the perfect excuse. Looks wasn't around, and there would be no interruptions at this time of night. His plan had worked brilliantly, and he enjoyed turning the tables on the clever minx.

He quickly dried his hair, wrapped the towel around his waist, and began to shave.

"Hugo?" Julie called from the hallway a few moments later. "I broke my pencil. Do you have a sharpener?"

"In the desk drawer in my office."

A faint unease stirred in him and grew more pronounced until he dropped the razor in the sink with a clatter and bolted towards the study. "Wait, Juliet, don't open the top drawer—"

Hugo was halfway across his bedroom when he heard her cry out as the booby trap tripped and the drawer caught her wrist in its wooden clutches.

Julie's face was white when he sprinted into the room. "I'll disarm it." Hugo reached behind the jam and released the latch, pulling her shaking hand out while wrapping his other arm around her.

"Damn. I am so sorry," he soothed, pressing tender kisses on the abused flesh of her wrist.

"I—it just snapped," she stammered. "Like a mousetrap."

"I know, sweetheart, I've done it myself. Howled like a banshee," Hugo murmured, feeling her body tremble against his almost naked one. "Grandfather had it installed. There was a footman that used to help himself to petty cash, and he wanted to catch him."

After a few moments, he felt her slowly relax against him, her body soft and pliant. He nuzzled the soft skin, inhaling her stimulating feminine scent that was making his blood run hot. The worn leather sofa was right behind them. It would be nothing to lay her on it, press against her, drop his towel, loosen her clothing, and—

"I should go back upstairs," Julie protested.

"Impossible," he murmured as his lips moved up the sensitive skin of her arm, feeling her pulse leap. "Land mines under the carpets. Cobras in the rubbish bin. You're safer here with me."

A deafening gong reverberated through the house. "Doorbell," Hugo said, not loosening his grip on Julie. "Pizza's here."

"Maybe I should get it?"

"He'll go away," Hugo assured her, but she pulled away, and he gritted his teeth, looking askance at the heavens and wondering what he had done to endure such curses.

"Wait, here's the money." He followed her out, taking the wallet from his dresser and pressing some bills in her hand.

Julie took them and hurried down the steps. Hugo finished dressing and came down the stairs barefoot, his hair still damp and tousled, buttoning his shirt as he went. Julie was struggling with the boxes and counting out money while the deliveryman looked at her closely and then at him. He quickly counted out the change and left.

"They smell wonderful." She handed him the boxes and tried to go back up the stairs, but he steered her back to the kitchen.

"No, I need to get back upstairs," she protested.

"See what's in this box first. You'll want some, too. It's the best pizza in London." Setting them on the kitchen table, he lifted their lids and handed her a slice of the onion and sausage. The aroma was enticing, and she looked truly torn. "Is this coming off my time with the book?"

"No. You can have all night." Hugo pressed her down into a chair and took a slice himself, eating hungrily.

"Did you make it to Wimbledon in time this afternoon?" Julie asked.

"Barely. Jason is always the last one to arrive, and I just made it in before him. But Mick Carr's new Aston Martin got a scratch from the launderer's delivery truck, and he was raising holy hell, so no one noticed. All the same, it was a close call."

"We'll have to tell Don and the students will be reprimanded. I have no idea what got into them."

"You'll do no such thing. I imagine they got a surprise when they watched the game or went down to let me out. But we'll have to say how you came to my rescue."

"But I didn't rescue you, I never even touched the door. You rescued yourself."

This made him laugh, and they ate in companionable silence. Accepting a second slice, she asked timidly, "May I ask you a question?"

"Of course. Anything."

"Why did you want *The Orchard*? The rest of your books are mostly history and geography."

Hugo chewed for a few moments. "It's not just *The Orchard*. I have the rest of them as well."

Her eyes grew wide. "All five?"

He nodded. "They came from the library at Wrothesley and were my grandfather's favorites. They'd been there as long as he could remember, and as long as his grandfather could remember, as well."

"How did *The Orchard* end up at Gladia's bookshop?"

"When we closed the house, Ian got half the library. He's been hocking them when he needs money."

Julie's jaw gaped open.

"He takes them to auction houses here in London," Hugo continued. "Gladia goes to the book auctions and buys them for me, and then I pick them up at her shop. She was out the day you saw *The Orchard*. It was behind the counter and wasn't supposed to have been put on display."

"Why didn't you tell me? I thought you were just being a..." Her voice trailed off and she struggled for words.

"An ass?" Hugo provided helpfully. "I didn't know who you were. I didn't know how much you cared. But Grandfather would have approved of you."

"Are they all marked up the same way?"

"Most, some more than others. The one about greenhouses and exotic plants hardly has anything."

"*The Greenhouse, Hot House and Stove*, 1838," Julie nodded. "That would make sense, the family didn't entertain much and wouldn't have needed the tropical plants. How do you think the books came to be at Wrothesley? They're about Haddonfield."

"I've thought about that. Grandfather said the gardens were laid out about 1860 by a rather accomplished headman who came from an estate in north London. He might have been the headman at Haddonfield and brought the books with him."

"It's an amazing coincidence."

---

Together they went back upstairs, and Hugo showed her the rest of the books. Both volumes of *The Book of The Garden* and *The Practical Gardener* were there, annotated by the same pen and spidery hand, noting dates plants were tried and the results.

Seeing she was completely absorbed by the books, Hugo silently left her and went to tidy his bedroom, picking up his clothing and smoothing the bed. Just in case.

Back in the library, Juliet was sitting at the table, reading. "He did plant currants, I was right! Whites and reds. I can order the stock right away," she spoke to herself, making quick notes. "And there were figs in the glasshouse. They were Green Ischias, easy enough to find. I bet I can put some in pots in the old glasshouse after the new polyhouse is up."

Hugo settled into a wing chair and watched her covertly while pretending to peruse a stack of endorsement offers Tom had declined months ago. "You don't mind if I stay and do some paperwork?"

"Not at all."

Her expression alternated between fierce concentration and excitement as she untangled the cryptic notes. Hugo watched, entranced, as confusion, elation, disappointment, and pleasure passed unfiltered across her face. Finally he gave up the pretext of working and gravitated to the table, where several pieces of paper were taped together and she was drawing a map.

"Pears..." she whispered, perplexed. "Ah! It's a Brown Beurre, not a Beurre de la Motte, that would make sense. They were a Belgian variety introduced in 1842, but the climate was too damp, and they never flourished. What luck."

Her pencil flew over the grid. "Hugo! Look!" She pointed to a page in undiluted joy. "There was a hothouse on this south bank. I knew it."

"What's there now?"

"Number eighteen, next door. There's an old brick foundation I saw when they excavated for their new garage."

She returned her attention to *The Orchard*, continuing a running commentary, which amused him greatly. "It's not a Black Eagle cherry? It's another May Duke, how did I miss that... ha, grapes failed, the winter of 1852 knocked them out. That will make Bonnie happy. She doesn't like grapes."

An antique grandfather clock in the corner chimed one in the morning. "Are you tired? You're welcome to use my bed," Hugo offered with calculated insouciance.

She didn't even glance up. "Thanks, but I'll keep working. I'm halfway through already."

"Come tomorrow night. I'll get another pizza."

"Mark's coming home tomorrow," she said, pursing her lips as she made a notation on the map. "We're having dinner with his boss."

"Oh. Yes, of course, you mentioned that. Another night, then. Actually, any night you like."

Hugo cheered himself, imagining Mark being detained at customs and having to submit to a full body cavity search. Moving to stand behind her, he looked over her shoulder, ostensibly to see what she was working on, but in reality to watch her unobserved.

Julie shifted slightly in the chair, leaning forward to write on her map. The breath locked in his throat as the waistband of her jeans gapped and sheer white panties were revealed.

They were lace. *Oh Lord, save me.* He had always loved lace on a woman, and white lace was his particular undoing. Not the trashy kind, which was obvious and tawdry, but the elegant kind, the Alençon, the Chantilly, the guipure. It hid, it revealed, it tormented, it enticed. But most of all, it aroused and never so hotly as it did now.

Hugo couldn't drag his eyes from the feminine display, so innocent yet so alluring. Her knickers were so delicate and sheer they would tear like gossamer in his hands. The coil of desire in his loins tightened, aroused beyond anything he had ever felt. His hand itched to slide down the length of her back, her skin warm and pliable as he explored under the lace to find the secrets it hid.

A guttural sound must have escaped him because she looked up in concern. "Are you all right?"

"Fine," he choked out, and with an almost superhuman effort, stepped away before he bent her over the table and took her like an animal. Raking his hand through his hair, Hugo knew he needed to get as far away from her as possible, or the deed was going to be done with her consent or not.

Muttering an excuse, he fled to the kitchen and splashed ice-cold water on his face till it stung. It took almost twenty minutes before he considered himself safe to return to his third-floor torture chamber, a book tucked firmly under his arm. Julie glanced at him over the top of her glasses and smiled as he flopped down on a wing chair and swung his feet onto an ottoman, forcing himself to concentrate on badly-translated ramblings of an obscure French philosopher. After three pages, exhaustion overwhelmed him, and he fell into a dreamless sleep.

# Chapter Twenty-Five

THE GRANDFATHER CLOCK in Hugo's library chimed 6:00 a.m. as Julie closed *The Orchard*, content in the knowledge that she hadn't been too far off the mark identifying the original plantings at Haddonfield. Yes, she'd mistaken two Fearn's apples that would have to come out, as well as a pear and a cherry, but the commercial nursery would have the correct replacement stock that could be delivered by Friday. Everything else was satisfyingly accurate.

Hugo lay asleep in the wing chair, his big body sprawled under the blanket Juliet had wrapped around him three hours ago. She savored the opportunity to watch him unobserved as he slept, his usually guarded features softened by sleep. His full lips were parted, and Julie filled with warmth as she remembered the feel of them against her own, passionate and intent. The urge to go to him and lie in his lap, feeling his arms wrap around her as he woke, was difficult to resist.

Quietly gathering her books and papers, she packed her bag and wrote a short note that she left with *The Orchard* on the table next to his chair. Gently tucking a corner of the blanket back under his leg, she cast one last look at him and then set off down the stairs.

In the second-floor hallway, Julie paused at the door to his bedroom, torn between the desire to explore where he slept and the risk of embarrassment if she were caught snooping. She listened for any sounds from the upstairs library. Hearing nothing, she took a few illicit steps into the room.

It was dominated by the massive four-poster bed that reached to the ceiling and seemed to be as wide as it was tall. The down comforter folded at the bottom was like a mile-thick cloud, making the bed a soft and cozy haven. The crisp white sheets felt luxuriously smooth against the back of her hand.

Next, Julie investigated the bath. The tiled shower was outfitted with an old-fashioned rainfall showerhead and met with her approval, as did the enormous claw-foot bathtub next to it. A handsome edition of Shakespeare's sonnets lay open on a side table pulled up next to it—so, Hugo liked to read in the bath as well. His shaving supplies on the marble counter drew her attention, and she held his shaving brush to her nose, inhaling his familiar lavender and pepper scent.

The dressing room, pungent with the smell of cedar and expensive leather, was lined with his collection of suits and white shirts, with handmade shoes in racks below. A collection of photographs in silver frames sat on a chest of drawers. The largest was obviously of his family; Julie recognized him and Ian as children, a younger Cynthia and a man who must have been Hugo's father. He looked almost identical to Hugo but had a much more relaxed and carefree attitude, with his arm around Cynthia and the boys. Julie smiled wistfully. They looked like such a happy family.

Next was a photograph of Hugo and another man in a wheelchair by a river, each of them holding a large trout and grinning. The last two frames were smaller, with one displaying a picture of Hugo and Ian, tanned and smiling on an alpine ski slope, and the other one, a team photo of younger boys, probably from Eton.

Julie took one last look around the room and went down the stairs to the foyer. She pulled on her coat and tried to decide which door to leave from. Choosing the wrong one might set off the elaborate security system, so she finally decided that the front door would be the simplest since nothing had happened when she'd opened it for the pizza deliveryman. She pulled it open and stepped outside, pausing on the stoop to pull on her gloves before skipping down the steps to search for the nearest bus stop.

Inside an unmarked van across the street, a camera with a very long telephoto lens clicked seventy-four times.

———◆———

Hugo awoke at nine o'clock to the ring of his mobile phone, still sprawled in the large chair with a warm blanket tucked around him. He glanced around for Juliet but saw he was alone, *The Orchard* on the side table next to him with a handwritten note folded on top.

The phone trilled again, and he dug it out of his pocket. "Tom. Thought you were in Cap d'Antibes watching Cassandra frolic about in a bikini."

"I am. But congratulations are in order, you work fast."

Hugo knew he wasn't talking about last night's match, and a faint sense of unease began to grow in his chest. "What are you congratulating me on?"

"I'm looking at pictures of that girl Looks has been going out with, leaving your house early this morning. The pretty blonde, what's her name, Julie? Paparazzi stalked her to the bus stop. You're getting cheap, old man—couldn't even spring for a taxi home?"

Hugo shot up in the chair. No, this was not happening. "Where did they come from?"

"*Daily Mail.* They sent it to the office first thing for a comment, and Nancy forwarded them here. They've got a story from a pizza delivery bloke who's saying she was dressed, but you were half naked when he delivered at twelve-thirty this morning."

Hugo cursed. "You have to block it, Tom."

"Calm down, they're fishing. The pictures are good, but they have no idea who she is."

"She was here doing research."

Tom chuckled. "Is that what you bachelors are calling it these days? I didn't realize I've been married so long."

"Look, Tom, I'll explain when you get home, but for now, this cannot get out."

"It won't, but only for now. They've caught a scent of something and will be on your tail. You'd best not forget that."

"I won't."

# Chapter Twenty-Six

"YOU LOOK RADIANT, darling. Glowing, in fact." Mark sat across the table from Julie in the restaurant after his boss had departed. "What have you been up to while I was away? Playing in your garden?"

Mark always meant it affectionately, but tonight his teasing made Julie bristle. "I turned two tons of soil double-digging this week," she retorted. "I laid new lines of straw bales by the Spanish tunnels, got the replacement saplings from the nursery, and took all the clippers for sharpening. Then on Sunday Hugo took me out to his family's house in Bedfordshire. "

"Really?" Mark considered this last piece of information. "Wrothesley, isn't it? I say! He fussed with his napkin, clearly put out. "He asked you out there, and you went? Did he know I was away?"

This was the first time Mark had ever sounded the least bit possessive, and Julie felt her heart pleasantly skip a beat. "I don't think he knew, but I told him."

"I wish you hadn't gone without me. I've always wanted to see that place myself, I've heard so much about it. Who knows if I'll get another chance like that again?"

Julie experienced a feeling not unlike an elevator falling two floors before coming to a lurching halt. "It was unplanned. Sorry."

"What's it like?"

"The house and grounds are beautiful, and Mrs. Auchincloss is very nice. She made us lunch."

"You got to meet her, too? She's a Russell, her cousins are the Dukes of Bedford. A few of them were in my year at Eton, never really got to know them. They're very tribal, keep to themselves."

"She's a duchess?" Julie asked.

"No, just an Honorable. But still. Next time, make sure I get an invitation as well, won't you, darling?"

Julie felt her temper flare and struggled to contain it. She wanted to blurt out that Hugo had hinted to be asked inside when he'd taken her home that first time. And had kissed her wrist just the night before. While wearing nothing more than a towel.

"Speaking of invitations," Mark continued blithely, "we're going to Pippa Donnell's birthday party Saturday night. Don't forget."

"Will everyone from the wedding be there?"

"Roughly the same group. Except for Hugo—ever since the wedding he's officially persona non grata around Pippa."

"What did he do?"

"He was nasty to her at the reception, and since she's remarkably thin-skinned, he's off the list. Not that he cares, I'm sure."

Mark walked her out to the street where the car waited. "You look beautiful tonight." He bent to kiss her, his lips soft against hers. "I missed you, darling."

Julie stifled a yawn. "I missed you, too."

"I'd love to have you come back to my place, but I've got early meetings," he murmured, but she was already sliding into the back seat of the car.

"Thanks, Mark, but I'm knackered. Some other time."

<hr />

Late Friday afternoon, Julie sat behind the wheel of the school van, idling in an endless sea of traffic, drumming her fingers on the steering wheel, and glancing at her watch in irritation. Half past five. Hugo would be leaving Haddonfield soon, if he hadn't already. Her day had been fraught with unusual delays, and routine errands had become anything but.

The traffic began to move slowly, but when she arrived at Haddonfield a few minutes before six, Hugo's usual parking spot was empty. Julie slumped in the seat. She hadn't seen him since she'd left his house early yesterday morning.

She unloaded the burlap-wrapped trees and set them in the shed and then went to the empty kitchen to make herself a cup of tea. Bonnie and Clive came in from the gardens and exchanged a few murmured words.

"Sit down, Julie. Clive'd like a word," Bonnie announced, taking a bowl of dough from the refrigerator and slapping it onto the worktable. Clive took a seat at the trestle table across from her.

"You and Hugo seem to be getting along better," Clive began reluctantly, glancing at his wife.

Julie scrutinized a plate of petit fours on the table and selected one that wasn't too badly burned. "You were right. He's a lot nicer than I thought. And he let me look at *The*

*Orchard*, and he has all the rest of the books in the series. He said I can see them anytime."

"That's fine," Clive nodded. "Yes. Fine. Fine indeed."

Bonnie coughed, and Clive ran his hand across his scalp. "But Julie, love... footballers. They're a bit different from other men you might know."

Julie bit into the cake and winced as a shard of eggshell scraped her tongue. "How so?"

Clive shifted his large bulk on the bench. "Footballers," he continued, "have a lot of women around. Women that make themselves very available to them."

"Available for what?"

Clive cast a beseeching look at his wife.

"For sex, Julie," Bonnie said, throwing the dough onto the table and kneading it ruthlessly.

Julie pursed her lips. "Well, that's not so bad, is it? I mean if they're dating and in a committed relationship and all that."

"No. Like, they go to meet them just to have sex," Bonnie said.

"Why would they do that?"

Bonnie shrugged. "Sometimes for the money. Maybe their lives are pretty boring, and they get swept up in the excitement. Sometimes they want to get famous themselves."

Julie wrinkled her nose in distaste. "That doesn't sound very smart. Why do the players sleep with them?"

"Because they're men. Not going to pass that up," Clive grunted, ignoring his wife's withering glare. "But it usually doesn't last," he continued. "It's all physical, do you understand? It might mean something to the girls, but it hardly ever means anything to the guys. But they get used to it, having any woman they want."

"So it's more of a one-night stand."

"More like a ten-minute stand," Bonnie said under her breath.

"And this goes on all the time?" Julie asked, and both Clive and Bonnie nodded. "Why are you telling me this?"

Bonnie wiped her hands on her apron and sat down next to her on the bench. "Julie, you're a smart, talented, and beautiful woman. Any man would be head over heels for you and might start making a play for you. You know, flowers, treats..."

"A trip to his country house," Julie added, finally getting the gist of the conversation. "But it's not like that with Hugo. I'm with Mark, and he respects that. We're friends, that's all."

Clive sighed. "I know, love, but that's from your point of view. Hugo is a man and is used to getting what he wants and, as a footballer, he gets it on a silver platter. And then goes on to the next."

"So you think he's paying attention to me because he wants to sleep with me?" Julie asked, laughing at the idea while she twirled a lock of hair around her finger. "I'm hardly one of those beautiful women that hang around him. I'm a twenty-six-year-old garden manager who can barely walk in high heels." She paused to lick her suddenly dry lips. "I just don't see it."

"Has Hugo ever kissed you?" Bonnie asked.

Julie squirmed. "Technically, no."

Bonnie frowned but let that go. "Julie, you're an adult, you're fully capable of making your own decisions. We just don't want you to get hurt."

"I appreciate what you're saying, really I do. And I will be careful."

———◦○◦———

Pippa's birthday party was in full swing, and everyone seemed bent on having an uproariously good time. Pippa met them at the door of her parents' house, clutching a bottle of champagne and wearing an outlandish birthday tiara. She proceeded to ignore Julie but gave Mark a soulful kiss that he enthusiastically returned.

"She's drunk," Mark offered by way of an apology as they pushed their way into the packed house.

That had been two hours ago. Julie sat next to Mark on an overstuffed settee while he held court, absently toying with the ruffled cuff of the shimmery pink peasant blouse she wore. It was blatantly romantic, and she'd dismissed it out of hand when it arrived from America, wondering what in heaven's name Rosie was thinking. Its full poet's sleeves fell loosely off her shoulders and were trimmed in additional ruffles, with a scooped neckline edged in lace and even more ruffles.

Wearing the blouse had been an impulsive decision, and she'd paired it with a short, black skirt and rather daring high heels. Standing before the narrow mirror in her bedroom, she let the impulse take full rein and released her hair from the neat chignon, shaking it until it fell in sensuous waves around her face and down her back. It made her feel beautiful and feminine. Sexy, even.

Which begged the question of who she was feeling sexy for. In the car on the way to the party, Mark had remarked that the color of the blouse looked nice on her and suggested a hair salon in Kensington that could add subtle highlights to her hair to warm her complexion and make her look younger. Somehow, she knew Hugo's reaction to her outfit would be a lot earthier, but Mark was correct about his banishment. He was nowhere to be seen.

A man next to her draped an overly familiar arm around her shoulders and leered at the cleavage the neckline displayed. "Can I get you another drink, Jules?"

She shook her head and tugged the blouse higher. "No, thank you, I'm fine."

"It's my turn to get her a drink, you b-bastard," another friend of Mark's hiccupped. "Can I get you another w-wine, Julie?"

A plump girl galloped through the room, screaming with laughter, and then swerved and fell into Mark's lap.

"Julie, you remember Sophie from the office, don't you?" Mark made the introductions. "She was out on Barbados with us."

"Yes, hello, Sophie," Julie said, vaguely remembering her. The sophisticated society girl had thick black hair piled luxuriously on top of her head and wide black eyes, like a doll's. Mark had confided that her father was a Member of Parliament, and that while she was officially called a production assistant, she did little more than get everyone tea and run the copy machine.

"So you know our Hugo," Sophie drawled from her perch on Mark's lap, her husky voice aristocratically accented like Mark's and Hugo's. "Heard you got quite cozy at Jillian's wedding."

Julie's glass wavered in her hand. "What do you mean?"

"He never dances with anyone, yet he danced with you. Pips told me all about it. What's your secret? Or can I guess?" she asked, smirking.

Julie's mind worked quickly. "He's volunteering at the school where I work."

Sophie snapped her fingers. "Oh, yah, that school for poor kids up on the Heath. Hugo told me all about it of course. You're the headman in the gardens, right? Wellies and manure and all that?"

Normally Julie would have laughed at that, but tonight it made her bristle. "I'm the horticulture instructor."

"Same thing. He said you're quite the workforce. Or was it workhorse? I can't remember, it was dark," she giggled.

For the first time in her life, Julie wanted to slap another woman. "So, you know him well."

"Gosh, yes, we've known each other ages. We're good friends," Sophie slurred as she accepted another glass of champagne from a passing server. "Very good friends. In fact, he's mad for me, can barely keep him off. Mark, reach in my skirt pocket and find the picture in there."

Mark complied, and she wiggled provocatively, almost spilling her drink in the process. Eventually he pulled out a small photograph and looked at it in surprise. "Is that our Hugo?"

"Yes, at the Clough twins' birthday party," she said triumphantly, showing it to everyone. "*Tatler* was going to run it, but it got pulled at the last minute. Probably bloody Tom interfering again."

Whoops of excitement went up as an ice sculpture of Michelangelo's *David* was wheeled into the room and parked in the middle. It was rigged up as a vodka dispenser, and Julie watched in astonishment as girls lined up to take hits while the men gathered around, shouting encouragement.

Sophie elbowed her way to the front of the line. "Join the fun for once, Jules. And no fair asking for a glass!"

"I think I'll stick with wine," Julie replied.

"Me, too," a beautiful woman said next to her, her dark eyes glinting with amusement. "I don't think David's been checked for STDs."

It was the first time that night Julie laughed.

"You're Julie Randall, aren't you?" the woman asked, holding out her hand. She was tall and slim and wore a beautifully patterned dress. "I'm Cassandra Bellville-Howe, Tom's wife. We're friends of Hugo's."

"Hello." Julie shook her hand with pleasure. "Hugo's mentioned you."

"May I introduce you to my husband? He'd like to meet you."

Julie followed Cassandra to a glassed conservatory at the back of the house that was blessedly less crowded. Her husband was chatting with a group of people, and his eyes lit up as they shook hands. "Julie! The pleasure is ours. I guess Looks is around here somewhere?"

"I think he's policing the ice sculpture," Julie said, taking an offered seat. "You're Hugo's agent?"

"Agent?" Tom snorted. "Easiest job I ever had. Bugger won't do any product endorsement deals, takes whatever contract Kingsbury Town offers because he's devoted to Sir Frank, and refuses all interviews. I barely have to lift a finger."

"Except to keep him out of the papers," Cassandra added. "It's Tom's specialty, he's the only public relations agent in London with an unlisted phone number."

"That's brilliant," Julie agreed, thoroughly enjoying herself.

"Kingsbury Town beat Blackburn this afternoon, and Hugo had an outstanding game. He'll be happy with that," Tom said. "Van Diesek got the better of him the last time they played, and he definitely evened the score."

"I hope he gets to celebrate," Julie said.

"Doubt it," Tom scoffed. "In fact, he's probably at home right now with ice packs and a book. Man's practically a monk."

Tom and Cassandra introduced her to the rest of their friends, and she joined their discussion. After a short time, Sophie loomed in the doorway. Spotting Julie, she marched across the tiled floor to stand before her.

"Jules! Mark's looking for you," she barked, focusing bleary-eyed on the rest of the guests. "Oh hullo, Tom. Honestly, Cassandra, would it kill you to eat a sandwich once in a while?"

# Chapter Twenty-Seven

HUGO SAT IMMERSED in the ice bath for twenty minutes after the match, the frigid therapeutic treatment excruciating but necessary. A Blackburn wing had dealt him a nasty tackle, which he managed to repay while the referee's back was turned. All the same, the swelling would be god-awful in the morning.

Six minutes remained on the timer, and he focused his thoughts on Juliet. She would be at Pippa's birthday party right now, an event he had pointedly not been invited to. Under any other circumstance, he wouldn't have given the snub another thought, but tonight it chafed. Tom and Cassandra were there, and Tom had promised to call and tell him how it was getting on.

Hugo shifted in the icy water, gritting his teeth to stop them from chattering. He hadn't seen Juliet since Wednesday night or, technically speaking, since Thursday morning. Looks was back in town and was obviously taking up her attention. She'd said they were having dinner with his boss Thursday night—had she stayed over at his flat? Had he missed her so much that he'd taken her to his bed and made love to her for hours?

It was impossible to stop torturing himself, imagining Juliet giving her body freely to Looks and enjoying all the ways he would try to please her. Did she fall asleep afterwards, sated in his arms?

The thoughts were poison, but Hugo could not dismiss them. He was in a hell of a state.

With four minutes still left on the timer, he fidgeted with his mobile phone on the table beside him. He wanted to see Juliet. He *needed* to see Juliet.

The rational part of his brain tried to insert reason. Everything was going brilliantly. Juliet was behaving exactly as predicted, and he shouldn't press his case. She was fighting her attraction to him and losing badly. If he pushed too hard now, he could blow it.

Unreasonable irritation flared, staunching any sensible thoughts. He missed her and wanted to see her. Ached to see her, actually. The fact that she could conjure an erection in the middle of an ice bath decided it.

Hugo picked up his mobile and tapped a number. "Tom. How's the party?"

Tom chuckled. "Undisciplined. The pavilion at the back of the garden is seeing more action than a cheap hotel, as usual. But it just became significantly more pleasurable—we've met Julie. She's lovely."

Hugo swallowed. "How is she?"

"Seems bored. Looks is being a twat, as usual, and she's got a crowd of admirers she's trying to shake."

Hugo half rose out of the icy vat. "Bloody hell, Tom—"

"Relax, she knows how to handle herself. We had quite a chat. She liked Wrothesley, and Cynthia especially."

"She said that?" Hugo's heart began doing funny things. "I'm coming over."

"Don't even," Tom advised. "Pips has a bottle of champagne in one hand and another inside her. She's a loose cannon."

"I don't care. Let me in the conservatory door."

"You'll regret it," Tom cautioned mildly, but Hugo had already rung off.

---

After another social round of the party with Mark, Julie was able to rejoin Tom and Cassandra's group in the conservatory.

"Look what the cat dragged in," Tom said dryly. Juliet looked up to see Hugo at the French doors, a crooked smile on his lips.

She ran to the door and opened it. "Hello," she said, unable to stop smiling.

Hugo stood mute, a lopsided smile playing on his lips, and her pulse leapt when she saw his eyes take in the rounded cleavage her blouse displayed. "You look stunning," he finally said, his voice choked.

Julie flushed under his approving gaze. "Thank you. Tom said you won today?"

"Won what? Oh, the match. Yes, two-zip. Good game, I had an assist. Sorry, my ears are still ringing. I swear the Blackburn punters bring bullhorns."

Hugo glanced around as if suddenly realizing there were other people in the room. Calling out greetings, he shook Tom's hand and kissed Cassandra's cheek.

"What a surprise to see you here," Tom remarked. "I hope you brought a peace offering for the birthday girl. Anything over one hundred seventy proof should do the trick."

Hugo wagged what looked like a hastily wrapped bottle. "Covered."

"Hugo!" A shrill voice yelled, and Julie saw his face darken as Sophie plowed through the crowd towards them at breakneck speed. She threw herself into his arms with a piercing squeal, pressing a full kiss on his lips.

Hugo moved quickly to disentangle himself. "Sophie, didn't know you'd be here."

"Gosh, Hugo, long time, no—" She broke off, trying to wrap an arm around his waist. "Let's just say it's been a while," she purred.

Pippa had followed her into the room, her face an ugly mask. "Who the hell invited you?"

"Happy Birthday, Pippa." Hugo shoved the bottle into her hand and gave her a perfunctory peck on the cheek. "Nice tiara. Suits you."

"Oh, let him stay, Pips," Sophie pouted, nuzzling his chest. "He's sorry for being mean to you, aren't you, Hugo?"

Hugo swallowed and seemed to be mentally framing an apology, but Pippa snatched the bottle out of his hands and lurched away. Seeing that Sophie had left a smear of crimson lipstick across Hugo's face, Julie fished a tissue from her pocket and handed it to him.

Mark appeared by their side and gave Hugo a hearty clap on the back. "Amazing game today, old man! Good show!"

"Come on." Sophie pulled Hugo's hand, laying claim. "You've got to see the ice sculpture!"

"Yes, come on, Julie, don't monopolize him." Mark took her by the elbow and led her back into the crowded house.

"Juliet—"

She heard Hugo's hiss loud and clear, but she walked away from him as fast as possible.

———◄◦►———

Julie followed Mark to an adjoining room while Sophie pulled Hugo around their groups of friends, her raucous laughter grating on Julie's nerves like nails on a chalkboard. Sophie seemed to have her hands full, trying to monopolize Hugo's attention while other girls flocked to him and flirted outrageously. She only kept her spot by brute force, resorting to stepping on one girl's toes and pinching another.

Hugo seemed to retreat behind his usual implacable facade, chatting with everyone and occasionally dropping his head to laugh at something Sophie said.

Julie shredded the cocktail napkin in her hand and forced her attention back to Mark and the lewd story he was telling. Minutes later, she glanced up and saw that Sophie and Hugo had disappeared. Feeling her heart turn to lead, she glanced around until she caught sight of them on the patio. Hugo was lighting Sophie's cigarette, his hand cupped around hers to protect the flame. He said something, and she threw her head back and laughed riotously.

Julie turned away and squeezed her eyes shut. *Would this night ever end?*

———◄◦►———

Sophie was drunk and intent on making everyone think they were together, and doubly intent on keeping him as far away from Juliet as possible. Juliet, for her part, wouldn't come within ten feet of him, and Hugo couldn't blame her.

He watched her from across the room, greedily noting every detail. Her hair fell in loose ringlets down her back, the frilly blouse revealing her alabaster white shoulders before it dipped to display the soft mounds of her breasts. Juliet was a combustible combination of guileless innocence and teasing allure, and Hugo watched her with unbearable longing. And judging by the attention she was getting from the other men, he wasn't the only one.

The adrenaline of the afternoon's victory pumped through his veins and he started scheming.

The party rooms were full of smoke, and he could tell Juliet hated it. She yawned, so she must be bored. She checked an empty cracker basket, so she must be hungry.

Perfect.

Two men, Oxford trash by the look of them, were monopolizing her attention in a corner across the room. Juliet was fidgeting with her bracelet, and when it snapped and fell to the ground, the buffoons practically fought for the damn thing at her feet. In a blind rage, Hugo stalked towards them and yanked the bracelet out of the winner's hand.

"*Sortir d'ici. Elle est à moi,*" he snapped. Get out of here. She's mine.

The men hastily obeyed the order, and Julie turned to Hugo. "Thank you, they were getting a bit overbearing. What did you say to them?"

"I suggested they leave because you are otherwise spoken for," he murmured, capturing her wrist and reattaching the bracelet.

Julie smiled. "I was just looking for Mark. He's disappeared."

Hugo was calculating the last time he'd seen Pippa when the blare of a badly blown hunt horn blasted from the next room. A drunken voice called out, "Who shall be the fox? I know—Julie! Where the devil did she get to?"

With quick instincts, Hugo pulled Julie down a hall and into a closet, slamming the door behind them.

———————◇———————

Julie stood pressed against Hugo in the dark amongst the coats. From the other side of the door came sounds of a large crowd galloping by, a hunting horn slurring loudly.

"There's a fur coat tickling my nose," Julie giggled before sneezing.

Hugo fished in his pocket and pressed a linen handkerchief into her hand. "Are you allergic to fur?"

"No, my sister is though."

"So you never had pets growing up?"

"I had the best pet in the world, Angelica. She was a goose."

"Is that a picture of her on your desk? She's beautiful." Hugo's voice was by her ear and she could feel his warm breath on her cheek.

Julie nodded and sneezed again, and Hugo put his hands on her hips to steady her. "Wasn't she? And don't think she didn't know it, too. She was a Brecon Buff. I had her for thirteen years."

"I didn't know they lived so long."

His hands stayed on her hips, warm and strong. "She was hatched at Clemson University," Julie said. "Our next-door neighbors were professors in the agriculture school, and they knew Rosie was allergic to fur. But Angelica was just as good as a dog or a cat, and she was an excellent watchman as well. I mean, watch-goose."

"Wasn't Angelica the name of the nurse in *Romeo and Juliet?*"

It was impossible to resist pressing herself closer to him. The warmth of his body was like a magnet. "My father's idea."

"So she was in charge of protecting your virtue."

Julie laughed. "More than I'd have liked."

Another round of hunters thundered past outside. "What did you do today?" he asked, his right hand moving to her back to trace lazy circles.

"Finished the seed order. Paid some bills. Took my landlady's dog for a walk on the Heath," Julie murmured, knowing his lips were only inches from her own.

"I thought about you at the game today," he said in the darkness, pulling her closer against the hardness of his body.

"Oh?" she asked thickly. "Problems with the turf? I've been reading up about it. Did you know there's a new fungicide treatment for anthracnose foliar blight?"

She couldn't decide if he was coughing or laughing. "No, I didn't, but that's not why I was thinking about you." He paused, and in the darkness she felt the steady beat of his heart against her chest. "Juliet, are you having a good time tonight?"

"Yes, of course," she answered automatically.

"I mean, really. Tell me the truth. Are you having a good time here tonight?"

Wrapped in the snug little world consisting of the coat closet and Hugo's arms, it was impossible to lie. "No. Everyone here seems childish and loud. And drunk. The party games are stupid. And I'm sick of the men pawing at me and the women being cold and standoffish. Except you and Tom and Cassandra," she added.

"Then let's leave."

"Where would we go?"

"Anywhere you want. We can get fish and chips, or we can go back to my house and get more pizza and look at the books, stay up all night." Hugo seemed to be holding his breath. "Or Paris is lovely this time of night."

"How would we get to Paris?" Julie countered.

"I'm a member of a private jet service. We could swing by your house to get your passport and be in the air by midnight."

He sounded dangerously serious. "But that would cost thousands of pounds."

"Miles called this morning, he's run the numbers on the changes you suggested, and we're looking to save over ten thousand pounds this year alone."

Dear Lord, he was completely serious. "Pizza sounds wonderful," she countered. "I'm famished."

Abruptly, the closet door was yanked open and another couple stood before them.

"Time's up, old man," was all they said before unceremoniously yanking Hugo and Juliet out of the closet, jumping inside and shutting the door firmly behind them.

# Chapter Twenty-Eight

THE MOCK HUNT collapsed, exhausted, in the living room, and Hugo saw that Looks and Pippa had reappeared, looking slightly disheveled. Juliet returned to Looks and began talking with him. Hugo could tell Looks was struggling to pay attention.

This was good. There was every chance she was going to leave Looks at the party and go home with him.

Pippa sauntered over, a nasty glint in her eyes. "Taking a break from drooling over Julie?"

"At least her skirt's not on backwards," Hugo observed, and was rewarded with having the contents of her champagne glass thrown at him.

Hugo found an unoccupied powder room off the foyer, where he blotted his shirt dry and splashed cold water on his face. He heard the door open and Sophie slipped in behind him, stealthily wrapping her plump arms around his waist and rubbing her ample chest against his back.

"Fancy a quickie?" she breathed, her hand dropping lower to fondle him. "Pips said the pavilion is awfully cold."

Utter and complete disgust froze Hugo for one second too long. Sophie smoothly unbuckled his belt, her fondling hand dipping beneath the waistband of his trousers while the other unzipped the fly.

"Get away from me, Sophie," Hugo commanded, attempting to elude her in the small space.

"What's the matter, Hugo, am I not good enough for you? Should I go rub some mud on my face, is that what you like now?" Sophie spat out the words. "You can't have her, you know."

"I bloody well don't want you," he retorted.

———◦◦———

After being evicted from the closet, Julie found Mark in the living room, collapsed on a sofa.

"Here you are. Where did you get to?" she asked.

"Oh, Pippa's cat got stuck on the pavilion roof, I said I'd help get it down." Mark yawned. "Having a good time, sweet?"

Julie ignored the question and plunged ahead. "Actually, I'm pretty beat. Hugo's offered to give me a lift and I thought I'd take him up on it."

"No problem," Mark slurred and gave her a goodbye peck on the cheek.

Never in her life had Julie done anything so reckless. If she went back to Hugo's house, she doubted she'd be able to keep her hands off him. It wasn't fair to Mark, but for once she didn't care. Leaving with Hugo just felt too right.

In the foyer, she bumped into Cassandra.

"Tom and I are leaving," the other woman said. "Can we give you a lift?"

"Ah, actually, Hugo has offered me a ride," Julie said, unable to suppress a small smile.

"Oh, yes?" Cassandra asked, and then both women jumped when Hugo strode out of the bathroom and into the crowded foyer, a furious scowl on his face.

Talk stopped as everyone's attention went first to his dangling belt and then to Sophie, who had followed him out, adjusting the bodice of her dress and straightening her skirt with a satisfied smirk on her face. Loud cheers went up, accompanied by a round of applause.

Julie felt the color drain from her face.

Hugo lunged towards her, but Cassandra stepped in his way. "I'm taking Julie home," she announced. "Julie, would you please get our coats. Mine's the red wrap with blue trim. I'll get the car."

Julie fled to the small room off the foyer where coats had been heaped on a low divan, her heart struggling to regain beating.

Hugo appeared in the doorway, his body tense. "Where are you going?"

She sorted through the pile, her hands shaking. "Home. Cassandra is giving me a lift."

"I'll take you."

"Take Sophie."

"Juliet, I know what it looked like. But nothing happened. She followed me into the loo, and I told her to shove off."

It was impossible to meet his eyes. "Oh."

"It's the truth. She came on to me."

"You're quite a victim, Hugo. Two women in a club wanted to go home with you, and now Sophie tried to have sex with you in the powder room. It's a miracle you can walk down the street."

Finally finding the proper coats, Julie pulled them out and clutched both to her chest. Hugo blocked her path, towering over her with palpable anger.

"Get out of my way," she demanded.

"Not before we talk."

"Go back to Sophie."

"Juliet, you're being ridiculous. Why would I want Sophie when I can have you?"

Her mouth dropped opened as he heard his own words. "I mean—" Hugo stopped to regroup. "I didn't mean it that way. I meant, I don't want anyone else *but* you. Come on, let's go somewhere we can talk."

"Like your house?" Julie suggested acidly.

"Yes! That's a great idea."

"Is that why you came here tonight? To get me to go home with you?"

"Yes!" Hugo nodded. "I mean, no! Not in that way. Damn it, Juliet, you get me so tied up I can't think straight."

Tucking the coats under her arm, she brushed past him. "I wouldn't go home with you if you were the last man on earth."

"But you would kiss me in a dark basement at a wedding."

Julie froze, stunned. *He knows.* Her mind flew over everything that had happened since the wedding, the time they'd spent together that had seemed like spontaneous magic. Sparks of mortification flamed to a roaring blaze, making the roots of her hair feel like they were on fire.

"It didn't mean anything." Her mouth was parched, but she managed to force the words out.

"The hell it didn't. It was bloody wonderful."

"It was a mistake."

"It wasn't a mistake." Hugo pulled her around to face him and cupped her chin, forcing her to meet his gaze. "It was real. You wanted me as much as I wanted you."

His other hand reached up to smooth the hair back from her face. "I want you, Juliet. I have never wanted a woman as badly as I want you. You're so beautiful, so desirable, I'll go out of my mind if I can't have you."

Hugo said it earnestly, as if it were the first time he was saying it to a woman instead of, in all likelihood, the hundredth. Julie had no doubt he was completely sincere—there was no mistaking the undisguised desire in his eyes.

Everything that had previously been so soft and lovely now came into sharp focus, revealing the harsh reality. Clive was right, Hugo did just want to sleep with her. But she'd let her emotions run wild and had even begun to fall in love with him. The humiliation was unbearable.

There would be time later, probably a lot of time, to wallow in her own stupidity. But for right now, she needed to be strong. Taking a step back, she forced herself to meet his gaze straight on.

"Then you can go to the back of the queue, Hugo. I've been dealing with guys like you for a long time, guys who want me for my body and can't see past it. I could fill a book with the offers I've gotten tonight alone. I'm not interested."

His eyes blazed with affronted dignity. "That's what you think I want? You think I'm like one of that lot?" he bellowed, jerking his head towards the party.

"No, I think you're a lot more sneaky and deceitful. There's only one man out there who respects me, who... who..." She faltered, groping frantically for words to describe Mark. "... who doesn't want me for a one-night stand."

"And that's Looks, I suppose?" Hugo retorted. "Juliet, where do you think Looks was when he went missing this evening?"

"For your information, he was helping Pippa get her cat off the pavilion roof."

"And you believe that?"

The pitying look he gave her infuriated her. "Of course. What else could they be doing?"

"The pavilion has been a prime make-out spot for years."

Julie paused, confusion tempering her anger. "You're saying Mark was cheating on me with Pippa in the pavilion?"

Hugo swallowed hard and nodded. "I don't want to hurt you, Juliet. But yes, that's exactly what I'm saying."

Seconds ticked by as Julie considered his words. "Is there no depth to which you won't sink?" she asked with equal amounts of contempt and loathing. "How dare you accuse Mark of what you just did yourself? He wouldn't lie to me."

"And I would?"

This time there was no pause. "Yes."

A blistering string of oaths flew from Hugo's mouth. When he finished, Juliet said, "I don't blame you for taking what you think I was offering, and I can see where it might seem that I led you on. I deeply regret my actions and take full responsibility for them."

Hugo glared at her, an ugly red flush spreading over his face.

"I admit I got confused for a bit. You can be very charming when you want to be. The bouquet, the Sunday outing—I fell for it completely. But I am not interested in being one of your conquests," Julie continued, wondering where she was finding the strength. "We have to work together. What happened between us was an unfortunate indiscretion, and I, for one, intend to forget about it. You've got three weeks left at Haddonfield, and I suggest you do the same."

———————◆◯◆———————

Juliet brushed past him, leaving Hugo alone in the little room, desperate to throw something heavy through the window. He had poured out his heart to her, and she'd thrown it back in his face. He'd told her the truth and she'd called him a liar, then quoted Looks Brooks, the one person who was lying to her more than anyone. That bastard was cheating on her left and right, but she thought *he* was the scoundrel? The injustice of it choked him and he wasn't going to stand for it.

Hugo pursued Julie into the foyer and out the front door. He had almost caught up with her when Cassandra stepped in his path, putting herself firmly between him and Juliet.

"Let her go, Hugo. I'm taking her home."

"Damn it, Cassandra, don't interfere!" he roared. Over her shoulder, he could see the tears streaming down Juliet's face and it destroyed him. "Juliet! I'm sorry!"

"Let her go," Tom snapped, using his wheelchair to block Hugo's way.

Cassandra swept Julie down the front walk past Ian, who was just arriving. They ignored his cheery hello and kept walking.

Ian's eyes widened when he saw his brother was at the party. "What are you doing here? I thought you'd been rusticated."

Seeing the wild look on Hugo's face, Ian glanced over his shoulder to where Cassandra was bundling Julie into the SUV and then back to Hugo. "Oh, boy."

At that moment, Looks Brooks strolled onto the front stoop and clapped Hugo on the back. "Thanks for keeping Julie occupied, Pippa wouldn't let up. I owe you." He winked and sauntered away.

Hugo's fists clenched as he saw nothing but a red haze around the son of a bitch who was the source of all of his problems. Without further thought, he lunged at Looks, intent on wiping the smirk off the man's face permanently. With barely a second to spare, Ian flung himself at Hugo before he could make contact and the two men went sprawling onto a patch of lawn. Ian outweighed his older brother by at least a stone, but Hugo was much stronger and after a short but vicious struggle, was able to fling his brother off. Hugo leapt to his feet, but Looks had disappeared back into the party, nowhere to be seen.

Hugo stood, heart pounding, his hands on his hips and still wild with rage. But he forced himself to take a few slow, deep breaths, shook his head to clear it, and gave his brother a hand up.

"Do I have to remind you that you are still on probation?" Tom hissed. "Get out of here now."

The Jaguar was designed for speed, and Hugo cherished every ounce of horsepower that took him as far away from the party as he could get. He hit the M1 at seventy miles an hour and pushed the pedal to the floor. The precision engine responded with an enthusiastic roar.

Juliet had made it clear she wanted nothing more to do with him, and her rejection had ripped his heart out with surgical precision. He admitted he'd messed up seriously, telling her he'd known all along that it was her in the basement. What made him blurt that out he had no clue, but it infuriated him that he had poured his heart out to her and she had denied her own feelings.

The fact that she refused to believe him was preposterous. Hugo let the indignity build, nurtured by his bruised ego. How was it that her boyfriend was cheating on her almost before her eyes and was getting off scot-free, while he, Hugo, who was telling her nothing but the truth, ended up getting his heart thrown back at him? The injustice threatened to choke him.

As the miles peeled by, Hugo resolved to face facts. Juliet Randall was a lost battle and it was time to move on. Not that she'd been that great to begin with, he decided; she was more of a challenge than was worth his valuable time and effort. She could be maddeningly gullible and stupefyingly naive on occasion, with a prickly nature and obtuseness that would tempt the saints. Plus, she insisted on acting like some unblemished rose even though she'd been dating Looks Brooks for the last seven months.

He had treated her like a queen. He had done more for her than he had ever done for any other woman, and would have done more, much more. He would have worshiped her. She could have had anything she desired—cars, jewelry, clothing—anything would have been hers for the asking. Yet she'd coldly rejected him and insisted that all she wanted was that jerk boyfriend of hers. Because she thought he respected her! Ha. She had a lot of heartache coming and, in his opinion, deserved every measure of it.

The extent of his infatuation sobered him. Christ, Juliet had almost become an addiction. He felt a twinge of compassion for Ian. If this was anything close to what the poor bastard had to cope with on a daily basis, maybe he should go a little easier on him.

But if she *was* an addiction, then he was going to be cured quickly of her. Because he, Hugo Auchincloss, had better things to do than chase after some awkward country lass who was so blinded by trust that she was going to pass him up. She and Looks deserved each other. Juliet was right, he had only three weeks left at Haddonfield, and it wouldn't be hard to avoid her, especially since he was certain she would be avoiding him like the plague. He had walked away from Trika and never given her a second thought. He could do the same with Juliet.

# Chapter Twenty-Nine

HUGO'S PLAN FAILED spectacularly from the start.

He considered skipping the Monday night dinner altogether but he was damned if he was going to let Juliet see she affected him that much. The best way to prove she meant nothing to him was to confront her and get that out of the way.

There would be no better way to signal just how over her he was than to bring a date. There was an unlimited supply of women he could call at the last minute who would jump at the invitation. He mentally ran down the list, rejecting each one out of hand. None of them could hold a candle to Juliet, and the thought of having to put up with any of them for an evening was exhausting.

Needing to prove he could function without her, he instead purposely didn't wear the cufflinks she favored, instead choosing another pair set with mother-of-pearl.

Ian was notably quiet on the drive north, and Hugo focused grimly on the road. Haddonfield was a hive of activity when they arrived. Don met them at the door and explained that Bonnie had the flu and had been ordered home for a week of bed rest, so everyone was reorganizing to cover her absence.

Juliet took over supervising the kitchens. She paused to welcome them with a pleasant smile, and Hugo knew immediately it had been rehearsed. A cool formality was quickly established between them, and he went to help the servers finish preparing the dining room, while Ian was assigned the job of supervising parking.

Juliet stayed in the kitchens and devoted herself to fully ignoring him, and the dinner went off with only a few hiccups. Hugo watched Clive warily, not sure what the man would do if he found out he'd upset her. But Clive was so completely distracted by worry for his wife that Juliet sent him home early.

At the end of the evening, Hugo put another hundred-pound note in the box and was sorely tempted to add four more just to annoy Juliet—anything to crack that cool facade she was hiding behind. Goodbyes were swift and formal, and he remained silent the entire drive back to town.

Ian wisely kept any remarks to himself.

———————

Haddonfield settled into a makeshift routine that kept everyone busy. Juliet took over the cooking classes, and Nerida was put in charge of the gardens. The girl positively glowed with her new responsibilities, and on the surface, everything hummed. Juliet was her normal cheerful self, but it was like an invisible drawbridge had been pulled up with a huge gulf separating them. Hugo could see and speak with her, but as the week wore on, her forced indifference began to cut him a thousand ways.

He wanted to tell her that practices had been terrible since Lars was put on the injured list, the Jag's windshield had suffered a tiny crack, and Gladia had called to say she'd gotten in a book on sixteenth-century French cartographers.

By Thursday afternoon, Julie's indifference was wearing him raw, and he actually looked forward to the away fixture at Sunderland that Saturday. Miles had called the night before, excited to tell him he'd gotten a packet of research Juliet had done. She'd even lined up an American seed company that was looking to market some new strain of hardy winter wheat and had suggested Wrothesley as a test site. Miles babbled like a bloody idiot for over ten minutes and finished by saying that the next time Juliet was at Wrothesley, he wanted to show her a new seed drill he'd bought. "You too, Hugo," he'd added as an afterthought.

At staff tea that afternoon, Clive introduced him to Richard, the farmer that Juliet bought straw and manure from. The farmer shook Hugo's hand heartily and Hugo instantly hated him. He was affable, handsome, wore no wedding ring, and was entirely too friendly with Juliet.

They visited over tea with an easy familiarity that made Hugo's blood boil. Richard produced a small bag of bean seeds from his vest pocket and dropped it on the table, explaining he'd found them in an old box in his barn and thought Juliet might be able to do something with them. Juliet was obviously delighted. Hugo gripped his mug so tightly the handle snapped, spilling tea all over the table.

The only things going right were the classes. The pace at which the students were learning had picked up dramatically, and he was mildly astounded. Maths became much easier, and they were able to understand topics the first time he introduced them, and the quality of their compositions improved greatly.

Everything was going extraordinarily well, with the exception of French, which was still a struggle.

As he sat grading papers at home Thursday evening, Juliet's words came back to him. "You're a natural teacher. You have a rare talent." It seemed that she was right. It wasn't hard, he discovered, it just took patience and being clear on things yourself.

Hugo thought back to some of his instructors at Eton, all of whom were excellent of course, but in some ways lacked the knack he seemed to possess. In quiet moments he began to imagine himself teaching at a school somewhere, leading an eager class in the history of the Peloponnesian Wars, the students' faces bright and inspired by his lecture.

Maybe he'd even be headmaster, someday.

He reluctantly brushed the images aside. Teachers went to university and toiled for years in academia. But still, at the moment the idea didn't seem so farfetched.

Hugo spent his evenings reading through the GCSE material and laying out a study plan. He and Matthew met twice a week at a coffee shop near his grandmother's house. The going was slow, and the boy was exhausted, but they were making some progress.

Actually, Hugo noticed, everyone was looking exhausted. The rest of the students seemed to plod through the day and Juliet's normal energetic attitude was waning as well. Yet everyone was doing outstanding work, and no one complained. He mentally shrugged. Some people just didn't know how to manage their workloads.

———————◇———————

When you're solving simultaneous equations in algebra, you use substitution. As you can see in this equation, we can solve for X and then use that result in the bottom equation to solve for Y," Hugo said as he wrote on the whiteboard Friday afternoon.

"That's not the way Julie explained it last night," Lalani whispered to Joanna. "She said we was supposed to find what Y is then plug it into the top equation."

"Shush!" Nerida whispered. "It's the same thing."

"No, it's not!" Lalani protested. "He's doing it backwards."

"She did it both ways," Alex hissed.

Hugo's head snapped around at the exchange. "Who did it both ways?"

The girls glanced between themselves, and Matthew frowned.

"Out with it," Hugo said, but the group remained stubbornly silent. "Has Juliet been helping you with your classwork?"

The silence was deafening. Hugo fixed his gaze on Lalani, who began to quiver in her seat, her frightened brown eyes growing wider by the second.

"Yes," Nerida spat out seconds before Lalani burst into tears. "She's been tutoring us."

"Since when?"

"Since when you first assigned us homework. But lately it's been hours and hours, every bleedin' night."

A dull ache began in his heart. "Why?"

"So's we'd do good for you. She didn't want us to fail," Tanda confessed. "We don't want to fail."

Nothing had ever felt so deflating in his life. The remarkable progress the class was making, the quality of the work they were handing in, everyone having their homework done—

suddenly it made sense—it was because Juliet was doing all the work for him. French was the only subject she couldn't tutor them in.

*Bloody hell.*

"You can't tell her we told you, though," Pax said and the rest nodded. "She'd skin us alive if she knew you'd found out."

"She's making you work too hard," Hugo protested.

"No harder than she's working," Phong said. "Not even close. And she's doing it all for us, and she ain't getting paid extra for it or nothing. Ain't nobody's ever done that before."

The group nodded their agreement.

"And besides," Tanda added, "she said it's only for a fortnight more. Then you'll be gone and done with us."

⚬

Julie stood in the baggage claim area at Heathrow early Friday evening, ignoring the admiring glances of male travelers while she waited for Mark's plane to arrive from Madrid. A small overnight bag was looped over her shoulder with the beautiful peignoir inside. Tonight was going to be the night. She looked at the clock and yawned.

Since Pippa's party, her embarrassment had settled into a dull ache that wouldn't go away. Hugo, for his part, seemed completely unaffected and when they'd had to interact, was unerringly polite and aloof. His expression returned to its original inscrutability, and he spent the week blithely unaware of her existence, choosing instead to load the students up with an avalanche of assignments that made them all bleary-eyed trying to keep up. The week had been nerve-racking, and she pushed herself to the point of exhaustion.

The worst part was that the excitement she always felt when he was around refused to be tamped down, no matter how many times she reminded herself of her own stupidity. Clive was absolutely correct—Hugo was a man and wasn't going to pass up opportunities like the one Sophie offered. It was her own fault she'd convinced herself that what he felt for her was more than lust.

That wasn't just being naive, Julie decided as she waited, that was bordering on a certifiable psychosis. The truth was that she'd fallen for him, hard, like a teenager with a desperate crush on a movie star she thought belonged exclusively to her. The reality was that he was one of the most eligible sport stars in Great Britain who had his choice of anyone he wanted. The depth of her feelings for Hugo was downright pathetic.

But regardless of how many times her head tried to explain this to her heart, it refused to cooperate, leaving Julie feeling confused and depressed. The continuous effort drained her. It was a blessing Bonnie was home sick, as she would have instantly picked up on the tension. With two weeks until he left time dragged on interminably. It seemed like a prison sentence. Was Hugo counting the days till he was free of her?

Julie decided she was going to have to do something radical. The reason Mark never made her feel like her blood was on fire the way Hugo did, she decided, was because they had never gotten that far. He said he wanted their first time to be special, but she was tired of being a virgin, and maybe it was just better to get it over with. The circumstances never seemed to be right, so she was going to help things along.

With grim determination, she selected a creamy, high-waisted dress with a very short hemline that caused Rosie to note, *"Watch the breeze!"* She paired it with strappy high heels and then dabbed, blended, and painted on makeup for over half an hour with fierce concentration until she didn't recognize herself. She looked... sexy. Very sexy and maybe even a little edgy, like the professional models. Hiding her chipped fingernails behind her back completed the picture.

A surge of passengers filled the baggage area, and Mark emerged, talking animatedly on his mobile phone. He shot her an appraising glance as he passed and then ground to an astonished halt when he realized it was her. "Julie?"

Pleased at his reaction, she kissed him full on the lips, making sure to press against him.

"I didn't know you were meeting me. You look amazing!" he gasped, taking a slight step back.

"I thought I'd surprise you." She attempted a quick twirl but ended up tripping over the spiky high heels.

"Outstanding! There's a driver waiting outside, and I have to stop back at my flat first, but then we can—"

"That's fine," she said firmly and linked her arm in his and marched determinedly out the door.

———◆◇◆———

Might be a bit messy, I'm afraid," Mark apologized as he opened the door to his small apartment. "Can I get you a drink?"

"Yes, thank you." Julie dropped her bag and perched prettily on the sofa. She definitely needed a drink.

"Okay then!" Mark rubbed his hands together and began searching the refrigerator. "I've got Diet Coke, some Perrier, a bit of ginger ale, and—"

"Any champagne?"

Mark paused. "Yes, I think I do." Rummaging a moment longer, he produced a chilled bottle and set it on the counter. "Sorry it's not Dom Pérignon, but maybe I'll get that account next," he said, popping the bottle and pouring two glasses.

"To us," Julie toasted as he joined her on the sofa, and she downed the contents of her glass in one motion.

"Refill?" he asked faintly.

"Yes, p-please," she said with a slight hiccup.

"Darling, are you feeling all right? You're not acting yourself."

"I just missed you and am very happy you're back." Julie looped her arms around his neck, closed her eyes, and pursed her lips expectantly.

Mark jumped off the sofa and refilled her glass with a shaking hand. "I'm damn glad to be back. Madrid was a nightmare. The office sent the wrong galleys of the Spanish print ads, and then we found out the labels on the commemorative bottles were printed with an ink the EU considers toxic, and—"

"Mark, why have we never made love?" Julie interrupted.

He blanched. "You said you wanted it to be perfect, darling, and I respect that. Perfect and romantic, and with all my work, I haven't been able to give you that."

"I never said I wanted it to be perfect, I just meant not as an afterthought. You know, somewhere quiet, private, peaceful. Like now."

"Now?" Mark squeaked but then got himself under control. "Wait a sec, I brought you back something special from Madrid. I passed this shop and thought of you immediately and knew you had to have it. Won't be a minute."

He fled to his bedroom and slammed the door shut behind him. After what seemed like ages, he reappeared, collected and calm, and presented her with a rectangular box. "For you."

She unfolded the decorative paper and opened the box. "A necklace made of wine corks?"

"Yes, clever, isn't it? They're from all the famous Spanish vineyards. Here, let me help you put it on." She lifted her hair and he fastened it at the nape of her neck before patting her hair back into place. "There. What do you think?"

With a huge effort she smiled, fingering the individual corks. "It's very interesting. Thank you."

"Ha! I knew you'd like it." Taking her hands in his, he lowered his voice to a soft croon. "Look, darling, I know this whole crazy thing has been hard on you and I'm sorry. You haven't been too lonely, have you? I mean, I know you've been spending some time with Hugo, and that's great, but I don't have anything to worry about there, do I?"

"He hasn't made any secret that he's interested in me," Julie admitted. "And it turns out he was the one who kissed me in the basement at the wedding."

Mark threw back his head and laughed like it was the funniest thing he'd ever heard. "Splendid chap, never one to pass up an opportunity."

When he saw she wasn't laughing, he slapped her knee. "Come on, old girl, you're still not upset about that, are you? You should feel flattered. Hugo makes a pass at every girl in our circle. He's rather well known for it. It doesn't mean anything. It's just something we aristocrats do. There's no harm in it."

"You make passes at the girls as well?"

"Of course not! I mean, I used to. Before I met you. Now I have eyes for no one else. How could I?" Mark watched Julie closely, for once fully observant. "I say, you're not feeling anything for him, are you? It's patently ridiculous. It was all in fun and there wasn't anything to it. Besides, I need you. How can I make it to the top without my best girl beside me?"

Maybe it was the champagne, but Mark's words sounded hollow and contrived. A bell began to ring in her ears, and it took Juliet several seconds to realize it was the church down the road chiming eight o'clock. She picked up her glass of champagne, drained it, and set it down firmly. "Mark, I want us to make love. Right here, right now."

His shoulders sagged. "Darling, not like this. I haven't had a shower in two days, there wasn't a bloody bite to eat on the plane, plus I have to be on a call at five a.m. That's not very romantic, is it?"

Smoothing her hair, he kissed her forehead. "I want everything to be perfect for your first time. Just like you described, quiet, peaceful, and private. It's just such a whirl right now. You've got your hands full in the gardens, and I've got this huge opportunity. But after the Bajan Gin launch, things will quiet down, and we can really spend some time together. I promise. And that's only a month away. Say you'll wait? Please?" he beseeched.

It was impossible to stay angry with Mark. When she nodded, he stood and clapped his hands. "Glad that's settled! Now, the gang from the office is meeting at Continuem for drinks and dinner, I'll just get changed and we can be off."

Mark's lightning-fast change of attitude was astonishing. And disheartening. "I've got an early morning as well," Julie said, gathering her bag and pulling on her coat. "Bonnie's been sick all week and I've got to get caught up on the thinning and sowing if we're going to have anything to serve in May."

"Really? But you look so spectacular, and everyone will be there. It will be a hoot."

Julie forced a smile. "I know, but I'm not really in the mood tonight. Have fun."

Mark trailed her to the door. "I can call for a taxi if you like."

"No, no need. I've got it covered," Julie answered with brittle cheerfulness. "Go change, you don't want to be late. I'll be fine."

She waved goodbye and waited in the corridor for the elevator, her knees trembling.

"Darling, wait!" Mark appeared in his doorway, and her heart gave a faint jump of hope. "Don't forget we're having dinner with Ramon Sanchez tomorrow evening at The Clevedon Grill. The car will be at your place at seven."

The elevator doors opened, and she stepped in swiftly, hot tears burning her eyes.

The humiliation was overwhelming. She had literally thrown herself at Mark and he'd seemed repulsed, yet all he could do was talk of their future. Hugo would have taken her up on her offer in a second and been gone the next. What in God's name was the matter with her?

The bus stop was three blocks away and the going was slow in high heels. Julie was making determined progress when she heard Hugo's voice call her name. She spun around in excitement, but it was Ian loping down the sidewalk towards her.

"Julie! Hello! What brings you down here?" he asked. "And looking amazing, if I might add?"

"You don't see me looking like a girl much, do you?"

"You always look like a girl—tonight you look like a babe," he corrected. "I say, is something the matter?"

"No, no." Julie rushed to frame a smile. "Mark just got back from a trip and wants to go out, and I'd expected a quiet evening at home. So I'm just looking for the bus back to Finchley."

"I think you need some cheering up," Ian decided. "I know, let's try and get into Bash Club. It's right down the road here and it'll be fun."

It was on the tip of Julie's tongue to refuse, but her life was a shambles and certainly couldn't get any worse. "*Fun* sounds like a good idea right about now."

Around the corner, the line for the club stretched down the street. "It's packed, we'll never get in." Julie frowned.

"Don't worry, I've got a secret weapon. Luckily, I wore a white shirt this evening." Ian winked at her and then took off his glasses, opened another button at the neck of his shirt, combed his hair back with his fingers, and scowled. "Don't slouch, Juliet," he muttered contemptuously.

She gasped at the transformation. Ian was a dead-on imposter of his brother. "That's amazing."

Ian grinned and nodded. "I've gotten good at it, comes in handy at times like these." They walked to the front of the line, Ian effortlessly adopting Hugo's superior air while Julie feigned a vapid attitude, her lips pressed together in mirth.

"Room for two more, old man?" Ian mimicked.

The bouncer immediately opened the velvet rope, and Ian and Julie swept through, accompanied by the flash of several cameras.

"I love this part," Ian confided.

# Chapter Thirty

KINGSBURY TOWN WAS going into the match against Sunderland on Saturday, ninth place in the Premier League rankings. A win today and an Everton loss against Chelsea tomorrow would move them into eighth place. As he shaved, Hugo forced himself to focus on his own mental preparations instead of letting his thoughts wander back to Juliet, where they would just get tangled up again and leave him upset and miserable.

Lars, the right wing, had been given a tentative green light to play, but his injury was well publicized, and Sunderland would almost certainly press him hard. But it was a relief to have him back, and the rest of the lineup was steady. The game plan was to work the ball down the left flank for the first half, then switch to a counter-attack strategy, limiting the space between the backline and goal with Jean-George as point man. The Sunderland attackers were wildly uneven, and it was a plan that had worked well against Tottenham the night he'd taken Juliet back to his house to see *The Orchard*.

Hugo nicked himself with the razor and swore, trying to block out the voice of Mick Carr next door, who was yacking his bloody head off to anyone who would listen. As he dabbed carefully at his chin, his mobile rang.

"What the hell were you doing in Chelsea last night?" Tom demanded.

"I wasn't in Chelsea last night, I was on the team coach to Sunderland."

"There's a rather good picture in the *Daily Mail* of you going into Bash Club last night with Julie on your arm."

"Come again?"

"Pick up a *Daily Mail*, page six, and call me back."

In the hotel lobby, Hugo bought the paper and flipped through until he found the photograph. "*AuchinClass*" the caption read. "*A rare sighting of Kingsbury Town blueblood midfielder Hugo Auchincloss seen here going into popular nightclub Bash with unknown blonde. The usually reclusive Auchincloss seemed proud to flaunt this beauty on his arm.*"

"It was Ian," he told Tom when he rang him back, "impersonating me to get into the club."

"As someone you pay a lot of money to keep you out of these papers, I'm going to start charging double if I have to keep Ian out as well."

Hugo sighed, the paper clenched in his hand. "I'll have a word."

"I'm serious, Hugo. The *Sun* already has pictures of her coming out of your place, and it's only a matter of time before they find her. If you want to protect her, you're going to have to be a lot more careful."

"That's not going to be an issue. It's over."

"Are you sure about that? I thought you might be able to patch things up."

"Not an option. She's made it clear she doesn't want anything to do with me."

Tom paused. "That's a shame. We liked her."

"Yes. Well. I'm moving on. Remind me, does Cassandra have any sisters?"

Hugo rode down in the elevator alone and took the opportunity to give his brother an early morning phone call. "What the fuck, Ian?"

"I'm sorry! I didn't think you'd mind. She was walking to the bus and looked really sad, and I thought she could use some cheering up."

Hugo gripped the phone. "Why was Juliet upset?"

"I'm not sure. She was very quiet. I think she and Looks had a bit of a tiff."

"Did she have a good time?" he pressed.

"We had a blast," Ian laughed. "It was early, and we only stayed for two hours, and then I treated her to a cab back to Finchley. I thought that's what you'd want me to do."

"You should have called me. I would have come down. The coach didn't leave till late."

"You? In a place like Bash? Besides, couldn't have you showing up twice—you were already there," Ian reasoned. "Say, would you reimburse me for the cab?"

When Hugo arrived at the breakfast table, his teammates were passing around a copy of the *Daily Mail* and whistling with appreciation for Juliet.

"Autograph it for us, would you, Hugo?" Brian, the goalkeeper, grinned before the paper was snatched out of his hands by Mick Carr, who scanned it critically, a wolf-like grin on his handsome face.

"Now that's a bit of all right," he murmured. "Where've you been keeping her stashed, Hugo? One of your museums?"

"I'd go to that museum," Jason chimed in, leaning over his shoulder to get a better look.

Blind fury gripped Hugo as he snatched the paper out of Mick's hand. "She's not your type, Carr. She can count past ten without taking her shoes off."

The table erupted in laughter, but Mick's eyes narrowed as he rose out of his chair. Darius quickly stood between them and clapped a hand on Mick's shoulder, shoving him back into his seat with a warning look. "Take it out on Sunderland, lads."

At dinner Saturday night, Julie sat between Mark and Ramon Sanchez, the president of Latin America operations for Dionysus, translating Ramon's rapid-fire Spanish into English for Mark, and Mark's sullen responses back into Spanish. Her dinner sat untouched as she tried to keep up with the heated conversation.

"He says you promised him the galley proofs two weeks ago," Julie told Mark.

Mark chewed his steak with irritation. "I said I'd try. I never promised."

Julie turned to Ramon. "He tried and apologizes for not being able to get them to you," she translated.

"This man, he is impossible," Ramon fumed. "No, don't tell him that—he won't hear it anyway. He has got his head between some pretty legs too much, I think."

It occurred to Julie that Ramon thought she was a hired translator.

"He is too young, too brash. I do not trust him," Ramon continued. "This new gin is a bad idea, and without targeted advertising in the Latin countries, it does not have a prayer. He does not understand this at all. Who wants to see that woman he says we must use? She is too skinny. My customers want a real woman with some life in her, some flesh on her bones, some passion. He just does not get it."

Ramon sipped his wine. "Tell him I will personally attend the photo shoot here next week, and that I will be very interested to see how it goes. In the meantime, I expect the proofs on my desk in San Juan by Wednesday."

"He's coming to the shoot?" Mark exploded after Julie translated. "He'll just interfere! Tell him absolutely not, it's a closed shoot."

Julie opened her mouth to translate, but Mark wrinkled his nose and sighed. "No, tell him that's fine. We'll be looking forward to seeing him. And I will personally make sure the bloody proofs are on his desk."

The dinner meeting adjourned, and Ramon paid her several warm compliments before departing. Mark shook his hand perfunctorily and flopped back into his seat.

"Bastard. He hates Rochelle and that's just going to make the shoot more difficult." Mark sulked, not even trying to conceal his bad mood.

Julie picked at the cold food on her plate. "You're doing the shoot here next week? In London?"

"Yes, I pushed for Prague, but Dionysus wants an 'authentic' English setting." Mark waved his fingers sarcastically. "And they are insisting on someplace fresh that's never been photographed before. Like I can just wave a wand and make a new stately country home appear!" Suddenly his face brightened, and he perked up. "Say, I don't imagine there's any way you could talk the Auchincloss family into letting us use Wrothesley?"

Julie recoiled. "Absolutely not."

Mark glowered and slumped back against the banquette seat. "I didn't think so, especially since you got papped going into Bash last night. Hugo's going to be furious."

Julie froze. "I'm in the paper?"

"*Daily Mail,* page six." Mark pulled the paper from his jacket pocket and handed it to her. "I figured you hadn't seen it."

It was a small picture but convincing. "That isn't Hugo—it was Ian pretending to be Hugo. I bumped into him in the road after I left your flat."

"Why didn't you call me?"

"You said you were meeting up with your friends."

Mark's lower lip thrust out in a petulant pout. "Still. I would have come. Bash is almost impossible to get into."

"Maybe we could try and get in now," Julie suggested. "The people at the door might remember me."

Mark glanced at his watch. "No, I'm meeting the art director to run out and look at the Cheeting Park Hotel in Richmond. It's an old place that might work for the shoot. Come on, I'll get you a cab."

In the lobby, Mark held her coat while checking his mobile for messages. Julie took it from him and looked him straight in the eye, her gaze steady and deliberate. "Mark, I'd like to go to the shoot next week."

"Whatever for?"

"I'd like to meet Rochelle. You said we should meet each other."

Mark squirmed, his annoyance clear. "Now might not be the best time."

"I won't be any trouble. And she might like to meet me."

For several moments, Mark appeared pulled by demons before warming to the idea. "It might be helpful having you there. Ramon will need a translator."

"Maybe you should start learning some Spanish," Julie suggested. "You said the Latin America countries are a huge growth area."

"Why would I do that when I have you, darling?" Mark quipped, his good humor restored.

From the start, the match against Sunderland was an unqualified disaster. Kingsbury Town narrowly averted an own goal in the first two minutes of play, and to be honest, they hadn't played that badly in ages. Giles pulled Lars at the half, but Dylan Rhea just didn't gel with the team despite damned decent play on his part. At forty-five minutes, Jean-George almost managed to knock one into the net on a rebound, but bloody Jason was offside, and it was called back. No one's head seemed in the game, Hugo's included, and Sunderland danced over them to win, 3–0.

After they loaded onto the coach for the trip back to Wimbledon, a milk lorry clipped them on the motorway, shredding two tires and twisting the rear axle. Fortunately, they weren't going fast and no one was hurt, but it jammed traffic for miles, delaying the arrival of the replacement coach. It was two o'clock in the morning before they were finally back underway.

Pozny lay collapsed in the seat next to him, exhausted from the match. Hugo felt for the kid, who'd played his heart out. He was a relatively new addition to the club, brought over from a Polish team in the middle of last season on the recommendation of one of Sir Frank's mysterious scouts. It was hard not to like the scruffy goliath; he was an outstanding center midfielder and a jolly decent chap to boot. His English was nonexistent, but he could speak passable schoolboy French, so Hugo was assigned to room with him on the road and they had developed a good relationship.

In the darkness, Hugo adjusted the ice pack on his ankle and surreptitiously reached into his jacket pocket to retrieve the page he had torn out of the *Daily Mail.*

Ian had done his usual amazing job of impersonating him, and he could tell by Juliet's smile that she was enjoying playing the role of arm candy. That tiny dress showed miles of leg, and her hair hung around her shoulders like a silk curtain. Jesus, she looked stunning. For a moment, he let himself pretend it was him in the photograph, his hand resting possessively on the small of her back, providing the distraction and comfort she needed.

Hugo didn't doubt Ian's explanation of the circumstances; if his brother found Juliet upset, the first thing he would want to do was cheer her up. Which, to Ian, meant going clubbing. He also knew Ian wouldn't dare make a play for Juliet without his permission. Ian was completely incapable of subterfuge or deceit, a trait that seemed to attract women like a magnet. Was there a possibility Juliet found his immaturity appealing?

Envy gnawed at him as he stared at the picture with equal parts craving and veneration. God, he missed her. Despite all his resolutions, he ached for her. The nameless yearnings that overwhelmed him had nothing to do with physical desire, as insistent as that was. He had always been comfortable with solitude, but suddenly being alone felt cavernous and empty. Alone felt lonely.

Sleep didn't bring any relief. Juliet was haunting his dreams as well. His mind made up its own potent fantasies of how it would be if she were his, willing and loving, sometimes teasing, sometimes playful, and always equaling his desire. Some of the dreams were shatteringly real, and he would wake in the middle of the night, shaken and aroused like an adolescent.

Ian said she and Looks had a tiff Friday night. What did they fight about? Maybe they broke up. Maybe she was home now, crying and needing comfort. Hugo sat in the coach, helpless, feeling his emotions careen out of control. Was there a chance she was missing him as well?

He knew he had to get ahold of himself; getting overwrought wasn't going to solve anything. He had to try to see her again. Anything was better than this living hell. She could yell at him all she wanted, call him every name in the book, but he didn't care. He just needed to see her.

Ian might have more details than he'd given up yesterday— best to check before he showed up on her doorstep. Pulling out his cell, he saw there was a missed call, and the number was hers. She'd left a message.

"Hello, it's Julie."

The recording of her voice was a like a tonic and his heart began to slow its pounding.

She paused for a moment, as if she were taking a deep breath. "I'm sorry to bother you. I guess you know about the picture in the *Daily Mail*. I'm sorry about going to the club with Ian and getting photographed. I know you pay Tom a lot of money to keep you out of the papers and it was inexcusable. Please don't be mad at Ian, he was just trying to cheer me up. I was... it had been..." She paused and regrouped. "I'd had a

long day and I'm very sorry. I hope your game went well.
Bye."

Glancing at his watch, Hugo saw that she'd left the message
four hours ago, right after the accident occurred. It was too late
to call her back, so instead he listened to the message a few
more times. Peace washed over him, and it seemed as if the
world had suddenly righted itself. Everything was as it should
be. His way forward was absolutely, perfectly clear. Juliet was
all he wanted, all he needed, and he was going to win her back.

Tom would know how.

# Chapter Thirty-One

CASSANDRA GREETED HUGO coolly at the door of their cottage in the country the next afternoon and accepted the bouquet he proffered. "Your sheepish expression is a nice touch," she said with a wry grin.

Hugo followed her back to the kitchen where Tom was chopping celery and wonderful aromas wafted from the stove.

Tom looked up. "Sunderland called. They want to send a thank you card."

"It was even worse on the field than it must have looked on the telly," Hugo recounted, helping himself to a beer from the refrigerator. "Dietl read Pozny like a book. They used to play together in the Eastern European under twenty-one league, and he knew every button to push. We're lucky we got off so lightly."

"How long is Lars out for?"

Hugo reached out to steal a bit of cooling pork roast, and Cassandra smacked the back of his hand with a wooden spoon. "He's going to see the specialists again tomorrow, but it could be the rest of the season. Wish to hell we had some options there."

He took a deep swig from the bottle and sat on a stool next to Tom. "I need advice from both of you on how to patch it up with Juliet."

Cassandra gave a disapproving snort as she added the celery to the sizzling sauté pan.

"Thought you were going to forget about her," Tom said.

"Turns out that's not an option. However, she doesn't want anything to do with me."

Cassandra stirred the pan with rapid strokes and added a generous measure of wine. "And you're surprised?"

"No, but there is a bit more to the story than me just being some Lothario."

"If we're going to help, maybe you should tell us everything," Tom suggested. "Start at the beginning."

Hugo began with meeting Juliet at the bookstore and ended with their confrontation in the coatroom at the party. Cassandra and Tom listened in compassionate silence until the very end.

Cassandra's stirring spoon clattered to the floor. "You told her you knew it was her you kissed in the basement?"

"You've gone insane," Tom concluded.

Hugo buried his head in his hands. "I know. She didn't believe me about Sophie and then she started talking about how wonderful Looks was, and everything spun out of control. I just blurted it out."

Cassandra looked at him with a mixture of pity and disbelief. "Why didn't you tell her about Looks and Pippa?"

"I tried, but she didn't believe me. Looks told her he was going to help Pippa get her cat off the roof of the pavilion, and she bought it."

"I've never seen you get like this over a woman," Tom said. "Not even Trika."

"I'm mad for her," Hugo admitted.

"Well, you're making a complete hash of it," Cassandra said. "The girl was devastated, Hugo. It was all she could do to hold back the tears on the trip home, and I don't blame her. I was standing right next to her, and it really did look like you and Sophie had just had a quickie."

"There is hope, though," Tom reasoned. "She really likes you. It was obvious when you showed up at the party. It was like night and day. She just came alive."

"Tom's right," Cassandra agreed. "And she wouldn't have been so upset if she didn't have some feelings for you. But what about this boyfriend of hers? Is he making a habit of hooking up with other women at parties?"

"It's a bit worse than that, darling," Tom said. "Looks is still carrying on with his ex-girlfriend, the rum model."

Cassandra looked between the two men. "Julie needs to know. Someone has to tell her."

"If she didn't believe me about Pippa, do you think she'd believe me if I told her about Rochelle?" Hugo said. "She believes everything Looks tells her. She's just stupefyingly naive."

Cassandra thought about this as she arranged the gravy, potatoes, and fresh peas in bowls and Hugo ferried them to the table.

"Not every woman is as worldly as the ones you're used to dealing with. Did it ever occur to you that perhaps she's truly inexperienced? Or even has no experience?" Cassandra offered, setting a platter with the lovely roast on the table.

Hugo rolled his eyes as they took their places. "Come on, Cassandra. She's been dating Looks for seven months."

"He's got a point, love," her husband said as he began to carve the roast.

"All the same, no woman likes her secrets thrown in her face, and I'm guessing it was probably a huge step for her to decide to leave the party with you. Now she's obviously terribly embarrassed and confused, and I'm not surprised she doesn't want anything to do with you."

Hugo tucked into the meal. "So what do I do? She thinks I'm some randy footballer out there snogging and screwing any girl I come across."

"Apologize," Cassandra said firmly.

"For what?"

"For being a randy footballer who snogs girls in basements and screws tarts in the loo."

Tom laughed at Hugo's look of disgust. "She's right, Hugo. It's the only way you're going to get anywhere."

"But it's not true!" Hugo protested. "I'd own up to it if it was the truth, but nothing could be further from it."

"Look, old man, you're arguing with a woman. They're a lot smarter than we are. Cassandra is correct. You're going to have to apologize and pray she discovers the truth down the road."

Hugo stabbed at a piece of pork and regarded Cassandra with a baleful eye. "This plan of yours better work."

———— ◆ ————

After lunch, Cassandra waved them off the dishes, and Hugo and Tom watched the later matches on the television in the sitting room.

"What are you planning on doing now?" Tom asked after Everton beat Aston Villa.

"I'm going to Juliet's, apologize for something I didn't do, and tell her about Looks. Cassandra's right, someone has to tell her."

Tom shook his head. "I agree, but that person shouldn't be you. You've already tried it and you got nowhere. If you try again, it'll just look like more of the same."

Hugo slumped in his chair. "So what do you suggest?"

"If you care for her even half as much as I think you do, you've got to be patient and let this thing play out."

"What would you know of patience?" Hugo snapped, but instantly felt contrite. "I mean, you and Cassandra met, fell in love, and got married, just like in the fairy tales. I didn't see anything but moonbeams and roses."

"It might have seemed like that but it wasn't. Marrying a man with a broken back was a big step, and I wanted Cassandra to take her time, be sure it was the right decision. We waited almost a year, so don't tell me I don't know anything about patience."

"Then what should I do?"

"You're going to sit tight, stay in her life, and let this work itself out. Julie has to come to the right conclusions on her own, and that may take some time. But you're a clever lad and you might find some ways to help that along."

Hugo's lips twitched, and he felt the first glimmer of hope in over a week.

"In the meantime," Tom continued, "have a chat with Looks and find out what he's up to. He was with Rochelle last week in Lisbon, and I heard they were all over each other."

"No time like the present." Hugo grinned and flipped open his mobile. "Hey, Looks, Hugo here. Care to meet up for a drink?"

———————◆◯◆———————

"She's beautiful, isn't she?" Mark Brooks mused as he stared over the bar at the poster of Rochelle with a bottle of Sam Lord's Castle Rum. "Beautiful, a Venus, with a heart as cold as ice."

"Is that so?" Hugo remarked, signaling the barman for another round of martinis, their fourth by his count. His drink arrived with no alcohol as prearranged, while Mark's was poured with a heavy hand and delivered with three olives. The bar's owner was a school chum.

"You have no idea. We were together for three years—three wonderful, horrible, magical, terrible years."

"Sounds like a bit of a roller coaster."

This sent Mark into peals of laughter that took him a long time to recover from. "Ripped my bloody heart out, the bitch. But you've been there, old chap, you know what I'm talking about."

Hugo's jaw tightened. "You're referring to Trika?"

" 'Course I am. Quite a mess. Whatever became of her?"

"She went to Australia and married a farmer, haven't seen or heard from her in years. No wish to."

"Lucky bastard. I see Rochelle everywhere I go, can't get away from her. Like tomorrow, I have to go to Amsterdam and be with her on a Sam Lord's Castle Rum shoot. Just can't seem to make the final break with her."

"Is it over?"

Mark turned red. "I'm trying. It's complicated. She's very upset, and I have to let her down gently. Things aren't going well for her now and she's being very emotional. I don't know what the hell's the matter with her."

"How does Juliet fit in?"

Mark took a deep swallow of his drink and sighed. "Julie. My angel. And she is an angel, completely pure and... angelic. But I guess all angels are angelic, goes with the job. Sorry," he belched, "got a bit pedantic there."

"She is wonderful," Hugo agreed.

"She's not too happy with you right now, old man. Look, I don't mind you having a quick snog with her in the basement, but she doesn't understand. Patch it up with her, get her a little trinket or something. I had to do that Friday night, gave her a gift from a distributor. Cheered her up immensely."

"I wanted to talk with you about that. At the wedding I—"

"She's completely different from Rochelle, you know," Mark rambled on, oblivious. "Completely. Her face isn't much to look at, but she makes up for it in other departments." Mark guffawed, making a lurid gesture of voluptuousness with his hands on his chest. "She's got Rochelle beat there easily— Rochelle's had two sets of implants done and Julie still outclasses her."

"So it's serious with Juliet?" Hugo interrupted, his fists curling.

"I guess." Mark took another gulp of his martini and wiped his mouth on his shirtsleeve. "I mean, she's a swell girl. All a chap could ask for, really."

"Swell?" Hugo repeated in disbelief.

"Entirely. Top notch. But she's got this thing, this problem almost, that I'm having the devil's own time dealing with."

Hugo was intrigued. "What kind of problem could Juliet possibly have?"

Mark laughed, a nervous, high-pitched sound. "Ah, yes. What problem could perfect little Julie possibly have? But I ask you, Hugo, what the hell am I supposed to do with a virgin?"

Hugo flushed and glanced away, pummeled by a wild volley of emotions. Holy hell, Juliet was a virgin?

"Don't suppose you've ever had one? Me neither. Had everything else, but virgins have been distinctly off-putting. And she's all over me—like last Friday night, she seemed almost desperate. But she wants it to be romantic, for God's sake. Who does romantic? Jolly good thumping is what I like."

Hugo stared at him, incredulous. "You're complaining?"

"No, not really." Mark chewed on the olive and then picked his teeth with the toothpick. "But God, Hugo, every time I kiss her I feel like I'm kissing my sister. If I had one, that is. I can barely bring myself to touch her."

"Then let her go," Hugo advised.

"No! I can work through this! Marriage isn't all about sex, old man. It's about making a family!" He pounded the bar with his fist to emphasize the point. "Settling down! Having some comfort and normality in your life, all the things that made England great. I can have that with Julie. She will be an amazing wife and mother. And the clients love her, my stock has gone up tenfold since I met her."

"What about her? Don't you think she'd want a husband that could at least kiss her?"

"I'll be able to, I know I will. Once we're married and it's impossible to keep going back to Rochelle. It will all happen."

"You're delusional." Unable to bear any more, Hugo stood and counted out a thick stack of bills to the eager barkeep and had him call two taxis—one for himself and one for Juliet's asshole boyfriend.

"Don't suppose you've got an extra ticket to the FA Cup this weekend?" Mark hinted as Hugo helped him down the steps to the sidewalk.

"Two tickets?" Hugo said coldly.

"I don't have to bring h-her." Mark's giggle was interrupted by a hiccup. "Figured you were put out about her getting papped with your brother outside of Bash."

A negative response was on the tip of Hugo's tongue but then he reconsidered. The idea was so perfect he could have kissed Looks. "There might be a ticket or two, let me look around."

Mark swayed before the waiting taxi and grabbed Hugo by the collar of his coat. "Look, Auchincloth. One more thing." He swallowed and tried to focus on the much taller man standing before him. "I know you're ver... very fond of Julie. Should be." He poked him in the chest to add emphasis. "But us chaps have to stick together. Now. Give me your word that what I've told you tonight goes no further, at least to Julie."

"There's no need to—"

"Your word, Hugo. As a gennnelman."

Damn him. Damn him to hell. "All right. You have my word. But I will also tell you that if you hurt her, you will answer to me."

"No worries there!" Mark snickered and stumbled into the cab.

Hugo waved the second taxi on and decided to walk home. A cold wind blew through the dirty streets, and he pulled his collar up and dug his hands into his pockets, passing shop windows decorated with red hearts and chubby cupids. Valentine's Day was quickly approaching.

Juliet was a virgin. Looks had never touched her. London was the most wonderful city in the world.

Traffic whizzed along the streets as he walked, his heart light. The paradoxes that had confounded him instantly evaporated. Cassandra was right. Juliet wasn't sleeping with Looks, and from all appearances he wasn't going to touch her. The way forward was clear, and a plan effortlessly came together in his head. He had twelve days left at Haddonfield, twelve precious days, and he intended to make the most of them.

He pulled his mobile from his overcoat pocket and pressed a few buttons. "Phillip, I'm going to need more tickets."

# Chapter Thirty-Two

BY MONDAY MORNING, Bonnie was back in the kitchens in full health and insisting she had never felt better. Clive hovered close by until he was banished to the attics to lay insulation, Bonnie muttering that she would never get anything done with that hulking Northerner under her feet all day.

Both Don and Bonnie insisted that Julie take the rest of Monday off, and Tuesday and Wednesday as well.

"You worked so hard last week and deserve some rest. Plus you have over seven weeks' vacation saved," Don reminded her. "Please take some of it."

A thousand objections leapt to mind but being able to avoid Hugo overruled everything. Calling him Saturday evening to apologize for being photographed outside Bash had been confusing and exciting at the same time, and Julie had dithered over what to say for an hour before finally resorting to writing it out. Getting his answering message was a curious letdown, but she read out her message and hung up.

And then lay awake for hours in case he called back.

At two in the morning, she put on her robe, completely disgusted with herself, and spent the rest of the night making detailed work lists for the remaining eleven days he'd be at

Haddonfield. She knew Bonnie would be suspicious that she'd planned so much outside work in the dead of winter, but she would rather freeze to death than risk making a fool of herself in front of him. Again.

Nerida jumped at the opportunity to continue running the gardens, and together they reviewed the multipage work list in Julie's office. "The alarm in my office will go off if the temperature in the glasshouse drops, and if it does—"

"—move the seedlings in here and get the bigger stuff into the hot frames," Nerida finished for her. "Relax, Julie, I can do this."

Julie ignored her and kept reading. "Make sure the carrots are watered twice a day and reseed the cut-and-come-again lettuce with the red bib seed I left out."

When they finished, Julie opened her desk drawer and withdrew a stack of papers. "Here's the corrected homework essays. Make sure everyone rewrites them tonight. We'll meet back here tomorrow evening for a study session."

Nerida shifted in the chair. "Julie, I've got to talk with you about that. We don't want you to tutor us no more."

"Anymore," Julie corrected. "Why ever not?"

"We've talked, all of us, and with half of us graduating in July, we know it's time we sink or swim on our own."

"Is Hugo putting you up to this?"

"No. It's what we want. Honestly, Julie, we love you and appreciate all you do for us, but we have to do this ourselves."

"You're sure? All right, I guess, it's only for another two weeks."

Nerida looked at her blankly. "Yeah. Two weeks. Then he's gone."

---

Her days off from work dragged. If Julie thought being around Hugo was torture, being away from him was doubly so. She made long lists of chores to keep herself occupied so she wouldn't give in to the urge to nip over to Haddonfield, ostensibly to pick up something she forgot or to just check in.

By Wednesday afternoon, she'd cleaned every inch of her house, talked with her parents, sorted her closet, and walked her landlady's dog five times. When her phone rang that morning, she dove for it, but it was only Mark calling from Amsterdam to say hello and fill her in on everything he was doing.

"Valentine's Day is Saturday," he added, "and there's a special treat planned. Dress warm, we'll be outside for most of it."

"Are we going to a garden?" Julie asked, anxious for a distraction.

Mark laughed uproariously. "Good heavens, no. And I can't say more—it's supposed to stay a secret, but I think it will be a day you won't forget for a long time."

That didn't sound encouraging. Julie tried to get more information out of him, but he was resolutely tight-lipped. She heard a sharp knock at the front door, so they said their goodbyes and Julie went to answer it.

Sophie stood on the front stoop huddled in a fur coat, smoking a cigarette, and tapping her foot.

"Sophie," Julie said after a moment, recovering from the surprise.

The girl took a drag of her cigarette and pointedly exhaled. "Jules."

Julie glanced to the street where a Range Rover was double-parked with Pippa Donnell at the wheel. "Care to come in?"

"No, thanks. Look. About what happened at Pip's party last weekend, with me and Hugo. It was a joke."

Julie eyed her warily. "How so?"

"Nothing happened." Seeing no recognition in Julie's expression, Sophie rolled her eyes. "In the loo, you moron, nothing happened. I came on to him and he told me to shove off."

"Oh."

"The truth is we're just friends." Sophie looked into the distance and wrinkled her nose. "Acquaintances, actually, if you look at it a certain way."

Julie could only stare at the girl in bemusement. Sophie was talking as if someone were holding a gun to her head.

"You're trying to decide if I'm telling the truth, aren't you? Well, I am. Hugo's never touched me. Bastard."

"Why are you telling me this?"

"Because Hugo's going to make my life a living hell if I don't come clean." Sophie stubbed out the cigarette and flicked it into the shrubs, enunciating each word as if she were speaking to a child. "It's you he's interested in, you daft git."

Julie gripped the doorknob behind her. "I'm with Mark."

Sophie gave her a pitying look. "Of course you are, love. So, are we square? Forgive and forget and all that?"

"Yes. Of course. Thank you for telling me."

"Right-o," Sophie called over her shoulder as she bolted down the path. "And you will tell Hugo I've been out?"

———— ◦ ————

Julie went back to work Thursday. The weather was beautiful, and she worked in the orchards, eating her lunch sitting on an old stump that offered a good view of the parking area.

Hugo arrived at noon, his Jaguar glinting in the sunshine. She stuffed the sandwich wrapper back in her pocket and returned to work, humming to herself.

Ian wandered through an hour later, announcing he wanted to take advantage of the nice weather and film more of the orchard.

"I thought you had class Thursday afternoons," Julie said as she stacked tree clippings on the hand wagon.

"We usually do but it was canceled. The professor is at a conference on international law or something," Ian said distastefully. "I say, are you always so busy in February?"

"Oh, yes," Julie replied quickly, "always. Did you come out with your brother?"

Ian glanced at the second-story window of Hugo's classroom. "No, I took the bus. I'm lying low. He's been acting very odd lately."

"He's not mad at you about the picture in the papers, is he? I called him and explained."

"No, not at all, and that's the remarkable thing. I thought he would have skinned me alive after he found out, but he was fine with it. Mostly wanted to know if you'd enjoyed yourself and did you get home safely. Didn't seem to give a fig that his, I mean my, face was in the paper. Like I said, damnably odd."

"It was just a small picture."

"Let me assure you, he's blown a gasket over much less. But the clincher was two nights ago at the scholarship fund raiser for Eton. He tore into Sophie Milkton-Sapp with a vengeance and made a terrible scene. Mummy was furious."

Julie's skin began to tingle. "What happened?"

"I'm not sure how it started, but he's never liked her, and I guess she pulled some stunt at Pippa's party that made him madder than hell. He chewed her out in front of everyone, called her every name in the book, even threatened to have her banned from Smith's Lawn. It's all anyone's talking about."

"What's Smith's Lawn?"

"Where the Guards play polo, for heaven's sake," Ian said in surprise. "I keep forgetting you're American. Anyway, that got her attention. Shocked he threatened it, though, but he wouldn't have if he couldn't follow it up. He's got tons of connections, so I wouldn't put it past him. In fact, the way he's been behaving lately, I wouldn't put anything past him. Something's got him tied up in knots."

# Chapter Thirty-Three

JULIE MET MARK Saturday afternoon at the Finchley train station, dressed in jeans, a sweater, and an overcoat—the only hint Mark had given her about his secret plans was to wear warm clothing. He greeted her with a hug and steered her to a train jammed with Arsenal fans kitted out in red and white, and Kingsbury Town fans who wore yellow and black, each keeping to separate sides of the aisle.

"Where are we going?" Julie asked.

"Can't you guess?"

"Kingsbury Town's FA Cup match?"

Mark's grin confirmed it. "Yes! Hugo got us the tickets but said it had to stay a secret. For some reason he thought you might not want to come."

Julie pressed her gloved hands together to keep them from shaking while Mark gave her arm a reassuring squeeze. "Come on, darling, it will be fun. And," he added slyly, "as a special treat, he threw in two passes for us to go up to the skybox for the party after the match. Valentine's Day doesn't get much better than that, does it?"

Emirates Stadium was overwhelming. As spectators thronged to fill the sixty thousand seats, Julie noted the grass was an unnatural neon green under lights that blazed from every angle. Mark was thrilled with their midfield seats, just twenty rows up from the pitch.

Julie began to feel pangs of anxiety for Hugo. These people were spending hundreds of pounds to watch him play—surely he was nervous about the match? Maybe his ego was justified. Anyone who would put themselves in front of all of these people must have a will of iron.

Arsenal took the field first and the crowd erupted in a deafening cheer. Kingsbury Town came on the pitch next, and the noise grew even louder, if that was possible. Hugo emerged from the tunnel about halfway through the lineup, his face an impassive mask, his body tough and lean in the form-fitting yellow and black kit. Julie frowned, noting very pretty women in the stands wearing replica number "9" jerseys with "Auchincloss" on the back.

As the teams warmed up, Mark pointed out the Kingsbury Town players. "That's Mick Carr, you'd know him from the tabloids, and Smith-Wessex used him for a sports drink campaign last year. Next to him is the captain, Darius Rutledge, and then Jason Edu and Fernando Garcia-Lopez. The midfielders are Hugo, Pozny Ostrowski, Jean-George Mayotte, and oh, hell, Dylan Rhea is in for Lars van der Beek again. Then up front is Marco Cantamessa and Samuel Lopuku."

"Who's the goalie?"

"They're called 'keepers,' darling. That's Brian Bathurst."

Mark pulled out his mobile phone and called someone to brag about where they were seated while Julie watched Hugo warm up. It might have been her imagination, but as the team met on the sideline, it looked like he scanned the stands and focused on her for a flash of a second.

Play started and Julie saw that Ian was right. Hugo was fast, perhaps the fastest player on the field. She watched in fascination as he blazed towards the ball and then retreated, darting forward and back, somehow seeming to know where the ball would be before it got there.

For a while the teams seemed to randomly pass the ball between them, with Kingsbury Town controlling it more than Arsenal. At the ten-minute mark, Arsenal was awarded a corner kick, and after some bobbing in front of the goal, a player sent it over the head of the Kingsbury Town keeper and into the net. The Arsenal fans launched into an incredibly bawdy celebration song that shocked Julie—there were children in the stands, after all.

Play resumed and she became engrossed in the game. It was much more physical than she would have imagined, with players stumbling, diving into the grass, or being tackled by other players. Twice Hugo had the ball and was dropped by an Arsenal defender, and once was awarded a corner kick. She became so engrossed in the game that when a whistle blew, she was surprised to learn it was already halftime.

"I'm sorry?" she blinked, realizing Mark was asking her a question.

"I said, would you like a cup of tea?"

"Oh, yes, please."

Mark patted his pockets and smiled sheepishly. "Rats. Did you bring any money? I only just realized I left my wallet at home."

Julie gave him some notes from her wallet and he scurried off. A longish scrap of yellow and black ribbon from someone's banner fell to the ground at her feet, and impulsively she picked it up and tied it in her ponytail.

Mark returned as the teams took the field, handed her the tea and, after some prompting, the change as well. The second half of the match began sluggishly, with both sides appearing to do nothing more than walk around and boot the ball back and forth between themselves. Julie chafed at the slow pace; surely Kingsbury Town was going to do something to even the score?

Minutes ticked by, and then, as if by an invisible signal, Kingsbury Town began pressing down the field with blistering speed. In an instant, she saw the play unfold as Hugo moved up and received a cross pass and dribbled, dodged, and flicked it into the open net at an impossible angle. The ball flew between the Arsenal keeper's outstretched hands and under the top of the goal with surgical precision. Julie leapt to her feet along with the rest of the crowd, her cheers lost in the deafening roar.

The Kingsbury Town fans broke into their own song, even bawdier than Arsenal's, as Hugo accepted pats on the back from his teammates. He jogged back to position, and this time there was no doubt that when he glanced into the stands, it was directly at her. Happiness washed over Julie as she stood clapping, immensely proud of him.

*It's you he's interested in, you daft git.*

Play resumed and Julie turned to Mark. "What kind of a cat does Pippa have?"

Mark, who was telling everyone around them that Hugo was a close personal friend of his, looked at her like she was mad. "How the hell should I know?"

There was no more scoring until the last three minutes of the game, when a Kingsbury Town player named Pozny Ostrowski lobbed a low side kick that caught the Arsenal keeper flat-footed. The Kingsbury Town supporters went crazy. Arsenal played in a frenzy for the additional two minutes of injury time, but Kingsbury Town held them off and ended up winning 2–1.

At the final whistle, Mark leapt to his feet and began to press through the throng of spectators, pulling her along. "Come on, darling, the party is in the Kingsbury Town skybox," he called over his shoulder. "They've never made it this far in FA Cup play. This will be a lark!"

Julie struggled to keep up with him. The players on the field exchanged jerseys and circled the field, thanking the spectators. Hugo stood, stripped naked to the waist, swapping shirts with an Arsenal player, a tattoo on his chest clearly visible. It was some kind of crest or shield. She remembered it from the night she'd gotten her hand caught in his desk drawer, and he had freed her.

Wearing only his towel. And kissing her wrist.

"Julie! Will you come on!"

⸻ ◆ ⸻

The skybox was packed, and Mark was in his element. Julie stood by his side as he began chatting with anyone and everyone, his outgoing personality attracting men and women alike. The mix of people was fascinating, and she heard a broad spectrum of accents and languages. The women were gorgeous and expensively made-up, their alert eyes reminding her of birds of prey.

Amid the hubbub, Julie found herself standing next to a glamorous woman with long black curls who looked her over critically.

"Where did you get those?" the woman asked, nodding towards her chest, and it took Julie a moment to realize she was referring to her breasts.

The team arrived in the skybox to wild applause, freshly showered and looking dashing in shiny suits and ties. A flame-haired woman with an Irish accent elbowed Julie out of the way, separating her from Mark in her eagerness to get closer to the players. As more people poured into the room, Julie retreated until she found herself by the elaborate buffet table set against a far wall.

A ruggedly handsome man reached across the table to pluck a strawberry from a bowl by her elbow. "Sorry, boardinghouse-reach, but can't help myself. I love strawberries."

"Don't apologize. Those are Buenavistas from Mexico, a real treat."

"That so?" Mick Carr said, cramming a handful in his mouth.

"They were developed to be resistant to Fusarium oxysporum," Julie chattered on, clutching her drink. "The cultivar produces a seventy-eight percent higher yield than Camarosa, which used to be the primary strawberry grown in Mexico's Central Plateau region."

His thick eyebrows rose fractionally. "You certainly know your strawberries."

"I grow them. Up on the Heath."

The man looked at her closely as if he were trying to place her face. "What, you have a little patch?"

"Close to half an acre. We grow Hapil and Symphony, although the soil is poor so we have to supplement with a high-potash fertilizer to encourage good fruiting," Julie heard herself babbling.

"So you're a farmer."

"Yes, I do the kitchen garden and orchards at the Haddonfield School in Hampstead."

The man's eyes coursed over her. "I have a farm as well, in Hertfordshire. There's an old apple orchard I'm having the devil's own time with."

"Really? Do you know what variety—"

"Carr," Hugo interrupted from behind them, "if you care to fill a plate, we can find someone to show you how to use utensils."

"Bugger off, Auchincloss, you're interrupting the lady," Mick Carr said darkly and then glanced at the two of them with a flash of recognition.

"Speaking of 'ladies,' Delia's lurking around the cloakroom," Hugo drawled.

A gleam lit in Mick Carr's eye and he moved off, leaving Julie alone with Hugo. He had changed into a tailored double-breasted suit that accentuated his broad shoulders and slim waist and wore his signature snowy white shirt with a black and yellow striped silk tie. The look was confident and aristocratic, and set him apart from his teammates, who looked and acted more like high-voltage rock stars.

"He was nice," Julie said, nodding in the direction Mick Carr had gone.

"Thick as a brick," Hugo grunted, helping himself to a wedge of cheese. Julie could see a nick on his chin that showed he'd just shaved and could smell his scent, the familiar blend of pepper and lavender and male.

"Did you enjoy the game?" Hugo asked with stiff formality.

"Yes, it was very exciting. Congratulations on your win." She glanced around the room, aware of how frumpy she looked in the sea of sophisticated people. A ponytail with a ribbon in it? For heaven's sake, she looked like a high school cheerleader. All she needed was a pair of pom-poms to complete the picture.

"Thank you, it was hard-earned. Do you realize you're the only woman here wearing Kingsbury Town colors?" He nodded to her hair ribbon. "Sir Frank pointed it out to me when we came in."

"Who's Sir Frank?"

Hugo pointed out a stout man in the middle of the room. "My boss, Sir Frank Poleski. He owns the team. And he doesn't miss much. Would you like to meet him? I'll introduce you."

She shook her head no, unconsciously shredding the paper cocktail napkin she held. "Another time. I mean, he's very busy with his guests." It was impossible to stand here chatting with him as if nothing had happened, and she struggled to find the words to begin to put things right. "Hugo, I want to apologize about the photo of Ian and me at Bash getting into the papers. I didn't think—"

Hugo took her arm. "Not here, it's too bloody crowded and my ears are ringing like bells. Come with me."

The observation balcony outside the suite overlooked a vast sea of empty red and white stadium seats. Hugo led her to a quiet spot at the end of the railing.

Resolutely she began again, "I'm very sorry about the photo —"

"I got your message. It's not a problem," he interrupted. "Ian's remarkably good at imitating me. I've actually sent him in front of the press a few times when I couldn't be bothered. Did it help? Did you have a good time?"

Julie shrugged. "It's hard not to have a good time around Ian."

Hugo snorted and waved a server over, selecting two canapés and handing one to her. "Yes, well, that's one of his problems. But his grades have been excellent this semester so I'm not too fussed."

"I also want to apologize for my behavior at Pippa's party," Julie continued doggedly.

"Damn it, Juliet, you are to take none of the blame—" he swore, but she shook her head.

"Sophie came to see me Wednesday and explained everything. She told me that nothing happened between you and her, and that it was just a game." Julie swallowed. "Your crowd plays a lot of games."

"They're not my crowd," he snapped, before getting control of himself. "I mean, I see everyone so infrequently. And I guess we're a bit dissolute when we let our hair down." He spoke as if the words were vinegar in his mouth.

"You're all a lot worldlier than I am, and I've got to learn not to take everything so seriously if I'm going to fit in," Julie said. "I told Mark what happened at the wedding, and he explained everything. He said it was to be expected, that you just took the opportunity to kiss a girl during a game. He said it's what your crowd does all the time and I shouldn't think anything of it."

Hugo brushed the canapé crumbs from his fingers and then, with exaggerated patience, placed his hands on the railing on either side of Julie, effectively trapping her. "I have never heard such a load of rubbish in my life," he began with deliberate calmness. "Now, you are to stop talking immediately. If you do not stop talking, I will clap this hand over your mouth—" he lifted his right hand to show her "—and use the other to hold you still until you've listened to everything I have to say."

He stared into her wide eyes, and she could see he was completely serious.

"I won't give a damn what anyone would say or do," he continued conversationally. "In fact, I think my teammates would rather enjoy the spectacle. So if you agree, nod your head."

Julie nodded, a warm shiver rippling down her spine.

"Good. First, your habit of taking personal responsibility for everything is very refreshing but entirely misplaced. My behavior has been unbelievably boorish, and it's me that's going to be doing the apologizing." He reached to tenderly tuck a stray hair behind her ear, his hand brushing against her cheek. "I was a lout to point out I knew it was you I kissed in the basement at the wedding, where my behavior was equally atrocious. You behaved exactly as a lady should by ignoring it. Telling you that I knew was rude and unbelievably crass.

"My only excuse," he continued, "is that you are very beautiful, and that has clouded my judgment on more than one occasion. But I don't want you to worry that I'll step out of line again. I've learned my lesson, which is that you are a lady and deserve to be treated as such. And from now on I will act as a complete gentleman."

Julie felt a faint pang of disappointment but nodded.

"Now," he said as he reached into his suit coat and took out a narrow, gift-wrapped box, "to show that I am truly repentant, I have a small gift for you."

She shook her head. "Hugo, I don't want anything from you —"

Swiftly pressing his index finger over her lips, he put the slim box into her hands. Seeing it was pointless to do otherwise, she opened the small card that was tucked into the ribbon. There was a simple red rose painted on it and a note written in his strong, slanted writing.

*The quality of mercy is not strain'd,*
*It droppeth as the gentle rain from heaven*
*Upon the place beneath. It is twice blest:*
*It blesseth her that gives and him that takes.*
*Have mercy on me.*
*Hugo*

She looked up at him and he took his finger off her lips. "*Merchant of Venice,*" she said, and with shaking hands untied the pretty red ribbon and pink paper. It was a bracelet box with the name of a jeweler embossed in gold above a coat of arms, and inside was a row of ten roughly-round green spheres on a bed of velvet.

"Pea seeds?"

Reaching inside his coat pocket, Hugo pulled out a thin envelope stamped Heritage Seed Library. "They came in this."

Julie's eyes widened, and she snatched the paper from his hands. "From the Heritage? What kind of peas are they?"

"Special peas. You have to guess."

She mentally ran through a list of heirloom and old-fashioned peas she knew the Heritage had in their collection. "Champion of England?"

"It seemed appropriate." Hugo grinned with a touch of arrogance.

"These are terrifically rare. They were bred in the 1840s and were very popular with the Victorians, but they haven't been available for almost a century," she exclaimed. "How did you get them? The Heritage makes it almost impossible."

Hugo chuckled. "That's an understatement. They acted like I was asking to borrow the crown jewels. They only agreed when they found out the seeds were going to you."

"They know who I am?"

"You have an excellent reputation," he nodded, watching her as she examined each seed. "So am I forgiven?"

"Yes, of course." The urge to pull his head down to hers and kiss him was overwhelming, but she forced herself to concentrate on the seeds. "Did you know that the grower in Kent who bred this pea used to correspond with Darwin?"

"No, I didn't," he laughed. "What did Looks get you for Valentine's Day?"

"That's rather personal," Julie parried, not wanting to admit it was a photograph of himself.

"Hey, Hugo, Sir Frank needs some help," a player interrupted. "He's trying to talk to some French bloke and can't understand a word."

Hugo reluctantly excused himself, and Julie leaned back on the railing, clutching the box to her heart.

# Chapter Thirty-Four

A MOMENT LATER, Mick Carr slid smoothly into the place on the rail Hugo had just vacated. "About time he shoved off," he said, giving her a dazzling smile and extending his hand. "I'm Mick Carr, by the way. Auchincloss needs to work on his manners. And who might you be?"

Julie shook Mick's hand. "Julie Randall."

"Now about my orchard. I just bought the farm adjoining mine, and it's got easily five acres in apples, but they've been left to run. And they taste disgusting."

"Where did you say it was?"

"Hertfordshire, near Tansbury."

"You said they taste bad? Are they astringent?" At his blank look, she added, "Are they bitter, sour, acid?"

"I'll say. I think I was sold a bill of goods on that, they're awful. Chap I bought it from thought they might be Black Kings."

"Kingston Blacks?"

"Yes. Exactly. That's what he said."

"Well, that's wonderful! You've got bitter-sharp cider trees. Kingston Blacks were popular all over the south of England for more than eighty years, and they're definitely not for eating.

Hertfordshire isn't really known for large-scale cider production, but many old farms ran cider orchards and pressed their own. They're one of the few cider apples that don't have to be blended, but they're very temperamental and actually do better in New York State where I went to school."

Mick studied her intently. "Would you have dinner with me tomorrow night?"

Hugo reappeared at that moment, escorting the stunning woman with black curly hair Julie had met earlier. "Seems Fanta lost you for a moment, Carr," he said, clapping Mick on the shoulder with a bit more force than was necessary.

Frowning, Mick shifted away from Julie and introduced her to Fanta de las Mercedes. Mark appeared as well, holding her coat, and it was Hugo's turn to introduce him to Mick and Fanta.

"What you've got there?" Fanta asked, examining the bracelet box Julie was holding. "Ooooh, something from Malbrey's?"

"Very rare pea seeds," Julie began to explain, opening the box and showing it to everyone. "They're called Champion of England, and are a strain of *Pisum sativum* that was—"

"Julie, don't be a bore, nobody wants to hear about your stupid seeds," Mark said grandly. He then pointed to an older couple standing near the door of the skybox and began to help her into her coat. "Darling, the Joneses live on the Heath and have offered you a ride home, isn't that lovely?"

"I can give you a lift home," Hugo offered, but Mark brushed him off and began to propel Julie towards the door.

"Are you kidding? You're going to want to stay here and enjoy the party after a match like that!" Mark said.

"It was a pleasure to meet you, Julie. We'll be talking again," Mick called after her, sending a withering glance at Hugo. "Soon."

Julie followed Mark as he led her towards the rather mystified-looking couple. "So you and Hugo have made up? He got you a nice treat and he's back in your good graces, then?" he asked.

"Yes," Julie said, annoyed by his crassness.

"Good show, old girl, I knew you wouldn't be one to hold a grudge. Though he could have done better than old pea seeds."

---

Hugo watched Looks drag Juliet off towards the door, the bracelet box still clutched in her hand. Bless Tom, it seemed to be working.

So Sophie had hoofed it out to Finchley, fessed up, and done a damn good job of convincing Julie nothing had happened. The stupid cow probably would have sworn the moon was made of green cheese if she thought it would keep her on the list at Smith's Lawn.

"Who the hell is that git?" Mick asked, nodding towards Looks.

"Her boyfriend."

"Wanker," Mick scoffed. "I'll make short work of him."

"Don't go near her, Carr," Hugo warned.

His teammate glanced at him, a predatory gleam in his blue eyes. "Fancy her yourself? She seemed to warm to me fast enough."

"She's kind to animals. I'm serious, Carr. You've made enough nuisance of yourself. Try it again and I'll make sure you regret it."

"It's worth trying just to see what you can dish out, Auchincloss," Mick chortled, and Hugo's hand rapidly began to curl into a tight fist.

"Lads!" Darius stepped between them. "Time to talk love to the sponsors."

---

The party was winding down when Mark sidled up to Hugo, who was talking with a group of French cement contractors.

"Thanks for the tickets, old man. Sorry you wasted one on Julie—she barely paid any attention to the game." Ignoring Hugo's carefully blank expression he continued, "We're doing a photo shoot Tuesday at Cheeting Park. Care to come along?"

"Cheeting Park, that's in Richmond, isn't it?" Hugo put off answering, mentally casting for a suitable excuse.

Mark nodded. "We're taking the entire house, staying overnight. It should be fun." Not seeing much interest from Hugo, he added, "Julie's coming along as well. She's insisting on meeting Rochelle. But she'll get bored quickly. Maybe you can keep her entertained."

Hugo immediately switched to feigned indifference. "I'll have to check the practice schedule. I'll let you know."

"Whatever you decide." Mark shrugged and winked at the blonde he'd been chatting up since he'd gotten rid of Julie. "Shall I send her your way when I'm done?" he asked slyly.

Hugo smiled. "No, thanks. I've got my eye on something else."

# Chapter Thirty-Five

HUGO'S TAILOR, WHO had been his father's tailor and his father's before him, prided himself on his extensive selection of shirting fabric. Customers could choose from over five hundred bolts of every color and pattern imaginable, but Hugo ordered only white shirts, preferably with French cuffs, although barrel cuffs were acceptable, and traditional turndown collars, but never those faddish spread collars Ian favored. He had a decided fondness for Egyptian cotton, but also liked linen and broadcloth, and had even experimented with poplin twill. The jury was still out on those.

A few years ago, Hugo had given in to Ian's nagging and let him pick out a fashionable striped pattern, but it made him look like a bloody zebra and he wore it only once before donating it to charity. So, as Hugo dressed for the dinner at Haddonfield Monday evening, he couldn't help but wonder if Juliet would appreciate what a radical sartorial departure the French blue shirt he pulled on was.

He buttoned it and stood before the mirror, looking himself over critically. It wasn't too bad, he decided, pleased he'd had two made up in the electric shade of blue. Brian Bathurst, the team's goalkeeper, wore one the other day and looked quite handsome in it. As a rule, Hugo considered his teammates' getups to be one step above gangster, but Brian's wife, Connie, had very good taste and Hugo wanted to take the risk.

Grabbing his herringbone tweed jacket, he leapt down the stairs two at a time and revved the Jag to pick up Ian. Twenty minutes later, Hugo pulled up to the curb and waited impatiently for his brother, who stood in the doorway of his Covent Garden flat, refusing to move. "What are you waiting for?"

Ian eyed him warily. "Mummy says not to get into cars with strangers."

"Shut up and get in the bloody car, Ian." Hugo grinned despite himself.

"So it's that serious," Ian mused as they drove north, a beatific smile on his face.

"It's just a shirt."

"How are you going to get rid of Looks?"

"I'm going to throw him out of a car at high speed, but I need some practice to make it look like an accident."

Ian couldn't stop grinning.

"You obviously approve," Hugo said.

"God, yes. But I'm damned intrigued how you're going to get her. This should be interesting."

---

The preparations for Monday evening's dinner service were in full swing. Julie waited until no one was watching before sneaking up the back stairs to the second-floor ladies' bathroom. Inside, she checked her hair and outfit in front of the full-length mirror, carefully inspecting the V-necked blue sweater for any spots or lint.

It was only natural, she reasoned, to be excited to see Hugo this evening. Things were different now; it was out in the open that they'd kissed and that there was a mutual physical attraction. They both agreed that nothing was going to come of it, and Mark knew about it and he didn't hold it against her. Hugo promised to be a gentleman and things were back on track. They could be friends, and that was what she wanted.

She dabbed on some light-colored lip gloss and adjusted her bra so that her cleavage was slightly more accentuated, then turned off the light and skipped down the hall.

Hugo and Ian were already seated at the staff table when she arrived. She noticed immediately that Hugo was wearing the most beautiful blue shirt she'd ever seen. Her favorite color.

"I put another hundred-pound note in the box, but then gave myself a proper scolding to save you the trouble," he quipped for her ears alone as he held the chair for her.

Don was telling everyone about a restaurant in Northfleet that was interested in taking some students as interns, and they chatted amiably as the soup was served, followed by the entrée of cider-braised cabbage and sausage.

"I had a nice visit from your teammate this morning," Julie told Hugo as she passed him the breadbasket.

"My teammate?"

"Yes, Mick. Mick Carr. He came out to see the orchard."

Hugo's expression became dangerously icy. "What did he want?"

"He has a farm in Hertfordshire with a grove of cider apple trees, and he wanted some advice. It sounds like it's been left to run, but properly managed he could probably get five to six hundred bushels a year to press a hundred hogsheads of cider. That's ambitious, of course."

"I meant," Hugo ground out, "what did he want from you?"

Julie was taken aback by the venom in his voice. "He asked me to go out to his farm with him on Sunday to look his orchards over and see what's salvageable."

"That's not all he wants."

"You're probably right," Julie agreed. "If he gets into replanting, he'll need help picking out good rootstock."

"For the love of God, woman, are you blind?" Hugo exploded. "He couldn't care less about his frigging apple trees!"

Julie drew back, astonished at his temper. "But he has Kingston Blacks."

"He's also got a dick that does all the thinking for him. He's a pig, Juliet."

"You're wrong, Hugo. He was here the entire morning and was a complete gentleman. He was even happy to sign autographs and stand for pictures with the students, which not all players do," she added. "He told me you're very critical of him because he dropped out of school."

With a swift motion, Hugo threw his napkin on the table and stalked out of the dining room.

Ian watched his brother storm out of the room and looked at Julie in slack-jawed surprise. "I say, what's gotten into him?"

"I have no idea. I was just telling him that Mick Carr came out today to see the orchards, and he went off the deep end."

Ian digested this bit of information while the conversation in the dining room returned to normal. "I assume you know about Hugo's old girlfriend, Trika?" he murmured, and Julie nodded. "Mick Carr was the one she was caught with."

Julie covered her mouth. "Oh, no."

Ian nodded. "It was an awful mess. I don't know how he's continued to play on the same team as Mick."

"Was Hugo in love with her?"

"It seemed that way at the time, though I doubt it would have lasted. She was spinning out of control, and getting married wasn't likely to stop it. Mick and Hugo have been at each other's throats ever since."

Julie folded her napkin on the table and slipped away at the first opportune moment. She found Hugo pacing in the garden, his agitation clear. It had started to rain, but he didn't seem to notice, and she approached him cautiously, unsure of his mood.

"Come on," she urged, "let's go to my office. It's freezing out here."

Once inside, he sat on the wooden bench while she prodded the woodstove fire. It jumped to life, bathing the room in warm light. Taking a thick towel from the closet, she began to dry his hair, luxuriating in the feel of it in her fingers.

The rain began in earnest and beat a steady rhythm against the window. He closed his eyes and pressed his forehead against her midriff.

"So, Ian just clued me in. I'm sorry, I didn't know," she said as she massaged his scalp.

A string of oaths erupted from Hugo's mouth, but she covered it with her hand. "Hush. I'm glad he told me."

Hugo looked at her, his expression tortured. "You're not going to see Mick again."

"No. Of course I won't," she assured him, smoothing his brow with her hand. "I'll put him in contact with an agricultural agent I know in that area who can look his orchards over, and I can give him the names of the nurseries where I get my rootstock. That should be all right, don't you think?"

"More than adequate. Keep drying," he demanded, and warm currents tingled through her as his nose began to tenderly nuzzle her stomach. Somehow he was edging the hem of her sweater up above the waistband of her trousers, and his lips were just fractions of an inch from the skin of her stomach, and he might—

A piece of firewood crashed audibly in the stove, snapping her back to reality. With tremendous willpower, Julie pulled away and stepped around the stove to hang the damp towel on a drying hook.

"Was Trika your first love?" she couldn't stop herself from asking as she smoothed her sweater down and turned on two lights for good measure.

Hugo sat back on the bench and crossed his legs. "I thought so at the time. We began dating just after I signed with Kingsbury Town. The team started climbing in the leagues, and we quickly became the hottest ticket in town. Trika loved that and all that went with it. You know all those people from Pippa's party? They were her crowd. Lots of energy, always running to the next party. It was fun for a while, and then the parties got bigger, louder, and much wilder. She liked seeing her face in the papers the next morning and started to get a taste for a very expensive lifestyle."

Julie sat next to him on the bench. "Were you living together?"

"No, I was still living at home. Miles was doing a stint in the Royal Marines, and I was trying to manage the farms, so I commuted to Hendon and Townsend Lane Stadium. She and some girls from school got a place in Kensington, and I visited when I could, but the team and Wrothesley took all my time. Most nights I was sitting in an ice bath, paying bills and scheduling harvesters, so she started going out without me.

"That went on for over a year, and then Ian started getting into serious trouble and needed me. I admit, she did have a case that I was neglecting her, but honestly, I felt like I was being pulled in every direction at once."

As she listened to Hugo talk, Julie felt irritation well up inside her. "She should have helped you. She should have taken an interest in Wrothesley and lightened your load."

Hugo shrugged. "It wasn't her fault. We were both young, and everything hit all at once. Kingsbury Town's success, Wrothesley needing me, Ian needing me. She was just looking to live life and have fun. We really should have parted ways then, but unfortunately she didn't want to give up her position as a WAG."

Julie blinked. "What's a WAG?"

"Wives and girlfriends. It's what the tabloids call the women around footballers."

Julie frowned. "You mean those women that were in the skybox Saturday night. They're gorgeous."

"They're trouble. A paparazzi caught her coming out of Mick's hotel room. They both swore it was the only time, but then it came out that there were other footballers, not from Kingsbury Town but other clubs, and that everyone knew. It was all over the papers. I'm sure Tom has a file an inch thick. There was a lot of drama."

"What happened then?"

"After I dropped her, no one would touch her. She came to see me, said she loved me and was sorry, and wanted to get back together again. Bit late by that point, and I told her to shove off. She went to Australia for holiday and never came back."

"People knew and didn't tell you?" Julie asked in disbelief, her heart breaking for him. "That's terrible. Do you wish they had?"

"Of course. Would have saved me a boatload of embarrassment and publicity. Last thing anyone wants is for their love life to play out in public. There's no worse death, let me tell you, and I never want to go through it again."

"What she did was horrible. Being betrayed by someone you love, and then to have it be so public. No one deserves that," Julie said, gripping his hand in hers. "I'm glad I never met her. I wouldn't have liked her. You'd just lost your father, you were trying to be a father to Ian, and still hold down a huge job. She should have stood by you, taken care of you, made sure that you knew she was there. You're much better off without her. You know that, don't you?"

He looked down at her slim hand in his, his expression unreadable. "I know it now. At the time, it was pretty awful. But I can see very clearly that it was the second-best thing that ever happened to me."

"What was the best?"

"Meeting you."

The fire crackled quietly in the stove as Hugo's thumb slowly traced a pattern on her palm. Julie stared at it, the soft pressure hypnotizing.

"In the basement, at the wedding, how did you know it was me?" he asked.

"I felt your ring on my face. And then I smelled your scent."

"I don't wear scent."

"Your shaving soap. It's like pepper and lavender and... other things. It's nice."

Slowly, giving her every chance to pull away, Hugo brought her palm to his lips and pressed a tender kiss to it. She watched spellbound as his lips moved to the sensitive skin of her wrist and then pushed the sleeve of her sweater slowly up her arm, his warm breath fanning her skin.

"Someone might come in," Julie whispered, her pulse jumping wildly as his lips burned a sensuous trail towards her elbow.

"Lock the door," Hugo murmured.

"I thought you were going to be a gentleman."

"Please lock the door," he corrected himself, and with a deep sigh, reluctantly surrendered her hand. "Sorry. I usually have more control than that."

She pulled her hand back and changed the subject. "Did Mark invite you to the photo shoot at Cheeting Park tomorrow? I think he was planning to."

"He mentioned it. Rochelle is going to be there, isn't she?"

Julie nodded. "I'm meeting her for the first time. Have you ever met her?"

"Once. Are you having second thoughts?"

She pressed her lips together for some moments as she grappled with the question. "I said I wanted to, but now I'm not so sure."

"Would it help if I were there?"

Julie slumped against the bench in relief. "It would."

It was time to return to the dining room. Before they left her office, Julie paused, placing a hand on his arm. "Hugo, I appreciate you telling me about Mick and protecting my relationship with Mark. You're right, I am naive and might have gotten myself into a situation I couldn't get out of. Thank you. You're a good friend."

He considered her for a long time. "I don't want to be your friend, Juliet."

# Chapter Thirty-Six

HUGO ARRIVED AT Juliet's house the next day promptly at noon. After repeated knocks, she finally opened the door and stood before him barefoot and more flustered than he'd ever seen her.

It was obvious she was in the midst of a huge dilemma over what to wear. She'd paired a flowered blouse with a plaid skirt and held two jackets, one pinstriped and the other crocheted.

"I'm sorry, I didn't hear you knock," she apologized as she led him into her small sitting room. "I've got to finish dressing. I'll just be a moment."

When she was safely back upstairs, he rifled through the contents of her desk, invading her privacy without a shred of remorse. There was a renewal notice for a crop journal, two pay stubs, a coupon for hand cream, and a bank statement that showed she paid an absurd amount of rent for the tiny house.

A letter tucked at the bottom of a stack caught his eye. It was a job offer from an American agricultural company. He read the details closely—they wanted to start a demonstration garden on their corporate campus. She would have a staff of five, a considerable budget, two greenhouses. Hugo read to the end, his agitation growing with each sentence. The salary offer was five times what he'd just learned she was making at Haddonfield, plus generous benefits. *Bloody hell.*

Hearing her footsteps on the stairs, he replaced the letter and was leafing through a copy of *Hamlet* when she reappeared.

"Ready," Julie announced, out of breath.

Hugo heartily approved of her final decision, a simple, high-waisted brown skirt and linen blouse with trim heels. She wore her hair down and looked fresh and natural—the exact opposite of Rochelle Chevelle.

As he helped her into her coat, she stopped and darted back up the steps. "Forgot my bag," she called over her shoulder and returned a moment later with an overnight case. "Mark said they're taking the entire hotel and we're staying over. Together," she added.

Separate rooms no doubt, Hugo thought cheerfully.

On the drive to Richmond, Julie stared out the window. "You're very quiet," he observed. "Is it the company?"

"I suppose I'm a bit nervous. You said you met Rochelle once. Where was that?"

"In Monte Carlo a few summers ago. We sailed in and she was with a party on another boat."

"What was she like?"

"The boat? Eighteen-meter racing yacht, cruising speed eight knots, bit of a pig to steer in tight quarters but lovely on the open water."

Julie glared at him in amused exasperation and Hugo grinned—at least he'd gotten her to smile. The idea that Juliet was afraid of meeting Rochelle was preposterous. What was Rochelle like? Self-centered, he wanted to say. Vain. Nasty to everyone. One of the ugliest people he'd ever met.

"She has terrible skin," Hugo said instead. "And the worst breath I've ever encountered in a woman."

"Oh, so you... got to know her."

"For about five minutes," Hugo said, repulsed at her implication. "I went to the dock to clear customs and then I found a wonderful old bookstore and spent the afternoon there. When I got back to the boat, she was gone but had dropped a cigarette on a deck cushion and burned a hole in it."

"Really?"

"Yes, really. Ivar said he thought Angela was going to smack her. And then after we pushed off, it was discovered she'd pinched a silver teaspoon."

That seemed to cheer Julie up a bit.

———◆◇◆———

Cheeting House was a boutique hotel nestled in a landscaped park in the Borough of Richmond. From the outside, it looked like a centuries-old Elizabethan mansion, but in reality was built in 1909 and turned into an exclusive accommodation ten years ago.

A valet met them and took the Jaguar, and together Hugo and Julie walked into the marbled foyer. "They're set up in the main drawing room," said the efficient woman who greeted them, pointing down a long corridor. "We'll have your bag sent up to your room, number twelve."

"Which room is Mr. Brooks in?" Julie asked, and Hugo listened attentively for the answer.

The woman glanced at the list and Hugo detected a slight pause. "He's in number twenty-two. The bachelor's wing." She made a game attempt at a wink and was saved by a ringing phone.

Hugo supposed they were on their own to find the main drawing room. They wandered through empty halls littered with furniture, boxes, and large cases of photography equipment. The place was deserted and everything eerily quiet.

The dining room had been set up as a temporary dressing room and held racks of colorful gowns hung on rolling carts, while a hairdressing chair sat empty in front of a full-length mirror and trunk of makeup.

"From the way Mark described it, I thought the place would be a beehive of activity," Julie murmured, looking around.

Towards the back of the house, they found a large reception room that was obviously being used as the set. Dozens of industrial-sized lights were directed at a magnificent fireplace, flanked by a grouping of chintz sofas and tufted chairs with needlepoint pillows. Thick oriental carpets, mahogany end tables stacked with silver-framed photographs, and distressed antiques and leather-bound books completed the setting.

"Mark said they had to fly decorators in from New York to make it look like an authentic British country house," Julie told Hugo in a hushed voice. "The London decorators just couldn't get it right."

Hugo studied the scene. "They missed one thing. There's not a wet Labrador in sight."

Julie laughed, her blue eyes dancing. Once again, his breath caught in his throat.

A nearly empty bottle of Bajan Gin sat on a side table. While Juliet wandered around the room, Hugo took a clean glass and poured a healthy shot. He sniffed the murky, peach-colored liquid and took a small sip, and immediately spat it into a potted palm. The noxious stuff tasted like a combination of juniper, pine tar, and cough syrup.

Hugo heard voices on the patio and followed Julie outside to where two production assistants lounged on deck chairs, smoking. They laughed when Julie asked where everyone was.

"Who knows? It was a bloody zoo all morning. First Rochelle was sick and arrived late, and none of the costumes fit her, and then she stormed out before noon. Brooks went after her, and we've been cooling our heels ever since."

Julie glanced at Hugo uncertainly.

"You can't mean they shut down the entire shoot?" Hugo asked, hoping for the worst.

"They certainly did. Then he got into the sample gin they sent out." The other assistant jerked her head to where a male model was passed out on a chaise lounge. The man reeked of stale cigarette smoke and sweat, and even Hugo, who was used to the close company of unclean men, was repulsed.

"Are they coming back?" Julie asked.

"Who knows?" The girl shrugged and took a long draw of her cigarette, then exhaled a cloud of blue smoke. "We're not too fussed. We're on the clock."

"Julia!" A distinguished grey-haired man called from the door and walked towards them, his relief evident. Julie introduced Hugo, and the men shook hands with stiff courtesy.

"Thank the Lord you are here," the man, Ramon Sanchez, continued in heavily accented English. "This is costing thousands of euros an hour. No model! Brooks leave as well!"

"*Mantén la calma*. Mark went to go bring Rochelle back," Julie tried to calm him. "He'll bring her back."

"No! Rochelle walk out for the last time, we are done with her. I say no more of these sticks! My customers do not want to see this skeleton. I want a new girl, one who is fresh and pretty." His eyes narrowed, and his lips curled into a cunning smile. "I want you, Julia."

Hugo frowned. "Juliet's not a model."

Ramon recognized the protective tone in Hugo's voice and paused to reevaluate him. "No, that is the wonderful part. Julia is so beautiful, but so natural. There is no, no..."

"Artifice," Hugo provided, frowning.

"*Sí!* No artifice about her. My customers want to see her," Ramon announced with absolute certainty. "And we pay."

"I don't want your money," Julie said, mortified.

"Then we make donation to your school," Ramon said craftily, and quoted an amount that Hugo knew was easily a third of what Haddonfield got in funding in one year. He felt Julie rock against him and put a hand to her back to steady her.

She licked her lips. "What would I have to do?"

"They dress you up like princess, they take pictures," Ramon said with a twinkle in his eye. "Will be fun, you'll see."

"Would I have to do it with that man?"

Ramon glanced to where the male model was now snoring. "He can be brought around."

Julie paled, and Hugo felt her begin to tremble.

"Juliet, this is nothing to jump into." Hugo tightened his grip around her waist and glared at the Spaniard. "Terms of the contract need to be negotiated, and your interests have to be protected. We should call Tom."

Ramon hung his head in a pantomime of shame. "Julia, I am embarrassed. Hugo is correct. Please to forgive me, this is too much to ask of you. This is all Brooks's fault. I call his boss."

Hugo saw the look of panic in Juliet's eyes and had to hand it to Ramon; he knew exactly which of Juliet's buttons to push.

"Excuse us a moment, Ramon," he said and pulled her a few steps away.

Once they were out of hearing range, Hugo turned Julie towards him. "This is Looks's mess. Let him deal with it."

Julie shook her head, clearly vexed. "Ramon is on the verge of having Mark fired. I have to do something."

From behind her, the male model staggered to his feet and dove for the patio railing, where he began retching violently.

"I'll call him." Julie fumbled in her bag for her mobile and tried several numbers, all with no answer. She left a message on each. "He's not picking up. I have to do it."

"Then I'm doing it with you," Hugo said.

"Are you crazy? It's for an advertisement, why would you do it?"

"I figure I owe Looks. I tried to steal his girl." Hugo caught Julie's hands in his own and smiled down at her. "Come on, it'll be fun."

The male model made more gagging sounds behind them. "All right, then," Julie agreed and followed Hugo back to where Ramon waited.

"We'll do it together," Hugo announced. "Triple the fee and it all goes to Haddonfield. One-time run, no appearances, no interviews. You can work the deal with my agent for both of us later, and when he's happy we'll sign the model releases."

A smile broke out on Ramon's face and he clapped his hands in delight. "Done! Please to get the dressers!"

# Chapter Thirty-Seven

AT RAMON'S WORDS, everyone jumped to life. The rest of the crew was summoned and the photographer, a sun-bronzed Australian introduced as Pierce, assessed Hugo and Julie.

"Blue one first," he announced, and two women dressed in identical black outfits took Julie to the makeshift dressing room while another led Hugo in the opposite direction.

A male stylist began to fuss with her hair while his assistant plugged hot rollers and curling irons into an industrial-sized power outlet.

"Strip," one dresser told her while the other held a measuring tape against different parts of her body.

Julie crossed her arms and nodded at the stylist. "I am not undressing in front of that man."

"I've seen it all before, love," the stylist assured her, but nothing would convince Julie to undress.

Heated words were being tossed back and forth when Hugo appeared in the doorway, naked from the waist up. "What's the problem?"

Julie slid next to him and eyed the stylist warily. "They want me to undress in front of him."

Hugo slipped a reassuring arm around her and frowned pointedly at the man. "How about you give her a moment?" he suggested. The stylist stomped out, and Hugo stood waiting expectantly.

"I'm not undressing in front of you either," Julie added.

"Can't blame a chap for trying." He winked and left.

After Julie shed her clothing, the dressers continued measuring while a girl brushed body-colored paint on her arms, chest, and neck.

"It smooths out all the colors in your skin, makes it easier for the retouching later," she explained. "Although yours is lovely. You're really healthy."

When she was done, they wrapped her in a thin robe, and the stylist returned to dress her hair.

"Who does your color?" he asked, yanking a comb through it.

"No one."

"You do it yourself?" he whispered in awe.

"No. I don't color my hair. This is its natural color."

He expertly fingered a piece and whistled under his breath. "I'll be damned. So it is."

As he curled and sprayed, Julie watched the dressers grab a strapless, sapphire-blue ball gown from the rack and attack it with scissors. They worked with brisk efficiency on what seemed like miles of satin, ripping seams and pulling out padding, deconstructing and then reassembling the dress in less than ten minutes.

The makeup artist came next. She worked fast and then handed Julie a mirror. "Done."

Julie looked at her reflection and was shocked at the transformation. A sophisticated and glamorous woman with sultry blue eyes and thick black lashes stared back, her coral lips full and perfect. The stylist had piled her hair in luxurious curls that tumbled down her back, with a few delicate wisps curling at the nape of her neck. It looked incredibly sensuous and she lifted her hand to feel it.

"Don't touch!" the stylist snapped.

The hair and makeup people departed, and the dressers helped Julie into the gown. They muttered to themselves as they laced up the corset back, and Julie stood awkwardly under their intent appraisal.

"Bloody hell," one said, using both hands to squish Julie's breasts together while the other yanked the laces tighter. "Turn."

Julie obediently moved around.

Both women frowned. "No good," said one. "They're all over the place. What do we do?"

"Blowed if I know," said the other. "I've only ever dealt with implants and they go right where they're supposed to."

"What's the matter?" Julie asked.

"Your boobs, they're too big. They have to go forward or you'll end up looking like you've had pillows stuffed down your front. Best go get Maggie."

An older woman materialized and assessed the situation. She repeated the squeezing and tightening, but to no avail. "Lucky for you lot I used to do costuming at the Royal Opera. It's been years since I've worked with the real thing, and there's only one solution. Tape."

Julie raised her arms over her head, and the women stripped off the gown and wrapped wide strips of duct tape under her breasts, drawing them together.

"Ow!" Julie complained, but was ignored.

When they finished, the gown was lowered back on. Her reflection in the full-length mirror showed a perfect silhouette with a deep valley of cleavage. But she could barely breathe.

The dressers draped a pendulous diamond necklace around her neck. "Is it real?" Julie asked.

"Ha! With Rochelle Chevelle supposed to be here? They'd need an armed guard. It's a fake—things tend to disappear when she's around. You're good to go!"

———◈———

In the main lounge, spotlights were blazing and the fire roaring. Hugo stood impatiently, already beginning to sweat in the tuxedo they'd sewn him into. The damn woman had left some pins where she'd let the shoulders out, and they were jabbing him unmercifully. He wore his own watch and cuff links. The diamond ones the stylist wanted were for bloody pansies. They had also smeared him with that greasy paint they liked to use, and it was beginning to run as he perspired in the heat. Plus, it made him look like a cadaver.

The stylist had also insisted on leaving the bow tie undone, explaining that the scene was supposed to be after a party, when he and Juliet would be relaxing and having a drink in the drawing room of their stately mansion. Which seemed odd—he wouldn't dream of being in a formal drawing room with an untied bow tie. It just wasn't done.

The male model had been removed, he supposed, to an upstairs bedroom to sober up. Hugo fidgeted as the photographer and his assistant moved lights and read meters, remembering exactly why he was violently opposed to doing this.

And then suddenly his heart stopped.

Juliet appeared in the doorway, looking like she had stepped out of his dreams. Her hair was swept up, with a luxurious cascade of curls falling down her back, revealing the long column of her throat. Her shoulders were creamy smooth, and he was overwhelmed by the urge to sink his lips into the tender flesh.

They had transformed her figure, which was stunning to begin with, into something close to perfection. The gown revealed her swelling breasts and the deep valley between them and then tapered to her narrow waist before flaring over her hips. A glittering diamond necklace, obviously a fake but magnificent nonetheless, circled her neck just above the generous swell of cleavage.

The effect she had on him was intoxicating. Thank God his jacket was cut longer and partially hid the protruding bulge she conjured.

She paused, holding her ballooning skirts aloft as if unsure of how to maneuver through the tangle of wires and equipment. He adjusted himself with a discreet motion and was at her side in an instant, offering her his arm.

"I say. You look gorgeous," he said.

"So do you." She clutched his arm as she tottered on high heels that made her almost as tall as he was. "I see we got the same makeup person."

"Ah, Julia!" Ramon came forward and kissed her hand, very pleased with himself. "You are *perfección*. We are ready to start."

The stylist arranged them in front of the fireplace while the photographer's assistant lined up a selection of cameras on a table. Pierce grabbed one and took a few shots to test the lighting, and then he and Ramon reviewed the shots on the laptop computer. More people drifted to the computer and began making contradictory suggestions, occasionally glancing to where Hugo and Juliet stood waiting. In all, Hugo counted nine people in the room, not including him and Juliet.

A prop girl repositioned the almost empty bottle of Bajan Gin on a side table and handed them cut-crystal glasses.

"Shouldn't they have something in them?" Julie asked.

"Added in post-production, love," the prop girl said.

"Okay, let's start," Pierce announced, and the assistants pulled back a few feet till they were just out of camera range.

"What do we do?" Julie asked, squinting in the bright lights.

"Just do, I don't know... stuff. Whatever you toffs do in drawing rooms."

Julie faced Hugo and forced a toothy grin. "It's starting to rain."

Hugo slouched against the sofa and gazed out the window. "Oh, yes? How much are we supposed to get?"

"Over an inch." She changed the glass to her other hand and cocked it at an angle. "It's supposed to get pretty strong around midnight and taper off by morning. Do you have to practice outside if it's raining?"

Hugo looked at his watch. "Depends. Playing on a muddy pitch can risk injuries."

Pierce ordered two lights adjusted and a footstool moved. "Julie, could you try looking a little less stiff? Relax your shoulders."

"I can't." At Hugo's quizzical look, she pulled back a section of the dress bodice. "They taped my breasts together. I can't breathe."

"I say," he looked in horror at the duct tape clinging to her soft skin.

"Redirect that flood," Pierce called to an assistant. "Julie, move to Hugo's other side. Hugo, put your arm on the mantelpiece."

"The thing's blazing!" he complained.

"And not so much teeth, it looks like you're snarling." The camera clicked a few more times, and Pierce let out a frustrated sigh.

"They're both so awkward," an assistant commented from behind the computer.

Leaning down, Hugo told Julie a ribald joke and she burst out laughing, which she instantly regretted when she couldn't catch her breath and her breasts almost tumbled out of the dress.

"No, no, no!" Pierce said. "Ramon, how am I supposed to work with this? Everyone take a five-minute break."

The wardrobe women took Julie back to the dressing room, and Hugo found Ramon. "We could use a bit of help out there. How about some music? And clear the room of these people."

Ramon nodded. "*Sí*, you are correct. Yes, good, I will make it happen."

# Chapter Thirty-Eight

TEN MINUTES LATER Hugo found Julie sitting morosely on a trunk in the impromptu dressing room. "Shall we try this again?"

She shook her head. "I can't do it. I'm making a fool of myself out there."

Waving the stylists away, he rearranged her skirts and sat down next to her. "No more than I am," he countered reasonably. "I spoke with Ramon, and they're making some changes. I wouldn't let you go back out there if I didn't think it would be all right. Do you trust me?"

How could she have ever thought his eyes were grey? They were so green. She nodded and he gave her his arm.

Hugo was right, the room was transformed. The fire had been banked to mellow flickers, her favorite bossa nova music played on the sound system, and it was empty except for Pierce and his assistant, who was hiding behind a wide palm.

"I love this song. It's called 'Desafinado,'" Julie declared in surprise.

"Then let's dance." Hugo took her right hand in his and held it at shoulder height, then slipped his behind her and pulled her against him.

Hugo's face was an impassive mask, and she followed his lead easily, but inside her nerves were churning. His hand on the bare skin of her back was electric and being this close to him devastated her will. Was it obvious to everyone watching?

Julie glanced at the assistant who was stealthily adjusting a strobe light.

"Don't look at him—look at me," Hugo commanded, and she obeyed. His eyes held hers as they slowly danced, his hand methodically massaging the tension from her back. "Flirt with me."

Julie blushed in consternation as the photographer began to shoot. "I don't know to flirt."

"It's easy—all you have to do is say something nice about the other person. Show them you're attracted to them."

"That's it?"

"Absolutely. Go ahead, give it a try."

As they danced, she considered various responses. "You looked very handsome in the blue shirt you wore to dinner last evening."

His arm around her waist drew her closer. "Thank you."

"Nice," Pierce muttered, moving around them furtively.

"Was that flirting?"

Hugo shook his head with mock regret. "Not really, it was more of a compliment. Try again."

Julie pursed her lips. "Would saying I like the tattoo on your chest be a compliment as well?" she queried prettily.

Hugo raised his eyebrows. "You naughty girl! How do you know I have a tattoo? Have you been looking through a peephole?"

"I've seen it a few times," Julie replied. "At your house. And at the match against Arsenal, when you were exchanging shirts with the other player. And back in the dressing room just now."

"You're very observant," he said, his voice a little rough.

"When did you get it?" She took her hand from his and lightly traced the part of his chest where she remembered seeing the insignia.

He licked his lips before replying. "After we won the Independent School championship, we all snuck out and got one. Our Housemaster almost had us rusticated."

"It's some sort of emblem, isn't it?"

"You'll have to find out for yourself," he smiled wickedly.

"That was flirting," she said decisively, and he nodded, his cool and sophisticated veneer seeming to melt away.

A spotlight dropped off its post with a loud clang, jarring them from the separate world they had drifted into. "Won't be a sec!" the assistant called and sprang to reattach it while Pierce changed cameras. Hugo and Julie continued to dance.

"Go on, try something else," he encouraged her. "Pretend you want to let me know you're interested in me. Try some Shakespeare."

"Turn her a bit to the left, get some motion going," Pierce directed, and Hugo complied, spinning her away and then reeling her back against him, her skirts swishing around their legs. A lock of Hugo's hair fell across his brow and she reached to brush it back, her fingers trailing across his forehead. *"In thy face I see a map of honor, truth and loyalty."*

He stumbled, missing a beat, but regrouped and shook his head sadly. "Sorry, that was flattery."

"No, *Henry VI.*"

That made him laugh out loud. "You're getting closer."

Julie bit her lip in mock dilemma. "This is trickier than I thought. You'd better give me an example."

He lifted his arm to twirl her under it. *"Thou art fairer than the evening air,"* he murmured, his nose nuzzling her ear as she brushed against him, *"clad in the beauty of a thousand stars."*

A delicious chill ran through her body.

"Wow," the photographer breathed, motioning for another camera. "Could you try not to get goose bumps, Julie? They're a pain to edit out."

Blushing furiously, she said, "That's not Shakespeare."

"No."

"Christopher Marlowe."

"Clever girl."

"Keep the glasses up!" a stylist yelled from the next room.

"Let them do whatever the hell they want. This is incredible," Pierce shot back.

"He better not let me do whatever the hell I want, there aren't many respectable magazines that would print the pictures," Hugo said softly into her ear as Pierce crept around them like a cat.

Julie looked up at a large oil painting of a beautiful horse that hung over the fireplace. "Who do you suppose that horse is?"

Hugo pulled his gaze from her face and glanced up at the painting. "I believe it's Zanzibar. He was a famous racehorse in the nineteenth century and was owned by the Duke of Portland. He won a lot of sprints and then went on to sire many successful racehorses."

Pursing her lips, Julie considered the painting closely. "So you're saying he was a very fast, aristocratic stud who knew how to please the ladies?"

Hugo shrugged. "I guess you could look at it that way."

Staring into his eyes, she smiled beguilingly. "You two have a lot in common."

Suddenly Hugo ground to a halt, his eyes searching hers feverishly with undisguised desire.

"Ha! I did it, didn't I?" Julie laughed in delight. "That was flirting!"

With a low growl, he wrenched her against him then bent her backwards over his arm, clamping his mouth over hers in a passionate kiss.

There was no teasing prelude to this kiss. He took complete possession of her mouth, invading it fully, his tongue tangling with hers in an erotic dance of passion and need. The intensity of his desire sent shockwaves through her as she dug her fingers into the thick muscles of his arms, clutching him to her.

She heard him groan savagely as she answered his rough, crushing kisses with wild pleasure, giving herself fully. The knowledge that she could shatter Hugo's much vaunted self-control with just a bit of teasing was intoxicating. She could feel his guise of the experienced, nuanced lover drop completely, replaced by something entirely primitive, completely elemental. He needed her. He needed more of her, as much as she needed him, and she needed more.

She gasped, wrapping one arm around his neck to draw him closer while the other fell helplessly to her side, the glass rolling out of her fingers, unsure if her desire for him was feeding his desire for her, or vice versa. It didn't matter, she vaguely realized, this was where she belonged.

"The Nikon!" Pierce hissed from next to them, followed by a frenetic series of clicks. "Damn it, which filter did you put on here?"

Reluctantly, Hugo ended the kiss, breathing hard. Julie recognized the obscenity he silently mouthed and tried to regain her breath as he gently eased her back to her feet. The music ended, and the camera went silent as they both stared into the other's eyes, acknowledging what had passed between them.

"Wow, it's pretty warm in here," Pierce announced, handing the camera off to the assistant. "Why don't we open some windows and take a look at what we've got?"

# Chapter Thirty-Nine

IN THE NEXT room, everyone huddled around the computer display, the wardrobe ladies sighing wistfully as the photographs flickered past.

"Julia, Hugo, that was *maravilloso*!" Ramon declared.

"How about we try the red gown next?" Pierce suggested.

Everyone agreed, and instead of watching Julie walk unsteadily through the cables and racks, Hugo simply swept her up in his arms and carried her back to the dressing room.

"They sewed me into the dress," Julie motioned helplessly when he set her down. There was no one to help her undress, so without further ado, Hugo took a fistful of fabric in each hand and rent the garment down her back with a loud tear. Julie barely caught it before it fell to the ground.

"I have to get this tape off," she pleaded and lowered the gown to her waist, showing Hugo the angry red welts under her arms. "Please, help me take the tape off."

For an instant, his eyes devoured the sight of her, naked to the waist, but he clamped his jaw determinedly. "Okay. This is going to hurt like hell but I'll be fast. Be brave."

"Just do it," she said and let out an involuntary yelp as he yanked a strip off. Immediately, he put his hand over the skin to stop the sting and then pulled off the next.

"Okay, okay, it's all over," he crooned against her hair after all the strips had been removed, keeping his hands pressed under her breasts.

"No, it's better already," she panted and indeed, after the initial burn, the relief was palpable. It didn't bother her that Hugo was holding her breasts so tenderly, his hands both cool and soothing as his fingers gently massaged the smarting skin. Her nipples furled tightly as his thumb brushed over one, jolting her with erotic bolts of lightning.

"No, don't stop," she protested when he moved to take his hands away.

"Juliet, I'm only a man," he tried to say lightly, but his voice was tight as he seemed to struggle with some inner demons.

The door slammed open and they froze. Mark stood in the doorway, his expression wild with anger. "What in the hell is going on here?" he demanded.

Julie snatched the dress back up. "Mark! You're back!"

"Damn straight I'm back, and what do I walk in on?"

"It's not what it seems. Hugo was just helping me take the tape off."

"Are you, or are you not, modeling for Bajan Gin?" Mark bellowed.

Hugo shoved Julie behind him and faced Mark. "Ramon asked her to be the model after Rochelle walked out."

Mark looked at Julie with loathing. "That's bullshit. You can't just push in here and do it."

"Can and did," Hugo said, his eyes narrowing. "Rochelle walked off the pitch and Juliet subbed in. And was bloody brilliant, I might add."

"How could you do this to me, Julie? Did you ever stop to think how Rochelle would feel?" Mark wailed. "This is her livelihood, her job."

"But she left," Julie tried to reason.

"She didn't really walk out, she just needed a break is all," Mark countered. "Ramon was beastly to her and she needed to clear her head."

Julie struggled to push Hugo out of her way, but he steadfastly refused to budge. "Mark, Ramon was going to call your boss if I didn't do it."

"He was bluffing," Mark said dismissively.

"Don't think so, old man," said Hugo. "He was completely serious, and Juliet stepped in and saved your sorry hide."

"And you no doubt egged her on. I don't suppose anyone considered how I'm supposed to tell Rochelle that she's out and you're in?"

Without waiting for an answer, Mark stalked towards the door, kicking a box of curlers across the room for good measure. "Where the hell is Ramon? I'll fix this with him." He paused in the doorway and glanced back to where Julie and Hugo stood. "And get out of that ridiculous costume, Julie. That color is hideous on you."

Hugo caught Julie as she tried to run after him. "Let him go."

"But I need to explain what happened," she protested, struggling in his arms. "I don't want him to think I did this on purpose."

"It doesn't matter what he thinks," Hugo said, privately hoping Looks was thinking the worst. "Ramon loves the photos and he's the customer. I'm guessing the photo shoot is over, and we'd do well to get out of these getups."

It took a moment, but Julie finally conceded. "You're right. I need my bag, I think they took it upstairs."

"Give me the key and I'll get it. Start getting changed and wait here."

Upstairs, he found her room and let himself in. A helpful maid had unpacked her bag, and he quickly collected her things and stuffed them back inside. Julie's nightgown was laid out across the bed, stopping him dead in his tracks. It was the kind of confection a woman would wear to tempt a man, creamy lace and ribbons and sheer gossamer fabric that would teasingly arouse some lucky bastard until he was insane with desire.

Hugo knew without a doubt that Julie would look like a flesh and blood goddess in that gown. Feverish bolts of jealousy ricocheted through him as he realized it was meant for Looks and not him, followed by the satisfying knowledge that Looks was screwing things up royally and would not be enjoying it.

Without a second thought, he snatched the gown and shoved it into the pocket of his jacket and then got the hell out of there. Back downstairs, he gave the bag to one of the dressers and instructed her to help Julie get changed, then went to wash and change into his own clothing.

As he returned to the drawing room, Mark was arguing with Ramon, who suddenly displayed a very limited grasp of English. "Julie, for Christ's sake I need you out here now! I have no idea what this man is saying!" Mark bellowed.

Julie emerged wearing her own clothing, remarkably composed. "He's saying we went ahead with the shoot without Rochelle."

"I can bloody well see that!" Mark raged. "Whose idea was that?"

"Mine," Ramon answered, seeming to enjoy taunting Mark.

Mark ignored him and began clapping his hands to get the attention of the crew. "It doesn't matter, I talked her into coming back and she should be here any moment. We need to get everything together."

People began to shift nervously but Ramon held his hand up. "No. Julia is our model now."

"Don't be ridiculous, Ramon." Mark snapped. "She's too fat to be a model."

Hugo's lips curled into a nasty grin as he balled his fist, grateful for the opportunity to finally deliver the punch Looks so sorely deserved.

Ramon saw his look of fury and stayed Hugo's arm before it could connect. "And Hugo model too. They do perfect," he added.

"What?" Mark's jaw dropped in shock and he focused on Hugo. "How the hell did they get you? Oh, let me guess, all Julie had to do was wag her little finger and you came running."

"Yes, actually, that's about right," Hugo smirked, shaking off Ramon's hand and taking a step closer.

"Mark, that's enough." Julie interrupted. "Hugo stepped in to help when the male model got disgustingly drunk. You owe him a debt of gratitude and me as well. Now, Hugo is going to take me home, and we can talk tomorrow."

# Chapter Forty

LONDON TRAFFIC WAS almost at a standstill. Hugo fidgeted in the driver's seat as Julie sat next to him, silent. She needed time to think, but she could never think clearly when Hugo was around.

Hugo finally exploded. "He's a dick, Juliet."

"No one is perfect."

"No, but not everyone is a complete bastard."

"I don't want to talk about it."

"Juliet, you must see it, he treated you like—"

"I said I don't want to talk about it."

Hugo shut up and drove the rest of the way in silence. When they reached her house, he took the keys out of her shaking hand and unlocked the door, then propelled her into the sitting room and deposited her on the small sofa.

"What?" she asked, trying to sound annoyed.

"We have to talk. Things are getting complicated."

"No, they're not. Nothing has changed."

"I dare say things have. What about us?"

It was impossible to meet his eyes. "There is no 'us.' I'm with Mark."

"What about me?"

"You're just an infatuation," Julie lied.

Hugo nodded. "I suppose I've been called worse."

Pulling a desk chair directly in front of her, he sat on it with his long legs stretched on either side of her, their faces inches apart. "Juliet, have you considered that Looks and Rochelle might still be involved?"

She clasped her hands in her lap. "Of course they're still involved. They have to work together."

"Looks is acting like it's a bit more than a working relationship."

Julie shrugged. "That's just Mark. He gets very swept up in things. Besides, it's none of my business."

"It's very much your business."

Blood began to pound in her ears. "He says he has to help her. He feels sorry for her."

"Or maybe it's not over."

The small sitting room felt suffocating.

"Are you in love with Looks?" Hugo asked bluntly.

"Yes, I love him," Julie replied automatically.

"No. I asked if you're *in* love with him. If you've ever really been *in love*, you'd know there's a big difference."

"Like how?"

"When you're in love with someone, it's more than just a physical desire or lust," Hugo explained. "You dream about them. You can't rest until you know when you're going to see them next. You become irrationally territorial and possessive and everyone else fades in comparison. The person is the only calm and happiness in your life, and you can't imagine the world without them in it. You literally can't live without them."

"Was it that way with Trika?" Julie couldn't stop herself asking.

"No, it wasn't that way with Trika, but I do know what I'm talking about. Is that what you feel for Looks?"

The answer was, of course, a resounding "no." She cared for Mark, but it wasn't anything like the feelings Hugo was talking about. He was describing her feelings for him. She'd known it for some time, the way she knew without a doubt that she could be perfectly happy with him for the rest of her life. But being in love with Hugo Auchincloss was the most wonderful, pointless feeling in the world.

"Romance like that is for daydreamers, not for ordinary people," she said, trying to sound sensible. At his look of disbelief, she continued, "I know I'm easy to deceive. I believe what people tell me because it seems a lot of work trying to figure out if they're lying. And when people lie, the truth usually comes out sooner or later."

"And what happens then? When you find out you've been lied to?"

"I... I don't know. I've never been in a position like this," she admitted. "But Mark respects me. He's the first man who's ever respected me enough not to try to... he's not all over me. I have to respect him as well. If he says it's over with Rochelle, then I believe him. If he feels he has to protect Rochelle, then he must have his reasons."

Hugo glanced around the room like he was looking for something to break. "All right, let's talk about reality. I'm going to be completely blunt, Juliet. You have to think of yourself here. You need to find out if your relationship with Mark is as exclusive as you think it is."

"What do you mean?"

"There are a lot of diseases out there. Both Looks and Rochelle have been around the block, several times according to some people, and you have to protect yourself."

Anger surged within her at the notion that Mark might be sleeping with other women but was immediately tempered by soul-jerking caution. Had Mark ever said anything about how exclusive they were? Her mind flew over potential hints but couldn't fasten on anything concrete. Yes, she knew he wanted to wait until things were perfect for them to make love, but was she taking it for granted that he was content to wait?

Razor-sharp doubt ricocheted through her mind, and she saw Hugo watching her intently. "That's funny advice coming from you. I thought you were the king of one-night stands," she said.

Hugo didn't flinch. "It's no secret that I choose not to attach myself to anyone, and I don't promise that it's going to be anything more than what it is. The girls know what's going on, and if they think it's going to turn into anything more, they're disappointed. But it seldom works out that way, and I don't think anyone has gone away unsatisfied."

His words sliced Julie's heart to ribbons. Of course no one went away unsatisfied. He was wonderful.

"I'm telling you this because I have always used precautions," he continued, taking her cold hands in his much larger ones. "Always, as much for my protection as for the girl's. You can be as naive as you want about everything else, but on this topic, you have to insist on honesty. Willfully burying your head in the sand could have very serious consequences." He searched her face, his own grim. "You have to find out what Looks is up to and then you have to decide if you can live with it. You have to know what you want."

"I want to make Haddonfield the premier restored, working kitchen garden in Great Britain," Julie replied with heartfelt certainty. "I want every graduate to be highly valued because they came from Haddonfield."

Hugo sighed. "No. I mean what do you want for yourself? Do you want excitement and adventure? Or do you want a home, a family?"

Julie glanced around her cozy sitting room. She had always envisioned marrying a man and having a house full of children and family, but it was almost impossible to see Mark living in the country or anywhere that could handle juice spills, handprints, and muddy wellies. "I think having a husband and a family and a career would be an exciting adventure. I want what my parents have. They adore each other, have a huge family, and love their work. It's all one thing."

"Can you have that with Looks? He doesn't seem the country sort," Hugo observed, seeming to read her mind.

"It's not his fault he has allergies," Julie snapped. "But living here in the city isn't so bad—I quite like it, actually. And there's a lot being done with urban micro-plots these days."

Hugo stared at her hands in his for a long time. "Juliet. I may be just an infatuation, but I care about you. Promise me you'll talk with Looks."

"I promise."

———— ◄O► ————

Hugo waited until he'd driven three blocks away from her house before he cranked up the Jaguar's stereo and let out a whoop of victory. Juliet was categorically not in love with Looks, and he had done a yeoman's job of planting the seeds of doubt in her mind about Rochelle. Let Looks talk his way out of that, the bastard.

Talking with Juliet about his past affairs had left a very bad taste in his mouth. She wasn't one of them, and in fact he couldn't even remember any of their faces. It had never bothered him before, his callousness and selfishness, but now he wanted to put that part of his life as far behind him as possible. Everything would be different with Juliet—she had already changed him completely without even trying. There was no one else but her.

He had come to the uncomfortable realization that he could have just told her the truth about Looks and Rochelle, but he rejected that immediately. There was no way to predict how she would have responded. If she confronted Looks, there was a chance the man might actually leave Rochelle and mend his ways. And that was a risk Hugo could not take.

The best course of action, he decided, was to let Juliet stew. He had planted enough doubt in her mind tonight, and in addition to Looks's behavior at Cheeting House, there was every chance she would come to the right decision on her own. Who had been there for her? Who had protected her? He had. Who'd treated her like dirt and screamed at her? Who'd behaved like the world's most ungrateful bastard? Looks. The choice was blindingly clear.

It was obvious she was in a terrible dilemma and his heart went out to her. She was desperately trying to be honorable and decent, unlike everyone else around her, including himself. But he knew Juliet well enough to know that when she made up her mind about something, she did it. Kicking Looks to the curb would be hard, and she would be distraught, but he would be right there to help her through it.

At the next stoplight, he pulled out his mobile and called Tom.

"I'm having you committed," Tom pronounced after Hugo explained what had happened at the photo shoot.

"That would probably be appropriate."

"You were doing this to impress Julie, weren't you?"

"No. Yes. I don't know—it all just sort of happened. Make sure all the money goes to Haddonfield. Call round to Smith-Wessex tomorrow and get it sorted."

Tom laughed, without pity.

# Chapter Forty-One

MARK WAS WAITING for Julie in her office the next morning when she returned from watering the gardens. He tucked his mobile away and sprang to his feet, smothering her in a crushing embrace. "Darling!"

Julie remained stiff in his arms, Hugo's warnings still fresh. Her resolve was firm. She and Mark were going to discuss their relationship, and no amount of cajoling on his part was going to put that off.

"I can't begin to apologize for what happened yesterday," Mark murmured. "It was awful, and I don't know what got into me."

Julie pulled away and stoked the woodstove, unmoved. "I suppose you want me to sign a contract."

Mark shook his head. "No. Not at all. In fact, I told them we're not going to use the pictures, any of them."

This was the last thing Julie had expected to hear. "But why? Weren't they any good?"

"They were amazing." He paused, his voice dropping to a silky whisper. "But you're too important to me. *We* are too important to me."

"But what will happen?"

Mark stared at the dull embers stirring to life in the woodstove. "I will, no doubt, get sacked."

"They wouldn't do that."

"Oh, yes, they would. They've been looking for the chance, and I'll be handing it to them on a silver platter. You see, darling, I really needed this win," he continued, casting a sideways glance at her. "I haven't wanted to worry you with this, but the distributors are ganging up on Dionysus and telling them the test marketing is going badly. All so they can get bigger up-front money for carrying Bajan Gin."

"But that's dishonest," Julie said.

Mark grimaced. "I've told you, the distilled spirit industry is a very rough crowd. And I don't want you to get mixed up with them—you're too important to me. So I'm going to do the right thing and tell Ramon and Dionysus that you will under no circumstances sign this release. Then I'll go and clean out my office." He looked out of the window at some distant point. "Dionysus will probably sack Rochelle as well."

"She did walk out on them," Julie said.

Mark laughed and dropped to the bench. "I know, darling. But none of it was her fault—it was all mine. I never realized how scared she was of meeting you and that she would panic and run off."

"Is that what happened?" Julie sat down next to him, her resolve wavering. "Why didn't she want to meet me?"

Mark patted her hand and smiled. "Darling, she's been very nervous about meeting you for a while. She's scared of what you might think of her because she's not educated at all, not like you. In fact, she never finished school, and she's afraid you'll think less of her. You're so smart, so respected, you don't even know how intimidating you can be. When she found out you were coming to the shoot, she just went to pieces."

"But I was afraid of meeting her," Julie admitted. Were they both really worried about meeting each other? Julie thought this over for several moments. "Mark, were you with her in Miami last month? When you told me you were in Toronto?"

Mark jumped out of his seat as if it were on fire. "How the hell did you find out?"

His words came out as a distinct snarl, and the transformation was jarring. "That night we were at Jesters, two women from your office were talking about it. I didn't mean to eavesdrop, but I overheard..."

Mark began pacing the room. "Yes. Yes, I was," he admitted. "Rochelle was in tears on a shoot—the director was being very mean to her because she'd gained some weight. I had to fly in and smooth things over. I couldn't tell you because if it got out, it would hurt her magazine work."

"I wouldn't have told anyone," Julie reproached. "How did you manage to smooth things over?'

A light sweat broke out on Mark's forehead. "Well, I... I talked to everyone. You know me—there's nothing that can't be solved with a good talk. I talked to the director, of course, I'd worked with him before. Then I told the caterer I wanted them to serve some healthier food than what they usually serve. Like what you grow."

Julie nodded. "Did that help? Was everything okay after that?"

Mark's lips pressed into a thin smile. "Everything was fine after that."

Now was the time to ask the question—right now, before she lost her nerve. "Mark, are you still involved with

Rochelle?"

"Of course we're still involved. We have to work together. I've told you that repeatedly."

"I don't mean that way. I mean... *involved*." Somehow it was impossible to frame her concern any other way.

Mark sat down next to Julie, crowding her on the bench, and took her hand. "Darling, you are everything I need, and there's no one else who can give me what I want," he crooned. "I would be a fool to take Rochelle over you. I love you."

This was the second time a man had told her he loved her— the first had been when she'd released Hugo from the cellar. Even though he'd said it in the heat of the moment, she'd believed him. Now Mark was saying the same thing, but his words left her numb.

*But are you in love with me?* It didn't seem fair to ask, since she wasn't in love with him. But that was a separate problem. Instead, she smiled wanly. "Really?"

"Of course, you silly. Everyone loves you—you're great!" He laughed as though it were the funniest thing he'd ever heard. "So now that you know everything that happened, how would you feel about us running the pictures?"

Repulsed by his complete about-face, Julie shifted away from him. "Of course," she shrugged. "I don't want you to lose your job."

"Darling, you're too sweet." Mark hugged her, his face wreathed in smiles. "You've saved me, again. The shots are brilliant, and everyone is thrilled. I wish it had been my idea instead of Ramon's. It's just that you and Hugo are so obviously mismatched, and I couldn't see past that."

"We are?" Julie asked, struggling out of his embrace.

"Well, of course. Women throw themselves at Hugo. He takes his pick of them. That's what makes those photos so amazing—in real life Hugo wouldn't have anything to do with someone as provincial as you. You're so innocent, and, and..."

"Virginal?"

"Yes, exactly! And he's so obviously the rake bent on seducing you. It's like one of those sexy book covers, only better, because it's got Bajan Gin in the shot. It's the perfect fantasy."

"What does sex have to do with gin?" Julie asked.

"Sex sells," Mark said bluntly. "And you and Hugo are sex on a stick. Now, there's one other thing we have to discuss."

Julie blushed. "You want to know why Hugo was holding my chest?" At Mark's blank look, she prompted, "When you walked in on us in the dressing room?"

"Of course! Yes, damn odd—" he puffed up "—not every day a chap walks in and sees another man holding his best girl's hooters. What was going on?"

"There wasn't anything going on. The dressers taped my breasts and I couldn't breathe. Hugo had to pull the tape off and was holding my skin so it wouldn't burn."

"Oh. I've heard they do that sometimes. Must hurt like the devil," Mark commiserated. "Actually, I wanted to talk with you about your fee. Ramon had no authority to offer you so much money."

A dull ache began to spread across Julie's forehead. "But it's all for Haddonfield. We wouldn't have agreed to do it otherwise."

"I know, darling, but it will completely blow the budget, and we're massively in the red as it is. Haddonfield will still get Hugo's half, which is more than generous, and there's no need to be greedy. You couldn't have worked for more than two hours."

An angry retort rushed to her lips. She wanted to tell him that it was more than the two hours of work, it was the fact that her face was going to help sell his gin in every Spanish-speaking country in the world. But it was impossible to argue without sounding mercenary.

Mark pulled a sheaf of papers out of his jacket and laid them on the table. "Excellent. You just sign here saying you're waiving your fee."

Julie rubbed her throbbing temple. "I should read the entire contract."

Mark dismissed her suggestion with an airy wave of his hand. "You needn't bother, it's going to Tom Bellville-Howe next. You're getting the same terms as Hugo, and I'm sure Tom is going to squeeze us for every concession he can get. See, here's the spot for Hugo's signature as well. You're just waiving your fee."

With strong misgivings, Julie signed and initialed in several places and handed it back to Mark, who pocketed the document and stood. "Excellent! I knew you'd save the day."

Julie walked Mark out to the parking area, where a car and driver waited. "The hotel didn't have anything for me this morning, did they? I can't find the nightgown I packed."

"I wouldn't know," Mark said. "I ended up coming into town last night as well. Call out there. They might have found it."

The driver discreetly passed him a small package wrapped in tissue paper and he pressed it into Julie's hands. "This is for you, darling, I found it in a small antique store in Notting Hill and knew it would be perfect for you. Now I'm off to New

York to show everyone the pictures. They're going to save everything!"

# Chapter Forty-Two

TEAM PRACTICE RAN late that morning, and Hugo chafed as Giles and his assistants tinkered with established set pieces, trying to work around Marco's injury and Lars's absence. He ran the drills perfunctorily, impatient to get to Haddonfield and see Juliet. She might be ending things with Looks this morning and would need him.

The team was dismissed at noon, and Hugo rushed to shower and change. On the drive out to Haddonfield, he checked in with Tom.

"Smith-Wessex sent their guy over this morning," Tom reported, "and I got you your deal, all of it to Haddonfield School. But I had to agree you'd show up at the launch party in two weeks."

Hugo grimaced. "Bother, Tom."

"Hey, they wanted you to stay for three hours and pictures, I got them down to ninety minutes and no pictures. But Looks obviously got to Julie—she signed off on the contract but refused to take any money, except one pound to make the deal."

Hugo swore violently.

"I couldn't agree more," Tom continued when he finished. "So we did the deal, and then things got interesting. The guy was Mister Chatty. Turns out Looks never told Rochelle that Julie would be at the shoot. She found out from one of the assistants and bolted."

Figured, Hugo thought. "Go on."

"What neither of them anticipated was the two of you stepping in to save the day, much less the pictures turning out to be solid gold. Everyone loves them, and Rochelle is most likely out."

"Serves them right."

"One more thing. This whole flavored gin idea is not doing well in the broader consumer tests they're running. It's failing everywhere, even the United States, where God knows they'll drink anything."

"It should fail. It's swill."

"Yes, well, let's not forget whose face is on that swill now, at least in the Latin America countries," Tom reminded him.

Hugo arrived at Haddonfield and sprinted to Julie's office. He hoped to find her in tears, desolate over her breakup with Looks. But instead, he found her sitting at her desk staring pensively at a crystal aperitif glass.

"How are you?" he asked.

Julie turned and smiled. "I'm fine. Mark came out this morning and explained everything. Rochelle was afraid to meet me, the poor girl. She thought I wouldn't like her because she doesn't have an education. Can you believe it?"

Hugo's crossed his arms and felt a tick start in his jaw. "No. I can't."

"And I was afraid to meet her. It's funny, really. I want to meet her now. I want us to be friends. I think we can be."

"So you and Looks have patched things up?"

"Yes. He admitted what he did was very wrong, but I can see where he felt backed into a corner." She glanced at the door and lowered her voice. "This isn't to be shared, but there are some problems in the test markets."

"Problems? Like what?" Hugo asked, dying to hear what drivel Looks had told her.

"Well, it seems that the distributors are trying to extort more money from Dionysus by saying the consumer testing is going badly. You know, so that Dionysus will pay them more money to carry it."

"Maybe the testing is going badly because it doesn't taste good and people don't like it," Hugo countered.

"That's ridiculous. Why would a big company like Dionysus put all that effort into something people don't want?"

"Have you tasted any?"

"No. Have you?"

"Yes, at the shoot."

"And?"

"Acquired taste at best. Tom said Looks got you to waive your half of the fee."

Julie shifted in her chair. "He said they're over budget already, and your half is already very generous. There's no need to be greedy."

"I suppose he gave you this as a peace offering?" Hugo picked up the small glass from her desk and turned it over in his hand.

"Yes, isn't it pretty? It's a kind of bud vase for flowers. There's some writing on it in French. I can read the word *amour*, which I think means 'love.' Can you tell me what it says?"

Hugo held the glass to the light. "'Joy of Love Pastis, One Hundredth Anniversary, Distributor's Annual Meeting, Paris,'" he translated. "It's an advertisement for pastis, Juliet, which is a French drink."

He set the glass down with a resounding thud and stalked away.

————◦————

For the next three days, Hugo made his irritation with Julie abundantly clear. He ignored her at afternoon staff tea, and when she saw him in the upstairs hallway, he only nodded and kept walking. It was subtle, and nothing anyone else would pick up on, but she knew he was annoyed at her for not taking the money. His censure hung over her like a dark cloud.

Julie felt uneasy and desperately wanted things to go back to the way they were. Even worse, she began to doubt her unquestioning acceptance of Mark's explanations. Everything had sounded so plausible when he had been standing in front of her, but as she thought back over it, unsettling questions began posing themselves. Had Rochelle really been afraid to meet her? Was there more going on between them than he was admitting to?

The answers seemed to be right in front of her but written in a foreign language. The harder she tried to focus on them, the more puzzling they became, leaving her confused and miserable.

————◦————

Saturday was Don and Gretchen's tenth wedding anniversary, and Julie offered to watch Philippa, age seven, and Alice, age five, while their parents went on a day trip to celebrate. In the morning, the girls helped her water at Haddonfield and then they went out for a puppet show and ice cream.

When they got back to the girls' house, Julie realized she had left her own house keys on her desk at Haddonfield. It would have been impossible to drag the exhausted children back to the school, but she remembered Ian had arrived as they were leaving to do some filming. Luckily, he was still there when she called, and he agreed to drop them off on his way home.

As dinner baked, the girls sat at the kitchen table making a raspberry trifle while Julie washed dishes at the sink. The doorbell rang, and Julie, up to her elbows in soapsuds, called over her shoulder, "That's probably Ian. Philippa, would you answer the door, please?"

The little girl climbed down from the chair she was standing on and marched to the front of the house, returning a few moments later. "This is Hugo," she announced, and scrambled back up her chair and dipped a spoon into a bowl of whipped cream.

Julie dropped the cake pan she'd been washing into the sudsy water, making a terrific splash and soaking the front of her long-sleeved shirt. "Oh, hello!" She spun around, tucking a stray hair behind her ear. "We weren't expecting you."

Hugo had come directly from his afternoon match and was wearing another of his expertly cut suits and a starched white shirt, open at the throat. There was a fresh cut on his cheek, she noted, where he must have gotten scraped by a Stoke City player's cleats.

"Ian said you'd left these at Haddonfield." Hugo dropped her house keys on the counter, his eyes coursing appreciatively over her wet shirt.

Warm currents began to pulse through Julie. "You didn't have to come so far out of your way. I thought he was going to drop them off."

"Ah. He had to go away suddenly."

"Where?"

Hugo paused, looking out the window at some distant point. "Wales."

At her look of surprise, he added, "Some friends of his were going to film something, last-minute thing, and he had to leave straight away. At least that's what he said. You never know with Ian. I said I'd bring these over for you."

"Thank you." Julie swallowed and made the introductions. "This is Philippa, whom you've met, and this is Alice. Girls, this is Hugo, he works with your dad and me at Haddonfield."

Alice looked up from the handful of vanilla pudding she was carefully dropping into the bowl. "Pleased to meet you. We're making a raspberry trifle. Do you like raspberry trifle?"

Hugo scrutinized the messy bowl. "It's my favorite. And this one looks especially amazing."

"You can help if you like," Philippa offered. "You can put the jam on the cake. Are you allowed to use knives?"

"Philippa, I think Hugo probably has plans," Julie interrupted.

"No, I'm not busy at all. And yes, I've been checked out on knives." Hanging his jacket on a peg in the hall, Hugo rolled up sleeves, exposing his strong forearms, and began spreading deep red jam on the golden cake. The girls told him where to place it in the bowl and spooned whipped cream and pudding on top with remarkable concentration.

"Am I doing this correctly?" he asked as the trifle continued to build.

"Yes. And Julie said you may eat the crumbs but not too much as it will spoil your dinner," Alice advised, looking at him closely. "You were on the telly this afternoon. We watched."

"Oh, yes?" Hugo glanced up at Julie in amusement, but she concentrated on the pan she was scrubbing.

"You ran around a lot," Phillipa said as Hugo put another chunk of cake in the bowl.

"That's my job."

"Why were you shouting at that man in the same shirt as you? The one with the mustache?" Alice asked.

"Because I wanted to pass him the ball, but he wasn't where he was supposed to be."

"That was naughty of him. Julie says you wiffed a cross pass because you were out of position," Philippa added importantly.

"Philippa, hush." Julie felt a blush cross her face with alarming speed.

"She's right, I faded too far left and I couldn't get the ball past my defender," Hugo agreed, handing Alice another slice of cake.

"And you made that other man fall down when he was trying to run with the ball," Alice pointed out.

Hugo feigned a look of injured innocence. "I did not. He slipped."

"He didn't slip!" Philippa crowed with glee. "You tripped him! And then when the man blew the whistle and pointed at you, you yelled. Julie said you've got quite a mouth, and your mummy might have to wash it out with soap."

"Wouldn't be the first time," Hugo admitted.

# Chapter Forty-Three

WHEN THE TRIFLE was finished, Julie sent the girls upstairs to wash their hands, and Hugo came to wash his at the sink next to her. "Thank you for bringing my keys over. Am I to take it you're no longer irritated with me?" she asked, handing him a tea towel.

"I wasn't irritated with you," he replied, drying his hands. "It's up to you what you want to believe."

"You've barely spoken to me for the last three days," she said. "I appreciate everything you told me Tuesday. I needed to hear it."

"You ignored it."

"I didn't ignore it. I took it under consideration. There's a difference. And Mark and I did talk about his relationship with Rochelle, and he admitted that he has seen her, but it's because she's going through a rough patch and needs his help. He swears it's nothing more than that."

"And you believe him."

How did he manage to heap so much scorn into a single sentence? Julie stood on tiptoe for the plates on a higher shelf, but Hugo reached over her head and handed them to her. "I know there are issues with Mark, but he's asked me to wait to talk about them until after the launch party," she continued. "That's only two weeks, and I said yes. He's under enormous stress and I don't want to add to that."

Hugo frowned. "He doesn't deserve you."

Julie shrugged and began to set the table. "He has to put with a lot of things with me as well. I'm not of much use to him. I'm not terribly social and can't do the late nights."

"Are you sure he's not your boss?"

Julie opened her mouth to dispute that but was interrupted by the girls galloping back into the kitchen. "Please, Julie, can Hugo stay for dinner?" Alice begged and turned to Hugo. "You should! Julie's making us macaroni and cheese. It's ever so yummy and we only get it when she watches us."

"If there's enough?" he asked her, seeming to offer a truce.

Julie smiled in relief. "There's plenty."

A squabble immediately broke out regarding who was going to get the honor of sitting next to Hugo, which Julie remedied by saying that the table could be pulled out and a bench moved in so both girls could sit on either side of him. They wiggled onto their seats with Hugo between them, and Julie took the golden casserole from the oven and placed it on the table.

Hugo entertained the girls as they ate while Julie quietly reminded them of their table manners. The girls had good appetites and ate two servings each, then were excused from the table with assurances that they would be called back for dessert. They scampered off to play, and Julie watched in amusement as Hugo finished a huge third helping and then cleaned up what the girls had left on their plates.

Finally sated, he leaned back. "The girls were right—that was delicious. And I haven't been fawned over like that in ages."

"You've collected two more hearts," Julie agreed.

"I suppose next they'll be expecting their picture in the tabloids and something glittery from Malbrey's?"

"Now that you mention it, Alice is partial to those rubbery bracelets they sell at the trinket store in Hampstead."

Hugo grinned. "Now there's a girl for me."

Julie made two cups of tea and they sat at the table and talked, just like her parents would do in the evening. The girls returned for dessert and Hugo carefully spooned out two bowls of trifle, explaining that he and Julie were still too full from dinner and would have some later.

When they finished, Hugo tucked a flowered dish towel into his belt and declared that he and the girls would do the dishes while Julie went next door to the dormitory to check on the students who had stayed for the weekend. As she walked back across the garden, she heard squeals of laughter and through the kitchen window saw Hugo juggling a sponge on the tops of his feet and then tossing it high in the air and heading it into the sink. The girls gave him a round of rapturous applause.

Julie opened the back door with a loud bang, and all three went back to washing the dishes, wearing angelic smiles. The girls then negotiated that Hugo would come up for story time after their bath, and they splashed happily in the tub as Julie washed the jam from their hair. Dried off and dressed in matching nightgowns, they scampered back downstairs to collect Hugo.

He arrived upstairs carrying one in each arm and deposited them on their twin beds, placing a chair diplomatically between them.

"Julie's going to tell us a story before bed," Alice said.

"She had a pet goose named Angelica and she always tells us a story about her," Philippa added, crawling under her thick comforter. "Angelica was a very naughty goose."

"Which story would you like?" Julie asked. "They've heard them all."

"Tell us about when the boy tried to kiss you!" Alice insisted.

"Oh, yes! Do!" Philippa agreed.

Julie squirmed. "Hugo doesn't want to hear that one."

"No, please," he insisted, "I do."

Julie began the story. "One evening a classmate of mine at Cornell came to my house to study for a test we were having in Principles of Virology."

"It was a date," Philippa giggled.

"And he brought her flowers," Alice added.

"Who's telling this story?" Julie rebuked before continuing. "And they weren't flowers, they were actually fronds from an experimental cultivar of an ornamental grass he'd been working with in lab."

"What a romantic," Hugo said. "I'll have to remember that one."

Julie ignored him. "Anyway, we were sitting on a bench in the backyard where Angelica had her pen, and he sat down very close to me."

"Did you like him?" Hugo interrupted.

"I'd only just met him."

"Tell him what happened when he tried to kiss you!" Alice ordered.

Philippa couldn't contain herself. "Angelica bit his ear!"

Julie rolled her eyes in exasperation. "Yes, when he leaned in to give me a kiss, Angelica snuck up behind us and bit his ear. Then what happened, Alice?"

"He jumped up and said some naughty words about geese and he ran away. And Julie said that anyone who would say nasty words about geese wasn't anyone she wanted to associate with and she was glad he left."

"And it turned out that he was a mean boy and Angelica was right to bite him," Philippa finished.

"He cheated on the final," Julie said. "And got caught."

Hugo nodded. "She was a wise goose."

"Now it's Hugo's turn to tell us a story," Philippa said.

"Yes, Hugo, let's hear a school story from you," Julie encouraged.

Hugo colored and shifted on his chair. "I went to a school with boys, and none of my stories are appropriate for a young lady's ears. But I have another skill you might appreciate. I can read palms."

"You learned that at school?" Julie's eyes widened.

"Eton specialty, got an A level in it," Hugo winked. "Learned it from a Romanian chap who swore his mother was a gypsy. Turns out she was a banking heiress from Cardiff."

He took Alice's little hand in his much larger one and turned it over, peering at her small palm intently. "This," he said, tracing a faint line, "is your head line. You are very considerate of others and like to read books."

At her enthusiastic nod, he continued. "And this is your life line." He pretended to consider it carefully for several moments, his brows knitted in concentration. "It says you have boundless energy but eat too many sweets."

This news was met with a bit of a pout.

"Now, this is your heart line," he said.

Alice looked at it closely. "What does it say?"

"It says that you will be very lucky in love but terrible at card playing."

Philippa's palm revealed that she was a very good leader, would be a brilliant student and go on to be Chairman of the Bank of England, but she needed to eat more vegetables.

"Now do Julie's!" the girls demanded.

"It's time for bed," Julie countermanded and pulled the covers up over them. She asked Hugo to turn off the main light, leaving a small night-light that cast a dull glow. In a quiet voice, she began reciting, "Repeat after me. One times one is one, one times two is two, one times three is three..."

<hr />

A half hour later, Julie collapsed on the sofa. "I don't know how Gretchen does it. The girls are wonderful but I'm knackered. We've never gotten as far as the five times tables before."

Hugo flopped down next to her and swung his feet onto the ottoman, draping his arm comfortably behind her. "I was beginning to lose all hope. Doing multiplication tables to get them to sleep is brilliant. I bet Mummy wishes she'd known that when Ian was a toddler."

"My mother used to do the same thing with us when we wouldn't settle down. I still can't do too much arithmetic without feeling drowsy."

It felt so nice sitting there next to him, so warm and comfortable, almost like they were a young married couple who had just put their children to bed at the end of a long day.

"When are Don and Gretchen due home?" Hugo asked.

"Sometime around ten," Julie yawned, and realized she was fantasizing again and that Hugo probably wanted to leave.

Reaching into the bag next to her, she took out some magazines. "I brought along my latest copies of *Farming UK* and was going to get caught up with them."

Hugo leaned across her and returned the magazines to the bag. "Has the New World discovered backgammon yet?"

"It's one of my favorite games," Julie said in delight. He wanted to stay. "I'll warn you though, I can be very competitive. It's a vice."

Hugo stood to retrieve the game from a nearby shelf. "Not in my line of work."

The first game went slowly as they tested each other's skill. It was close, but Hugo ended up winning. Julie easily won the second.

The third game became an intense match of wills. Julie ruthlessly sent him to the bar twice, his teasing entreaties for mercy making her laugh so hard that he put his hand over her mouth and pointed upstairs.

"If you roll doubles one more time you lose a turn," she pointed out as he rolled a third time.

"You wish. Six and three, I take that point. So where's Looks?"

Julie concentrated on her roll. "Five and two. Traveling."

"Where?"

Julie pondered her strategy. "New York, showing our pictures around. He said they look even better with the retouching and that I wouldn't recognize myself."

"If they're gorgeous then they look exactly like you."

Julie felt herself blush. "You're trying to distract me."

"Is it working?"

"You tell me." In a series of moves, she sent him back to the bar and moved three of her pieces off the board. In two more plays, she beat him.

"I didn't realize you were quite so ruthless," Hugo said. "Now take your shirt off."

"What?"

"Your t-shirt, take it off," he repeated, his green eyes glinting with deviltry. "We've played a match, now we're supposed to trade. You take off yours and give it to me, and I take off mine and give it to you. It's a tradition I'm very fond of."

Julie bit her lip. "Well, okay, if it's a tradition," she murmured, grasping the hem of her long-sleeved t-shirt and pulling it over her head, revealing a thin, short-sleeved t-shirt underneath.

His disappointment was palpable. "I wear a lot of layers," she explained, handing him the shirt. "Your turn. Do I get the cufflinks as well?"

———◆◇◆———

Hugo grinned as they put the game away—the clever little minx was obviously very proud of herself.

"Time for dessert," Julie announced, scrambling to her feet. She headed to the kitchen, her ponytail bobbing fetchingly.

Hugo hung back, needing a moment to get himself under control. He had suggested they play backgammon because it was an innocent game and he'd needed an excuse to stay, but leave it to Juliet to turn it into the most heated foreplay he'd ever experienced.

Watching her delight in the game sharpened the pleasurable urges that always stirred whenever she was around—make that *uncomfortably* pleasurable urges. His body was demanding he go further, and his promise to be a gentleman was becoming steadily more impossible to keep.

But then again, he hadn't been a gentleman to her for most of the week. He'd been a right bastard ever since she'd accepted her boyfriend's word as gospel. It was obvious Looks wanted her to forgive and forget, but that was not an option. Hugo needed to keep the issue in front of her. Making his disapproval clear usually worked well with Ian, and while he hated doing it to Juliet, there wasn't any other choice. She wasn't listening to his warnings, and she obviously wasn't listening to her own common sense. So, the unspoken ultimatum was clear—it was either him or Looks.

Which worked up to a point, the point being he couldn't stay mad at her yet couldn't stay away from her, either. He'd come tonight because he'd given up trying to figure out the mystic pull she had over him. And it was a bit of luck when Ian called and said she'd asked him to drop off her house keys, which saved him the trouble of coming up with an excuse to explain why he was on the door stoop. Being with Juliet and the girls was remarkably fun. In fact, this was the best evening he'd spent in a long time. And now he'd promised to be a gentleman, so he'd damn well better get ahold of himself.

# Chapter Forty-Four

HUGO'S RESOLUTION WAS blown as soon as he stepped into the kitchen and saw Juliet bending over to take the trifle out of the refrigerator. A snap of pure longing jolted him as he soaked in the sight of her delicious bottom.

His desire strained at its tight chains as she stood and held the glass bowl before her, framed between the peaks of her breasts. With an immense effort, he shackled his lust and took a spoon from the counter, plunging it deep into the thick custard layers.

"This is the best," he said, devouring the huge spoonful.

"There are bowls," she objected, but he dipped his spoon in again and held it to her mouth. She paused for a moment and then lowered her lips. "Mmmm. It's delicious. They did a good job."

Where he found the willpower to continue standing there like he didn't have the world's biggest hard-on, he didn't know. Beads of sweat broke out on his forehead as she ran the tip of her tongue over her lips. He took another mammoth spoonful for himself, the cream soft and sweet in his mouth.

"You got more raspberries than I did on that spoonful," Julie pointed out.

"Greedy," he grinned, and refilled the spoon with a more reasonable portion, carefully choosing the best raspberry for her. He brought the spoon to her mouth and watched spellbound as she licked the wayward custard off her lips.

Hugo set the bowl down and took her hand. "It's time to read your palm."

"Hmmm, let me guess. I like to work with my hands, have a kind heart, and will be prime minister if I eat all my rhubarb?"

He smacked her palm playfully and began to examine it. "This," he said, tracing a curve with his finger, "is your head line. You are creative, enjoy physical achievements, and have enthusiasm for life."

"That's true," Julie agreed.

"And this," he continued, "is your life line. It says you have plenty of energy but are cautious when it comes to relationships."

She pursed her lips. "That's true as well."

"Now this," Hugo ran his finger across her palm, "is your heart line."

"What does it say?"

"It says that your heart breaks easily, but that you recover quickly and move on."

Julie frowned. "I've never had my heart broken."

He traced a line around the base of her thumb. "The last one is the Fate line."

"Does it say how many inches of rain we'll get this summer?"

"Saucy wench. It says your road to true love will be a little rocky, but that the man you fall in love with will worship you completely and love you forever."

"Really?" She looked up at him with those big blue eyes and batted her long lashes. "So I have a chance with David Beckham?"

"Minx!" he scoffed and plucked a full raspberry from the bowl and pushed it playfully into her mouth. An errant dollop of cream dropped to her chest, landing on the gentle swell of her breast, and with a slow motion, she picked it up with her finger and held it to his lips.

———————◇———————

Julie knew there was a line and she crossed it without hesitation.

Hugo grasped her hand in his and with a slow, deliberate movement brought it to his mouth and licked the cream from her finger, his lips and tongue working sensuously over the tip, his eyes intent on hers.

She realized he was giving her every opportunity to pull away. As if she could—every intimate part of her felt like it was turning to molten lava. But he was letting the decision be hers.

What was she waiting for? It was different this time—no confusion, no surprise. They were alone, the lights were on, and both knew clearly what they desired most. Without hesitation, she grasped his head in her hands and pulled his lips down to hers.

Hugo pinned her against the counter, crushing her in his arms as his mouth worked over hers with a delicious thoroughness. Julie responded eagerly, her tongue sliding around his, drawing him into her mouth in the same way he'd done to her the last time they kissed. She couldn't get enough of him—she wanted him to kiss her everywhere. They plundered each other with tender desire, exploring, intent, all teasing abandoned.

He seemed to have no control over himself as she gave herself freely, and the same current of desire flowed hotly through both of them. His hands moved down her back to clasp her bottom and draw her to him, and a moan escaped between their lips as she shifted to fit against his rock-hard desire. He peppered her face with demanding, ardent kisses and she arched in ecstasy, her fingers digging into the broad expanse of his back.

Keeping one hand on her hip, his other traveled to her waist and dipped under the hem of her shirt, her heart leaping in excitement as he stroked the smooth skin. Dropping his lips to nip her neck, he continued to explore, moving steadily upwards until his fingers brushed her lacy bra. He teasingly traced the edge as she writhed in his arms, then pushed it away to capture her breast.

The pleasure of his big hand caressing her sensitive skin was intoxicating. A small whimper escaped her lips and he laughed, bending her back over his arm and lowering his lips to hungrily feast on the tender mound.

"That feels so good," Julie gasped.

"It's just the start, love," Hugo murmured.

Like a starving man, he kissed her satiny skin and then moved to the incredibly sensitive point to claim the rosy tip with his mouth. The shock of pleasure was so violent, her knees would have collapsed if he hadn't been holding her. He suckled her greedily, lavishing attention on the stiff peak before moving to taste the other. Her fingers splayed in his hair, holding him as he pleasured her.

With a throaty growl of masculine satisfaction, his lips retook hers, warm and devouring. "Tell me I'm more than an infatuation, Juliet," Hugo demanded.

She ignored his words and nestled her hips closer against his, needing to feel his hardness against her softness. With a harsh breath, Hugo sank his lips into the tender flesh of her neck, sending flames of liquid delight spilling through her.

"Tell me it's me you want," he insisted.

Why did it matter? Why did he need to hear it from her own lips? She willed herself to look into his eyes and almost cried at the fruitlessness of her feelings for him. "Of course I want you," she whispered. "Every girl wants you."

"I don't care about them."

"I'm not like them."

"I should say not," he agreed.

"No, I mean I'm not like the women you've been with. I can't be like them. You said you want women who have no problem just sleeping with you, with no strings attached. You're very up front that it's just a physical thing, and I appreciate that honesty. But I can't do that."

His expression turned foreboding. "What I said doesn't apply to you."

"I know I'm naive," Julie said, "but I'm not that naive. I think you're wonderful. You make me laugh, you make me feel like I'm the only woman in the world. That's a lot to get heated up over. But I could never be one of those women, the kind you want. I think making love should mean something and be more than just a fling or a burst of passion."

Hugo grasped her shoulders. "Juliet, that's not the way it would be. I swear it would be different with you."

"Maybe at first. But I know I'm completely out of my depth with you. I'd just end up getting hurt."

A little sound interrupted them. Alice stood in the doorway, rubbing her eyes. "Julie, I have the hiccups."

Hugo reluctantly released her and scooped the little girl up in his arms, while Julie filled a water glass and followed them back up the stairs. Quietly, so as not to awaken Philippa, they tucked Alice back into bed and Julie gave her sips of water and had her hold her breath. Slowly the hiccups faded, and the little girl began to nod off.

Hugo stood. "I should leave now."

"Hugo," Julie eased off Alice's bed and followed him to the doorway. She fumbled, trying to explain the complex emotions battling inside her. After several false starts, Julie realized it was impossible, everything was so jumbled and confused.

"I'm really glad you came over this evening," she finally said, and impulsively stood on tiptoe to kiss his cheek, inhaling his scent.

Hugo paused, motionless, once more the remote and aloof aristocrat she had met at the bookstore. "Good night, Juliet."

# Chapter Forty-Five

THURSDAY NIGHT, JULIE sat in bed, her freshly washed hair wrapped in a towel and the latest issue of the *Journal of Soil Science* in her lap. There was a very interesting article on modeling soil water retention she was trying to focus on, but after rereading the same paragraph four times, she tossed the magazine to the floor and buried her face in the pillow.

Tomorrow would be Hugo's last day at Haddonfield. There was some irony in the fact that she had been longing for the day to come, but now that it was here, she dreaded it. A small party was planned. Don would say a few words, there might be a speech or two, and Hugo would be gone.

But Julie didn't want Hugo to leave.

Would he try to see her alone? The idea triggered a flurry of emotions, adding trepidation and excitement to the already chaotic mix. He was very good at finding her almost anywhere on the property. If she was alone in the glasshouse, he might come out and see her there. Or in the workroom where she needed to sort beans—that was secluded and a good place for a private conversation.

And then... what should she do then? She'd talk with him, of course. They were colleagues and had a good working relationship. And if he wanted to say more? She would be kind but firm. She hoped they could stay friends. Good friends. Very good friends.

The memory of what had happened in the kitchen Saturday evening was still fresh and potent. They hadn't spoken of it since, and by tacit agreement had taken pains to make sure they were not alone together. For four days Hugo had been a complete gentleman—calm, composed, and charming. It had been exhausting, trying to emulate his behavior.

What if he attempted to kiss her again? Things between them tended to get out of hand fast, and returning his kiss would be a fatal mistake. Julie pondered this for a while and then decided the smartest thing to do would be to remain passive in his embrace. That would be the best way to demonstrate she wasn't interested in him.

Minutes ticked by. One kiss, but no more than one. It would be a goodbye kiss, and it would have to last her, well... forever.

Unable to find a comfortable position in bed, Julie turned on the light and went to her closet. There wasn't much choice of what she would wear tomorrow, as the forecast was for more raw weather. But she chose her nicest pair of khaki work pants and a snug blue turtleneck sweater that his eyes had lingered over in the past. Seeing the bottle of scent on her dresser, she dabbed a touch behind her ears and her neck and then between her breasts where his lips had so passionately scorched her skin.

Rapidly replacing the lid, she turned off the lights and crawled back between the sheets. Starting with the ones, she methodically began reciting the times tables, concentrating on visualizing the numbers and products as her mother taught her. The rhythmic monotony helped settle her nerves and she quickly became drowsy. Her last thought before falling asleep was that her bed was too short and Hugo would never be able to fit.

---

The school was gathered in the dining room, and Don clinked his glass to get everyone's attention. "Students, we need to give Hugo a big round of applause and thanks for all the help he's given us."

Enthusiastic clapping broke out, followed by a chorus of "For He's a Jolly Good Fellow." Hugo shook Don's hand while Ian filmed from the back of the room, and on cue three students emerged from the kitchens with a cake. It was inscribed, "To Hugo, who made us better than we ever thought we could be."

Julie saw Hugo brush some moisture from his eyes and it took him several moments before he could speak. "I'd like to thank everyone for their hard work. You have all done exceedingly well. Thank you for having me here." He coughed and continued. "I have everyone's exam scores here and I'll pass them around. I think you'll be very impressed. I certainly was."

As Hugo sliced the cake, exam papers were circulated and squeals of joy erupted. The students surrounded him, and he posed for pictures and shook hands.

"You were right," Julie told him as she accepted a piece of cake. "They needed to be pushed."

"Aye," Clive agreed, "I never thought you'd get so much out of this lot. Plus French."

Hugo laughed and devoured an enormous slice.

Soon it was time to say goodbye. "I hope we'll be seeing you again soon," Bonnie said.

"It would be a pleasure," he replied, giving her an affectionate hug. He shook Don's and Clive's hands, brushed a kiss on Julie's cheek, and then followed Ian out the door without a backward look.

Julie stood unmoving for several moments, stunned.

That was it? That was all he was going to do?

She fled to her office and collapsed on the bench.

*That was it? That was it? That was it?*

The three words pounded a relentless staccato in her head. Panic gripped her, the worst panic she'd ever felt in her life— she physically felt as though someone were squeezing her heart. The future stretched before her like a fathomless black hole reaching to eternity.

———◦○◦———

That night the barometer plunged, and the weather service issued a storm warning with gale force winds. Julie privately considered this a blessing—there were preparations to be made and she would need to work nonstop. Which meant there would be no time to go down to the Plaid Elephant and watch the Kingsbury Town versus Manchester City match Sunday afternoon.

Clive met her at Haddonfield early Saturday morning, and together they filled emergency buckets and added a second line of straw bales to protect the low Spanish tunnels. Seeing dark clouds billowing ominously on the horizon, Julie called the dormitory house to see if any of the students could come up and help.

Gretchen apologized, saying they all had decided to visit a museum and weren't expected back till later that evening.

"A museum?" Julie repeated.

"I know, I'm curious about it as well. There's something going on, although I don't think it's anything bad. But I'll come up and help."

---

By Sunday morning, the wind had worked its way up to thirty knots. Julie spent the day updating her logbooks and anxiously peering out her office window. After hearing the overnight forecast, she decided to spend the night on the bench in her office. She scavenged the kitchens for leftovers and warmed them on the woodstove, then took a blanket from the closet and tried to get comfortable on the hard bench. A dull night-light flickered occasionally, but the power held and the temperature alarm in the glasshouse remained silent.

As she lay in the dark listening to the ominous creaking of the ancient oaks overhead, she wondered what Hugo was doing that night. The radio said Kingsbury Town had beaten Manchester City. It was impossible to follow the announcer's excited babbling, but it seemed another club had also lost, so Kingsbury Town had gone up in the rankings by two spots, their closest ever to the top. Townsend Lane Stadium had been pandemonium, with heightened security to ensure the celebrations remained peaceful. The team's party, no doubt, would be raucous.

Julie pushed that thought out of her head and closed her eyes. One times one is one, one times two is two, one times three is three...

---

It's like they're catering the Armada," Ian whistled under his breath Monday evening as they watched the students roll tall stainless-steel shelves into a van for the evening's service at the Belevedere. "Do they have to do all the work here at Haddonfield?"

"They do the prep work here. The grilling and sauces will be done at the Belevedere," Julie said, sipping a cup of strong tea. The winds had subsided slightly around noon but were due to pick up again at sundown.

"Who's in charge tonight?"

"Joanna. She's planned poached salmon and pork medallions. She's been on staff there three times and knows the drill. She'll be fine."

"If she can stay awake," Bonnie added. "The rest of them as well. I have no idea what's the matter with them, they've been dead on their feet for the last three weeks. Gretchen says they've been leaving after dinner and not coming back until curfew at eleven p.m. And Matthew's grandmother called me this morning. She's very worried about him. She said he's been out very late, she doesn't know where, and is coming home exhausted."

"Aye," Clive chimed in, "he's been looking terrible."

"They go out unsupervised? Is that allowed?" Ian asked.

"Yes, they're not locked in. They can come and go as they please," Bonnie said.

"Matthew has been miserable and grumpy around here, too." Julie agreed.

"Sounds like an epidemic," Ian said. "Hugo's been knackered as well. There must have been quite a party after the drilling Kingsbury Town gave Man City last night. They moved into sixth place. I went over to his house this morning and he looked like hell, said he'd only just gotten to bed."

Julie's heart turned to lead. She returned to her office and took out a dried yellow rose from the bouquet Hugo had given her, inhaling the faint fragrance it still held. Had he forgotten about her completely? The brotherly peck on the cheek was the last thing she'd expected, and she was trying hard not to be devastated. She toyed absently with the rose and stared at her mobile phone. If she pushed three buttons, Hugo's mobile would ring. He might answer it, and then she could hear his voice.

What would she say? Hello, I miss you, and I'm regretting having pushed you away the night you came to Don and Gretchen's house?

With an abject groan, she buried her head in her hands. She was in love with Hugo. Utterly, miserably in love. There was no hope for it, and she knew instinctively that staying here in England would just prolong her misery. The Virginia job offer was in her mail basket at home, waiting to be declined. It had come out of the blue on the recommendation of one of her professors at Cornell, and she was flattered but hadn't even considered it. Perhaps it was time to go home and reread it.

# Chapter Forty-Six

THE WINDS INCREASED violently the next day, and Julie moved the most delicate seedlings into her office in the event they lost power to the glasshouse. She also took the precaution of taking all ten pots of the Champion of England peas home with her for safekeeping.

After lunch, Nerida saw a rip develop in the plastic covering of a Spanish tunnel, and together they managed to mend it and re-cover the area, grueling work in the bitter wind. When they finally returned to the kitchen, Bonnie had a strange half smile playing on her lips. "Julie, you've got a visitor."

Pure joy filled her but instantly deflated. "Oh, hello, Mark."

"Darling!" He pulled her into his arms and kissed her.

"Not in front of the students," Julie whispered, squirming out of his embrace. "It's nice to see you. When did you get in?"

"Just now. I had the driver stop here first."

"Is everything okay?" Julie asked with concern.

"Yes, of course. I just missed you."

"Would you like to take some tea back to your office, Julie?" Bonnie asked sweetly. "I've made up a tray."

Mark trailed her back to the office, maneuvering through the trays of tender seedlings that lined the hallway and the floor of her office. "Gosh, darling, you don't know how good it is to see you."

Afraid he was going to maul her again, Julie set the tray on the low table between them and sat in her desk chair, offering him the bench.

"How was New York? You look exhausted." It was true. His color was waxen and there were dark circles under his eyes.

"I am. Planning on going home and sleeping till tomorrow, but I wanted to see you first." Mark swallowed a large gulp of tea and wolfed down a cookie. "I say, these got a little burned on the edges."

"We get the rejects."

"Oh. Well then. Anyway, they loved the shots and forgot about everything else. So, that's done and I'm home now, and don't have to travel again until after the launch party. That's almost a full two weeks we can be together!" Mark announced with delight. "And I've got another surprise for you, but you have to come into town Thursday to see it."

Julie yawned. "A surprise?"

"A good surprise, darling. You'll be excited. We can go out for dinner afterwards, anywhere you like."

"With whom?"

"It will be just us. I promise."

A blast of wind hit the house, rattling the windows and shaking the foundations. Julie looked out the window in time to see another cover blow off a Spanish tunnel.

Nerida was already out the kitchen door as Julie struggled into her coveralls. "I'll try to make it, Mark, if the wind dies down by then," she apologized. "I've got to go out now and fix that tunnel or we won't have anything to eat next month."

Mark stared helplessly as she fled out the door. "Bloody nuisance, Julie, can't you let those students do all that?"

———————◦○◦———————

By Thursday, the storm had blown itself out, and Clive announced Haddonfield had come through reasonably unscathed, although the neighborhood was harder hit. The staff and students spent the morning helping clean up storm debris in the road and adjacent properties and then moved the seedlings back to the glasshouse and hauled the straw bales from around the Spanish tunnels back to the barn.

Julie was exhausted and had to drag herself to meet Mark in Chelsea that afternoon. She hadn't had much sleep, was hungry and irritable, and didn't really care what she wore.

The address Mark gave her was a modern high-rise building on a street lined with chic restaurants and expensive boutiques. He was waiting for her in the glassed portico and waved enthusiastically when she walked up. "Finally! I didn't think you were going to make it."

"The bus got stuck in traffic."

"Whatever. Come on, let's go in."

They rode up the elevator to the eleventh floor. With a quiet swoosh, the doors opened into an elegantly appointed foyer with deep white carpeting. There were three apartment doors, each one in its own vestibule niche. Mark went to the nearest and fished in his pocket for a key. After a brief process of trial and error with the electronic key, Mark swung the door open with a flourish. "Ta da!"

Julie stepped into the flat, expecting someone to greet them, but it was empty. The hall opened into a living room with a slippery, blond maple floor and a breathtaking view of London. Behind it was a gleaming kitchen of stainless steel and granite and a dining area off to one side.

"Well?" Mark said from behind her. "What do you think?"

"It's very nice. Whose is it?"

"Belongs to a girl I work with at Smith-Wessex. Her husband is in finance in the City and he's just been transferred to Hong Kong. They have to sell up."

"Oh." Julie looked around for a few more moments. "Oh! Are you thinking of buying it?"

"Sort of. I thought *we* might think about buying it."

Julie's feet felt rooted to the floor.

"There's lots of wonderful things about it," Mark enthused. "There's lots of light and over here there's a small balcony you can put some plants on."

"It faces north."

"Yes, we'll have a great view of the King's Road. And look, she said orchids do really well here!"

Indeed, a regal purple dendrobium sat next to a delicate white *Phalaenopsis aphrodite,* their flawless stems twining elegantly from antique porcelain cachepots.

Mark grabbed her hand and pulled her along. "And through here is the bedroom and en suite. It's spectacular."

The bathroom was indeed impressive, small but expertly designed with marble tiles and a glassed-in shower. Julie spent several moments wiggling a sink faucet trying to get water before giving up. "There's no bathtub."

"Bathtubs are so old-fashioned," Mark scoffed. "And this shower has individual temperature controls and a sauna setting."

The bedroom had a row of closets against one wall, and an enormous flat screen television hung on the other. Mark flicked the remote control and it sprang loudly to life. "Ah. Home theater surround sound. Brilliant."

Julie followed Mark as he poked around, obviously pleased with every modern amenity he found. "So, darling, what do you think?" he finally asked.

She thought she'd been in cozier dentists' offices. "It's nice. But what's the rush? I've still got months left on my lease in Finchley."

Mark brushed that detail aside. "Darling, all last week in New York I thought about how important you are to me. How special. And how it's bloody well time I did something about it! Don't want someone sneaking in and stealing you away from me, do I?"

"Like who?"

"Like Hugo Auchincloss, for one," Mark spat. "You're my own darling angel, and I'm keeping you for myself." He came to her and kissed her, his breath warm and smelling of rum. "I know we've been putting off getting more intimate," he continued, his lips soft against her own, "and I can't for the life of me understand how I could have been so crazy."

His arm wrapped around her back and pulled her against him as his other hand slipped inside her coat and cupped her breast through the thin fabric of her blouse, squeezing it. Julie stood like a statue, revolted by his clumsy fondling.

"You look amazing." He nuzzled her ear and clasped her bottom, grinding his groin into her. "And it's so quiet here, so peaceful, we won't be interrupted—"

"Mark!" Julie heard herself screech and dropped her voice to a frigid whisper. "This is someone's home!"

She spun and fled the apartment.

Mark joined her in the foyer, looking ashamed. "Darling. I'm so sorry. You're right. It's just that you're so damn desirable, and I lost my head for a moment. Forgive me? Hmmm?" He pressed her hand to his lips, giving her the charming little boy look that used to melt her heart but now left her feeling repelled. The elevator finally appeared and took them to the ground floor in silence. Julie shrugged into her coat and pushed the building door open into the brisk spring sunshine.

"I'm sorry, Juliet, I panicked." Mark scurried to keep up with her on the sidewalk.

"Don't call me Juliet," she snapped.

"Julie," he hastily corrected. "I'm sorry, I'm screwing up all over the place. I feel like I don't know which way is up. But I do know you mean so much to me."

She just kept walking faster.

"Would you be up for a trip to Essex this weekend to meet my parents?" he asked from a step behind her.

"I'm painting the baby's room for Clive and Bonnie this weekend." Julie tried to sound apologetic but with a streak of meanness she didn't know she possessed, she added, "Would you like to help?"

"Paint? Ah, actually, there's so much to be done for the launch party next Thursday, I'll be swamped. You're right, Essex is out of the question, at least for this weekend. But you will go with me, won't you? And soon?"

"We'll see."

"And don't forget about the launch party on Thursday. There's three hundred on the guest list, it's going to be the event of the season."

"Will Rochelle be there?"

"Absolutely not. I managed to save her contract with Dionysus, and she knows she has to toe the line. She's booked to be at the launch party in New York. I'll send a car for you at six."

Julie sat on the bus back to Finchley, fighting the tears that seemed ever-present nowadays. What was the matter with her? Suddenly everything she wanted was coming true. Mark was ready to make a commitment, Mark had gotten rid of Rochelle, and Mark wanted to make love to her.

And she wanted someone else.

# Chapter Forty-Seven

BONNIE CHOSE A lovely yellow for the baby's room and Julie took the entire weekend to paint it. Mark was busy coordinating the multiple launch parties that would take place Thursday in four cities around the world and called frequently to check on her progress and apologize for not being able to help. For once, Julie heard the sounds of a busy office in the background.

Sunday afternoon, the nursery was finished, and Bonnie set out lunch in their snug sitting room. Clive arranged a footstool and some pillows for her and made sure she was settled comfortably on the sofa before turning the television to the FA Cup match. Julie sat on the floor and watched as Kingsbury Town jogged onto the field, followed by Liverpool. Ian was right—Hugo did look tired, and her heart went out to him. Was he eating enough? Was he so busy taking care of everyone else that he wasn't taking care of himself? Or was someone special taking up his time?

Her sandwich sat untouched as she hugged her knees to her chest and watched him play. Clive was a lively commentator, and it was obvious from the start that Kingsbury Town was having difficulties.

"They're working through a lot of injuries, and they tend to overthink things when they get behind. Bunch of oddballs, really—brilliant but oddballs," Clive snorted. "Hugo fits right in."

With thirty seconds to go before the half, a Liverpool striker booted in a short ball on a rebound that caught Brian Bathurst off guard, and the teams went to the locker room with the score 1–0 Liverpool.

"Where the bloody hell Carr and Rutledge were on that one, I have no idea," Clive grunted. "That striker could have driven a lorry into the net from that angle. Don't you want your sandwich, Julie?"

"Wrap it up and put it in the fridge please, Clive," Bonnie said. "She can have it later if she likes."

Clive took the plates into the kitchen, and Bonnie folded her hands over her stomach. "You've been very quiet," she observed. "Have you heard from him?"

There was no need for Bonnie to specify who "he" was. "No."

"How long has it been?"

Julie picked at a stray thread on the carpet. "Nine days."

"I see." Bonnie considered this for a moment. "You don't have to answer this question if you don't want to, but how close did you and Hugo get?"

"Close." At Bonnie's raised eyebrows, she added, "Not that close. But we kissed a few times."

"And?"

"And it was wonderful. More than wonderful—*he's* more than wonderful. I thought he was cold and arrogant and aloof, but he's not. He's warm and kind and actually very humble. Compared to Hugo, Mark is the cold and arrogant one."

"I think they're both very different men. And Hugo is not Prince Charming—far from it. But I've come around quite a bit on him."

"It's so easy to be myself around him," Julie said. "It doesn't seem to matter to him what I wear or what I do—he just likes being with me."

"That's good. That's the way it should be."

"No, it's not. It turns out that you and Clive were right, what you told me about footballers. He wants me, but he's not interested in a romantic involvement. For him it would just be physical. He was very upfront about it."

"Are you sure, Julie?" Bonnie asked.

Julie's shoulders sagged. "I told him I couldn't do that. Now he's been gone eight days and hasn't tried to call me or see me or anything."

"What about Mark? Is he still involved with Rochelle?"

"He says he doesn't want anything to do with her, and after the photoshoot, I believe him. But he feels like he has to help her. She's gained weight and has been very difficult to work with."

Bonnie's eyes widened, and she pressed her lips together.

"I know you don't like Mark," Julie continued, "but he's under a lot of stress right now, and I'm not being fair by comparing him to Hugo all the time. And he swears that after the Bajan Gin launch, it will all be much better." She paused and drew a deep breath. "He wants me to meet his parents."

"Are you ready for that?"

"I don't know." Julie buried her head in her hands. "Everything is a jumble. I wanted to spend more time with him and now I'm avoiding him. I thought I wanted to make love with him, and then when he wanted to, I didn't. What should I do? Throw Mark away for a fling with Hugo? Because that's all it would be, a fling."

"Look, Julie, I don't know what either of them is playing at, but I don't think anything is as it seems. I've watched Hugo and I think it's more than just a physical thing with him. You made it clear you're with Mark, yet he still followed you around like a lovesick puppy. And Mark..." Bonnie paused and thought for a moment. "I don't know what's going on there. But something is, and it's not good."

"No, it's not good. I'm a twenty-six-year-old virgin who's got a crush on a famous footballer. I have no idea how I'm going to behave at the launch party on Thursday night. What if he brings another girl, Bonnie?" Julie asked in desperation. "I don't think I could bear it."

Bonnie patted her shoulder. "I think you should go to the party and let your heart tell you what to do."

Julie cheered up a bit at this advice. "May I borrow some nail polish?"

———— ◆◇◆ ————

Hugo swung around to Malbrey Jewellers on Wednesday afternoon to pick up his cuff links, which were in for an emergency repair. He'd taken them off at Sunday night's study session when he'd rolled up his sleeves, and Tanda had accidentally dropped three heavy literature books on them, flattening the hinge pins. They were Juliet's favorites, and he intended to wear them to the launch party.

Parking in Mayfair was impossible, so he caught a bus and walked the few blocks to the landmark store. It fussed him mildly that his favorite jeweler also did a brisk business with other Premier League players, but he knew they spent outrageous amounts, and he could hardly begrudge the store for indulging their rather flamboyant tastes. But they knew him there, his family had been customers for decades, probably centuries, and they catered to his discernment. The repair was undertaken without delay, a privilege available to few customers. Which was a good thing, because everything had to be perfect for when he saw Juliet again.

Hugo had counted the hours, waiting for tomorrow night. He'd deliberately left her alone for exactly fourteen days, knowing he had to give her the opportunity to miss him. The time had dragged, and it had been damn near impossible to stay away from her, to say nothing of the physical discomfort his desire was causing.

Luckily, the GCSE tutoring was occupying all his time. In addition to Matthew, he was now tutoring Nerida, Tanda, Lalani, and Alex as well. Their progress was encouraging, but the time commitment was enormous. His mother had found a common room at the Finchley Art League where they met almost every evening, including after Kingsbury Town's momentous win over Manchester City. They had studied till two o'clock in the morning that night, as well as after their loss to Liverpool in the FA Cup.

His loneliness was assuaged somewhat by the fact that he knew everything Juliet was doing almost every minute of every day. The students had readily participated in a tacit agreement that payment was to be any and all information about her and had proved to be remarkably observant. Between the five of them, they contributed bits and pieces that added up to a near-perfect timeline.

He knew that Juliet had planted strawberries in the hot frames, added another beehive, and was happy with the tomato seedlings in the cold beds. Richard, the farmer, stayed for tea on Wednesday, and his jaw tightened when Joanna added that Juliet had been invited to his house for dinner that evening. The windstorm kept everyone busy, a windowpane broke in the glasshouse, two letters arrived from her parents in America, and Looks had paid a surprise visit on Tuesday.

"Useless posh git," Matthew grumbled, and glanced at Hugo. "Sorry, no offense."

"Was she surprised to see him?" Hugo asked sharply, having long ago discarded any pretense of disinterest.

"I'll say. Practically mauled her in the kitchen. Get a room, I say. He stayed for a half hour, then another cover blew off and she had to scurry. Thursday, he took her to look at apartments in Chelsea, and he wants her to go to Essex this weekend to meet his parents."

That last bit of information caused Hugo undeniable panic. Had the mess at Cheeting House forced Looks to reevaluate things? He mulled this over as he turned onto South Audley Street, and as if on cue, his mobile phone rang.

Hugo checked the number and scowled. "Looks. How was New York?"

"Stupendous. The shots of you and Julie are going viral and now all the regional vice presidents want them. We need to redo the contract."

"No way. They were a one-off."

"We can make it worth your effort," Looks parried smugly. "Corporate's wild for you. At least let's sit down and talk."

"Absolutely not."

"Come on, Hugo, everyone has their price. Even you."

It was on the tip of his tongue to tell Looks to go to hell, but Hugo had an epiphany. "You're right. There is one thing I

MARINA REZNOR

want."

"Name it."

"Juliet."

"You can't be serious," Mark sputtered.

"I've never been more serious about anything in my life."

There was a pause, and he could tell Looks was weighing the possibilities. "And we'd get you?"

"Lock, stock, and barrel of gin."

"No," Mark decided. "You'll be retired in under three years and then you'll be a nobody. I'm in this to get to the top, and to get there I need Julie. Besides, she'll never go with you. She thinks you're the worst sort of rake. See you at the party Thursday night, and don't forget, we get three hours with pictures."

"Ninety minutes and no photos."

"Whatever."

With a sigh, Hugo tucked his phone back in his pocket and walked past Malbrey's grand portico to a discreet side entrance.

"Mr. Auchincloss." Robert Paulson, the manager, greeted him and showed him into a private display room. "We have your cufflinks finished. Just a slight repair to the pins."

Hugo checked them over and nodded. "I'll take them with me. And this watch needs to be cleaned, it's my spare so there's no rush."

"Very good, sir."

As he settled the bill and turned to leave, a glint of dazzling blue caught his eye. A display cabinet at the end of the room held a sapphire and diamond necklace that glittered warmly in the expert lighting, and he walked towards it, hypnotized.

The color of the blue gems was varied and gradated, exactly like Juliet's eyes. Some were as light as the sky, others almost indigo, and a few the exact shade of her eyes in candlelight. They were surrounded by marquis-cut diamonds, interwoven with graceful arcs of glittering baguettes in a winsome platinum setting, like lyrics to a love song. He couldn't take his eyes off it.

The manager slipped a key into the display case lock and withdrew the necklace, handing it to Hugo to examine. The brilliant gems winked brightly, their size generous but not garish. Hugo examined it from every angle, amazed by its lightness and flexibility.

"It's spectacular," he murmured.

"Quite, sir. It just came out of the workrooms this morning. You're the first to see it."

That sealed it. He had to have it—Juliet had to have it. He didn't know when, or how, but this necklace was going to be hers. "I'll take it."

"There is a choice of clasps." The manager produced a black velvet tray with samples and they spent some time discussing the merits of each. In the end, Hugo chose the simplest, a deceptively clever lock that lay flat and hinged invisibly, which of course, also ended up being the most expensive. But he couldn't have cared less.

Robert Paulson made careful notes on the work order. "It should be finished by next week. That would make the total price—"

"I said I'll take it," Hugo snapped. Bugger the cost. He wasn't out there busting his ass on national television every week so he could haggle over the price of a necklace. "Have it sent around when it's done."

# Chapter Forty-Eight

JULIE BARELY SLEPT Wednesday night. The next morning, she arrived at Haddonfield before daybreak, did her chores with lightning speed, and was home by lunchtime. She soaked in a hot bath and scrubbed her nails, then spent a full forty minutes on her makeup. Reaching into the back of her closet, she pulled out a dress with a note: *"Save for a special occasion."* If the launch party wasn't a special occasion, she didn't know what was.

The dress was made of white Alençon lace backed with flesh-colored netting and came to just above her knees, with long, snug-fitting sleeves and a straight, horizontal neckline that skimmed her shoulders. It was unadorned and hugged her figure becomingly, although test runs showed it wasn't the easiest thing to sit down in.

After three evenings of experimenting with updos, Julie settled on wearing her hair down with a few strands caught up and pinned at her crown with a pearl barrette. A small clutch purse completed the outfit, and she glanced at the clock, surprised to see she was ready to leave a full two hours before the driver was due to pick her up.

She nibbled two crackers, her stomach full of butterflies, and in desperation reorganized her bookshelf in alphabetical order by author's last name to keep herself from pacing a path in the carpet.

————◆————

Julie's knees knocked together as the doorman approached the car, the enormous hotel in Regent's Park looming behind him. What if Hugo brought a date? Even worse, what if he greeted her with the same affectionate friendship he'd shown on his last day at Haddonfield?

She licked her dry lips and walked up the broad steps, smiling for a few photographers who'd arrived early to stake out their spots. Mark said Smith-Wessex was working out of a suite of rooms on the fifth floor, so she took the lift up and knocked on the door and waited, and then knocked again.

The door was finally opened by Sophie. "Jules."

"Sophie."

The two women stood facing each other. "May I come in?" Julie finally asked. "I think Mark's expecting me."

With a sarcastic flourish, Sophie opened the door wider, revealing a beehive of activity. Julie spotted Mark at a wide table, poring over a floor plan with several staffers.

"Darling!" Mark said, scurrying over. "It's been a madhouse all day, but I think we're finally set. I just have to nip into the loo and tidy up." He dropped a kiss on her forehead as he headed to the bathroom. "We ordered in some curry, help yourself—I made sure to get that vegetarian dish you like. I hid it in the back. These vultures will eat anything!"

A desk in the corner held a littered assortment of half-eaten takeaway boxes, with one bearing a warning, "DON'T

TOUCH OR YOU'LL BE WORKING ON THE KITTY LITTER ACCOUNT!!!"

Realizing she was famished, Julie ate hungrily. After several bites, she detected some off flavors and put the box down, sipping from a bottle of water.

Mark emerged from the bathroom freshly shaven and looking handsome in a dark suit, crisp white shirt open at the throat and diamond cufflinks in the French cuffs.

"I look like Hugo, don't I?" he laughed, seeming to read her thoughts. "Quite dashing, I decided imitation is the sincerest form of flattery."

People began clamping on headsets and departing the room in groups with clipboards tucked under their arms. "Guess we better get going as well," Julie said.

"Darling, wait, a word." Mark paused and drew her aside. "I want to apologize for last week. I realize now the apartment was completely unsuitable for us. You need to be much closer to Haddonfield, don't you?"

"That would help," she conceded.

"I have a girl looking. She said there's a lot available that should be convenient for both of us. And if this launch goes well, we might be able to afford a bit more, maybe even something with a small garden. Would you like that?"

"We can talk about this later, Mark. You need to concentrate —"

"No, I want to say this now. I'm also sorry for pressing my attentions on you. I feel like I've been on a roller coaster these last few months, and you've been the only steady, dependable thing in my world. I want you to know how much I appreciate that. And how much I care for you."

Mark looked soulfully into her eyes, and Julie felt her stomach lurch. "You'll be finding out soon how much," he added, kissing the tip of her nose.

A frantic assistant swung around the corner. "Mark, the duchess is arriving! You're wanted downstairs!"

"Shall I escort you?" Mark offered.

"I think I need to use the restroom. I'll be down right after that."

"Of course, darling. You should make a grand entrance. Just don't be too long."

---

Hugo and Ian arrived a few minutes after seven and followed the glittering crowd across the cavernous hotel foyer towards the club. Hugo sent Ian in through the main doors and let the cameras click on him while he entered via a side corridor, completely unnoticed.

The club was already jammed with beautiful people sparkling under the skillful lighting. A Caribbean band played on a stage under banners hung from the rafters heralding Bajan Gin, while servers circulated with trays of neon-colored drinks garnished with tropical fruit.

Four of the banners were images of him and Juliet, and Hugo was taken aback by how outstanding they were. For once, Looks was right; the chemistry between them was undeniable. They were sizzling.

He found Ian chatting with a camera crew. "Everyone looks remarkably sober," Hugo noted as he scanned the crowd for any sign of Juliet.

"That's because no one's drinking," Ian said. "They're all holding the glasses but they're still full. And I see Mongo

Montieth over there, passing a hip flask around. That's not a good sign."

Nodding to groups of acquaintances, Hugo and Ian passed through the crowd before joining a group of footballers who were admiring a poster of him and Juliet.

"You've never looked lovelier, Hugo," a defender from Chelsea grinned.

"Wish Nike would give me a model like her to pose with," a midfielder from Everton chimed in.

"She just had twins," Hugo provided helpfully. "Certainly got her figure back fast."

"I'll say. Damn, is that her?"

They turned in unison and Hugo felt time pause, just like the first day he met her. Juliet walked into the party looking more breathtakingly beautiful than he'd ever seen her. She was wearing a pure white lace dress, and Hugo stood transfixed as she walked across the marble floor. She looked like a bride coming down the aisle. Like *his* bride. The spell continued to build with delicious momentum until she was standing before them, a vision in white.

"Hugo," she said, "it's so nice to see you again. I'm so glad you could come."

His lips moved soundlessly as once again words fought to tell her that Sunday's FA Cup loss had been painful, Miles had just finished the first application of the fungicide she recommended, and that he had never seen a woman as beautiful as she.

"Juliet," he finally got out, raising her fingers to his lips. "Lovely to see you." Hugo held her hand a moment longer than necessary, the blood pumping hotly through his body. "You look amazing."

"Thank you."

Ian leaned down to brush his lips against her cheek. "You do look spectacular, Julie."

She looked each brother over from head to toe. "Same charcoal-grey suits and white shirts, so I'm guessing it will be you tomorrow in the papers, Ian?"

Both men laughed while Hugo continued to hold her hand. "Did you cut yourself?" he asked in concern, looking at the almost invisible scratch on her finger.

"It's just a small cut. A window broke in the glasshouse Monday, and I replaced it."

Looks appeared, a huge smile on his face. "Hello, chaps, good to see you. Doesn't Julie look smashing? And see, she even got a manicure!" he kidded, wrapping a proprietary arm around her. Hugo fought the urge to bend it back till it snapped.

A waiter appeared and flourished his tray of tropical drinks, each one a strangely vibrant color. Looks inspected them carefully and handed one to each of them.

"Excuse me," Ian declined, "but I think I'll get a soda at the bar."

Hugo's drink was an iridescent yellow and Julie's, a dark purple. Mark selected a murky green and proposed a toast. "To Bajan Gin!"

They clinked glasses, and Hugo took a tentative sip, almost gagging on the cloyingly sweet combination of alcohol and juice. "What are these?"

"Some of the designer cocktails they've come up with. Julie has the 'Plum Good'—it's made with the dried plum gin."

"Prune-flavored gin?" Julie wrinkled her nose.

"Not prunes. Dried plums. World of difference. We hired some of the best mixologists in New York to come up with signature cocktails—it's all about creating a buzz. You've got the pineapple-flavored gin and I've got the kiwi-orange. We can try the coconut, if you like."

"I'll pass." Hugo grimaced and gamely tried his drink again. "How is everything going?"

"Brilliant! Couldn't be better. Almost the entire guest list has shown up. All that's left to do is enjoy the night—" he squeezed her waist "—with the most beautiful woman in the room on my arm. Oh look, the lead singer for that new boy band just came in. Come over and join me in a few moments, won't you darling?" he said and darted off. "Tonight is going to be a very special night!"

———◆———

Finally, Hugo was alone with her. "How is Bonnie feeling?"

Julie took a tissue out of her clutch and dabbed at her forehead. "Wonderful. We painted the baby's room this weekend, and it turned out so well. We're going shopping for furniture Saturday, and then it will be finished."

A waiter circulated with a tray of hors d'oeuvres. Hugo selected one and handed it to Julie, then chose one for himself.

"No, thank you. I'm not hungry," she declined. "It's odd not having you around at Haddonfield. We've missed you."

"I've missed being there," Hugo said. "I've missed everything about it."

"Ian comes out quite a bit."

"If he's being a pest, let me know."

"No, he's fine. We honestly forget he's even there."

"Lucky you," he said, and Julie laughed weakly, a faint sheen on her skin. "I say, do you not feel well?"

"I had a quick bite to eat upstairs and I'm not sure it agreed with me," she admitted, patting her neck. "There might have been some shellfish in it. It was a curry and hard to tell. But I'll be all right."

Sophie appeared and glared at Hugo. "Mark's looking for you," she told Julie. "I told him I knew just where to look."

# Chapter Forty-Nine

JULIE JOINED MARK as he greeted the guests who continued to pour into the party, taking care to keep the purple drink far from her nose. His smile was genuine, and Julie realized it had been ages since she'd seen him so relaxed and happy.

Across the club, Julie could see Hugo had been waylaid by a fervid Kingsbury Town supporter and was doing his best to be charming. She couldn't resist watching him, and when he glanced in her direction it was impossible to look away. He smiled as if they were sharing a secret joke, and for a moment it seemed like they were the only two people in the club.

A woman next to her gasped, breaking the spell. "I can't believe it!"

A surge of excitement rippled through the crowd, and Julie heard Rochelle's name whispered in multiple amplitudes. Guests surged to look out the windows to see a white limousine that was being swarmed by photographers.

A Smith-Wessex staffer slid next to Mark and whispered in his ear.

"She's supposed to be in New York!" he exploded. "Is she coming in?"

"She says she won't until..."

"Until what?" Mark demanded.

The staffer glanced at Julie and pulled Mark aside. Julie stood alone, frozen to the spot as grim-faced Smith-Wessex executives joined the huddle and cast furtive glances in her direction. Her hands began to shake as the queasiness in her stomach grew.

Julie felt a steadying hand on her back. "What's going on?" Hugo murmured.

"Rochelle is here. I think people want me to leave."

"You'll do no such thing. Just stay where you are and tell me how the Champions of England are doing."

This made her smile. "I got germination from nine seeds, which is a huge number."

"Remarkable. Tell me more."

Hugo kept her talking while the chaos around them grew. Mark reappeared, his earlier composure replaced with flat-out panic. "Julie, darling, can I have a word?"

He took her arm and pulled her behind a large pillar. Hugo followed grimly.

"Darling, Rochelle is here and she's making some serious drama."

"She's refusing to come in until you leave," Sophie announced, joining them with a fresh drink in her hand and giving Hugo a spiteful look.

"Is that true?" Julie asked.

"Well," Mark squirmed. "You see, she is still the face of Sam Lord's Castle Rum..."

Julie glanced at Hugo and straightened her shoulders. "Then tell her to come in. I thought you said you wanted me to meet her?"

Mark paled. "I did! But not like this, for Christ's sake, not when she's being so unreasonable."

"Why don't you just leave, Julie? Make it a lot easier on the rest of us," Sophie suggested.

"She's not going anywhere," Hugo announced, facing Mark. "Grow a backbone and go tell Rochelle she can either leave or join the party. But Juliet is staying."

"She'll make a scene!" Mark hissed, his eyes wild.

"Fine, you should welcome the publicity. Tell her to come in or announce she's leaving."

"But that would humiliate her!"

"And you'd let her humiliate Juliet? Go and give her the ultimatum." With a strong hand, he turned Mark around and pushed him towards the door. But Mark had turned to stone.

Julie followed his stare across the room, to the arching entrance where Rochelle Chevelle emerged under the spotlights.

She was breathtaking. She stood like a statue, swathed in an intricately pleated white gown, her short hair slicked back and her pale skin luminous. Her dark eyes flashed over the crowd before settling first on Mark and then Julie.

Her escort was a handsome Latin man dressed in a flawless tuxedo. His black hair was slicked back like Rochelle's, and together they made a stunning pair, she entirely in white, he in black, their teeth gleaming like porcelain.

A server appeared by their side with a tray of drinks. The man chose a purple one and handed Rochelle a green one. She sipped it and smiled, then raised her glass to Mark in salute. The room broke into rapturous applause. It was as deft a performance as Julie had ever seen.

Mark lurched forward as if released from a spell and hurried to Rochelle's side, escorting the pair from group to group, the billowing folds of the model's gown undulating around her as she walked. There were frequent pauses to smile for photographers while Mark hung nervously in the background.

"He seems very upset about something," Julie murmured. "I thought he was happy with the way the evening was going. Now he seems to be melting down."

"That's putting it mildly," Hugo said. "Keep smiling."

"Rochelle looks amazing, doesn't she?" Julie asked as the willowy woman moved inexorably closer to them.

"I told you she has terrible breath. Now you can see for yourself."

Ian joined them, holding a green cocktail. "That's Eduardo Mantegna. He's a film star from Ecuador."

Hugo frowned. "I thought you weren't drinking."

"I'm not. I saw the bartender mix up one of these green things for Rochelle with no alcohol, so I asked for one as well. It's vile—can't imagine what it tastes like with that gin in it."

As the threesome approached, it occurred to Julie that both she and Rochelle had chosen to wear white. To the crowd, though, the two women could not have been more different, and they mobbed around, anticipating their meeting.

"Rochelle, this is my friend Julie." Mark hurriedly made the introductions. "And you've met Hugo Auchincloss, and this is his brother, Ian."

"I remember," Rochelle simpered, extending her hand to be kissed. "We met on your little sailboat in Monaco two summers ago."

"That's right," Hugo shot back, ignoring the proffered hand. "You were teaspoon shopping."

Her dark eyes flared at Hugo's words.

"Rochelle, do you need another drink?" Mark asked, sweat erupting on his brow.

"Here," Hugo said, taking a pink-colored concoction from a passing server's tray. "I think this one is the passion fruit-flavored gin." He extended the drink in a subtle challenge.

Rochelle paused. "No. Pink won't look good in the pictures. Mark, go tell that adorable bartender with the mustache to make me another just the way he made my first, there's a good boy."

Mark dashed off and Eduardo shook both men's hands. "*Señorita*," he murmured, pressing a warm kiss on Julie's hand.

"*Un placer conocerle*," Julie replied in Spanish. A pleasure to meet you.

The man's eyes lit up. "*El placer es mío, cariño*," he said in a deep voice. The pleasure is mine, darling.

A venomous flame lit Rochelle's eyes as Julie and Eduardo conversed easily in Spanish. Standing back, she looked at the huge banner of Hugo and Julie that hung over their heads.

"You seem to enjoy getting your picture taken, Julie," Rochelle said loudly to no one in particular. "You should really consider doing more modeling. Virgin Airlines might be able to use you. I don't think they've ever had a real one in the ads before."

Julie gasped, and Rochelle smiled, knowing she'd made a direct hit. If Rochelle had reached out and slapped her, the effect could not have been more direct.

Hugo's eyes narrowed. "You sodding bitch—"

"Julia!" Ramon interrupted, tugging Julie's elbow. "I must to introduce you to some people!"

# Chapter Fifty

HUGO NOTED WITH relief that Ramon was keeping Julie busy at the opposite end of the room, as far away from Rochelle as possible. Julie, for her part, seemed to be devoting herself to socializing with serene charm despite her growing pallor. Seventeen minutes left to go, according to his watch, until he could whisk her the hell out of there, Looks be damned. It was time she knew everything, and it would be a pleasure to clue her in.

Across the room, Rochelle dismissed Looks and began flirting with her escort. Looks, for his part, was being eaten alive by jealousy, which was obviously exactly what Rochelle had planned. He stood with a group of Smith-Wessex staffers, downing drinks like his throat was on fire. Every time Eduardo touched Rochelle, she would make sure they were in Looks's direct line of sight. It was an over-the-top performance, and Looks was melting down—literally, if you went by the sweat dripping off him.

The final straw came when the film star bent Rochelle backwards in a dramatic kiss caught by the photographers. Sweeping his palm across his forehead, Looks marched to Julie, grabbed her wrist and hurried her along to the podium.

The band stopped mid-song as he tapped a glass to draw everyone's attention.

"I say, she looks awful," Ian said next to him.

Hugo frowned. "She's ill, not sure what the problem is."

"Sure someone didn't give her a poison apple?" Ian asked, nodding to where Rochelle was staring at the podium.

---

Julie struggled not to squint in the blazing spotlights. Mark stood at her side, beaming down at her, and she tried to smile back, but her stomach rolled queasily, and the smile came out as more of a grimace.

"Thank you so much, all of you, for joining us on this monumental evening," Mark began, pointing out the glory of Bajan Gin and recognizing several important guests. Sweat began running down Julie's face as her abdomen clenched, and she wished Mark would finish. What in heaven's name was she doing up there?

"And not only do I have the luck to have been given the opportunity to promote one of the most exciting new drinks of the decade, I also have the good fortune to be blessed with a wonderful girl in my life, talented and loyal, and a better helpmate a man could not hope to find. So before one of you lot steals her from me, I decided it was time I made my move."

Mark bent to one knee and with a theatrical flourish, pulled a black velvet box from his pocket. "Julie Randall, will you marry me?"

He snapped the lid open and angled it towards the crowd, who gasped in unison. When he turned it back to her, she saw a large diamond ring, the center jewel surrounded by a swirl of other diamonds. The setting looked bigger than a coin. She'd never be able to get the dirt out of it.

Mark took her limp hand and slid the ring onto her finger. The glittering piece was too large, and the diamonds rotated around to her palm, but Mark patiently returned them to the top. "You can get it resized right away," he whispered.

The crowd burst into applause and flashbulbs began to go off, temporarily blinding her as Mark wrapped his arm around her waist and gave her a huge squeeze. People descended on them from all sides, clapping them on the back and offering congratulations and best wishes, which Mark accepted gleefully. Julie looked to where Rochelle had been standing a moment ago, but the spot was empty.

Unable to fend off the queasiness any longer, Julie slipped the ring from her finger and pushed it into the pocket of Mark's jacket before discreetly bolting down the hall to the bathroom, reaching a toilet just in time.

Her body was wracked with convulsive heaves as everything in her gut forced its way out. Coughing between the repeated waves, she tried to catch her breath and steady herself against the stall wall.

A cool hand pressed to her forehead and a wet paper towel was held to her lips. "Relax, I've got you," Hugo said, kneeling next to her.

"You can't come in here," she gulped before another bout gripped her.

"They can throw me out," he said as he held her hair back from her face, an arm around her waist to support her. When her body slackened, he wiped her lips and sat on the tile floor, cradling her in his arms.

"I think I drank too much Bajan Gin," she whispered, her teeth chattering.

"You barely touched your drink," he said, wrapping her in his jacket as she trembled. "Did you eat something bad? Or are you upset about Looks proposing?"

"No, I'm happy," she sobbed, struggling to catch her breath. "Very, very happy."

"I've never seen anyone vomit with happiness before."

"Well," she gasped as another bout gripped her, "shows how much you get out."

Hugo held her as her stomach continued to reject everything in it, leaving her for only a brief moment to get more towels. When it seemed nothing more was forthcoming, he held her again as she sobbed uncontrollably.

"Juliet, what's the matter? Should we get you to hospital?"

"No. It's almost over. There must have been some shellfish in the curry. Nothing else makes me so sick."

"That's not what's upsetting you, though," he persisted.

"I can't grow orchids," she sobbed.

He paused, trying to make sense of what she was saying. "I'm sure you could if you put your mind to it. You're a brilliant gardener, you can grow anything."

"And... and I don't think I could live in Chelsea."

"Why in God's name would you want to live in Chelsea?"

She buried her face in his chest. He stroked her hair, trying to soothe her, and after a while, the trembling subsided, and it felt like she could breathe again.

"It's true, what Rochelle said," Julie whispered. "I am a virgin."

Hugo's arms tightened around her. "Hush, it doesn't matter,"

"No, it does. Mark and I have never slept together. I know you think we have—everyone does. But he didn't want to, and now I don't want to, and I don't know what's the matter with me."

"Juliet," Hugo said, "there is nothing wrong with you except that you're exhausted, and sick, and frankly, making no sense whatsoever. I'm going to go find Looks and tell him I'm taking you home. I'm sure he's worried about you."

———◆———

"Oh, she's not here?" Looks glanced around in surprise when Hugo caught up with him. "I say, is she all right?"

"She'll be okay, but she's exhausted. I'd better take her home."

"Okay, yes, she wouldn't want me to leave on my big night," Looks said, waving to someone across the room before returning his focus to Hugo. "Julie and I are glad you could be here for our big announcement. You can see why I turned you down the other day. And now that we're engaged, everything will be perfect."

"She hasn't said yes, has she?"

Mark laughed. "Didn't you see the look on her face? She was speechless."

Hugo kept his fists unclenched with a great effort. "Do you want to say goodnight to her?"

"She's not still being sick, is she?"

"No. She's waiting in the kitchens with Ian while the valet gets the car."

"I won't disturb her. Tell her I'll call from New York tomorrow," Mark said, and turned to chat with a tall brunette.

Fine by me, Hugo thought as he ducked out to the back of the hotel. The valet pulled the Jaguar up, and Ian helped settle Julie in the front seat.

"I think I'm going to stick around," Ian said. "Let me know how she's feeling then."

She rested in the seat with her eyes closed while Hugo carefully navigated the busy streets, anxious not to jar her. He began to make conversation until he realized that she was fast asleep.

Turning onto her street, he got lucky and got a parking spot very close to her house. He found her house key in her purse, lifted her in his arms, and carried her to her door. She murmured sleepily, wrapping her arms around his neck.

Inside a plain car parked down the street, a man raised a camera and began snapping.

Upstairs in her bedroom, he laid her across the bed, gently tugging off her shoes. With an effort, she began to sit up, and he slid an arm around her to help the rest of the way.

"What do you need?" Hugo asked, noting with relief that her color was looking healthier.

"I want to brush my teeth."

Julie emerged from the bathroom wearing a simple white nightgown that buttoned at the neck with a pearl and crawled under the covers of her bed. Turning off the light, he kicked off his shoes and lay down on the bed next to her, drawing her into his arms with the thickness of the blanket and counterpane separating them. She immediately snuggled closer, shivering slightly as he stroked her hair, and slowly her breathing became more even.

"You can get under the covers with me," she offered.

"Not if you want to get any sleep tonight."

"I don't think Rochelle was scared of meeting me," Julie said, nestling against his chest in the darkness. "I think she hates me."

"I told you she was quite a piece of work."

"I didn't plan it, you know."

"Plan what?"

"Still being a virgin. I wish Mark hadn't told Rochelle." Hugo tightened his arms around her in the darkness and she snuggled deeper. "We moved around a lot when I was growing up, and in college I'd be up at four in the morning to work on the farms and was in bed by eight. Didn't leave time for much of a love life, and I wasn't into getting drunk and making out."

"I'm glad," he murmured as his fingers traced the smooth line of her jaw.

"And having a father steeped in Elizabethan ideals of love and courtship didn't help."

"There's nothing wrong with wanting to be wooed and courted."

"Yes, there is. It makes me look naive and ridiculous, like tonight. Everyone else is so sophisticated—you all take it so casually. I tried to be that way, too, I even went on birth control. Stupid."

"Someday you are going to be very, very glad that you waited for the right man and the right situation. I promise." Taking her hand, he kissed each finger and prayed that the day would come very soon. "Juliet? Did you miss me these last twelve days?"

"Fourteen days. Yes," she yawned. "Missed you so much... thought you'd forgotten me... 'fraid you'd bring another girl tonight..."

He felt her breathing gradually become deep and regular, everything about her soft and warm. In her sleep, she turned to her side and he pulled her back against him, her back and bottom fitting against him with perfection. He felt her every breath, her chest rising and falling in his arms. She was safe.

# Chapter Fifty-One

A WONDERFUL FEELING of lassitude enveloped Julie as she woke. It was like swimming to the surface of a lovely pool, and when she finally opened her eyes, she never wanted to get out of bed. She remembered grumbling earlier that morning when Hugo had gotten up, disgruntled that her source of warmth was leaving. He'd laughed and tucked the covers back over her.

The world felt different this morning. She had slept all night with a man for the first time in her life and might be engaged to another man she wasn't sure she wanted to marry, but she felt very, very happy. Buoyant.

After a while, she decided to try sitting up and winced. Her stomach was sore and it felt like she'd been kicked by a mule. There was a glass of water sitting on her nightstand with a note propped in front of it.

Good morning, sweet princess, and flights of angels sing thee to thy awakening.

You look too beautiful to wake. I'll call Bonnie

and let her know you'll be late.

Call me when you get up,

—H

Her mobile phone was propped next to the note, with Hugo's number already entered. She smiled and pressed the button.

He answered right away. "How are you?"

"Sore but better. I think there was some shellfish in the curry I ate last night. Nothing else makes me that sick."

"That's what you said, and I'd have to agree. Look, we're flying to Blackpool for a makeup match tonight and will be back very late, but I want to see you. I'll come up to your house when we get back, okay?"

"But you'll be exhausted."

"No worries, it's imperative that we talk. There are some things you need to know."

"If you say so. Good luck this evening."

After hanging up with Hugo, Julie let herself savor the warm afterglow he always left her with. It took a long time for her to dial Mark's number.

"Darling! Good timing, they're just about to call my flight. And guess what? I've been told to fly directly to Los Angeles —that's where the bigwigs are. There's going to be a huge meeting, and they want me there."

"That's wonderful," Julie said, happy for him.

"Isn't it? Oh, and how are you feeling?"

"Better, thanks. I'm sorry, dinner just didn't agree with me."

"Hope it was the food, darling, and not the ring or the proposal. Did Hugo get you home all right?"

"Yes. Yes, he did. And Mark—" Julie took a deep breath and plunged ahead "—he ended up staying the night. It was to take care of me," she rushed to reassure him, "but I think we need to talk. I'm... I'm having some feelings for Hugo that are confusing me." Running her fingers through her hair, she groped for how to continue. "Actually, I'm not sure how I feel about anything anymore. But we've always been honest with each other, and I don't want to hide anything from you." She paused and waited. "Is any of this making any sense?"

The silence from Mark's end was deafening. "None of this is you!" she continued. "You've been wonderful. I'm just having a hard time sorting out how I'm feeling. I mean, we're sort of engaged now, and we've never talked about how we feel about big things, like having children, or our jobs, or anything like that. I'm just afraid we're rushing into something very permanent, and we need to talk. Don't you think?"

Seconds ticked by and the silence became unbearable. "Mark?"

"Pardon? Oh, sorry, darling, I was texting on my other mobile. So you got home okay? Capital. Now, I'm scheduled to fly home Sunday, but in the meantime, look at your calendar and start thinking about a wedding date. The sooner the better as far as I'm concerned."

"Don't you want to meet my parents first?"

"Whatever for? Hey, they're starting to board my flight, I'll call you tonight when I get in. This is all so exciting, darling. Now gotta hop, take care."

Julie stared at the phone for a long time before she set it back on the nightstand.

———————◆○◆———————

Hugo stayed as long as he could at Juliet's, and then rushed home to shower and change before speeding to St Augustine School, where the club coach would take the team to the airport for the flight to Blackpool. Of course, if the new training facility in Hendon were finished and he were living with Juliet, that would have shaved two hours off the blasted odyssey, but there it was. He wasn't too fussed. Things were going to change for the better very, very soon.

He checked his mobile as he waited in traffic. There were five missed calls from Ian, and Hugo wondered what bee had gotten into his bonnet. But he waited to return them, knowing his brother rarely got out of bed before ten in the morning. There was also a terse command from Tom to call him.

"I see Looks and Julie got engaged last night," Tom said. "He got Dionysus to put out a press release."

"Technically, but not really. She never said yes."

"Oh, that will make all the difference in the world," Tom replied tartly. "The *Daily Mail* has an awfully good shot of you carrying her into her house around midnight last night. Over the threshold, nice touch. Very gallant."

A violent string of curses flew out of Hugo's mouth. "She got sick at the club right after Looks proposed. I took her home."

"Calm down, lucky for you the street lighting was a bit off. It's obviously you, but Julie's partially obscured. They're fishing. But they're close. Very close."

"You have to bury it, Tom," Hugo demanded.

"I will, but I'm not a magician. You have to be more careful. They're smelling something big here and if they find it, there'll be no helping anyone. One other thing," Tom continued, "fallout from the launch parties last night is bad. Very bad, especially in Los Angeles where they were pouring so much of it down the drain, the fish are protesting. Same for Tokyo and New York, but evidently the theatrics in London made everyone forget what they were drinking. Dionysus is scrambling and might pull the entire line. Looks is under a lot of pressure."

"Good."

"In the meantime, is there any way I can convince you to stay away from her until things settle down?"

"No, but I will be more careful," Hugo promised. "And, Tom, there's something else. What are the chances Rochelle could be pregnant?"

Tom whistled. "Why do you say that?"

"She wasn't drinking last night, and that dress she was wearing had lots of fabric. You couldn't see her waist."

"I'll be damned. I'll look into it."

Once at St Augustine School, Hugo changed into his club windsuit and decided to run some laps while he waited for the rest of the team to show up. This gave him some time to think and plan, because God knew he needed a good one. There was no way he was going to let Juliet marry Looks, and the faster he shut that down the better. The bastard might suddenly decide they should elope to Barbados.

Juliet seemed on the fence enough as it was, especially if last night was any indication. She had lain wrapped securely in his arms, snuggling her bottom against him and leaving him with a raging hard-on all night. Only the memory of her violent, retching illness kept his hands chastely at her waist, content with holding her.

Tonight he was going to tell her everything he knew about Looks and Rochelle. He would do it somewhere private and emphasize that he was only telling her for her own good. He would be firm and let her know that he had agonized over it, and then encourage her to confront Looks with everything he told her, even about the pregnancy, which Hugo suspected the man was in the dark about. Juliet would be very upset and had every right to be angry, but she was a sensible girl and would come around in the end.

It was going to be hell for Juliet. Her trust in everyone would be rocked, even in himself. She would feel used and humiliated, but by getting ahead of the issue, he would show her he was the one person she could trust.

The engagement would be called off, of course, and Tom could help with that. People broke engagements all the time, and a short statement would do the trick. Looks would keep his mouth shut— Hugo would see to that.

It would take a month or two for some of the attention to die down, and Hugo forecast that August would be a good time for them to take a holiday. The team was supposed to do a short tour of the Far East at the end of July, and then there was a two-week break until practices started again for the new season. They would go to Philadelphia to meet her family, although he knew from experience that part of America could be hotter than the hinges of hell at that time of year. By then it would be September, six months after the engagement was dissolved, not an indecent amount of time to think about presenting her with a ring of his own.

"Save it for Blackpool, Auchincloss," Darius called from the bench as he sprinted past. Hugo slowed down, realizing he'd gotten into another one of his trance-like states. "And I think your brother wants a word."

Darius pointed to the gate where Ian stood, his face drawn. Hugo was shocked; Ian had never come to a practice before. Grabbing a towel from the bench, he loped over to him, wiping the sweat off his face.

Up close, Hugo saw Ian was more upset than he had ever seen him. "What's up?"

"It's Julie." Ian's face was a mask of convoluted anger. "No! She's okay, at least I guess she is. The question is for how long, though."

"Ian, slow down, tell me what happened."

"Last night, after you left, I stayed at the party and snooped around. Looks and Rochelle had a huge row."

"What about?"

"Something about the gin, Rochelle kept insisting that he quit and walk away from it. Then she started screaming about him and Julie getting engaged. It was terrible."

"I imagine Rochelle was pissed."

"She was," Ian continued. "Looks managed to get her calmed down, promised her a lot of things, told her it was her he really loved and that Julie was just there for his career."

"And then?"

Ian swallowed. "And then they went at it like rabbits."

"You're sure?"

"I'm sure. It was pretty vocal." He looked at his brother closely, understanding slowly dawning. "You're not surprised. How long have you known?"

"Looks told me weeks ago they were still involved, and Tom said it's pretty much common knowledge."

"How are you going to tell Julie?"

"I'm not sure. It's an impossible situation, Looks has got her completely buffaloed. I've already tried, and she just can't fathom the idea of someone lying to her."

"But you are going to tell her. She needs to know." Ian drew himself up to full height and looked his brother straight in the eye, mustering more courage than Hugo had ever seen in him. "Hugo, if you don't tell her, I will."

"Ian, of course I'll tell her. Do you think I want her marrying Looks? But I have to be careful, Tom just told me Looks has gotten the announcement into the press."

Ian frowned. "She's got a bit of heartache coming to her then."

"Yes. But I'll be right there to pick up the pieces."

# Chapter Fifty-Two

"HELPMATE?" BONNIE PUT down the butane torch she was using to melt sugar on crème brûlées and repeated Julie's quote in disbelief. "No one says 'helpmate' anymore."

"I think it was just a figure of speech," Julie said.

"Where's the ring?"

"It was too big. Huge, actually. I gave it back to him before I went into the bathroom to throw up."

"So, are you engaged or not?"

"I don't know."

"Do you want to be?"

Julie buried her head in her arms. "I don't know, Bonnie. I know I want a family, I want companionship, and I'd like a bit of passion. I just don't seem to be able to get it all in one man."

"Do you love him?"

Julie raised her head. "Who?"

Bonnie's eyebrows shot up. "Your maybe-fiancé, Mark."

"I'm very fond of him," Julie conceded.

"Fond." Bonnie took the stool next to Julie and patted her back. "What about Hugo?"

"I'd like it to be more than sex."

"I think you should have a talk with him when he gets back."

"Hugo or Mark?"

"Both."

Julie nodded. "Hugo is flying home from his match in Blackpool tonight, and he said he wants to talk then."

"I think that's a very good idea."

———◦———

Kingsbury Town lost their match against Blackpool in a fog-shrouded downpour. Hugo knew before he came off the pitch that the flight back to London would be canceled, and indeed the small airport was completely socked in. No amount of Hugo's pleading, coercion, or bribery could entice anyone to get a plane in the air.

The train would take all night, a car about the same, and besides, he was knackered and had planned on getting some sleep on the flight back. Giles assured everyone that the weather would be clear by morning, and an 8:00 a.m. flight was arranged. The team was then sent off to a nearby hotel where half the players hit the bar and the rest went to bed.

Once in his room, Hugo called Julie.

"It's okay," she reassured him. "Come out tomorrow in the afternoon. I'm going shopping with Bonnie in Hampstead in the morning. Unless you'd rather talk now?"

"No, this has to be in person. I'll come out straight from St Augustine."

They talked for a few minutes more about the match, and Hugo got the pleasurable impression she'd seen quite a bit of it. It was intensely difficult to say goodbye to her—he wanted to keep her on the phone all night. But he heard her yawn and forced himself to finish the call.

Hanging up, he lay back on the bed, relishing the feeling of contentment that Juliet always brought, even when she was far away. Along with another raging hard-on that accompanied any interaction with her, but that was his tough luck.

Soon. Hopefully, soon.

What baby furniture do you need?" Julie asked Bonnie the next morning, absently rocking a baby swing at a shop in Hampstead.

"Gretchen and Don are passing down the girls' high chair and crib, and my mother is sending down a pram. So aside from a changing table, we should be in good shape, at least in the beginning."

After Bonnie selected one and arranged delivery, they walked down the busy high street looking at interesting windows. "Bonnie, how did you know you were ready to marry Clive?" Julie asked.

Bonnie laughed. "It was the easiest decision of my life. I knew I loved him, knew he was everything I wanted in a man, and he certainly made it clear he loved me and wanted to marry me."

They stopped in front of a shop window displaying three beautiful bridal gowns. Julie stared at them and tried, but failed, to imagine herself in any of them.

"I'm guessing it's not so easy for you," Bonnie said. "Have you spoken with Mark since he got to Los Angeles?"

"No, I haven't heard from him at all. I've left messages, but he hasn't returned them."

"Do you think something's wrong? His office would have called you, right?"

"Yes, of course. I'm sure he's fine. He was so excited about meeting all the senior management. He thinks he's going to be rewarded for everything he's done. I hope he gets everything he deserves."

A man darted across traffic towards them, his eyes glinting. "Miss Randall?" he called, approaching them with a broad grin.

"Yes?"

"I was wondering if you have a comment?"

"About what?"

"Rochelle Chevelle's marriage in Las Vegas yesterday."

Julie heard Bonnie's rushed intake of breath. "Oh, well, I wish her every happiness. Whom did she marry?"

"Your fiancé," the man replied. "Mark Brooks."

# Chapter Fifty-Three

THE TEAM'S FLIGHT finally landed at ten the next morning, and it was almost noon by the time they arrived back at St Augustine School. Hugo was on his way out the door when his mobile rang.

"I can't keep it out, Hugo. I'm sorry. It's just too big," Tom sputtered, so agitated Hugo could barely understand him. "Where are you?"

"We just got back to St Augustine. What's going on?"

"Looks got married."

"What the hell?" Hugo dropped onto a bench, feeling like someone had taken a cricket bat to his knees. His guts turned to jelly. Dear God, no. No, he needed more time. Anything for more time. He'd spoken to Juliet just the night before and she hadn't said anything. How had this happened?

"And in Las Vegas of all places," Tom continued with disgust. "Guess it suited Rochelle's taste."

Hot waves of relief flooded through his body. *Not Juliet. Not Juliet. Juliet is still mine.* Hugo took a moment and pulled himself together. "Why would they think he's married Rochelle?"

"Because her agent has put out a press release, that's why. She followed him to Los Angeles, where they pulled the plug on the gin yesterday. She saw it coming, but he didn't. And you were right, she's pregnant. They're keeping a lid on it for now until they cut a deal with Dionysus. But I confronted her agent, and he confirmed it."

As Tom filled him in on the details, Hugo felt like it was Christmas, his birthday, and the time he'd caught the biggest perch in the River Ouse, all in one day. There was no way Juliet would go back to that idiot now. It felt obscene to be so happy, knowing the wrenching sorrow she would be going through, but there it was. The way was clear for him, for them, for their future. Nothing had ever felt so certain.

"That's outstanding news, Tom."

"You better get to Julie—they're going to be all over her. I didn't like the way the call went with Rochelle's publicist. We both know she's got to get some good publicity for herself, and I'm hoping they leave Julie out of it."

"Make sure that happens," Hugo said as he fished in his pocket for his car keys. "I'm going out right now."

"Let me know what you need."

Five minutes later, the Jaguar was leaping to overtake every car in its path on the M6. As the first flush of euphoria passed, Hugo's mind raced to plan the next steps. This was going to be an awful shock to Juliet, and he needed to give her space. Tom had warned that the paparazzi would be looking for her, so it would be best if he whisked her away for a few days. Paris was the obvious choice—it was close enough to get there quickly and large enough to engulf them. They could leave immediately after the match tomorrow and be there in time for a late dinner at a romantic restaurant he knew on Rue des Gravilliers. He made a mental note to arrange the private jet.

---

Julie sat on the bench in the kitchen clutching a mug of tea, while Bonnie stood at the worktable, chopping any vegetable she could get her hands on, a habit those who knew her took warning from. Ian's coat hung in the mudroom, which meant he was somewhere on the property with his camera, but no one had seen him.

Immediately after the reporter in Hampstead had begun barraging her with questions, a photographer had started snapping pictures, his lens only inches from her face. Bonnie had pushed Julie into a bakery and told her to stay put, and then drove the car around to the back to pick her up. They sped back to Haddonfield, where Clive slammed the gates shut behind them. He was outside now, patrolling the perimeter, and had already thrown two paparazzi off the property.

"Do you think it's true? That they got married?" Julie asked Bonnie.

"I think no matter what the truth is, the bastard has a lot of explaining to do," Bonnie muttered. She raised her cleaver and chopped a cabbage in half with one savage blow.

"They were together a lot, but Mark always said it was for work. He said he was completely over her, and a lot of times, when he came back from shoots she was on, he just hated her. I could tell."

"Doesn't mean he was over her." The cleaver was replaced by a glinting French chef's knife that diced the cabbage in a furious blur of finely honed steel.

Clive returned from checking the gates, accompanied by Hugo. Julie rushed to him and he caught her in his arms, wrapping her in their secure warmth.

"Are you all right?" he asked, checking her for any signs of distress. "Clive said they found you in Hampstead."

She nodded. "We're okay. Is it true?"

"It's true. Tom called and it's confirmed. They were married last night or early this morning in Las Vegas."

"Why?" Clive asked. "I mean, why go to all the trouble of proposing to Julie and all that, just to turn around and marry that bit of muff?"

Hugo pulled Julie onto the bench next to him, taking her ice-cold hand in his warm one. "They pulled the plug on Bajan Gin Friday morning. All of the launch parties were disasters, and things had been going badly for a while. Looks got the blame. So Dionysus sacked Smith-Wessex, and Smith-Wessex was going to sack Looks, but Rochelle got to him first."

"That's terrible," Julie murmured, feeling a brief pang of sympathy for Mark.

"Evidently Rochelle saw the writing on the wall and tried to get him to resign the night of the party. But he wouldn't hear of it, so she followed him out to Los Angeles and talked him into nipping off to Las Vegas to get married before it could happen."

Everyone was dumbfounded by the news. "So he married her because he was going to get fired?" Julie asked.

"No, because of something else." Hugo tightened his arm around her and took a deep breath. "Rochelle's pregnant."

Julie looked at him blankly.

"It's Mark's baby," Hugo clarified.

The pain was immediate and piercing. Bonnie dropped her knife and rushed to Julie's side, while Clive paced back and forth, muttering a string of curses. Hugo held her and stroked her hair while Bonnie crooned soft words.

"Get us a wet washcloth," Bonnie told Hugo.

Bonnie wiped Julie's face and handed her tissues as they were needed. The tears subsided, and Julie sat back and took several deep breaths.

"You're sure, then?" Clive asked, his face a mask of barely contained fury.

Hugo nodded. "Tom's had it confirmed. It's true."

A string of curses flew from Clive's mouth. "Bonnie, where's my passport—"

"There will be plenty of time for that later, dear," Bonnie interrupted. "Hugo, exactly what happened?"

"Rochelle knew that she was on the chopping block as well, so she and Looks snuck off to Las Vegas and got married, and then had it announced right away. Her agent is in negotiations with Dionysus and Smith-Wessex to work a settlement with them."

"Why would they pay off that lot?" Clive asked.

"Pretty damn difficult to fire a pregnant woman and the baby's father. Rochelle is clever, you've got to give her that. But she knows their hand is weak. Mark walked out on Juliet, after all. So they're going to do anything they can to stir up positive publicity for themselves, hoping they'll get more money."

"So he didn't need me anymore," Julie said.

"He's been using you all along, Juliet. Forget him," Hugo advised.

"Do you think it was a one-time thing?" Julie asked him. "Or do you think it's been going on for some time?"

Hugo searched her eyes, his mouth working soundlessly. "I think it doesn't matter. The deed is done, and that's all there is to it. Now we need to come up with a plan to handle what's coming next. Tom said they might try to drag you into this."

Julie rubbed her pounding temple. It was too much to absorb, and she needed some fresh air to help her sort out her thoughts. "I need to go for a walk in the garden," Julie said. Clive helped her on with her jacket and held the door for her, and she stepped into the cool afternoon air.

"No, let her go," Bonnie cautioned as Hugo made a move to follow her. "She'll be back. She needs to collect her thoughts."

# Chapter Fifty-Four

OUTSIDE, THE MARCH sun shone brightly as Julie walked the paths of her gardens, taking solace in their familiarity. Spring was making itself forcefully felt and the garden smelled fresh and alive, with green shoots pushing through the rich brown earth and birds singing to each other in the orchard.

*Rochelle is pregnant. Rochelle is pregnant. Rochelle is pregnant.*

Maybe it had happened in Fiji, or Madrid, or Miami, depending on how far along she was. And it must have been just once, she reasoned—Mark's vexation with Rochelle was real, and he never made any effort to disguise the fact that her temper tantrums and erratic behavior tested him sorely.

Stopping to check the brussel sprouts under their cloche pots, she considered that perhaps Mark was in just as much shock as she was. He certainly must have been blindsided by Bajan Gin being canceled and then by Rochelle's pregnancy. She almost couldn't blame him for going along with Rochelle's plan. Almost.

Burying her hands in her pockets, she turned the corner and saw Ian with his camera filming a tufted titmouse building a nest.

"Hello, Julie! Come see what I've found... I say, you don't look well at all," Ian said. "Is everything all right?"

Julie ran a hand through her hair and blotted some tears away with a tissue. "Not really. I just found out..." She trailed off and tried to collect herself. "About Mark and Rochelle."

"Did Hugo tell you?" Ian asked anxiously.

"Yes. He told us everything."

Ian exhaled as if the weight of the world had been taken off his chest. "Buck up, old thing, it's best you knew," he said, wrapping a supportive arm around her shoulder.

"It's just such a shock."

"I know. But it was time Hugo told you. If he hadn't, I would have. This is a relief." He gave her a compassionate squeeze.

Julie heard Ian's words, but they seemed jumbled and wouldn't settle into something that made sense. Their meaning seemed impossible, and it took her several moments to turn them over in her mind.

"How long has he known?" she forced herself to ask.

"About what those two were up to? Weeks, I guess. Maybe months. He said Looks told him everything, but he'd already had it from Tom. He only told me yesterday because I caught them..." Ian blushed. "... *in flagrante delicto* in the cloakroom at the launch party. Hugo had to keep it mum, though—he gave Looks his word as a gentleman he wouldn't tell you. But getting engaged changes everything—you couldn't marry him not knowing that. Glad he finally told you."

The world wobbled darkly, and Julie would have fallen if Ian hadn't supported her. It was like being hit—she literally couldn't draw a breath. Her heart was paralyzed, and coldness began to spread everywhere.

Hugo had known. He had known all along.

———— ◆◇◆ ————

"It's Julie!" Ian burst into the kitchen, frantic and out of breath. "She's... it's like she's had a seizure or something. I, I..." he stuttered, looking wildly from Bonnie to Clive and finally to Hugo. "Oh God, I think I really screwed up."

Hugo got to Julie first. She was sitting motionless on the edge of a raised bed, her arms wrapped around herself protectively. He reached out to her, but she jerked away from him as if his touch scorched her. Ian, Bonnie, and Clive had run after him, and came to a stop next to her.

"You knew all along," Julie said, staring at him as if he were a complete stranger.

"Yes," Hugo admitted as the world crashed down around him.

"Knew what?" Clive asked.

"That Mark and Rochelle never broke up. That they never stopped..." Julie had difficulty forming the words. "... never stopped... you know. Why she's pregnant."

"Hugo!" Bonnie erupted.

"I thought you told her," Ian told his brother, looking like he wanted to die. "Because Looks proposed. I thought you told her everything."

"He married Rochelle yesterday," Hugo explained tersely. "Shotgun wedding in Las Vegas."

Ian went white. "Oh, my God. Julie, I'm so sorry."

Her unflinching stare never left Hugo. "No, Ian, thank you for being honest. At least someone was. I'd like to hear the rest of the truth now."

It was impossible to know where to start, Hugo realized.

"Out with it," Clive growled.

"The truth is, they never stopped," he began, the words like dust in his mouth. "Looks did try to break it off, but Rochelle wasn't having any of it. She caused huge commotions on her shoots so that he'd have to be sent in to calm her down. Everyone had so much money invested in her that they needed to play along, and Looks knew that as long as he could keep her under control he'd be the golden boy."

"Were there others besides Rochelle?" Julie asked, her eyes never leaving his.

Ian looked at him pointedly, and Hugo gritted his teeth. "Yes."

"Pippa Donnell?"

Hugo nodded. "And more, but I don't know their names. A lot more."

She flinched as if he'd slapped her. He could see her nails digging into the flesh of her palms. "What happened at Cheeting House?"

"He never told her you were going to be there, but she found out and threw a fit."

Julie was silent for several moments, and he could see her putting things together in her mind. "Where was she staying?"

"At his flat."

"She stayed there a lot, didn't she?"

"Yes." Jesus, this was killing him; he no idea what it was doing to her.

"Did you know she was pregnant?"

Hugo swallowed and looked to the sky. "The night of the launch party, I guessed. She wasn't drinking alcohol."

A cold wind picked up and a light patter of rain began to fall. Julie's voice came out as a sort of croak. "And you knew all this since the beginning."

It was all so damning. "There were rumors, and I wasn't the only one who suspected," Hugo glared at Clive. "I wanted to find out what the hell was going on, so I got Looks completely soused and he told me everything. But he made me give my word to not tell you."

Julie lifted her eyebrows. "Your word. Well. Can't have you breaking your word to another old schoolboy."

"But I was coming here today to tell you," Hugo rushed on. "This is what I wanted to talk with you about, and I was going to make you listen no matter what. I tried before and didn't have much success."

"Yes, you did try to warn me, and I didn't listen," she acknowledged bitterly. "And then Clive and Bonnie tried to warn me about you, and I didn't listen. I certainly have no one to blame but myself."

"What the hell did you tell her about me?" Hugo flared at Clive, and Ian grabbed his arm to restrain him.

"Now't that wasn't common knowledge," Clive replied grimly.

Juliet's gaze went to a distant point and she seemed to retreat deep into herself, effectively making him disappear. She sat motionless, in shock. Desperate to keep her attention, he knelt before her and took her by the shoulders, forcing her to look at him.

"Juliet, I know what you're going through right now. It seems like the end of the world, but it's not. We'll get through this together, and everything will be fine. You'll see."

With an effort she focused on him, her voice almost a whisper. "There's one other thing you told me that I should have listened to, Hugo. You told me you weren't my friend and you were right. I didn't realize what you meant until now."

No. This was impossible. This was not happening. "Juliet, I know I should have told you, but I couldn't stand to see you hurt. I thought I could handle it all and protect you. I did it all for you," he pleaded, feeling more scared than he'd ever felt in his life.

Julie pulled away from him, tears coursing down her face unheeded. "For me? What more could you do for me, Hugo?" she lashed out. "Would you like to burn my crops down? Matches are in the tin on my desk. Help yourself."

Clive stepped between them and pointed to the parking area. "Clear out, you lot," he ordered, his voice a roar.

"Juliet, there's more, I need to tell you more," Hugo said desperately. "There're pictures, and Rochelle is going to use them."

Bonnie held Julie as the sobs wracked her body. "I don't want to hear anymore," she whispered.

"You've said enough," Clive announced and grabbed Hugo's arm.

"No, damn it," he swore, shrugging off Clive's beefy hand. "She has to hear everything—she's going to be targeted—"

"You're going to be my target if you don't leave right now. Clear out you bloody toffs, the pair of you," Clive snarled. "I warned you what would happen if you upset her. You've got thirty seconds to clear off the property or you'll wish you'd never heard of Haddonfield."

Seeing no other alternative, Hugo grabbed Ian and dragged him to his car and drove off, gravel flying behind them.

———◦———

A cold sweat engulfed him as he raced the Jaguar through the narrow streets of Hampstead, cursing whoever got in his way and slamming the steering wheel with his fist. No, no, no! This was not happening. He was not losing her. He would not let this happen.

Ian sat next to him in terrified silence and bolted from the car as soon as Hugo pulled to the curb in front of his flat. The city was in gridlock and seemed to be filled with every bloody tourist on earth. After what felt like an eternity, he reached the shelter of his street and saw two paparazzi stationed outside his house. Hugo gunned the car towards his garage with relish, and they jumped out of the way with satisfying yelps.

Inside the house, he paced the rooms. *Bloody Ian. What to do now, what to do now?* He needed another plan, and kidnapping Juliet was at the top of the list. There was no way she would listen to him now unless he made her. And he had to make her listen. He had to make her understand.

Understand that he was in love with her.

# Chapter Fifty-Five

THE MEMORY OF Sunday's home match against Hull City was a blur, but Hugo knew it was easily the worst game he'd ever played. He got a yellow card, which was horrifying, and made even more so because he couldn't remember what he did to deserve it. All he recalled was being elbowed by a Hull midfielder and feeling a pure, directionless fury overwhelm him.

The referee was a decent sort he'd played with many times before, and who took almost thirty seconds to book him out of complete surprise. Darius tried to talk with him afterwards, and then Giles, but he refused to explain his actions to anyone except to say it wouldn't happen again. He couldn't even explain them to himself. All he knew was that his world was collapsing.

Hugo spent Sunday evening hunkered down in Tom's office, while Tom tried to get the situation under control.

"She never wants to see me again," Hugo said, pacing the office like a caged tiger while Tom dialed numbers on his mobile.

"Smart girl."

"She thinks I betrayed her."

"You did."

Hugo collapsed in a chair. "Bloody hell, I didn't mean to. I have to see her, Tom. I have to protect her."

Cassandra, who had come to help, gestured to the stack of tabloids on the table before them. Small photographs of Julie appeared in many of them, either snapped on the streets of Hampstead or from the launch party. At the moment, she was a subtext to the drama of Rochelle and Mark's elopement in Las Vegas that was captivating the tabloids, fed by Rochelle's agent.

"Hugo, the poor girl is embarrassed, her heart is broken, and on top of all that, it's been made very public," Cassandra counseled. "Tom is going to make sure that part goes away, but she's going to need some time to get over it and sort out her feelings. You have to give her that time. She might come to some good conclusions on her own."

"Like what?" Hugo asked, raising his head.

"Like maybe she's miserable without you, too."

"But what if everyone is talking me down? Her friends all hate me—what if they're telling her I'm bad for her?"

"She doesn't strike me as someone who would be so easily swayed," Cassandra said. "She seems like a very sensible girl and one who doesn't make rash decisions. She needs time to work through this. You have to be patient."

Tom slammed the phone down and snorted. "My beautiful wife is right, as usual, and you'd do well to take her advice. Go fishing in Ireland or something—just get away and let us protect her. It's going to get worse before it gets better."

Hugo's jaw tightened. "How much worse?"

"That was the *Sun*. Your pictures hit tomorrow and they're going with 'Jezebel Julie.' They've already gotten an exclusive with Rochelle, plus the *Observer* said they have a special feature, an interview with your current girlfriend that you were cheating on with Julie. Complete with pictures."

"I don't have a girlfriend. Who the hell is it?"

"That's my job to find out, and I'll let you know. In the meantime, keep your head down and don't talk with anyone— you're making enough work for me as it is. I've already told the gang there's going to be a great bonus this Christmas."

———— ◆◯◆ ————

The tabloid press found Julie's house and by evening, were milling about on the sidewalk until her landlady chased them away with a broom, calling them a disreputable lot. Bonnie and Clive didn't give her a choice but immediately moved her into their spare bedroom. Julie balked, protesting it was set to be the nursery.

"I hope to God this will be over by the time the baby needs the room. In the meantime, you're our guest, and there's no more to be said," Bonnie announced.

She lay on the bed Saturday night, forcing herself to come to grips with the situation. It felt like a blindfold had been brutally ripped from her eyes, and the reality was harsh and humiliating.

Her mind raced over all of the things that had confused her in the past but were now as plain as day. Mark hadn't taken her back to his flat because Rochelle was probably there often. And he wasn't interested in sex with her because he was getting plenty with everyone else. The only thing Mark wanted her for was to further his career.

It was exhausting to remember the effort she'd put into dating him, all the concerns about getting things just right. She felt a savage desire to go home and start a bonfire with Rosie's dresses, starting with the one she'd worn to the wedding. And then the one she'd worn to Wrothesley. And especially the one she'd worn to the launch party.

She ached to crush the crystal vase Mark had given her that Hugo said had come from a distributor's conference. No wonder he barely spoke to her for three days afterwards. It must have been impossible for him to not laugh in her face.

Of course, the signs were all there, but she had been blind to them. Hugo had flat out told her that Mark went to the pavilion with Pippa, but she was so devastated by the thought of him being with Sophie that she ignored it. The truth was, she had been so swept up by her infatuation with Hugo that Mark's behavior could have been painted on the side of the barn and she would have ignored it.

As she lay in the dark, she realized Mark had been someone to hide behind when her feelings for Hugo overwhelmed her. Aside from that, he was frequently an afterthought, when she thought of him at all.

Mark had used her, but in all honesty, she had used him as well.

She had fallen head over heels in love with Hugo Auchincloss, and there was no one to blame but herself. The humiliation was total.

———————◦———————

Clive went to her house Sunday morning to get some clothing and came close to punching a photographer who tried to take his picture. A growing group of paparazzi also began to stake out the gates at Haddonfield, and a call was put in to Don, who was attending a conference in Leeds. The decision was made that the local police, as well as the Haddonfield neighbors, needed to be informed about the situation.

The realization that soon her foolishness would become common knowledge in the neighborhood made Julie nauseated.

"I have to tell the students," she said.

"I'll tell them," Don interjected over the phone. "I'm presenting this afternoon and if I cancel, it'll just draw more attention to the situation. But I'll go over and talk with them when I get home this evening."

Bonnie refused to let Julie see the Sunday papers, only relenting when Julie persuaded her she had been in the dark long enough and wanted to know everything. Rochelle and Mark's marriage was a major gossip story, with a dozen photographs spread over four pages. Mark looked grim and Rochelle's smile was strained as they left the Las Vegas wedding chapel, with Rochelle holding a bouquet of carnations. With a jolt, Julie recognized the engagement ring on Rochelle's finger.

"Mark looks miserable. He must have hated the tawdriness of it all," Bonnie observed.

Julie scrutinized the pictures closely. "Rochelle doesn't look much happier. They're going to have a baby, after all. They should at least try and make the best of it."

"That's a lot more kindness than they deserve, especially after all the commotion they're causing around here," Bonnie huffed.

As they scanned the pages, Julie saw she'd earned only minor billing, escaping with just two sentences beneath a picture that had been snapped in Hampstead and captioned Jilted Julie.

"That's not so bad," she said with relief.

Bonnie mulled over the page. "I don't get it. If that's the extent of it, why are more of them flocking around you instead of less? It's almost like they know the story is going to get bigger."

"They'll have to announce that Rochelle's pregnant soon, and I suppose they'll keep wanting to hear how I feel about that. Aside from that, there's nothing else to know."

Bonnie shook her head. "No. There's something else, something bigger. They smell blood and they're not going to go away until they find it."

———•◇•———

Later that evening, Don arrived at Clive and Bonnie's and flopped in a chair, his boundless energy for once deserting him. "I just met with the kids."

"How did that go?" Julie asked, wrapping her sweater tighter.

"Odd. Damn odd," Don murmured, accepting a cup of tea from Bonnie. "When I got to the dormitory, they were all there and were very quiet. I told them about Mark and Rochelle eloping, but they knew all about it from the papers, of course. They're very concerned for you—in fact, that was most of our discussion. But I swear they were acting guilty, almost like they'd had some hand in all of this."

"Did you tell them about Rochelle?" Bonnie asked.

Don nodded. "They just about went through the roof. It turns out they've known about Mark for some time, which explains their violent dislike of him. Evidently one of Tanda's neighbors is an exotic dancer at a club he frequents, and..." he paused after catching a warning look from Bonnie, "... and he was a very good tipper, let's say. I hope Mark never plans on eating at one of their restaurants—he's very likely to be poisoned."

"The kids knew, too?" Julie's stomach plunged. "Am I the only one who was in the dark?"

Guilty looks were exchanged between her friends. "Julie, you know as well as I do that MI5 has nothing on a bunch of street kids." Don patted her hand. "And I think I speak for everyone when I say we thought you'd be getting past him on your own, without us interfering. If any of us had any idea this would blow up the way it has, of course we would have told you."

Julie ran her hands through her hair and tried to soldier on. "It doesn't matter. Is that why you think they were acting guilty?"

"No, not quite, I'd bet my hat there's something more going on there. Lalani was a mess and blurted out that they'd set you up."

"How so?"

"I don't know. Nerida hustled her out of the room before she could say anything more. But they know not to speak to anyone and not to pick any fights. That would be the last thing we need."

# Chapter Fifty-Six

ON MONDAY, CLIVE went to Haddonfield first and called home to say that the swarm of photographers at the gate had tripled. They mobilized to snap pictures of Bonnie's little car as it darted through the gates with Julie crouched in the backseat under a blanket, and then retreated as Clive slammed the gates shut behind them. Neighbors walking their dogs glared at them.

Inside Haddonfield, the students swarmed Julie, crushing her in their embrace. Lalani wept openly and Tanda clutched her hand while Matthew glowered.

"We're sorry we didn't tell you 'bout Mark and those clubs he goes to," Lalani sobbed.

"You're better off without the likes of 'im," Tanda added.

"Those people outside the gates, they're trying to talk with us. Matthew told them where to go," Joanna confided. "Slimy bastards, that's what me granny says."

"And we're not believing anything those rags are printing about you and Hugo," Nerida said. "None of it."

Before they could say more, Bonnie shooed them out of the kitchens to meet the dairy delivery.

"Why are they dragging Hugo into this?" Julie asked Clive. "He didn't have anything to do with Mark and me."

When Clive wouldn't meet her eyes, Julie panicked. "Is there more? Is that why there are so many photographers? How bad is it?"

Clive sighed. "You don't want to know."

"Clive, I need to know what's happening!" she demanded, her voice trembling.

He pulled two tabloids out of a drawer and laid them on the table. "That lot out there threw them over the gate this morning."

JEZEBEL JULIE! screamed the full-page write-up in the *Sun*. It featured a dark picture of Hugo carrying her into her house the night of the launch party, and a sharp photo of her leaving his house the morning after he'd let her read *The Orchard*.

*It looks like Mark Brooks might have been the one who was the cuckold here!* the story blasted, before going into details. *Julie Randall, Mark Brooks's fiancée, has been carrying on an illicit affair with Kingsbury Town midfielder Hugo Auchincloss for some time now, apparently behind Brooks's back. The two even socialized in town while Mark was out working!*

"That was the night I was sick!" Julie stabbed the large picture with her finger. "And that one is from the night I studied *The Orchard*! Nothing happened, I stayed up all night and was going to get the bus."

"It doesn't matter, love, they'll push it together to make it look the way they want," Bonnie said.

"It does matter," Julie said, reaching for her coat. "I'm going out there right now and set the record straight. I will not let them smear me like this—"

"Julie Randall!" Bonnie thundered, raising her voice for the first time since Julie had known her. "I will personally lock you in the basement if you set one foot outside that door. They want to provoke you. It's what they're looking for. You have to ignore it."

Julie slumped on the bench, her forehead beginning to throb. Of course, Bonnie was right. She continued to read, feeling sicker by the minute.

The *Observer*'s headline was even more crass—CHEATER! —and featured an exclusive interview with Sophie Milkton-Sapp. She'd been photographed clutching a tissue while standing on an empty football pitch over the caption, She broke us up, too!

*Hugo and I were so happy, but then she came along and broke us apart. I even went out to her house in Finchley, thinking we were friends. But she betrayed me, too!* The article featured the picture of Sophie sitting on Hugo's lap at a party.

Julie silently mouthed an obscenity.

Hugo was featured prominently on the next page with the headline, HELLO, YELLOW! He was shouting at a referee, his face wild, next to a Hull player who was lying face down on the pitch. Her heart lurched.

"What happened?" Julie had never seen his face so contorted, as if he had completely lost control of himself. "What's a yellow card?"

"It's a citation for misbehavior on the field," Clive explained. "Most players get a few, but he's never gotten one his entire career. I think that includes when he played at school. It was bizarre, Rouet was blocking and Hugo tackled him ugly, really ugly. Everyone was shocked, took the ref almost half a minute to blow it."

The phone rang, and Bonnie answered it. "That was Don. He's been called down to the Magness Foundation offices."

"Am I going to be fired?" Julie asked.

"Of course not. But they're concerned about the security, and Don is trying to figure something out. Clive, he wants you to go with him. Now let's get to work. The sooner we get some normalcy back around here the better."

Julie walked into the gardens, and for the first time in her life had no idea what needed to be done. Her thoughts wouldn't leave Hugo. Why did he get a yellow card? Was he all right? He looked drawn and haggard in the photograph, his fists clenched and the muscles in his arms strained.

It must be the publicity. He was being smeared right beside her and of course resented being dragged into all of this. Was he angry that she'd been photographed leaving his house? Did he think she'd done it on purpose? And he must be livid about the picture of him carrying her into her house. He had just been helping, after all. It didn't mean anything to him.

---

Tuesday night, Hugo waited for the students at the Art League in Finchley, rubbing his chin and realizing he'd forgotten to shave that day. It hardly mattered, he mused, everything seemed pointless now. Eating, sleeping, it was all impossible. There was no getting over what had happened, no recovery, no pulling himself together and just getting on with his life. He couldn't do that without a heart, and he had left his at Juliet's feet.

It seemed impossible that just four days ago, Julie had lain in his arms the entire night, her exquisite softness molded against his like they were made for each other. He was so damn certain of what he wanted, so cockily assured of the way it was going to be, that he'd never considered the potential for catastrophe. Now he was paying the price for his hubris.

The students filed in silently and grouped behind Matthew, who stood before him.

"We have something to say to you," Matthew said. "We all wrote this." He took a piece of paper from his shirt pocket. "We love Julie. She's the best thing that's ever happened to us. All the work she does, we know she does it for us, and she doesn't get paid almost nothing for it. She deserves only the best, and we did wrong by not telling her what we knew about him and we shouldn't have told you so much about her neither because it's gotten her in a lot of trouble. We're going to keep up with this because we know if she knew, she'd make us keep going. We appreciate what you're doing, but we won't talk about her, and you'd do best to leave her alone."

When Matthew finished, Lalani burst into tears.

Hugo looked from one student to the next, reading nothing but contempt in their expressions. "I just need to know if she's okay."

"If you mean is she alive, yes. Beyond that we're not going to say." Matthew's jaw was set.

Hugo nodded, feeling one hundred years old. "I understand. And I agree. Sit down and we'll get started."

# Chapter Fifty-Seven

BY WEDNESDAY, CLIVE had hired a security guard for the gate. Sophie had given two more tabloid interviews that featured Julie's college graduation picture and her staff photograph from the Magness Foundation, and Rochelle had been pictured sunbathing on the roof of a hotel in Las Vegas in a bikini, her protruding stomach very obvious, spurring a fresh wave of drama. Mark was nowhere to be seen.

That afternoon, the guard opened the school gates to admit a sleek minivan. In the parking area, the doors slid open and a man in a wheelchair maneuvered to the front door.

"Tom," Julie said, kissing his cheek. "It's good to see you."

"You, too. Cassandra sends her love. How are you holding up?"

"There's been better weeks." She tried to smile but failed. "Let's go inside. Everyone would like to meet you."

In the kitchen, Julie introduced Clive, Bonnie, and Don. They sat down around the trestle table, Tom's eyes lighting up at the plate of cookies Bonnie placed before him.

"I see you've gotten security. Good," Tom began, pulling papers from his briefcase. "Send me the bill."

"How long do you think we'll be needing it?" Clive asked.

"Two weeks at the most, but that can change at any moment," Tom said. "I've been able to shut down Rochelle's publicist. Dionysus and Smith-Wessex have settled with them, and keeping their mouths shut is part of the deal they're getting for walking away. That happened yesterday."

"Does Dionysus want their donation back?" Don asked.

"Good heavens, no," Tom said. "In fact, I think they'd probably double it if you asked. Anything for some good PR at this point."

"What about Sophie?" Julie grumbled.

Tom's lips curled into a cold smile. "Hugo's friends have been sending me a remarkable assortment of photographs they've rounded up, plus two videos that my assistants are reviewing this afternoon. I'm having drinks after work tonight with her father's private secretary. Did I mention Mr. Milkton-Sapp is angling to be the next home secretary?"

"Are there any more pictures of me out there?" Julie asked. "I didn't know we were being followed."

"Not as far as I know. And the ones that were out there would never have seen the light of day if a certain footballer had been using his head. But it's my job to make him use it, and I let you down badly there."

"What should I do?"

"You need to leave here and let this all die down."

"No," Julie shook her head. "I will not run away from this. Let people think of me what they want. The people who know me, know that none of it is true."

Tom sighed. "There's a lot of truth to that, but you have to think of the students and the Magness Foundation. As long as that lot at the gates know where to find you, it will just prolong this."

"Tom's right, Julie, it's for the best and just for a few days," Don said. "I met with the Foundation yesterday and while they're very supportive, they're also concerned about everyone's safety. But I have to say," he continued, "that Hugo had been there ahead of me and taken the blame for everything. Made my job a bit easier."

"Will I have a job when I come back?" she asked.

"Of course you'll have a job! You have seven weeks of vacation saved. This will hardly put a dent in it."

"Where will I go?"

"To our country house in Bedfordshire," Tom announced. "And I can take you there right now."

---

"When will all of this be over, Tom?" Julie asked as they drove north, a hastily packed bag on the seat behind her.

"In the blink of an eye," Tom assured her. "There's nothing we can do in the short term to reverse the damage to your reputation, because it's all circumstantial and just really rotten luck. But in the next few months, I think we can do quite a bit of reconstruction."

"How much will I owe you for all you're doing?"

"Nothing. Even if Hugo wasn't insisting on paying for everything, I still wouldn't take a dime from you. I've known for ages about Looks and I could have just as easily clued you in as anyone. But I'm cynical and jaded, and that blinded me to the truly innocent parties."

They drove north, the traffic easing as dense housing gave way to open fields and picturesque farms.

"How is he?" It almost killed Julie to ask, but she needed to know.

Tom glanced at her. "He's a mess. I've never seen him in such a state."

Julie nodded. "He must be hating all the publicity. He said he never wanted to go through again what he went through with Trika."

"This situation is completely different. He was never in love with Trika," Tom said. "And he doesn't remember, but he was actually relieved to be rid of her. In fact we all were. She was a very cold person." Tom paused and continued with care. "Julie, I've never seen Hugo happier than when he's with you."

The countryside rolled by her car window unseen. "He used me, Tom. He knew everything that was going on and he let it happen. He could have told me about Mark and Rochelle a long time ago and saved me being 'Jilted Julie' and 'Jezebel Julie.'"

Tom sighed. "I agree, and under normal circumstances, I'm sure he would have. But there was nothing normal about what was going on with Hugo."

"He seemed normal enough to me."

Tom laughed out loud. "Hugo and I have known each other since we were lads in short pants, and I can assure you that the day he met you, his world turned upside down. In just under three months, he's been photographed for an advertising campaign, danced in public, allowed Miles to change the farming plan at Wrothesley, made a huge scene at his mother's fundraising party, and gotten a yellow card." Tom exited the motorway and turned onto a busy local road. "Our tailor even told me Hugo ordered a French blue shirt run up, but I'm drawing the line at that. Old bugger is obviously senile and should have retired years ago."

A smile tugged at the corners of Julie's lips.

Tom glanced at her, astonished. "Really? I say, that clinches it. Look, I'm not sure if any of this is making any sense and it's up to Hugo to make it clear, but it's obvious you're both in this muck because his feelings ran riot over his common sense."

"You mean his lust."

"No, I mean his feelings for you, feelings I don't think he's ever had before. And the fact that he's also damned attracted to you just made it even more of a mess. My meddling didn't help any either. After Sophie's prank at Pippa's party, he was determined to tell you everything, and I talked him out of it."

"Why?"

"Because I knew Looks would lie through his teeth to you. I lived with the SOB and I know exactly what he's capable of. Smith-Wessex wasn't going to make him a partner without a nice little wife like you, and he wasn't going to let anything stand in the way of that happening."

Tom's words sent a chill down Julie's spine. The thought of how she'd let herself be manipulated sickened her.

Tom continued grimly, "Cassandra and I knew right away you were a bright girl and that you would eventually see Looks's spots. So I convinced Hugo that you needed to find these things out on your own."

That seemed to have been the current consensus, Julie thought. "I was getting there."

"In hindsight, I should have realized that nothing would be that simple with Looks involved, and that Rochelle would do anything to get him back, including getting pregnant. Of course, that's all water under the bridge now. But suffice it to say, if everything played out according to plan, you were supposed to wake up one morning and realize that Hugo was the man for you and tell Looks to shove off, and you would both live happily ever after."

The memory of her doing almost exactly that the morning after the launch party hit Julie with a jolt. "Hugo's not in love with me, Tom. He was very upfront about what he was interested in, and I turned him down. So he might be frustrated, but he'll get over it."

"Hah!" Tom laughed as they drove into a small village. "Is that really what you think? Good heavens, he's mucked things up worse than I thought. Look, Julie, all I can tell you is that Hugo is the best man I know. His life is brutal. He's got the burden of Wrothesley, the team, and Ian. He puts himself on the line every week in front of millions of people, all waiting for him to screw up and make a fool of himself. The accident last November? It's true what they say—Ian was at the wheel and Hugo took the blame. The boy already had one drink-driving citation and the courts would have been merciless on him—not that Hugo's been any easier. But he got Ian into a program and is making sure he's sticking to it, and it's working. Ian is doing really well."

Tom glanced at her. "All I ask is, if he asks for a chance, you consider giving it to him."

"Are you going to tell him I'm here?"

Tom blew his cheeks and turned into a short lane off the high street. "No. Things are still much too chaotic. He's been on lockdown at our place in town since he got the yellow card. I suppose you know about that? He's got to be on his best behavior at Saturday's match, and that means staying focused. My staff and I have started to get control of the situation, but we need another seventy-two hours to move the story out of the public eye. After that, things will sort themselves out. Do you trust me?"

Julie wiped her eyes with the back of her hand. "Yes."

"Good lass."

# Chapter Fifty-Eight

FRIDAY AFTERNOONS WERE Bonnie's usual marketing day, and Hugo waited impatiently in the car park of the supermarket for her to come out.

The week had passed in a trough of misery. Practices were wretched and unproductive, and the press was hounding him mercilessly. He couldn't have cared less, but he was desperately worried about Juliet.

He'd had no news of her in days. Tom had gone to see her, and aside from telling him that Clive had hired security and that she was safe, wouldn't say anymore. She wasn't staying at her house—he had lurked around the neighborhood for several evenings, and there were never any lights in her windows. He thought she might be staying with Bonnie and Clive, but a cautious look around their house revealed nothing as well.

Bonnie emerged from the store and crossed the busy lot with her cart. He slipped in next to her as she began loading grocery bags into her car.

"Hugo!" She startled and nearly dropped a sack of oranges. "What are you doing here?"

"Hullo," he said, helping her transfer the bags to the boot. "I wasn't followed. I need to know how Juliet is."

Bonnie sighed. "She's okay. She trying to sort things out."

"Does she hate me?"

"I don't think she knows how she feels. It's impossible to think with all those photographers at the gate."

"I need your help, Bonnie. I need to see her."

"She's gone away. It was your friend Tom's idea, and I think it was a good one. I'm not going to say where, but maybe when she gets back, she'll be in a better mood to talk."

"Will Clive let me near her?"

Bonnie slammed the lid of the boot closed and turned to face him. "That's an entirely different matter."

"I just want her to know that, whenever she's ready, I want to see her. And that I'm sorry."

She held his gaze for a long moment. Finally, she nodded. "I'll tell her."

<hr>

Tom showed Julie around the charming whitewashed bungalow filled with comfortably worn furnishings. It had been extensively remodeled for wheelchair accessibility, with a sitting room, dining area, a large kitchen with a well-stocked pantry, and two bedrooms, each with its own bath.

"It's lovely," Julie breathed. "I was worried it would be something grand on the scale of Wrothesley."

Tom laughed. "This was my parents' house. Dad was a transportation engineer and mother taught school. I went to Eton on scholarship. It's a great bolt-hole, although it's going to be a bit small for us soon, so we're planning some major renovation work. But I think you'll be very comfortable here."

Julie declined his offer to have the local grocer send around more provisions. Her appetite had vanished. The cans of soup in the pantry would suffice.

After Tom left, she explored the rest of the house. The guest bedroom was furnished with a large wrought-iron bed covered with a beautiful quilt, and Julie lay across it, exhausted. Hugo must have visited here many times—he was in several photographs in the sitting room. She had looked at them closely, and then turned them facedown, unable to bear seeing him. Did he like the cozy house? It was completely different from his own. Did he mind the slightly shabby furniture? Did he hit his head on the low doorways? Had he slept in this very bed?

Tears overwhelmed her. She pulled the quilt around her and cried, and then amazingly, she slept.

———————◆○◆———————

Julie woke the next morning feeling much better. Her stomach growled in hunger as she lay in the bright room, listening to a corn bunting chirp outside the window. She tried to remember the last time she'd slept so well and realized it had been the night after the launch party, when Hugo had stayed with her. Her appetite abruptly vanished.

There were a few staples in the pantry, but she decided to walk down the lane to the village, where she had coffee and a few bites of scone in a bakery. The town looked like a picture postcard, and she spent some time exploring the bustling high street and a few side alleys. Passing a news vendor, she saw a headline announcing Kingsbury Town's match against Birmingham City in two days' time. She winced at the sight of another article mocking Mick Carr for thinking Barcelona was the capital of Spain, accompanied by a photograph of him at a news conference, his handsome face flushed and sullen.

Julie worked up the nerve to buy two tabloids and flipped through them quickly. The front pages were devoted to news of a Hollywood starlet who'd been caught using cocaine while visiting a children's hospital. Steeling herself, she carefully scanned through each publication, looking for news of herself, Hugo, Sophie, Rochelle, or Mark. But there was absolutely nothing.

That would make Hugo happy.

She tossed the papers into a waste bin and returned to the cottage. After she explored the large garden, she found a pair of nippers and spent the rest of the morning pruning the mature gooseberry bushes. She broke briefly for lunch and then returned to her work, trimming the ornamentals and cleaning dead leaves out of the flower beds. She worked by rote, thinking of nothing but the task at hand. By sunset, she was exhausted. Dinner was a bowl of soup and after washing up, she found a book on the sitting room shelf about Joseph Paxton, a noted Victorian garden designer. He was from Bedfordshire, just like Hugo. She took it to bed and fell asleep reading.

Saturday morning a courier arrived with a thick envelope, sent by Tom. "This is for you, miss, and I'm to ask if you need anything."

"No, nothing, thank you."

Inside was a short note from Tom. *"Things are simmering down. You should be able to go back to work Monday. Enjoy yourself, Tom and Cassandra."*

He'd also sent along her mail. There were two horticulture journals, an inquiry from a man in Dorking who was having trouble growing heirloom short horn carrots, and a letter postmarked from Los Angeles five days prior, addressed to her in Mark's scrawling script.

> *Dear Julie,*
>
> Look old thing, I've been a shit and there is no way to ask for your forgiveness so I'm not going to waste your considerable patience in doing so. They've pulled the plug on the gin and I guess you know about the baby, so for once I decided to do the right thing and knew you'd be the first to understand. We're getting married and are going to try and make the best of it.
>
> Anyway you are far better off with Hugo because he loves you madly and is a better man than I ever will be. Know that I swore him to secrecy.
>
> I will make this up to you I promise.
>
> Mark
>
> PS — Rochelle says sorry too.

Julie carefully folded the letters and laid them on the table, then took a bike from the shed and set off on a ride through the countryside.

The morning was overcast, which matched her mood. For over an hour, she forced herself to identify the trees that grew in the hedgerows and small forests she rode past, seeing ash, hemlock, and willows. Flocks of fierce-looking sheep sporting two pairs of horns glanced up from their lush pastures to watch her pass before resuming their grazing.

She came to a stop in front of an old stone church and took a drink from her water bottle, then walked around to shake out her legs. As her breathing slowly returned to normal, Julie examined her feelings.

It turned out they had sorted themselves out with impressive speed.

It was impossible to stay angry at Mark; he was weak, and certainly hadn't set out to betray her. She cared for him, but she wasn't in love with him, nor was he with her. In fact, she probably owed Rochelle a debt of gratitude for helping her avoid a big mistake. But the memory of the tabloid attack squelched any generous feelings.

The sun emerged from behind the clouds. She didn't miss Mark at all.

Hugo, on the other hand, was a different matter. Walking around the well-tended graves, Julie felt a restless, pointless anger. She wanted to find the man and yell at him, loudly. Why hadn't he tried harder to make her see the truth?

Yes, it was easy to understand why he'd thought she wouldn't believe him, Mark did have her completely bamboozled. But couldn't he have just, well, made her listen to reason? Carried her off somewhere and forced her to think about all the warning signs? No, he couldn't have. He was a gentleman. She kicked a stump in vexation.

A pair of eighteenth-century gravestones lay canted to one side, a husband and wife who had been married for over fifty years. That's what she wanted, Julie knew with blazing certainty. She wanted to be married to Hugo for as long as she could have him.

Dropping to her haunches, she plucked a few weeds from around the couple's headstones. There was no one to blame for her blindness except herself, but the reality that nothing was going to work out was hard to accept. Mark hadn't worked out, Hugo hadn't worked out, and her career at Haddonfield was probably ruined as well.

Her future had changed in the blink of an eye, and it would take some time to get adjusted to the much different one that lay before her. Tom had assured her that other scandals would displace her from the papers by the end of the month. But as long as she stayed in England, she would always be "Jezebel Julie," and the notoriety might taint Haddonfield.

Was there really anything left for her at Haddonfield? Every inch of the gardens and orchards had been planned out, and the new polyhouse would be up by May. A less ambitious gardener could come in and take over. Maybe Nerida would even consider going on to a local college and then come back to run things.

The church bell rang as she tried to come up with a plan for her future. The job in Virginia was very good, and she doubted anyone there was aware of her notoriety. Career-wise, it was a plum offer, a huge step up, and there was a nearby university where she could work on her doctorate.

The church bell chimed eleven times as she tried to muster enthusiasm and convince herself of the merits of the offer. But in the end, she found it impossible; there was no challenge in the position, and the thought of leaving England filled her with inexplicable sadness. This was her home now, and she wanted to see Bonnie and Clive's baby born. Maybe after that it would be time to move on.

The bell finished tolling as she looked out at the vast green fields of winter wheat. Did Hugo have any idea how blessed he was with farms the size and quality of Wrothesley? The seed company she'd contacted in America had jumped at the suggestion of using the estate as a test site. Just her three-sentence description of the growing conditions alone had set them to salivating. He was sitting on a gold mine.

His soil was rich and well-drained, and she would bet her hat that there'd once been a kitchen garden at Wrothesley—the house was grand enough that the kitchen garden might even have been walled at one point. Now, *there* was a challenge she could sink her trowel into. The old cow barn would have plenty of room for a proper tractor, the neighbors wouldn't fuss about the smell of the manure, and there was every chance she could work more closely with the Heritage Seed Library to develop a demonstration garden.

Ideas flooded her mind and she jumped to her feet, brushing grass off her pants. Strong emotions bubbled to the surface, feeling remarkably like happiness and astonishingly, *hope*.

She was not going to let Mark, Rochelle, or any tabloid in Great Britain dictate the path of her life. She was in love with Hugo and if she had to fight for him, so be it. He was right. It was much, much different than simply loving someone. She wanted to know where he was at that exact moment. She wanted to know if he was happy, if he'd had enough to eat. She wanted to show him the Joseph Paxton book. If he were here, maybe he would notice she was wearing a yellow t-shirt and black jacket.

Tom said there'd been a lot of misunderstandings, so maybe it was best to just put everything on the table and let the chips fall where they may. Hugo had a match this afternoon against Birmingham City at three thirty, and Tom said it was important that he stay focused on that. Tomorrow would be soon enough. She'd take the first bus to London and go directly to his house.

Getting back on her bike, she resolved to tell him everything, including how she felt about him. She pedaled for several minutes, getting used to the liberating idea. It would cost her some dignity, but there wasn't much left of that. Everyone in the United Kingdom already thought she was a slut. No matter what happened, it would be cathartic. There would be no remorse to live with, no "what if." And if things didn't work out, she would leave and get on with her life.

Upon her return to the village, she realized she was ravenous. The bakery featured a local pastry called a clanger, a turnover filled with meat at one end and a pie filling at the other. She bought one and then decided to add a second to her order. If nothing else, she could eat it on the bus back to London tomorrow.

Passing the station notice board, she saw there was a bus the next morning at 7:05 a.m. and she planned to be on it. A flyer on the notice board announced a string quartet concert in the town hall that evening. Impulsively she decided to go, knowing she would need the distraction. Back at the cottage, she packed her small bag for the morning and set about dividing clumps of daylilies in the garden to keep her occupied until the concert.

# Chapter Fifty-Nine

SATURDAY'S HOME MATCH at Townsend Lane Stadium against Birmingham City seemed doomed before it even started.

Sir Frank himself insisted the team use St Augustine School for their pre-match warm-up instead of Townsend Lane and then travel up by coach as if they were the visitors instead of the home club.

The reason was obvious enough when they were greeted at the stadium gates by television cameras and crowds twenty-deep. They were hoping for another blowup, and Hugo had every intention of disappointing them with ninety minutes of cold, efficient, and ruthlessly focused play. He was not going to make a spectacle of himself again, not when there was a chance Juliet might be watching.

The team ignored it all, and Hugo was heartened by the tact they were showing. Not a word about his problems had been said all week. Even Mick Carr had kept his bloody yap shut, perhaps preoccupied with something else.

Surly Birmingham City punters waved yellow hankies at him during the singing of "God Save the Queen." The match began sluggishly, which was part of Kingsbury Town's strategy, and things brightened considerably when Kingsbury Town scored in the eighth minute of play, a simple set piece that caught Birmingham City flat-footed, letting Fernando boot the ball in with ridiculous ease.

"They won't let us do that twice, lads," Darius cautioned. "Saddle up."

Kingsbury Town began to move the ball up and down the field, following their plan to let Samuel test a revamped Birmingham City back row a few times to discover where the holes were. Hugo chatted in French with his opposite, a recent arrival from Cote d'Ivoire who was momentarily distracted by the banter and failed to notice Hugo setting up a quick cross pass that Marco almost knocked in. This was all good. The solace he'd felt after talking with Bonnie still held, and while he was not exactly cheerful, he felt he was at least keeping his head together.

They were up 2–0 at the half. Back in the locker room, they decided their opponents were looking tired and needed to be run around a bit more. A string of long plays with broad passes was selected, and if Kingsbury Town could successfully maintain control, it would be devastatingly effective. They would wait until the last three minutes to press, sending Jean-George forward and Pozny back, leaving Dylan and Hugo wide.

But unfortunately, Birmingham City also had a plan.

At eighty-five minutes, Jason Edu deflected a brilliant Birmingham City corner shot, which Hugo picked up and was moving up the field when Joss Jenkins, who was playing out of position, tackled him. Joss was easily two stone heavier, and Hugo twisted and brought the defender down with him. Both men crashed to the pitch as the ball rolled out-of-bounds. The whistle blew, and the line judge marked the spot where Hugo would throw in.

"Clive says that in case you're thinking of trying to see Julie, you'd best not," Joss cautioned Hugo jovially as they got back on their feet. "Sounds like good advice to me."

Unbridled rage exploded in Hugo and he launched himself at the Birmingham City defender, delivering a solid punch to his grinning face. Joss reeled with the force of the blow. Hugo was preparing to follow it with another when Pozny threw himself between them and both teams rushed to circle their own players to keep them out of the fray. The blare of whistles and the roar of the crowd drowned out everything else, while Hugo lashed against his teammate's restraint, desperate to grind Joss into the pitch.

Ignoring the string of vitriol Hugo was spewing, the referee pulled a red card out of his pocket and flashed it high over his head. "Auchincloss, I have no idea why you've suddenly gone insane, but for God's sake, put a lid on it!" he ordered over the thunder of the crowd, and with a nod to Giles Roberts, Hugo was pulled from the game. He stalked off the field and disappeared back into the locker room.

"I can't quite remember ever seeing Auchincloss so violent," one announcer commented. "Do we know what Jenkins said to him?"

"No clue, but it was obviously something. Auchincloss is usually the coolest character on the pitch," his partner replied. "First yellow card of his career last week, and now a red. It's like he's got eleven years of aggression pent up and is only now letting it out. And all this on the heels of a rather brilliant second half-year."

"He's been in the tabloids recently with some mix-up over a girl and he can't be happy about that."

"I'm looking at Kingsbury Town Captain Darius Rutledge and he looks as flummoxed as we are," the second announcer continued. "Auchincloss is facing a three-game suspension, and Rutledge and Manager Giles Roberts better get a leash on him or they can kiss the rest of their season goodbye."

---

Playing with a man short, Kingsbury Town managed to hold back Birmingham City and clinched the win, much to the satisfaction of their fans. After the match, Hugo sat despondently on a bench in the locker room as Giles screamed at the top of his lungs, pacing madly and waving his arms.

"What the hell did Jenkins say to you?" Darius demanded between Giles's rants.

"He wanted your sister's phone number," Hugo sneered.

Darius just shook his head sadly. "For Christ's sake, I've got you going mental and Mick mooning over some girl. Since when did Kingsbury Town turn into such a bloody drama?"

Pozny joined him at the locker next to his. "You have been sad," the young Pole declared in rapidly improving English.

Hugo took off his match shirt. "Yes."

"*La belle femme*?" Pozny suggested, lapsing into French. The beautiful girl?

"*Oui.*"

"Have you tried to see her?"

"She has a friend who doesn't want me to."

"Ah. And they send you message." Hugo nodded, and Pozny shook his head in understanding. "Then we must talk with her friend."

Hugo snorted. "He's big."

"Pozny is big!" the young Pole announced, thumping his chest. "And Hugo is fast. We go see him together, I think."

"This isn't your battle, Pozny."

"Ah," Pozny scoffed, "Hugo is smart, Pozny not smart at all! But Pozny know something Hugo don't. Life is short, *mon ami*. You have nothing to lose, you lose it already. We go."

"I'll go by myself."

"No. I do this. This girl, she make you happy. Very, very happy. I see it. And you help me bring Mama over from Polska. No one else helps. So I make sure you have friend there."

Hugo's chest constricted at Pozny's words. He'd never really had any friends on the team before. Now this teammate was willing to get in a serious fight with him. "Okay," he relented. "Let's go."

———•◯•———

The Black Thistle was doing a good business Saturday evening. Hugo and Pozny nodded to a group of Fulham players gathered at the bar as they entered. A dark-haired girl behind the counter asked if they wanted beers, but they shook their heads and joined a group at the darts area.

"Hugo, Pozny." Bev Jenkins, who was even larger than his brother Joss, greeted the men.

"I'd like a word, Clive," Hugo said.

Clive lined up his shot. "Answer's no. Leave her alone."

The shot landed millimeters from the bull's eye. Clive grunted with satisfaction and then turned and walked squarely into Hugo's fist.

The force of the blow, square on the chin, rocked Clive back on his heels. He paused, working his jaw, and focused on Hugo, his eyes blazing. Fulham players swiftly surrounded them as Pozny snatched an empty beer bottle from a nearby table and stepped in to guard Hugo's back, muttering taunting threats in Polish.

"This isn't your fight, Bev," Hugo warned, not taking his eyes off Clive. Clive nodded and waved everyone off.

"Take it outside!" the barman yelled.

"Auchincloss will never get the better of Clive," a Fulham fullback noted as they watched the men leave out the back door.

"I've got ten quid says he does," another player wagered. "He's been a wild man since the dustup over that girl."

"What, the one that got thrown over by her boyfriend for that rum model?"

"Aye. And he got a red today. Joss Jenkins knew just which button to push."

"Now, lads, let's think this through," a Fulham striker cautioned. "We need Kingsbury Town to take out West Ham in two weeks if we're going to move up to tenth, and they're not going to do it without Hugo. Maybe we better make sure it's a fair fight."

The Fulham captain finished his beer, pulled out his mobile, and pressed some numbers. "If we're going to be the cavalry, we better call his team, they'll want to wade in, too. Darius would never forgive me if Fulham saved the day."

———◦———

The alley behind the bar was poorly lit and reeked of every excrement known to man. Hugo and Clive faced off next to a rickety wooden fence that did a poor job of blocking the sharp drop to a loading dock below, the garbage-strewn ground slippery with rain.

"Come on, lad, take another swing and do it properly this time," Clive urged him. "That last one was a cheap shot."

Hugo tried a right hook, which Clive evaded easily, and then ducked a fist Clive threw and landed a solid blow to the larger man's gut.

"I see they taught you to fight at your toff school," Clive said, as the pair exchanged a volley of punches.

"If you have a message for me, send it yourself," Hugo snarled, feinting a right hook but delivering a vicious hit.

A cut opened above Clive's eye and he wiped away the blood. "Right, the message is keep away from her. Your kind is poison."

"Then you're going to have to kill me to keep me from her."

They circled each other warily for several moments before Clive landed a solid crack to Hugo's jaw that sent him sprawling back against a reeking dumpster. "What makes you think she wants you?"

Raising himself on one elbow, Hugo focused unsteadily on Clive's hulking form. "I love her and I'm not going to let her go. And you're not going to keep her from me."

The fight then began in earnest. Within minutes, a crowd of Kingsbury Town footballers poured through the Black Thistle and out to the back alley. By this time, Hugo was also sporting a nasty cut above his eye and Clive had a scraped hand and a bloody lip.

"Fuck off," he snapped as Darius and three other teammates tried to restrain him.

"Come off it, Hugo, she's not worth it," one called out, which only made him fight more viciously. He clamped an arm around Clive's neck and twisted his body with a vicious jerk, and then hooked Clive's ankle, causing the much larger man to career backwards. With Clive still hanging onto Hugo, both men slammed against the fence which promptly collapsed under their weight in a sickening crack of rotting wood, sending them crashing to the pavement below.

———————◆○◆———————

Two hours later, the door to a very discreet physician's office flew open and Bonnie marched in. "Clive Connelly! You're going to be a father in less than two months and you're getting into bar fights?"

Clive held an ice bag to his jaw and kissed the top of her head, wincing with the pain of a cut lip. "Couldn't be helped, love. I had this one coming."

A violent string of curses came from the adjoining treatment room and Bonnie glanced around. "Is that Hugo? I thought he never fought."

"Aye, but you wouldn't know it by this evening," Clive sighed. "I had Joss Jenkins send a message to him during the game today, and that was out of line," he admitted, genuinely shocked by how wild Hugo had been. "I think letting him use me as a punching bag made him feel better."

"What kind of message?" Bonnie glared at her husband.

"To leave Julie alone. I was testing him, but he passed. He's in love with Julie, I'm convinced of it."

"How do you know that?"

"Because I know I'd be behaving the same way if I thought I'd lost you."

# Chapter Sixty

THE CONCERT STARTED late, and the pitch-black of the starless night made Julie grateful she'd tucked a flashlight in her purse for the walk home. It was almost eleven o'clock when she turned down the lane to the cottage, humming a tune the quartet had played. The concert had only improved her happy mood, and she thought about the trip back to London in the morning with impatient excitement. She wanted to go now, this very instant. She didn't want to wait.

Lost in her thoughts, she unlocked the front door and, unable to find the light switch, took off her boots in the dark foyer. As she hung her jacket on the coat rack, a tall figure emerged from the darkness and loomed before her.

"It's me," Hugo said, reaching for her as she stood frozen with terror. "Don't be scared."

Joy flooded through Julie as she threw herself into his arms. *He's here*, she thought with wild relief.

Snatching her against him, Hugo kissed her like a starving man, his lips crushing hers. She kissed him back fervently, the familiar smell of him filling her senses—warm wool, lavender, pepper, and the subtle musk of healthy male. The scents mixed with alien smells, sour and fetid odors, but nothing else mattered. Hugo was here, with her, and everything was right and good.

Pulling back, he searched her face in the dim light, his breathing labored. "Are you all right, Juliet? Have they followed you here? Should I—"

"I'm fine."

"I couldn't keep away from you, Juliet," he whispered, their breaths mingling, breathing life back into her. "Yell at me all you want. Bitch at me. Please, I deserve it. But just let me be with you."

"I'm not angry." She pulled his lips back to hers, needing him, needing to feel the security of his toughness and strength. Her hands splayed over his shoulders, feeling the play of his sinewy muscles, loving the rough silk of his hair in her fingers.

Abruptly, she paused, her exploratory fingers encountering grit and swollen flesh. Pulling back, she saw the faint outline of dried blood near his hairline, and her relief was immediately replaced with concern.

"Hugo, you're hurt." Against his protests, Julie pulled him into the sitting room and flicked on a lamp. She cupped his face and turned it towards the light, shocked to see the numerous cuts and scrapes. Dear Lord, one eye seemed to be swelling shut.

She quickly examined the rest of him. "Your shirt is torn and there's mud on your trousers. What on heaven's earth happened?"

"I was in a fight," he confessed, drawing her back into his arms. "Two fights, actually."

"You never fight." She gasped as he sank his lips into the base of her neck.

"I've never had anyone worth fighting for before."

Tears stung her eyes as Julie gave herself up to the desire that engulfed her, her need for him absolute. She leaned back as he pressed her against the wall, his arms molding her body to his as she surrendered to his kiss.

"Tell me to stop, Juliet, and I will," Hugo said, covering her face in hard kisses.

Stop? Was the man insane? "I don't want you to stop."

"No, this has to be about what *you* want," he insisted, his hands roaming her body.

"It is," she assured him.

"But I want you to know that I respect you, and I'm willing to—"

She pulled his lips back down to hers, silencing his words as she unbuttoned his shirt.

"I'm staying in the guest bedroom," she told him.

With a grin, he swung her into his arms, carried her through the house, and laid her down on the bed. "Wait here."

Hugo left the room, leaving her confused and very aroused. When he returned, he thrust a tissue-wrapped package into her hands. "Put this on."

Julie unwrapped it with curiosity. "My nightgown! Where did you find it? I thought I'd lost it at Cheeting Park."

"I stole it," he confessed. "It's meant for me and me only. Go put it on."

---

When Julie emerged from the bathroom, she saw that Hugo had lit two candles, bathing the room in gentle light. He approached her warily, feasting hungrily on the sight of her. The slit up the front of the gown revealed a flash of bare leg, and the thin ribbons of the bodice strained across the soft mounds of her breasts.

"You look like an angel." He swallowed, and the unmasked desire on his face made Julie's nipples tighten under the thin lace of the bodice of her gown. "I have never seen anything as beautiful as you. I'm afraid if I touch you, you'll disappear."

"I bought this the same day I found *The Orchard* at Gladia's. It's why I didn't have enough money with me to buy the book."

Moisture rimmed his eyes. "We have guardian angels, Juliet."

She stood immobile while he circled her, intent on seeing every facet of her. He stopped a safe distance away. "Juliet, you have to be sure this is what you want. Because if I touch you, I swear I won't be able to stop."

She took his hand and placed it over the spot where her heart beat wildly, his palm rough against her warm skin. "*You* are what I want, Hugo. Only you."

And then she kissed him, her touch breaking the invisible chains that had held him back. He groaned, running his hands over her body, and with impatient fingers, Julie finished unbuttoning his shirt. His skin pressed against hers, smooth and hard.

She fumbled with his belt, but he took over and unbuckled it swiftly, letting his trousers drop to the floor, followed by his boxers.

He pulled her against him, the warmth of his skin shocking her. Hugo was lean and finely-sculpted, and she pressed her face against the downy golden hairs of his chest, his skin tasting salty where she licked it.

His arousal was pressed intimately between them, and she could feel the searing heat of it, sizeable and intent. He reached for the first ribbon between her breasts and pulled it slowly, watching in fascination as the satiny strand unwound. "I feel like I'm unwrapping the world's best present."

As each ribbon gave way, she shivered, wanting to feel his lips where his hands had been, until finally her breasts were fully exposed.

The feel of the silky pelt of the hairs on his chest against the sensitive peaks of her breasts drove her wild, and she arched against him, desperate for more. Effortlessly, he lifted her in his arms, laid her in the center of the bed, and followed her down. The slit of the gown parted, and he cupped her calf and ran his hand up her bare leg. His touch was calming and soothing and remarkably arousing.

"All of you is so soft," he murmured, his hand moving up to caress the sensitive flesh of her stomach.

He pressed her back into the pillows and kissed her passionately, making her feel drugged with desire. She pulled him to her, her hands exploring the strong muscles of his back. With studied concentration, he lavished full attention on her breasts, tenderly teasing the incredibly sensitive peaks till she moaned with pleasure.

She gasped as his hand slipped between her legs, making her body jolt upward in surprise.

"No, Juliet, you're so beautiful," he coaxed, using his own body to compel her back into the pillows as his fingers continued to gently explore. "You're so ready for me, let me show you how good it can feel."

She wanted to feel him as well, all of him, but he caught her wrist as it moved lower and he laughed.

"Later. There will be time for that and more. But I want you so badly that if you touch me now, everything will be over way too quickly. It has to be good for you first."

He continued to suckle her breasts as his hand gently sought out the most sensitive parts of her body, chuckling deeply as she begged him for release. He stroked her with deliberate rhythm as Julie thrashed in complete abandon, her gasps driving him to a frenzy. She begged him not to stop—not that he could have. He felt her pause at the pinnacle, quivering, then pulse in wave after wave of ecstasy.

She lay back, gulping air. "That was amazing."

"It's just the beginning," Hugo murmured, bending his head to lick her breast. As her breathing settled, he pulled the gown over her head and lay over her, reveling in the feel of her completely naked body beneath him. Finally she was here, in his arms, his to explore and pleasure.

He nudged her legs apart and settled his hips between them, nestling into her moist recesses, her hips shifting to accommodate his weight, pulling him closer. He closed his eyes in pleasure as she moved again, rubbing upward and against him in a light thrusting motion. The breath caught in his throat and he moaned out loud and then kissed her with a passion that bordered on frenzy.

Suddenly he pulled back, panting heavily.

"Did I do something wrong?" she asked in confusion.

"You said you're on contraceptives," he stated hoarsely, and she nodded. "I've always used protection, always. And the team tests for everything every six months. There's no issues."

"I trust you," she said simply and tried to draw him back down, but he resisted.

"I've always used protection," he repeated earnestly, "but I don't want to, not now, not with you."

"Okay," she agreed.

"It will make it easier for you," he explained desperately.

"That would be nice."

"And I want to feel all of you."

"Do people always talk this much before having sex?" she asked.

He smiled. "We're not going to have sex. We're going to make love."

There was nothing between them now. He wanted her so damned badly, wanted to be inside her immediately. Swiftly he moved over her, his desire raging, yet he knew he needed to be gentle, wanted to be gentle, and he trembled with the restraint it took. Her eyes were filled with tenderness as she pulled him down to her, welcoming him into her body.

As he pressed into her, the lusciously hot tautness stunned him, enveloping him. She arched beneath him and he pushed into her blindly, knowing nothing but the sensation of her softness.

Their fit was intensely tight, and he nudged hard, hating that he was causing her pain. Her eyes were shut, and he whispered endearments, hesitating, almost ready to withdraw. He knew it must be hurting like hell.

Instead, he felt her hands on his hips pulling him closer against her, her nails digging into his skin. "Don't stop."

With a last thrust, he filled her completely, and she jerked reflexively beneath him, letting out a small cry. Intense sensations enveloped him in a grip of erotic pleasure. Julie shifted from side to side, trying desperately to accommodate him more comfortably, but the motion shot lightning bolts through his body.

"No, sweetheart, stay still," he begged, but it was too late—the heat, the smell of her, her throaty cries, the exquisitely hot velvet feel of her, the endless desire—all joined together to lift him to a height he could have never imagined.

"Oh, Lord," he gasped, and felt his heart climax at exactly the same time the rest of his body did.

# Chapter Sixty-One

AFTERWARDS THEY LAY sated, their bodies entwined, and she felt the strong beat of his heart where her head lay on his chest. "I'm so sorry I hurt you," he murmured. "But it won't hurt like that ever again."

Julie smiled languorously. "If I was concerned about it not hurting, I would have chosen a much less well-endowed man."

"So I please you?"

"Tremendously. But you made it last so long for me, I wanted it to be wonderful for you, too. But it was over so quickly, did I do something wrong?"

Hugo had never heard anything funnier in his life. "I swear I've never felt anything so amazing, you have no worries there. And it will last longer next time."

"You're sure?"

"I'm sure."

———◆○◆———

Sometime in the middle of the night, Julie awoke to being lifted in Hugo's arms and carried to the bathroom, lit by one candle. The shower was already running, and he walked in and set her down on the tiled bench that ran across one end, the warm water splashing over them.

He washed Julie lovingly, his hands coursing unhurriedly over her soap-slick skin. His hands cupped the fullness of her breasts, his thumbs brushing over the sensitive peaks that tightened under his caress.

Gently he held a hot washcloth between her legs, blotting tenderly, then to her shock, replaced it with his lips.

Julie slid away from the almost-too-intense intimacy and took the soap and lathered it on his skin, seeing faint traces of his wounds in the flickering candlelight. Shyly, she moved her hands over his body, anxious to explore him as well. Hugo was hard again, and she touched him hesitantly, her fingers lightly tracing the powerful length of him. Her touch was evidently too light because he groaned as if in pain and wrapped his hand around hers, clenching it strongly along his shaft.

Getting the idea, she brushed his hand away and tried it herself and was extraordinarily pleased with the results. She watched as his eyes rolled back in his head and his knees practically buckled, but her laugh of delight was cut short when he swiftly backed her against the tile wall and grasped her bottom firmly, then lifted her and nudged himself between her thighs.

The fit was easier this time, and although the abused flesh protested, she shifted her hips rhythmically, loving the feel of him. Hugo groaned and buried himself inside her, his hands supporting her hips as she wrapped her legs around him. He drove into her, and she cried out in a combination of delight and pain until he lost control. With three intense thrusts, he climaxed, and then clasped her tightly against his body, their breathing ragged.

"See?" he laughed unsteadily. "I lasted almost a full twenty seconds longer that time."

———————— ✦○✦ ————————

Dawn broke brilliantly the next morning as sunlight streamed in through the cottage windows. Julie woke wrapped in the crook of Hugo's arm, his naked skin warm against hers, her leg wedged intimately between his. His head lay on her hair and his deep, even breathing told Julie he was fast asleep.

She lay in the bed, luxuriating in being able to watch him as he slept, his aristocratic features relaxed in slumber. In the clear morning light, she could see the full extent of his wounds. There were some scrapes on his cheek, and the eye she could see looked slightly puffy, but he was still a devastatingly handsome man.

Tentatively, she flexed different parts of her body. She felt different, tender in places that had been stretched and loved just hours before.

What was it like in the morning after two people made love for the first time, she wondered? Did someone make the coffee and the other fetch the morning paper?

Anxiety began to slowly wrap her in its insidious grip. Hugo never stayed the night with the women he slept with, and he might not want her there when he woke up.

It seemed impossible that it could be that way after the night they'd spent, but she knew she wouldn't be able to bear his cool indifference. Making love with him solidified all the feelings she had for him, and his indifference would destroy her.

She knew she couldn't stay and find out.

With more bravery than she'd ever felt, she carefully pulled her hair out from under Hugo, taking great care not to wake him, and dressed quickly. Her bag, which she had packed the afternoon before, was by the front door, and after taking one last regretful glance around the cottage, she pulled on her coat and hat and steeled herself to walk out the door.

Her feet felt like lead as she trudged down the narrow lane towards the village, which was deserted at this hour of the morning. Turning the corner to the street where the bus would stop, she gasped as a hand snaked out from a shop vestibule and Hugo stepped into her path, his face a wreath of anger.

"Where do you think you're going?" Hugo demanded.

Julie tried to regain her composure. "Oh, good morning. Sorry, did I wake you?"

"You mean when you snuck out of my bed? Yes, you bloody well woke me. Now I repeat, where the hell are you going?"

"Home," Julie said, trying to sound practical. "Then over to Haddonfield, the cut-and-come-again lettuce needs to be reseeded, and I forgot to tell Nerida to mound up the sea kale."

Hugo glowered. "You can't be serious."

"Actually, I'm being sensible. You made it clear you prefer, um... brief encounters, and I completely understand. I... I've done a lot of growing up this week and I realize having no attachments is definitely the way to go." She composed her face into a cheery smile and groped for more platitudes. "The bus will be here in a few moments. Say, last night was great, I really enjoyed it. Thanks. We'll see each other around, I suppose?"

"No."

Julie faltered. "No?"

Hugo's mouth worked silently, as if he were grappling with a huge quandary. Then he seemed to reach some decision and picked up her bag.

"Hey, I need that!" Julie protested, but was cut off when he bent down and threw her over his shoulder.

"What are you doing?" she demanded, dangling upside down.

"What I should have done the very first day I met you," he said, walking back towards the cottage.

"But you'll hurt your shoulder!"

He turned down the lane, striding easily. "Then don't wiggle around so much."

"Put me down!"

Hugo shook his head. "And have you try to run away again? Not a chance."

"You said it doesn't mean anything to you."

"I changed my mind."

"I only slept with you because I'm on the rebound," she declared hotly.

"Is that so? Damn you, I feel so cheap."

Back in the cottage, Hugo walked straight through the sitting room and dumped Julie unceremoniously on the bed, glaring down at her. "I didn't stop to ask last night, but do you want Looks back? Is that it?"

Now it was Julie's turn to be appalled. "No. I was fond of Mark but that was it. I haven't missed him at all."

"Who have you missed?"

"You. I've never missed anyone so much in my life."

"Then listen to me carefully, Juliet. If you ever try to leave me again, I will find you and you won't like the consequences."

"But you said you had an understanding—"

"I see I'm going to be blessed with a woman with an excellent memory," Hugo sighed as he unzipped her coat and pulled the boots from her feet. "I appreciate your sentiment," he continued conversationally, "but I said a lot of things that you'd best forget because things are completely different now. That is not you, and it's not me either. Not ever again."

"How can you change so quickly?"

"For the love of God, woman, haven't you been listening to me?" Hugo bellowed. "I'm out of my mind in love with you! My life has been heaven and hell since the first day I met you. The last week being pure hell and last night being pure heaven."

He moved over Julie, pinning her to the bed, his hands holding her wrists to either side and his weight holding her immobile. "I've been captivated since the first day we met. You haunted me, and I couldn't forget you. Then fortune smiled on me, and I found you again. After that, I got to know you and just kept being more and more drawn to you.

"I went through hell watching you with Looks. I followed you to Edward's wedding because I needed to see what you and Looks were like together, to see if there was any affection. And then when I kissed you in the basement, everything changed, and I realized I wanted to keep you for myself. But you had to make up your own mind, had to choose me over Looks."

"I was getting there," she protested. "I was very close."

"At Pippa's party I thought I'd finally won you—I thought you were choosing me. And then Sophie ruined it all, and I was furious, so furious that I blew everything."

Julie made a face at Sophie's name and Hugo laughed. "You don't have to worry about hearing any more from her. She's on her way to Canada for an extended vacation, or so I've heard. Her grandfather has a ranch in Alberta."

"Good riddance. What did you do next?"

"I tried ignoring you, and that was impossible. Your every movement had me on a torture rack. I knew I needed to find out what was going on between the two of you, so I got Looks very, very drunk. It took four martinis to get him loosened up enough to tell me that he was still carrying on with Rochelle and that you were a virgin."

Julie pursed her lips. "So. You'd known about that as well."

"It meant you weren't sleeping with him, so I was thrilled," Hugo countered. "It was the best news I could have ever hoped for, because it meant I had a chance. So I tried every way possible to make you see that we were meant to be together."

"You did," Julie admitted. "And I think I didn't want to see it. I love you so much that it overwhelmed me, and I didn't know how to cope with it. Telling my boyfriend, 'Shove off, I've found the man of my dreams who also happens to be much wealthier and successful,' just didn't seem right."

"So, if I was a poor stiff slaving away in Level Seven, things would have gone a lot smoother?"

Julie thought about that for a moment. "Probably not."

"Well, after yesterday I might find myself looking for a job there," Hugo said, pressing her onto her back and covering her body with his own. "But no matter what happens from now on, we're together—we are one. And you better hope that you have some affection for me, because you're going to be stuck with me for a very long time."

"Are you sore?" Hugo asked solicitously much later, idly winding lengths of her hair through his fingers.

Julie smiled with sleepy pleasure. "You kissed away the soreness. And then some."

"Your body is like a playground." She felt him stretch next to her, then raise himself on one elbow to look down at her. "Why did you leave me this morning?"

"I panicked," Julie admitted. "Last night was so wonderful, I didn't want to wake up and have it ruined because *you* wanted to leave."

"I never want to leave. You've introduced me to the delights of waking up with a beautiful woman." His hands slid possessively over her warm skin and began to trace delicious patterns on incredibly sensitive parts of her body.

"Hugo, you can't possibly be ready again," she gasped, pushing away his already insistent erection and changing the subject. "You said you were in two fights last night."

"The first was during the game. I got a red card."

"That sounds worse than a yellow card."

"It is, and I'll be paying the piper for that one. And the second one was Clive."

Julie pulled back from him, her hair tumbling down around her, her eyes wide. "Why did you fight Clive?"

"He wouldn't let me see you."

She scanned him quickly for broken bones. "What kind of shape is he in?"

"About the same, but he said Bonnie wasn't done with him yet." He caught her hands. "It's okay, Juliet. We're friends again. We talked, and he told me where you were. I got in the car and drove straight here."

She collapsed back against the pillows. "You fought for me?"

"Of course. And I will always fight for you."

"You won't have to. I'm yours," Julie whispered, as she pulled his head down to hers and kissed him.

# Chapter Sixty-Two

"YOU NEED SOMETHING to eat," Hugo told Julie later that morning. "You're going to need your strength."

He pulled on a pair of pajama bottoms and helped her into a paisley silk robe from the guest bedroom closet.

"Wait," he paused. "I have something to go with that outfit."

Sitting her on a chair by the mirrored dresser, he went to the bag he had hastily packed the night before. "Now close your eyes."

Smoothing her hair away, he draped the diamond and sapphire necklace around her neck and hooked the clasp at the nape. "Now you can open them."

Julie gasped when she saw her reflection in the mirror. The gems twinkled brightly in the morning sunshine, the blue of the stones indeed matching her eyes.

"Oh, Hugo, it's so pretty. I love it!" She spun around, delighted. "Where did you get it?"

It occurred to Hugo that Juliet didn't realize the necklace was real. "A shop in town," he shrugged. "I saw it and knew you had to have it."

She kissed him warmly. "It's very nice. Do lords of the manor always treat the virgins they ravish so well?"

"We have to. We're only allowed one per nowadays," Hugo said, loving the feel of her lips against his. "There's a vast shortage, and we have to make do. They must be well taken care of."

Julie pressed closer against the full length of him. "You certainly do."

"And they must be ravished on a regular basis," Hugo added, cupping her buttocks and fitting her against his intent hardness. "I'm sorry, but it's the rules."

She made a delightful sound as his lips continued to explore her satiny skin. Hugo was nudging her back against the bed when he felt her stiffen. "What was that noise?"

They followed the unmistakable sound of kitchen cabinets opening and closing to find Ian seated at the table, reading the newspaper and munching on a clanger.

"Good morning," Ian said, a smile spreading over his face.

Hugo saw Julie's mortified blush and pulled the robe closer about her, almost losing her in the rich folds. Tightening the sash, he sat and pulled her onto his lap, wrapping his arm around her.

"Learn to knock," Hugo told his brother, a faint smile on his lips.

"Pretty sparkler, Julie," Ian said, helping himself to another slice of clanger. "That's nicer even than some of Granny's stuff."

Hugo felt Juliet stiffen in his lap, and she dropped her lips to his ear. "It's real?" she whispered.

*Bloody Ian.* "Yes."

She swallowed. "I can't keep it."

"You can have it for as long as you stay with me."

"I don't deserve it."

Hugo smoothed his hand over her hair and kissed her forehead. "You deserve it. You've put up with a lot. You went through hell because of me."

"Where'd you get that shiner?" Ian asked his brother.

"Fighting some dragons. To what do we owe the pleasure of this visit?"

Ian stood, wiping his hands on a napkin. "Tom sent me. He wants to see you both this morning, you're to go straight to his office. Say, is there another clanger in that box?"

---

"So, you two are now officially together." Tom grinned later that afternoon. "And about bloody time, if you don't mind my saying. But as of now you're officially shut down."

Hugo rolled his eyes in disgust. "Bother, Tom, you're being ridiculous."

Tom ignored him and turned his attention to Julie. "If you're going to keep him around and expect to maintain your sanity, you're going to have to let me handle it and do as I say."

"For how long?" Julie asked.

"Not long. Three months."

"Two weeks." Hugo countered.

"This isn't negotiable. Right now you're 'Jezebel Julie.' It's my job to make sure you don't become 'Rebound Randall.' The Premier season has nine more weeks left, and then you can have the summer to yourselves. By then you'll be old news, and by the start of the next season, the pair of you can run down the high street naked and no one will blink an eye. But until then, you're shuttered."

Hugo turned to Julie. "You don't want this, do you? Bring it on, I say. I don't want to hide the fact that we're together."

"I have you, and that's all I want," she said. "And I'd like our privacy, or as much as we can get. I'm going to be flat out for the next few weeks with the gardens anyway, so it works for me."

Hugo turned back to Tom. "Just till the end of the season. And I'm not staying away from her."

"You don't have to. Just keep your heads down, assume you're being followed. They'll try to provoke you. But there is some good news—I've got it on good authority that there's going to be rumors of another royal engagement erupting. That should take the heat off for a bit."

"Oh, yes? Who?" Hugo asked.

"There's nothing to it. Now, Julie, I need to represent you as well. And you're in luck—today my fee for unlimited representation is one pound. There's an agreement drawn up for you on Nancy's desk. Why don't you read it and pay up."

"Not you," Tom snapped at Hugo, who had turned to go. "Sit down." He waited until Julie closed the office door and fixed Hugo with a steely stare. "You can't marry her for at least another six months."

"Why not?" Hugo roared with outrage.

"For her sake. We need to get control of the situation."

"I've had too much control. For once I'm going to go with my gut instincts, which I should have done in the first place."

"Hugo, I couldn't be happier for you. But you're walking a thin line, and they will destroy her if you let them. Figure out a way to distract them from Julie for the next few weeks. Make it look like you're after someone else. It's the only way."

Hugo frowned but nodded in agreement.

"And there's some other news," Tom added.

"Great, what now?" Hugo snapped.

Tom's face broke into a broad grin. "Cassandra's pregnant."

Julie was walking from Hugo's cavernous kitchen to the front sitting room when she heard him speaking in a low tone to someone on his mobile.

"No, don't come over. She's here."

She stopped dead in her tracks. There was a pause, and Hugo continued. "No, she doesn't know anything. So don't come over until I call." Again, another pause. "It will be fine, I promise. I'm okay. I'll call you later."

Sickening waves of betrayal hit Julie, worse than she had ever felt in her life. The horrible pain of what had happened with Mark came flooding back and she stood frozen like a statue.

Hugo walked around the corner and ground to a halt when he saw her. "Juliet, what's the matter?"

Her mouth moved but no sound would come out. From deep within herself, she found the resolve to lick her lips and force the words. "Who were you talking with on the phone just now?"

Hugo paled. "You heard?"

"I wasn't eavesdropping. I was just coming to find you."

He pulled his mobile from his pocket and placed a call. Seconds passed, and then someone obviously picked up. "I need you to get over here as soon as you can. Juliet needs to know." There was apparently an argument from the other end, for he snapped, "I don't care, and you shouldn't either. I know what I promised. But this is too important."

He returned the mobile to his pocket. "Have a little faith in me. I promise you won't be disappointed."

Back in the sitting room, Hugo collapsed into a thick club chair and Julie sat on the staircase steps, unwilling to share a room with him until she found out what was going on. She was unconsciously picking at a tuft of wool carpet when the doorbell rang fifteen minutes later.

"Would you get that?" Hugo asked.

With a heavy heart, Julie went to the door, squared her shoulders and opened it. To her surprise, it was Matthew on the door stoop.

"Matthew! What are you doing here?"

"Matthew is who we're expecting," Hugo said from behind her.

Julie glanced between the two men. "I don't get it."

"Hugo's prepping us for our GCSE's."

She looked at Hugo, and he nodded. "Why are you trying to take those?"

"I've got to pass them. I've got plans." Matthew followed them into the sitting room and sat in an offered chair. "I want to go on to school, this school," he said, handing Julie the brochure. "Hugo's helping me get in. Nerida, Pax, Joanna, Tanda, and Lalani all want to do something, too. So Hugo's tutoring us."

Julie read the brochure carefully, relief flooding through her. "How long has this been going on?"

"It's been seven weeks now. Almost every evening, for hours and hours. He's worse than you," Matthew lamented. "Or close to."

"Matthew, your grandmother is beside herself. You're all exhausted, and we're very concerned."

"I know, Julie," he said. "It's been grueling, but it's worth it. Only don't blame Hugo—we swore him to secrecy. We don't want everyone else knowing, on account of we might not pass."

"You'll pass," Hugo shot back.

"Swear you won't tell anyone," Matthew begged. "Gran... if she knew, she'd try and talk me out of it. She means well, but she don't know the plans I've got. I need five GCSE's and this is the only way to do it."

"How's it going?"

"A mixed bag," Hugo replied. "Matthew's math is good, all of their science is actually quite good. But the composition is rough, and we've still got a long way to go on the poetry and grammar. The test is at the end of May, and it's going to be close."

"I wish you had told me."

"He couldn't," Matthew said vehemently. "We made him promise and give his word as a gentleman. And he's kept it. He said a real gentleman always keeps his word and he has, even though you probably thought we was girls he had stashed on the side."

That truth was closer than Matthew knew, and Julie shifted in her chair.

"Believe me, Julie, if Hugo's had any time for anything in the last seven weeks besides footballing and teaching us, he'd have to be a superman," Matthew added for good measure.

She looked between the two men. "Don needs to know. I have to tell him what's going on and that you're all okay. He won't say anything—he'll want you to succeed. But you've got to start getting some rest."

"We will, Julie, I swear. But that's all you can tell," Matthew said. "It has to be a secret. If I fail, which I jolly well might 'cause I'm drowning in this rubbish, no one can know. The others don't want anyone to know, neither."

"Either," Hugo corrected. "And tonight is a good night to get some rest. Tell the others. We'll be back at it tomorrow."

# Chapter Sixty-Three

THE STAFF AT Haddonfield sat slack-jawed the next day as Julie filled them in.

"Hugo's tutoring all six for their GCSE's?" Don finally asked.

"Who put that daft notion into their heads?" Clive asked.

"It was Matthew's idea," Julie said. "He wants to apply to the Hampstead School of Management Science, and they want five GCSE's. And a good five. The rest decided they want to take the tests as well."

"So that's what they've been doing, studying for the tests with Hugo? How long has this been going on?" Bonnie asked.

"Since the beginning of February. No wonder they've been so exhausted," Julie said.

"I'll help," Don announced, and Bonnie and Clive immediately nodded in agreement.

"I told Matthew that we'd all want to help, but he's adamant that it be kept quiet. They're scared of it getting out if they fail."

Don sprang to his feet. "We can respect that. I'll put together a study schedule right now and we'll work it into the schedule so it's not noticeable. Good God, we've only got eight weeks. Did Hugo say how they were doing?"

"Not too badly. But it's overwhelming."

"Right then. Let's get cracking."

———— ◄◯► ————

Don, Gretchen, Clive, and Bonnie all took over test sections to tutor, but even with everyone pitching in, Julie knew success was not assured. She and Hugo spent every night with the students, and afterwards would go back to her house in Finchley and lie on her sofa, sometimes opening a bottle of wine while Julie massaged Hugo's aching muscles.

The ease with which Hugo blended into her life made Julie happy, and the past faded into a distant memory. In no time they had settled into a regular routine, usually spending the night at her house. Tom had been right, the rumor of a royal engagement had made the paparazzi evaporate and life felt normal once again.

The first thing Julie learned was that her body was no longer her own. Hugo claimed it, fiercely and possessively. He casually took what felt like amazing liberties, undressing her as he pleased, exploring every inch of her body, worshiping her. His desire seemed to know no bounds, or decency for that matter, especially where lace was involved.

At night, they would lie in bed and explore each other. He was a tender and patient lover, teaching her what pleased him, but more remarkably, what pleased her. He taught her how things were better when they lasted longer, but then he would take her swiftly when she innocently did something to arouse him.

Afterwards they would lie in each other's arms, sated from making love, and Hugo would open up about his worries about Ian and Wrothesley. The weight of his responsibilities seemed staggering, much more than one person could handle.

Hugo sat out his one-game suspension with good grace. The following week, they snuck into the Plaid Elephant to watch the FA Cup match. She put her foot down, however, when he suggested she come to their midweek match against West Ham.

"Tom says no. We're not supposed to be seen together."

"Juliet, he meant nothing public," Hugo reasoned.

"What's more public than a football match? And besides, Tom called and said the press is getting wise there's not going to be a royal engagement. We have to be careful."

<hr>

Hugo reluctantly conceded, and the next day a small television was installed at her house so she could watch from there. But he still chafed—he wanted Juliet at his matches.

On Thursday, Matthew stayed back at the dormitory, sick. The other students didn't know anything except that he didn't look well and was refusing to leave the television room.

"I'm concerned about the visit to Hampstead College he's got lined up for Saturday. He was asking me a lot of questions about it yesterday and seemed nervous," Julie told Hugo.

"How about I go down to the house and have a chat with him?" Hugo suggested.

Julie nodded. "I think that would be a good idea. I can take the poetry you're doing tonight, while Pax and Tanda review maths."

"You're amazing, do you know that?" Hugo smiled down at her.

He walked the few blocks to the dormitory and found Matthew sitting alone, staring at a muted television.

"Hello, Matthew," Hugo said, shrugging off his overcoat and pulling up a chair next to him. "We missed you at school today. What's up?"

Matthew continued to stare at the television, motionless as a statue.

Hugo leaned back in the chair and crossed his legs. "I was in my last year at Eton," he began casually, "and I got a letter from a scout inviting me to a tryout for a football club. I had no idea which club it was—they usually don't tell you until you show up—but I was on cloud nine. The tryout was set for four days away, and I couldn't wait to get to the pitch and show my stuff.

"To prepare, I scrimmaged with some friends and made a few stupid mistakes. The next day I scrimmaged again and played worse than a granny. I began throwing up, and by the morning of the tryout, I literally couldn't get out of bed."

"What'd ya do?" Matthew asked, his voice sharp.

"I didn't do anything, I just lay there. I was supposed to go myself—it was an easy train ride. But the thought of disgracing myself in front of whichever team wanted to see me and losing my only chance of ever playing professional football paralyzed me. I wasn't exactly in great demand."

"You obviously made it."

"No, I didn't. I missed the tryout." Hugo laughed at Matthew's look of surprise. "It was set for eleven in the morning, and at noon my housemaster found me still lying in bed staring at the ceiling."

"What happened then?"

"He literally dragged me out of bed, made me get dressed, borrowed one of the don's cars, and drove me to where the club was practicing. Then he threw a cup of cold water in my face and pushed me onto the pitch. That water got my mind off my terror, and I snagged the ball off an old veteran and wouldn't give it back. Five minutes later I was laughing, and forty minutes after that I had a spot on the team."

"That's pretty good," Matthew said, relaxing a bit. "Why're you telling me this?"

"Because I think you're worried about going up to Hampstead College on Saturday to see their restaurant management school."

Matthew grew rigid again. "I can't do it. I don't know why I ever thought I could. We take those practice tests and I do lousy, and that means I'll flunk the real one. At the interview they'll see that, they'll know I'm not good enough."

"It's not really an interview, it's more of a go-see," Hugo reasoned. "You know, take the tour, talk with some of the professors, see what it's all about. We've got you kitted out nicely so you'll make a good impression."

Matthew hung his head. "They'll laugh."

"I don't see why they should," Hugo countered, truly perplexed. "It's just as much their job to make a good impression on you."

"The place is huge, you should see the map of the campus they sent. I'll never find where I'm going."

"Then I'll go with you."

"No. I'm not walking in there with you, everyone will be wanting your autograph and treating me special because I'm with you."

"Then Juliet will go with you."

Matthew snorted. "That'd be like showing up with me mum."

The answer was obvious, and Hugo was irritated he hadn't thought of it sooner. "Then you're going with Ian. He knows a lot about getting into schools because he keeps getting kicked out of them—God knows it's the only practical skill he has. You'll be in good hands."

Hugo messaged Ian, and it was agreed they'd meet up the next morning at King's Cross Station.

Matthew still looked nervous, but Hugo had a sudden brainstorm. "And your reward for going tomorrow will be a ticket to our match against Fulham on Sunday."

Matthew's eyes lit up. "I've never been to a Premier League match before. It's at Townsend Lane Stadium, isn't it? Gosh, Hugo, you've been great about all of this. I don't know how I'll pay you back."

"I said there's no need to pay anything back. But if you want to do me a favor in return, you could convince Juliet to go with you. I would consider that a very great favor indeed."

# Chapter Sixty-Four

SATURDAY AFTERNOON, HUGO leaned nonchalantly against a pillar in the locker room of Townsend Lane Stadium while his teammates wandered about waiting for the call to the pitch. The congestion and bustle in the half hour leading up to the match was usually a time Hugo hated, but today he felt completely relaxed, almost like he could play Fulham by himself and win.

Because Juliet was in the stands. There'd never been anyone in the stands for him before. Trika had stuck to the skybox and admitted she barely watched the game, and Mummy and Ian watched from home. Matthew had done a good job convincing Juliet to go with him. Hugo had hoped they'd watch the match from the skybox, but she'd flatly refused, noting that Matthew would be overwhelmed.

Ian had called yesterday afternoon and reported that while he'd had to pry Matthew off the train, they were greeted warmly at the college and Matthew finally relaxed. They had taken the tour and talked with the dean of the program, who coincidentally had grown up down the road from Matthew's grandmother's house.

"He had such a good time I couldn't get him to leave," Ian said. "So we stayed and had an early supper on campus, walked around some more, and then took the train back. I'd say he's hooked."

Feeling mellow, Hugo thought back on the night before. Juliet had been adorably reticent and shy at first, but he had coaxed and wooed her till she panted shamelessly. He teased her and tormented her, taking them both to heights he'd never dreamed possible. Finally, he had entered her, but damn him, he'd exploded almost immediately. Again.

This wasn't quite a problem—yet. But it was something he was going to have to figure out. He knew he could last longer, but he was so overstimulated that the feel of her welcoming warmth and enthusiasm drove him instantly over the edge. The second time last night had lasted, by his estimation, ten seconds longer.

But he had given her pleasure. And that was all that mattered.

---

"I've never been to a proper football match. These seats are great." Matthew was beaming as he and Julie settled in their seats at midfield behind the Kingsbury Town benches. "Do you think we'll get on telly? Gran's watching just to see."

The fans roared as Kingsbury Town took the field. Hugo was near the back of the pack, and when he looked towards them in the stands and smiled, heads snapped around in surprise. Julie felt herself glowing with pride.

The match started with a great deal of ball passing. "Kingsbury Town's just testing Fulham," Matthew explained, "because they're better at pacing themselves. They'll let

Fulham drive down a bit and see where their weaknesses are. Then they'll go to town."

While Matthew explained strategies, Julie watched Hugo, his long muscles flexible and supremely well-conditioned. Twenty minutes into the match, Hugo crashed into another player and both were knocked to the ground. The referee blew his whistle and talked with them.

"That Fulham player, he tried to do a nasty tackle on Hugo. The ref, he told him to watch it."

"He should have gotten a yellow card for that!" Julie said, fuming. "Hugo landed on his bad shoulder, it will take me hours to massage that out."

As the match progressed, Matthew pointed out that Fulham had a lot more in their game than Kingsbury Town had guessed. At the end of regular time, the score was tied 0–0 and both teams looked exhausted. Two minutes of injury time was added to the clock, and play began again.

Matthew pointed to a tough-looking man standing in the walkway in front of them. "That guy's trouble. He's got a huge camera under his jacket."

Julie didn't take her eyes off the field. "Maybe he's here to take pictures."

Matthew shook his head. "Him and that other bloke over there, they've been outside of Haddonfield."

Sharp nerves pricked the back of Julie's neck. "Let's leave, Matthew."

The crowd roared as Kingsbury Town drove the ball towards the Fulham net and scored with only five seconds left on the clock. Matthew stood and began working his way down the row of cheering fans, away from the two thugs with the cameras. Julie began to follow.

"Teach them lads to leave it to the last minute," a man next to her groused.

Julie paused. "What do you mean? They won."

"Aye, and if Dylan Rhea hadn't been out of position most of the time, they would have had two more goals."

"Come on, Julie," Matthew called from halfway down the row.

"They worked very hard out there!" Julie retorted. "And it's their thirtieth game of the season! I'd like to see you—"

"Julie Randall, will you come on!" Matthew said.

Hearing her name, the paparazzo whipped around, focused his camera on her and began to snap away.

Matthew hurried to her side to block his view, but the other paparazzo grabbed her shoulder from the other direction and spun her around.

"Get your bloody hands off her!" Matthew bellowed, trying to knock the camera out of his hands. The thug shoved him backwards, knocking Julie to the ground in the process. Matthew landed in a heap on a wiry man behind him.

Matthew leapt to his feet and struggled to get to Julie, but the man he had fallen on swung a beefy fist aimed at his head. Matthew ducked, and the blow hit another man directly behind them, and suddenly the area was filled with screams and the sound of fistfights. Both photographers started pushing their way through the throng of spectators, who pushed right back. Many people trying to escape either fell or tripped, and soon the entire section was brawling.

Julie lay on the cold cement, stunned, listening to the screams all around her. In seconds, Hugo was at her side and pulled her to her feet as guards and stadium security flooded the area, adding to the pandemonium.

"Down there!" Hugo yelled to Matthew, and together they all jumped the fence onto the field.

Hugo pointed to a tunnel and once they'd made it safely inside, he grabbed Julie and held her. "What the hell happened up there?" Hugo demanded.

"Those two blokes, they're paparazzi—I recognized them from Haddonfield," Matthew gasped, a trickle of blood coming from his mouth. "One started snapping pictures of Julie, and when I tried to block him, he knocked me aside. Then the guy I fell on hit me, and after that everything just sorta boiled over."

"Jesus," Hugo muttered over the din of sirens. "We need to get someplace safer. Come on."

———◇———

Julie and Matthew sat on chairs in the team's locker room while the uproar swirled around them. Tom arrived with a man introduced as Alex, who turned out to be Tom's brother and Hugo's lawyer. The three men conferred, and Alex accompanied Julie when the police took her statement.

Hugo wanted to go as well, but she squeezed his hand. "Let Alex handle it, he seems to know what to do. I'll be fine. See to Matthew and call Don."

The police had a video surveillance tape playing in the small office they'd commandeered. Julie could see herself and Matthew in the stands, and at Alex's urging, she began to narrate the action.

"There, that's where Matthew saw the first one," Julie said. "He's pointing him out to me. And there, that's where Kingsbury Town scored the goal, and where that nasty man next to me started saying mean things about the team. I was giving him a piece of my mind when Matthew called for me, using my full name. You can see the paparazzo turn around and start taking my picture. And then Matthew is trying to block him from me..." Julie's voice trailed off as she watched, horrified at the violence.

After the police finished asking questions, she was excused and found Hugo anxiously waiting outside.

"They want to talk to Matthew next," Alex said. "I'll go in with him. He's an adult, yes?"

Julie nodded. "He is, but you have to know he has a criminal record. Can it wait until Don gets here?"

"I called, he should be here momentarily," Tom said.

Don arrived as Alex emerged with an exhausted-looking Matthew. "It's okay. They've seen the tapes and they're not pressing charges. It's clear the photographer was taking your picture and pushed Matthew."

"So Matthew is cleared? He's free to go?" Don asked.

Alex mopped his brow. "Yes. There's something else going on they're not talking about, like how the paparazzi got in there in the first place. Damn strange, but it seems one of the WAGs called them to be photographed. Some sort of publicity stunt, only they stumbled onto you."

"But that's ridiculous, the WAGs never leave the skyboxes," Hugo said. "All of them know what a security risk it would be."

"I agree, it's damn strange, but eleven spectators have been sent to the hospital. None of the injuries are life-threatening, but it's a mess. It's got something to do with Mick Carr."

"That would explain a lot," Hugo said.

"They're trying to untangle it now, and I don't think Sir Frank is going to get much sleep until they do. But everyone is free to leave."

Hugo drove Julie back to his house, insisting it was much safer than her own. Once there, he poured a hot bath and made her drink a stiff swig of aged brandy, which gave her the hiccups. He gently undressed her and led her to the tub, then quickly doffed his kit and followed her in. He pulled her between his legs and held her, gently sponging hot water over her.

Julie shivered. "It was terrifying, I've never been so scared."

"When I heard you scream," Hugo said, running his hands up and down her arms, calming her trembling, "the thought of you in trouble, or hurt—I went mad."

"What did Alex mean when he said the police thought it was a publicity stunt?"

"The WAGs are in some turf war over Mick Carr, but no one ever dreamed they'd dare bring it into the stadium."

Julie closed her eyes and relaxed against Hugo's slippery chest. "And I thought Rochelle was scary."

# Chapter Sixty-Five

KINGSBURY TOWN BEAT Newcastle handily the next weekend, with Hugo picking off a rebound that he punched through for his twelfth goal of the season. He was pleased with his performance and to everyone's amazement, even stood in the interview corner for a thirty-second interview. Even the presenter was initially at a loss for a question. But Hugo went through with the interview because he knew Juliet would be watching at Clive and Bonnie's.

Hugo left the interview area puffed up with pride and eager to go home and make love to her all night. Instead, he showered and changed into a bespoke suit and rode the elevator with the rest of the team to the reception in Sir Frank's skybox, checking his watch with irritation. Thirty minutes was the absolute minimum he could stay.

Once in the skybox, Hugo scanned the room and saw Mick's new girlfriend, Marie-Claire, or MC as everyone seemed to call her. She seemed like a nice girl, an American like Juliet, but with none of her spark and wit. She had a dreamy look about her, almost like she was seeing the world through a different set of glasses. Definitely a free spirit and obviously unaware of her boyfriend's checkered past. Tom said she was a bit dim—the FA had completely exonerated her for causing the riot, but she had gone to their offices and insisted they arrest her anyway.

Mick, Hugo noted, was looking uncharacteristically nervous around her. Perfect.

He waited until Mick was called away to do some photos with sponsors and introduced himself to MC in French, just for the effect. She responded flawlessly with a slight Languedoc accent, much to his surprise, and they chatted for several minutes until Mick approached, furious. Hugo left, satisfied that many people in the room had noted him hitting on Mick Carr's new girlfriend.

———◇———

Friday afternoon, Julie collapsed into a train seat heading north to Birmingham. She planned to surprise Hugo, who'd wanted her to come up for the night before their match against nearby Wolverhampton the next day. The visit was to be a surprise—the students had just finished sitting the two-day GCSE exams, and everyone was bleary-eyed and ready to celebrate. Don and Gretchen had arranged a party at a restaurant in Camden Town, and Julie had told Hugo she should go.

Don, however, had shooed her away. "Go. Go up to Birmingham and stay with Hugo, you both deserve a little trip, even if it's just for the night."

Hugo had left a message on her mobile saying he was in room 471, and that a key would be waiting at the desk in case she could make it. He'd be at the team dinner at a nearby restaurant until about seven.

When the train pulled into the station in Birmingham, Julie awoke, refreshed from her nap. Night had fallen, and she walked the brightly lit streets to the hotel, where a desk clerk apologized that no key had been left.

At her request, he was checking again when another clerk approached. "Sorry, miss, there's been a mix-up on the rooms, you're wanting number 464 now, almost right across the hall. Here's the key."

Julie rode the elevator to the fourth floor, and once in the room, she kicked off her shoes and began unbuttoning her blouse. Suddenly, the door swung open. A large man stood in the doorway, obviously as surprised to see her as she was to see him.

Julie clutched her blouse to her chest. "Who are you?"

"I'm Darius Rutledge. Who are you?"

"I'm Julie Randall, Hugo's girlfriend."

"Excuse me for asking, but what the hell are you doing in me and Mick Carr's room?"

"I... I came up to surprise Hugo. This is his room. Where is he?"

Upon hearing her words, Darius appeared to stop breathing. "Oh, no. No, no, no," he intoned. "Oh, bloody hell. I am going to kill Mick. Come on, get dressed, we've got to get you out of here."

Julie pulled back into her blouse while Darius grabbed her bag.

"Did anyone see you come in?" he asked.

"Yes, lots of people," Julie said, tugging her heels back on. "What's going on? Why did they give me your room key?"

"I don't even want to guess. No! Do not go out there!" Darius commanded when she moved towards the door. He fumbled with his mobile and pressed some numbers, cursing when there was no answer. "We've got to get you out of here before Hugo finds out what's happened or there'll be hell to pay."

"The man at the desk said the rooms had been changed."

"I'm sure he did," Darius grunted and spoke into his mobile. "Phillip. I need you to detain Hugo. Do not let him leave dinner... How the hell should I know? You're the college boy, you think of something. I need ten minutes."

Darius shoved the mobile in his pocket and went to the door, listening while a group of people came down the hall. After they passed he waved her over. "Look, love, I'm going to go out into the hall and see if the coast is clear. When I knock twice on the door, you run down the hall and take the stairway. I think it empties into the kitchens—find the alley and run like hell. Give me your bag, I'll meet you at the train station."

"Why is this happening?"

"I'll explain at the station."

Julie shrugged back into her coat and picked up her bag, then waited by the door, her heart pounding. Several players went past, and she heard Darius joke with them. After what seemed like hours, there was a quick double tap on the door.

"Go!" Darius whispered.

Julie fled the room and ran down the stairs past the lobby level to the ground floor. She found a door that opened to the outside and plunged through it into a dark alley, running like the bats of hell were on her heels.

At the station, she spotted Darius at the ticket counter. He completed his purchase and walked casually to where she was hiding behind a kiosk, his eyes alert. "Here's your ticket to London."

"What happened back there?" Julie demanded, her heart still pounding after her mad dash.

"Mick set you up, is what happened," Darius said, scowling. "He wanted you to be found in his room, so I'm guessing he paid off a desk clerk to tell you the rooms had been rearranged and to give you the wrong key."

Julie felt a chill pass through her. "He wanted Hugo to find me in his room, the way Trika was."

Darius nodded. "Thank God I left early. Mick didn't see me leave or I'm guessing he would have stalled me. As it is, I think Phillip delayed Hugo long enough that you made a clean getaway. Here's your train now."

He walked her to the platform. "Julie, I'm really sorry about this," he said. "I have no idea why Mick did this, but please don't say anything. He and Hugo are already at each other's throats. I'll deal with Mick. Just go home."

# Chapter Sixty-Six

HUGO STOOD WITH Julie in the little church in Finchley the next morning, suppressing a grin as he thought back to the wanton vixen he had turned her into the night before. After he'd arrived home from the Wolverhampton match, he'd allowed her almost no sleep as he mercilessly teased and ravished her.

There was no other woman like her.

A young couple sat in the pew in front of them, not much older than Juliet and himself. The father held a baby girl dressed in a charming green pinafore, blissfully asleep on his shoulder. The pretty young mother sat with their little boy on her lap, patiently showing him the pages of the Bible, her expression loving as they turned the pages.

A jolt hit Hugo, as if an earthquake had hit the small church, but one that only he could detect. It filled him with a blazing certainty, more intense than anything he'd ever felt. This was what he wanted—this quiet love, this devotion to a life and family together. He wanted more than just the physical pleasure he shared with Juliet. He wanted a future.

After church they drove out to Wrothesley.

"Aren't you going to ask me how Wolverhampton went yesterday?" Hugo asked as he drove.

"Oh! Yes! Good game?" Julie asked brightly.

"We won, but it was a battle from start to finish. And it turns out it was a good thing you couldn't come up, I didn't get to bed until almost one a.m. the night before."

Julie nodded, looking straight ahead. "Oh, dear. What happened?"

"After the team dinner, Phillip Trent told me a journalist from *Country Life* magazine wanted a word. Mummy would have my hide if I declined that, so he shoved me in a cab and we went on a wild goose chase looking for some pub called the Horned Grebe. Then he decided it wasn't important and told the cabbie to take us back to the hotel."

"That's... extraordinary."

"And then Darius called a completely ridiculous team meeting that lasted an hour and accomplished nothing. Pozny came up to me afterwards and said he saw a girl that looked exactly like you in the hotel lobby right after dinner, but then Darius called him over and he wouldn't say anything after that —he just kept muttering in Polish. Isn't that the oddest thing?"

Julie nodded, her hands clenched in her lap.

———————•◦•———————

Cynthia was on holiday, so when they arrived at Wrothesley they checked on her house. Miles stopped by with his records for Juliet to review and then insisted they drive out to look at some runoff issues in a far field. Hugo was annoyed but Juliet seemed to think it was important, and several of the local farmers joined them on a rise where she spent another two hours discussing the probability of a Septoria tritici blotch infection migrating south.

By four o'clock, Hugo's patience had worn thin. "I hope you'll be having much more of Miss Randall's time in the very near future," he told them, "but for now I would like some of hers for myself."

The men grinned and quickly dispersed. Hugo suggested they walk over to Wrothesley in the fading afternoon light, and once inside, he showed her the narrow staircase leading to the flat roofs.

"How did your mother keep you away from here?" Julie asked when they emerged onto the broad expanse. "It's like the world's most dangerous playground."

"That was Dad's job. For years he told me they kept a lion up here, and he'd occasionally make sure I saw him taking birdseed and suet up, saying he was feeding the lion."

"You thought lions ate birdseed and suet?"

"He told me that Bedfordshire lions did and he could be very convincing. And when I started to doubt it, he'd let one of the dogs run around up here for a few hours."

"How old were you when you finally caught on?"

"Eight. Dad was away on a business trip, and I got worried that no one was feeding the lion, so I worked up the nerve and went up with the birdseed and suet." Hugo pointed to a large birdhouse mounted on an exhaust vent. A hand-painted sign over it read "Lion House."

"That's ingenious," Juliet said, laughing.

They watched the sun setting in the west, casting a dramatic golden glow over the rolling fields. "Do you like it here, Juliet?" Hugo asked, wrapping an arm around her shoulders.

"I love it," she replied.

"There's nothing more you want? Something more?"

"We're together. I love you and you love me. What could be better than that?" she asked.

Hugo dropped his arm and walked to the edge of the roof, running a hand through his hair in distraction. "It might be working for you but it's not for me."

"What's not working?" she asked from behind him, and he could hear confusion in her voice. As well she should.

"You and me. The way we are. All of it, to be truthful. It's not your fault," he said, continuing to walk along the roof wall. "I know it's mine. But still, the way things are at present is just not working, but I'm damned if I know what to do about it."

"I would think that would be obvious," Julie said.

"You do? What?" Hugo spun around eagerly and then froze in terror.

Tears were streaming down her face, soundless sobs wrenching her. "We go our separate ways."

"Have you gone mad?" In an instant he was at her side, sweeping her into his arms. "Juliet! What's the matter?"

"You're breaking up with me," she sobbed.

"Why in God's name would I do that? I'm out of my mind in love with you," Hugo said, laughing. "You've completely turned my world upside down. I suffered when I thought you loved another. I tried to forget you, and it was like trying to rip out my own heart."

He held her as she cried, running his mind back over the discussion. "Juliet, what's not working for me is having to hide my love for you," he crooned, kissing away the tears. "I hate not being able to go out in public with you."

"But you told Tom it wouldn't be a problem."

"I didn't think it would be. I thought I could wait, but I can't. What I want is too important."

She sniffled. "What do you want?"

"I want you forever. I want us here, together at Wrothesley. I want us to make a family, a home. There's so much I want, and I can only have it with you. And I bloody well don't want to wait. I've already waited long enough."

Pulling the signet ring off his finger, Hugo held her left hand and dropped to one knee before her. "Juliet Randall, since the day I met you, my life has been nothing but wonderful. I want us to spend the rest of our lives together. Would you marry me?"

Julie sat on the vent box, her eyes wide.

"You're supposed to say 'yes,'" Hugo prompted.

She furiously wiped her nose and the tears that were brimming in her eyes. "Yes," she said, and he slid the ring onto her finger.

Where it immediately fell off. "Wait," she said, pulling a piece of twine from her pocket and wrapping it efficiently around the ring before sliding it back on. "Much better."

"I'll get you a proper engagement ring, but first I want to talk with your father. And I want to meet your mother, and your sister and brother-in-law."

"They're planning on visiting in August."

"No. Next week."

"Hugo, you're at the end of your season, and your most important games are coming up. Let's make plans for after that." She hiccupped through her tears, holding his face in her hands. "I love you, and I can wait for you. For us, and for our family, as long as I know that you love me."

# Chapter Sixty-Seven

AT MIDNIGHT ON Wednesday, Hugo came home to Finchley from his midweek game at Reading to find Julie sitting at the kitchen table, her wallet and checkbook open in front of a stack of envelopes. He kissed her and slumped into a chair.

"You're still awake?" he asked.

"I wanted to wait up—you sounded pretty cross on the phone."

"In the press conference, everyone thought we lost because Mick Carr's girlfriend wasn't there. I've never heard such a load of rubbish."

"Is it true?"

"You mean have we won every match she's been at? Yes, but we've been playing bloody well. However Reading is facing relegation and cleaned our clock. What are you doing?"

"Paying bills. Are you hungry? I made some soup for dinner. There's quite a bit left over."

Julie turned to the stove and ladled soup into a bowl, adding a slice of buttered bread. When she turned back around she saw Hugo going through her checkbook. "What are you doing?"

"Your landlady is charging you more rent because I'm staying here?"

"Twenty pounds a week. She said I'm using more utilities. But it's okay."

"It most certainly is not," he fumed. "I'm already paying for use of that ancient garage of hers."

"You're awfully grouchy tonight," Julie said, moving the stack of bills aside and setting the dinner before him. "Would you like to know what else I was doing tonight?"

"Besides paying extortion money to your landlady?"

She took the seat next to him while he ate. "Yes, besides that. I was cleaning out some drawers in my dresser to make more space for you, and I found a nightie I had completely forgotten about."

"Oh, yes?" Hugo paused between spoonfuls.

"Mmmm. It has a lace top," she continued, "and a satin ribbon that gathers under my breasts, right here..."

"What color?" he growled.

"White, with little blue flowers embroidered in the skirt."

Hugo twisted in his seat and pulled Julie onto his lap, but in the process knocked her wallet to the floor. Pound notes and receipts tumbled out.

He bent to retrieve them and paused when he saw two train tickets amongst the scattered papers. Julie became very still.

"You were there. Last Friday night, in Birmingham. Pozny was right," Hugo said, looking at the stubs.

Julie swallowed. "Yes."

Hugo held her arm, his eyes a steely grey. "Start talking, and don't stop talking until you've told me everything."

"You're going to get upset."

"I'm already upset. But I need to hear what happened. You got there Friday night, didn't you?"

Julie nodded. "I went to the hotel desk and asked for the key. They said there'd been a mix-up and gave me a key to a different room. I took it and went up."

"And then what happened?"

Julie shifted in her chair. "Darius came in."

"You were in Mick Carr's room?"

"Evidently. Darius got very upset and said I had to leave. He snuck me out, and I ran back to the station, and he met me there and got me a ticket back to London. I got the train back."

"You said you couldn't come up."

"No, I didn't, I said I had to cancel the trip because a gutter burst. And it did. But it burst on Saturday."

A string of violent oaths erupted from his mouth.

"Don't be angry. I wanted to surprise you. Why would Mick do that?"

"To get back at me."

"For what?" Julie asked, her eyes narrowing. "You've been taunting him, haven't you?"

"I'm not doing anything to him that he hasn't done to me. And Tom told me I have to get the press's scent off you."

Julie's eyes widened. "You're pretending to be interested in his girlfriend, aren't you?"

"Mick doesn't care about her. He'll be on to the next one by next month. She's a student for God's sake. What would she want with an imbecile like him?"

"So you're using her."

"Of course I am," Hugo snapped. He released her, got up from the table, and began pacing the small room.

"You're doing it to get revenge on Mick. For sleeping with Trika."

"No, I'm not," Hugo denied hotly. "We were over long before she hooked up with him, it was just the nail in the coffin. Mick will do anything to top me and this proves it. He wants to show everyone he can get you."

Julie recoiled. "He can't have me."

"Then show everyone he's wrong. There's a gala Sir Frank sponsors for the hospital on Sunday. Come with me."

"I'm staying the weekend with Bonnie. Clive is going up to Birmingham to see his mother."

Hugo dismissed her excuse with a contemptuous glare.

"You said you would give it three months," Julie reminded him. "They have all the pictures. I don't want to be 'Rebound Randall.'"

"I hate this."

Julie leaned forward and began to collect the papers on the table.

Hugo paced the kitchen in irritation. "You know, when you sat like that at the library table the first night you came to the house, it nearly drove me crazy. I had to go down to the kitchen and douse myself with cold water."

"You mean like this?" She adopted an innocent air and leaned forward, casually arching her back and stretching her shoulders up, which made her shirt rise.

Hugo's mouth went dry. "You were doing that on purpose?"

Julie's lips curved in a smile.

"Do you have any idea how impossible you made it for me to even move?" Hugo demanded.

"Poor Hugo," Julie purred sympathetically and went to him, brushing her breasts lightly across his chest. "Did you suffer?"

"Yes!" He choked, indignant.

She clucked her tongue. "What would you have liked to have done?"

Hugo grinned and with a quick movement, clenched her bottom in his hands and lifted her onto the counter, pulling her jeans off and pushing himself between her legs. He peppered her face with kisses, and she wrapped her legs around his hips, pulling him against herself. With one hand he unbound himself, then pushed his hips forward and filled her to his hilt in one flaming thrust. Molten pleasure shot through her, the raw feeling of desire and possession overwhelming her senses. Lust fought with sensual pleasure, urgent and unbound.

"That, my lady," he breathed huskily after claiming her with a blistering passion that left them both breathless, "is what I wanted to do to you every time I saw the flash of your knickers."

<hr />

The clock on the mantelpiece at his house chimed six o'clock, signaling it was time to get changed for the gala Sir Frank and Lady Poleski hosted each year for the hospital. Player attendance was mandatory, so Hugo grabbed a bottle of cognac and went upstairs to change into his tuxedo. He threw back one glass of the excellent brandy while he tied his bow tie and downed yet another while he waited for the cab.

If Juliet had been there, she would have been putting the finishing touches on her outfit for the evening. He would be placing the diamond and sapphire necklace around her neck and then sinking his lips into the warm skin of her shoulder. By all rights, she should be on his arm tonight—his woman, his jewel.

Flopping into a club chair in his sitting room, Hugo looked around the grand rooms and yearned for Juliet's snug little terraced house in Finchley. It shredded his heart the way she was so charmingly domestic and had turned it into a little home for the two of them. But her bed was too small and the adjoining walls so thin that she didn't feel free to moan and gasp.

That was a problem in need of a solution.

His mother had recently mentioned a cousin who was thinking about selling her house in Highgate, which was only a mile from Haddonfield. He'd been out to the house and found it delightful, built ten years ago with four bedrooms, a lovely kitchen, and a small garden. It was a house for a family.

---

The gala was crowded. Hugo arrived late and once inside, spied MC Wentworth, who was scantily clad in some sort of gold fabric that looked like several napkins sewn together. In full view of everyone, he kissed her hand and glared at Mick tauntingly.

MC stiffened, and Hugo almost felt sorry for her. Almost.

"Good evening, my love, may I say you look ravishing," he said loudly.

Darius Rutledge smoothly interceded and steered him away, hissing, "Hugo, I swear Sir Frank will have your arse if either of you cause a problem tonight. And then he'll turn you over to Lady Poleski."

Hugo shrugged and went to find a table at the back of the room.

The night dragged on and he picked at his meal. The people at his table were lovely, and Juliet would have enjoyed them immensely—two surgeons from the hospital with their husbands and three sets of parents. His mood lifted as they told stories of how their children had been helped by the hospital and how much the team's support meant to them.

The auction began during dessert, and soon the Master of Ceremonies held the crowd in the palm of his hand. Hugo glanced at his watch, desperate to leave but knowing he had to stay till the bitter end.

"Next on the block," the emcee trilled, "a watercolor painting of a Brecon Buff goose, water-color on parchment, 140 centimeters by 160 centimeters, signed by the artist, Miss MC Wentworth of the Lady Warwick College of Arts and Design."

A loud round of applause erupted, and Hugo stood to get a look at the painting. It was indeed a portrait of a Brecon Buff, almost identical, from what he could see, to Juliet's photograph of Angelica. His heart leapt recklessly, and he knew that he would spend every cent he had to his name to get that painting for her. Juliet had to have it.

The bidding began, and Hugo bided his time. The price crept slowly past one thousand pounds before Hugo raised his voice and announced a bid of five thousand pounds—it was for the children, after all.

Above the gasp of the crowd, Mick Carr immediately overbid him by a thousand pounds. That bastard, how did he know about Angelica? There was no time to wonder—it was obvious Mick was bidding to win it for Juliet.

Hugo's temper ignited. He knew his net worth was a hundredfold over Mick's. The other bidders dropped out, and now it was between him and his rival, the bidding fast and vicious. Mopping his brow, the emcee called for a momentary break, but the war raged on, Mick apparently desperate and Hugo deadly calm.

Finally Hugo called out the astronomical sum of twenty thousand pounds. An audible gasp went through the room, and Marie-Claire stood up and stopped the bidding. She awarded Hugo the painting and offered to paint whatever Mick wanted for the same donation, netting forty thousand pounds for the hospital in under ninety seconds.

Hugo was ebullient as he pushed his way towards the front to claim his painting, giving Mick a spiteful glare on his way past. Dashing off a check, he shook hands with the dignitaries, ignoring Sir Frank's quizzical look.

The crowd of photographers swarmed outside as he hailed a cab, and one snapped him holding the painting, a triumphant smile on his lips.

# Chapter Sixty-Eight

JULIE WAS BRUSHING her teeth early the next morning when her mobile phone rang.

"Are you at Bonnie and Clive's house? Good, stay put," Tom barked. "On no account are you to go to Haddonfield."

"What's the matter?"

"Your boyfriend's brain. Or lack of one. I'll call back when I know more. Why in God's name he spent twenty thousand pounds on a painting of a duck, I have no idea."

Bonnie was still asleep upstairs, so Julie pulled on a jacket and walked to the nearest newsstand.

TWENTY THOUSAND BOB FOR A BUFF? blazed the *Sun*. Hugo had made the cover, clutching a painting, alongside a photograph of MC Wentworth and Mick Carr leaving the auction, Mick's face thunderous. Other tabloids had the same picture with varying degrees of clever captions.

Julie paid for a copy and hurried back to the house. When she arrived, Bonnie was awake and having a cup of tea.

Julie put the tabloid on the table and Bonnie's eyes widened. "What a beautiful painting! It's just like Angelica, isn't it?"

Julie nodded and turned to the story inside. "It says Hugo and Mick got into a bidding war over it at the charity auction last night. Hugo left me a message on my mobile after I'd gone to sleep and said he'd gotten me something I'd like but that it was going to be a surprise."

"Where is he?"

"He left this morning for Lyon. He'll be there for two days at the sports physiotherapy specialist. Tom called, I'm supposed to stay put."

"Probably not a bad idea," Bonnie said.

———◆○◆———

"You left quite a mess here," Tom told Hugo after he arrived in Lyon.

"I had to have it, Tom. The bird in the picture, Juliet used to have a pet goose just like it. Mick was bidding against me to give it to her as well."

"Well, the tabloids are making it look like you're in love with this American."

"Good. Wasn't I supposed to be distracting attention from Juliet?"

"Yes, you were, and top marks to you, but it's backfired badly. The press has practically set up camp outside Haddonfield. The word I'm hearing is that MC's school has had enough of all the publicity she's drawing to herself."

"So? They chuck her. There's a lot better art schools in London than the Lady Warwick."

"Wasn't she your aunt?"

"Great-aunt, married into the family, nuttier than a fruitcake. Kept every Christmas tree they ever had in the attic. My great-uncle was terrified the place was going to go up in smoke like a chimney. Look, I will sort this all out when I get home. I'm at the clinic now and flying home tomorrow afternoon."

"No! Don't come home until the team does—you're keeping the press with you. In the meantime, keep your head down and don't talk with anyone. I've laid on extra security again at Haddonfield, but I'll warn you, they are not happy."

―――――◄○►―――――

It seemed an eternity before his plane finally touched down late Thursday afternoon at Luton. He had followed Tom's instructions and not left Lyon until he knew the team had departed from Milan.

Juliet's mobile was turned off and he drove directly to Tom's office.

"What the hell is going on? I haven't been able to get ahold of Juliet for two days!"

"That's because I have her phone. She gave it to me right before she left for Heathrow."

Hugo collapsed in a chair. "She's gone to her parents?"

"Yes. We decided it was the safest thing," Tom said. "They chucked MC Wentworth from school and then pressed deportation on her immediately. You're being blamed."

"Me? What did I do?"

"We've been trying to tell you," Tom said in exasperation. "This is all exploding out of proportion. There's something else going on as well, something much murkier involving Manchester United. One of their big supporters got his hand in this and helped trump up some flimsy excuse for the school to sack her. Sir Frank is trying to figure it out, but it's all happening so fast."

"Why would a Man United supporter want MC out?"

"She seems to be a good luck icon. When she's at your games, Kingsbury Town wins. Psychological play, and with

Mick Carr being arrested in Milan, it looks to be working."

"Those charges have been dropped."

"I know, but not soon enough. Like I said, everything's gone to hell in a handbasket and you've got yourself a ringside seat. Now, go home, pack a bag, and get over to our house. You're on lockdown."

"You're exaggerating. How much worse could it get?"

———— ◄O► ————

*Much* worse, Hugo reflected later, worse than he ever would have thought possible.

MC had indeed been deported, and Mick became completely unhinged. Not that Hugo was doing any better. Juliet had left her mobile with Tom, and Tom had confiscated his as well, so he was without any way of communicating with her. He appealed to Ian but was steadfastly refused.

"Tom says you're going to have to trust that she really does love you. It's going to be over in a week," Ian said, "so just sit down and shut up."

Both Hugo and Mick had been forbidden to practice with the team, but their presence was required at the Manchester United match. Old Trafford Stadium in Manchester was never the friendliest place under the best of circumstances, but the crowd was positively ugly and taunted Kingsbury Town unmercifully. Mick, who was seated at the opposite end of the team seats from Hugo, looked comatose. Kingsbury Town allowed three Manchester United goals and never got near their net. Hugo felt the waves of hatred against him before he and Mick were ushered out in the last five minutes of play and driven away in separate cars.

Back at Tom and Cassandra's house, Hugo paced their sitting room. Would Juliet come back? What if she was going to that job interview that was offering her the earth, sun, and moon?

"Get me on a flight to Philadelphia tomorrow morning," he pleaded with Tom.

"No can do, you have Sir Frank's award ceremony in Hendon tomorrow afternoon. And," Tom continued pragmatically, "no amount of cursing is going to change that. You have to go, and no more trouble."

# Chapter Sixty-Nine

OF COURSE THERE was more trouble.

The award ceremony recognizing local heroes in the Hendon area was a tradition with Kingsbury Town Football Club. Player attendance was mandatory, and Ian drove Hugo with strict instructions to not let him out of his sight. He took undisguised delight in the role as his brother's keeper for once, and Hugo chafed under the restrictions.

Hugo sat on the stage with his teammates while dignitaries spoke, baking in the heat of the spotlights, a headache pounding a merciless rhythm in his forehead. What was Juliet doing right now?

After an interminable amount of time, the team stood for pictures. The photographer took for-bloody-ever to arrange the honored firefighter and his family who stood with them, and then realized Pozny was taller than Hugo and asked them to switch places. Hugo took the spot in the second row and stared straight ahead while the photographer finally started clicking. Ian sat in the audience grinning, thoroughly enjoying his brother's discomfort.

Finally the damn pictures were over and Hugo spun on his heel, coming face-to-face with Mick Carr, who had been standing behind him the entire time. This was the first moment they'd been in close proximity since the auction, and in the blink of an eye, both knew that the other man was the cause of all personal misfortune.

Mick's fist connected a fraction of a second before Hugo's, and from there it was a blinding flurry. The screams of bystanders barely registered as they fought across the stage amid camera flashes and people scrambling to get out of their way. Hugo, lighter than Mick by three stone, was able to parry most of Mick's attack. Mick, for his part, seemed inured to the punches Hugo landed and only fought harder.

It was several minutes before anyone could get near them, but finally they were separated. Ian pushed him into the Jaguar and took off.

"I have to take you back to Tom's," Ian said, passing his brother his handkerchief to staunch the blood flowing from his nose.

"Take me home, Ian," Hugo said, breathing hard. "Please, they're following us. We can't take them back to Tom and Cassandra's."

"That was smart thinking," Tom agreed when they called him. "There were photographs?"

"Evidently." Hugo sighed. "And don't try to block them, I deserve whatever comes. Best to let it all run its course. I take responsibility for everything."

⸻ ◆ ⸻

Ian refused to leave, and Hugo was truly touched. He returned from an emergency meeting at Sir Frank's office the next day and collapsed in a chair. The thick velvet sitting room drapes were pulled across the windows, plunging the room into gloom.

"What happened with Sir Frank and Lord Lambton?" Ian asked, handing him an ice bag.

"Mick and I got a two-game suspension."

"But they need you both for Manchester United this weekend!"

"We know. Lambton wouldn't budge, and Sir Frank said he'd double it."

There was a loud commotion on the street, followed by a knock at the door. "It's the press. Let it go," Hugo said, but Ian had already gone to answer it.

As Hugo held the ice bag over his swollen eye, Mark Brooks walked into the vision of his good one.

"What the hell do you want?" Hugo asked in disbelief.

Mark stood before him, thin and pale, all crass self-confidence gone. "Believe it or not, I think I can help."

"The hell you can," Hugo bit out.

"I know who's behind this mess. Or at least part of it," Mark continued despite Hugo's disbelieving look. "He's a businessman up north. He owns a distilled spirits distributorship in Manchester, one of the biggest in the UK. He's completely ruthless, came up from the streets, and thinks Man U is God.

"I found out he bribed a student at the Lady Warwick to help get rid of that American girl Mick Carr was dating. He was bragging at a conference yesterday that getting rid of Julie was a side boon. With both of you out, Manchester United is going to skate in."

Hugo ran a hand through his hair in distraction. He and Mick had handed the win to them.

Mark took a business card from his suit coat pocket. "This is his card. The student's name is on the back—he's hiding out somewhere in the East End. You're going to have to find him and haul him in front of the FA."

Hugo turned the card over in his hand, anger pulsing through his body. "Why are you doing this?"

Mark's lips curled into a bitter smile. "I'm doing this for Julie. And, believe it or not, for you. I know you kept your word, I know you didn't tell her. I'm the scoundrel, and I need to make things right. Tell Julie I'm sorry. She deserves only the best, and that's you," Mark said, and turned to leave. "Tell her I'm sorry for all that I put her through."

———◦◦———

"This bloke?" Clive's eyebrows raised when Hugo showed him the business card. "He's trouble, mate."

"So I've been told. He's been paying a guy, an art student, to do his dirty work, and this student is now hiding out in the East End, lying low until after the match. I need to find him."

Clive nodded to the gardens where Nerida was directing work. "That lot knows every inch of that part of town."

"I can't drag them into this mess."

"No, but they'll put their ears to the ground. Bloke like him, an artsy-fartsy, he's going to stand out like a sore thumb, 'specially if he's flashing money."

Clive was correct. Matthew called him the next morning.

"We found your guy. Meet me and Pax at the Anchor Bar at five o'clock tonight. We'll be playing darts, and we'll point him out."

"I don't want you involved," Hugo said.

"We won't be. But bring some help, some big help."

"Will there be trouble?"

"No one's going to stop you. He's been making a proper pest of himself."

"I can't thank you enough."

"Huh," Matthew snorted. "You can get Julie back here right quick. Nerida's like to drive us all mad."

---

Hugo worked feverishly to arrange everything and then drove to Wimbledon to track down Mick. It took some convincing, but he agreed to go with him to Tottenham Green.

Hugo parked the Jaguar on the street in front of the bar, and the two men waited in tense silence. Finally, Hugo's mobile chirped. "Okay, let's go."

Matthew and Pax were in the bar playing darts, as prearranged. Matthew nodded towards a squat young man seated on a barstool with two women, one on either side.

When the young man looked up and saw Mick, he fled with impressive speed down a back hall. But he wasn't faster than Hugo.

Hugo bolted after him and followed him into the dirty alley, where Clive tackled him to the ground.

"Ruddy little swine," Mick said, hoisting the whimpering man to his feet, and together he and Clive threw the man into the school's van.

Pax and Matthew caught up with them, and Hugo tossed them the keys to the Jaguar. "Follow us!"

The first stop was the Lady Warwick School, where Hugo's mother was holding an emergency session of the Board of Regents. The story came out quickly, and the group unanimously voted to reinstate Marie-Claire. They then drove to the FA offices, where Sir Frank, Lord Lambton, and several detectives waited for them.

Mick seemed to be in a haze. "Does this mean I can go get Marie-Claire and bring her back?"

"Soon," Hugo said. "We still have to show up for the last match, even though we're suspended. But I think everything is going to be okay."

Mick considered him for a long time and then stuck his hand out. Hugo shook it firmly.

# Chapter Seventy

JULIE'S TRAIN PULLED into the Thirtieth Street Station in Philadelphia. It was a beautiful May afternoon, and she decided to walk the ten blocks to her parent's house in West Philadelphia, rolling her suitcase behind her along the uneven pavement. She steeled herself against the fact that there could be word waiting for her at home that she'd been fired from Haddonfield. The job offer from the Virginia agriculture company was tucked in her bag.

It had been two weeks since she'd heard from Hugo—Tom had told her he'd be taking away his mobile as well, which she knew he'd hate. She wore his signet ring looped through a thin gold chain around her neck and touched it often.

By the time she turned onto the leafy street lined with huge Victorian houses, she was hot and thirsty. Carrying her bag up the broad wooden steps, she went around the porch to the kitchen door.

A tall man stood at the sink intently peeling potatoes. He was barefoot, wearing loose jeans and an untucked t-shirt stretched across his muscular back. She glanced at him— obviously another of her parent's graduate students staying for dinner.

"Hello." Julie took a glass from the shelf and went to the refrigerator for a glass of water.

"Juliet."

It was Hugo. She spun around in amazement, and he took her in his arms and kissed her soundly.

"Oh, my God, what have they done to you?" she asked, blinking in astonishment. "Where are your shoes? You're wearing jeans! And a t-shirt..."

"Ken took me shopping," Hugo said, grinning. "And Rosie took me to Independence Hall. You didn't tell me she's got quite a sense of humor. We stopped and had cheesesteaks. Marvelous things. I ate two."

"You met Ken and Rosie? How long have you been here?"

"Since last Saturday," Hugo said, taking the glass and pouring her water. "We've gone to a baseball game, the Philadelphia Phillies. I'm bagging football—baseball is my sport from now on. Same salary, gain four stone, stand around for three hours. That's the job for me."

"You've been here the entire time?"

Hugo nodded. "Ken and Rosie wanted me to stay with them, but your parents insisted I stay here. I've been hanging out with everyone for the last week. They're wonderful people, Juliet."

Julie could only gape in astonishment.

Hugo handed her the glass. "How was Virginia?"

"It was very interesting," she said, taking a swallow of the cold water. "They offered me the job."

"Okay," Hugo nodded. "I think we should do it. I'm willing to move here if this is where you want to be. Your dad's been taking me to his classes at Swarthmore, and, Juliet, I could do it. I could go to college here."

"You'd be willing to give up everything and move to the States?"

"Yes. As long as I can be with you. But your job is waiting for you back at Haddonfield, and they want you back desperately."

"But how? It was such a mess."

"Mick and I have gotten it cleared up. He should be in Maryland now, trying to convince MC to marry him."

"You're friends now?" Julie asked suspiciously.

"It's a long story, and we had some help, but yes. I think everything is resolved. Everything except for one thing."

"What's that?"

"I want my ring back." Hugo reached around her neck and unhooked the clasp to her necklace, slipping his ring off and putting it back on the little finger of his left hand. "Ah, excellent. I've missed it."

"Don't look so put out," Hugo chastised, seeing her startled look, and reached in his pocket. "I've brought you a replacement. And this one will fit."

Taking her left hand, he slipped a flawless diamond solitaire engagement ring onto her finger. Julie held it up to the light in wonder. It was, indeed, a perfect fit.

Just as they were for each other.

# Epilogue

THE ENTIRE SCHOOL was gathered in the kitchens. Don stood in front, holding seven envelopes, while Lalani clasped Julie's hand and Hugo helped Clive settle Bonnie into a chair. She was four days past her due date and couldn't have been more miserable.

"So, gang, here are the GCSE results," Don said.

Matthew ran his hand over his forehead, and Pax licked his lips. Tears rimmed Lalani's eyes behind her thick glasses. "Don't open them, Don."

Alex paced behind the worktables. "Wish I had never taken the bloody thing."

Tanda nodded. "This was a bad idea."

"Come on, Don, open them," Gretchen said, apparently the bravest of the lot.

"Just get it over with," Nerida muttered as Bonnie winced and shifted in her seat.

"All right, then." Don fumbled with the envelopes for a moment before dropping them on the table. He took a deep breath. "I can't do it. Hugo, you do it."

Hugo squeezed Julie's shoulder and went to the table, where he opened the first one and smiled. "Lalani, full pass."

The crowd gasped, and he opened the next one. "Joanna, full pass."

"Do me next," Pax pleaded, and Hugo complied.

"Pax, full pass."

The boy's legs gave out and he crumpled onto the bench. "Jesus."

"Nerida," Hugo continued, "full pass with distinction. Tanda and Alex, also full pass with distinction."

"And lastly, Matthew." Hugo tore open the envelope and began to read. After several moments, he turned to the second page and then reread the first.

"Oh, Jesus," Matthew began to whimper.

"Hugo!" Bonnie yelped sharply.

"Matthew," Hugo began, a faint smile playing on his lips, "full pass—"

"Oh, thank God." Gretchen broke down in tears.

"—with A's across the board. And a commendation for finishing in the top quarter of all takers."

A cheer exploded from the group, and Matthew was surrounded by his friends. The letters were passed around and closely inspected while tissues were produced and eyes wiped.

Bonnie struggled to her feet. "Clive, it's time."

"It certainly is!" Her husband beamed. "Time for a ruddy good party!"

"No, Clive, it's time for the baby. It's coming now."

Julie had never seen such fear strike a man's face. "Matthew, catch him!"

Celebration turned into pandemonium as they maneuvered a shocked Clive into a seat, his lips working soundlessly as he stared at his wife.

"Hugo, bring your car around," Julie said. "We'll follow in the van."

Bonnie was helped into the Jaguar and Hugo sped away to the hospital while they loaded Clive into the van and followed. Four hours later, a beaming Clive emerged from the hospital room and announced that Charles James Connelly was hale and hardy, and mother and son were doing fine.

———————◆O◆———————

That evening, Hugo filled his enormous bath with hot, sudsy water and reverently undressed Julie and carried her into it. He then stripped naked and joined her.

"We haven't had time to talk about the wedding," he said, sinking into the hot water.

Julie sighed, relaxing back into his arms. "I think we should elope."

"Not likely. You're going to be the first bride Wrothesley has seen in forty years."

"We'll have to work around your match schedule."

"Yes, and now that everything has worked out, you'll be coming back to my matches, right?"

"I suppose."

"You do like watching me play, don't you?" he asked in concern.

"Oh, yes," Julie said, rubbing a bar of soap over his muscles. "I just don't like seeing other women enjoying watching you play."

"Really?" Hugo asked in delight.

"Yes. I get a bit jealous."

"How do you know which ones are watching me?"

"They're the ones wearing the number 'Nine' jerseys, Hugo," Julie pointed out.

"Oh, them. You'll never have to share me. But it's a two-way street, Juliet. I don't share. If you have feelings for someone else, you should tell me now. Because I won't share you with anyone, ever."

She rubbed her slippery body over his rampant arousal, enjoying the feel of his sinewy muscles. "There's no one but you."

"I'm serious, Juliet. Tell me now." At her uncomprehending stare, he continued, "Like that farmer who gave you the seeds?"

"Richard? But he's a great guy."

Languorously, Hugo pulled her hands over her head and clasped them with one hand while with his other, he began to do delicious things to her budding nipple as he pressed kisses into her throat. "I hate him."

"Whatever for?"

"Because he's handsome and charming and a thoroughly decent chap. You pay too much attention to him. I want to bash his face in."

Julie pulled back from his embrace. "You're jealous of Richard?"

"Yes."

"Hugo," she said, trying to keep a straight face. "Richard is gay."

"Really?"

"Really. He has a partner, Arthur, who's a solicitor in the City. They've been together for years." She laughed and pulled his lips down to hers. "I should be the jealous one. Richard said he thought you were cute."

Hugo laughed out loud. "Too bad. I only have eyes for you."

# About the Author

**MARINA REZNOR** lives with her rugby-player husband and their two Labradors in Birmingham, Alabama. She became interested in English Premier League football (or soccer as she occasionally slips up saying) when American television began broadcasting matches and she realized there were almost no commercials.

Impressed by the players' agility and stamina, Marina began following their exploits off the field. As fiction authors know, the start of a good book often begins with "I wonder what would happen if…" From the first chapters of *Fowled*, the characters formed themselves and wrote their own story. Marina swears she just wrote it down as it happened.

In the course of researching English football, Marina fell in love with Hendon Football Club, a semi-professional club based in West Hendon, in the London Borough of Brent. The Kingsbury Town Football Club series is dedicated to their spirit.

Visit Marina at her website, marinareznor.com, and join her on Twitter @MarinaReznor and Instagram @MarinaReznor.

While you're at her website, keep in touch with Marina by joining her charming, interesting, and very infrequent newsletter. Infrequent as in "My goodness, is the next ice age here already?" Sign up at https://marinareznor.com. She doesn't share and she doesn't spam.